Aberdeenshire Library and Information Service
www.aberdeenshire.gov.uk/libraries
Renewals Hotline 01224 661511

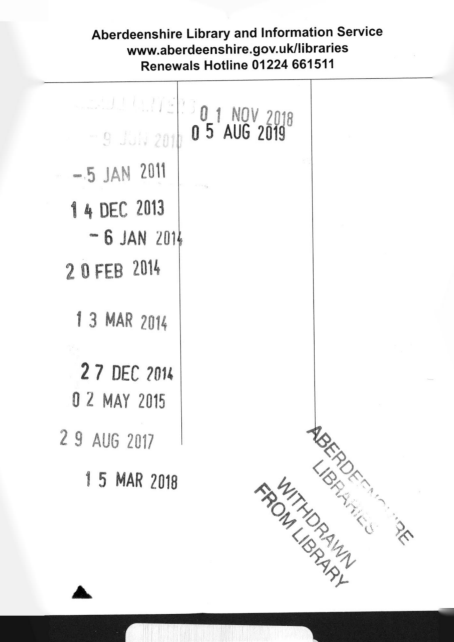

0 1 NOV 2018
0 5 AUG 2019

- 9 JUN 2010

-5 JAN 2011

1 4 DEC 2013

- 6 JAN 2014

2 0 FEB 2014

1 3 MAR 2014

2 7 DEC 2014

0 2 MAY 2015

2 9 AUG 2017

1 5 MAR 2018

ABERDEENSHIRE
LIBRARIES
WITHDRAWN
FROM LIBRARY

PANZER IV

By

PETER PRINCE

First published in Great Britain in 2009 by Peter Prince,
Peter Prince Publishing,
P.O. Box 519., Paddock Wood.
TONBRIDGE. Kent. TN9 9AR.

Cover illustration by Peter Prince
© Peter Prince.

Typeset and Printing by
Windsor Print Production Ltd.
2 Sovereign Way, Tonbridge. Kent. TN9 1RH.

Binding by Wayte Binding,
6 Chalkin Business Park,
Longfield Road, Tunbridge Wells. Kent TN2 3UG.

ISBN 978-0-9562348-0-3

FT

2

Contents

Disclaimer

In some parts of the story I have used the names of real people. However the characters and actions of these people as written in this book are total fiction and derived from my imagination. At no point in the story do I intend to imply that any character from my story is in any way representative of the real person.

At other times I have included events similar to those that actually took place during the period covered by the story. The characters who take part in these events are also totally of my imagination and in no way represent any person living or dead who may have participated in any similar event depicted in this book.

C. J. Thorne Feb 9th 1966 "The Chief Constable of Durham was quite correct - it's not hard to buy a tank!"
Courtesy, The Argos Newspaper, Crowhurst Rd., Brighton.

Dedication

I dedicate this book to my grandfather Charles James Thorne.

I wanted to record something of the major events in my grandfather's life which led to the supply of so many military vehicles for the making of films such as *Scott of the Antarctic, Mr Drake's Duck, The Red Berets, The Heroes of Telemark* and *Dunkirk*.
After his death in 1972 most of his vehicles were sold either for restoration or for scrap.

I hope this book is a suitable memorial to my grandfather and the men and women who created the stories in which his military vehicles were depicted.

LIST OF DIAGRAMS AND MAPS   Page

9

TANK ANATOMY

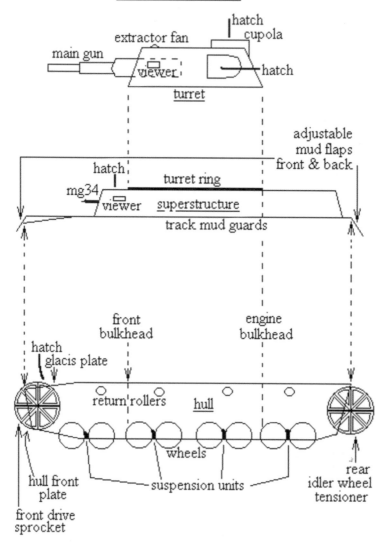

main gun

extractor fan

hatch
cupola

viewer

hatch

turret

hatch

adjustable
mud flaps
front & back

mg34

turret ring

viewer   superstructure

track mud guards

front
bulkhead

engine
bulkhead

hatch
glacis plate

return rollers   hull

wheels

front drive
sprocket

hull front
plate

suspension units

rear
idler wheel
tensioner

EXTERIOR TANK PLAN

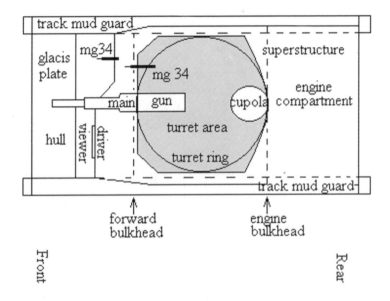

Front

Rear

INTERIOR HULL PLAN

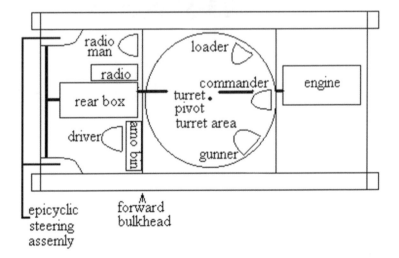

CREW POSITIONS

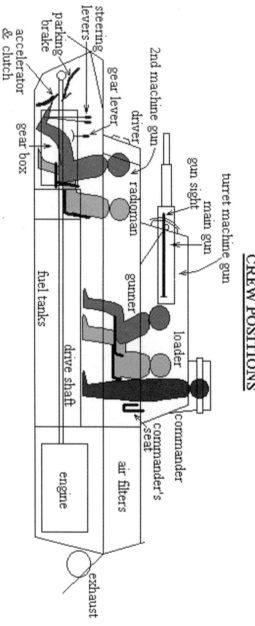

steering levers
gear lever
parking brake
accelerator & clutch
gear box
2nd machine gun
driver
radioman
fuel tanks
drive shaft
turret machine gun
main gun
gun sight
gunner
loader
commander
commander's seat
air filters
engine
exhaust

75 mm MAIN GUN ANATOMY

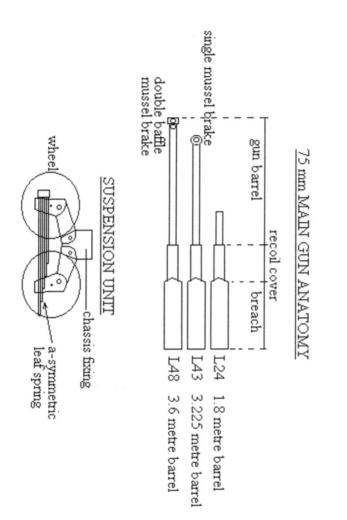

gun barrel	recoil cover	breach

single mussel brake

L24   1.8 metre barrel

L43   3.225 metre barrel

double baffle
mussel brake

L48   3.6 metre barrel

SUSPENSION UNIT

wheel

chassis fixing

a-symmetric
leaf spring

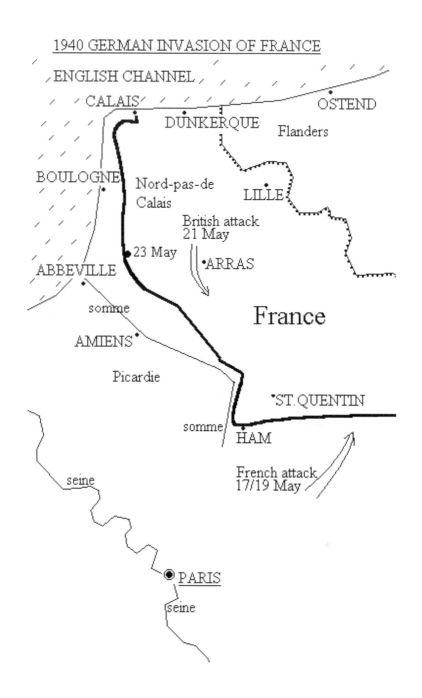

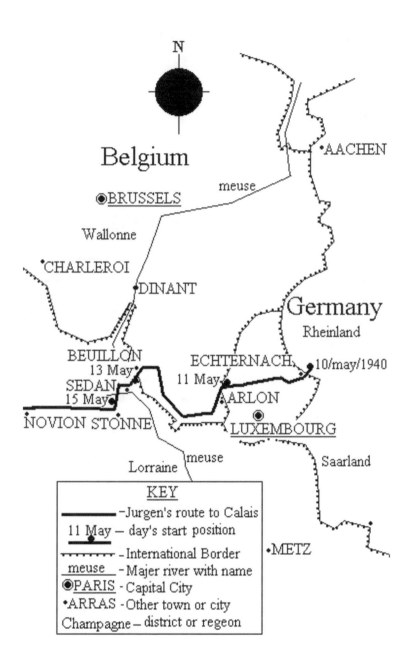

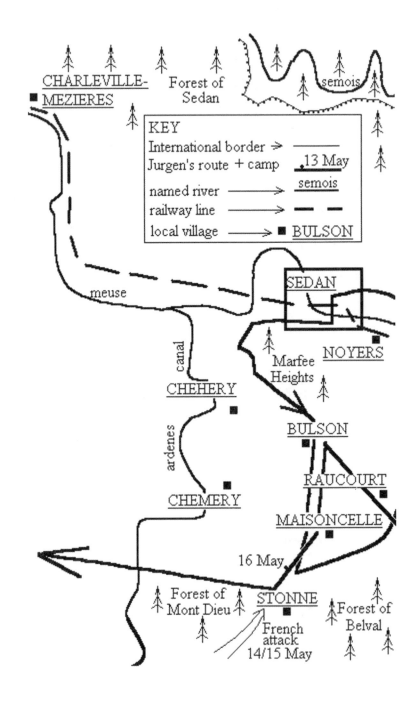

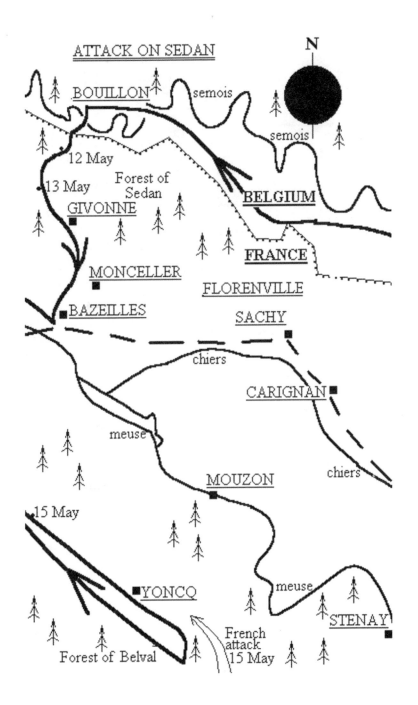

ATTACK ON SEDAN

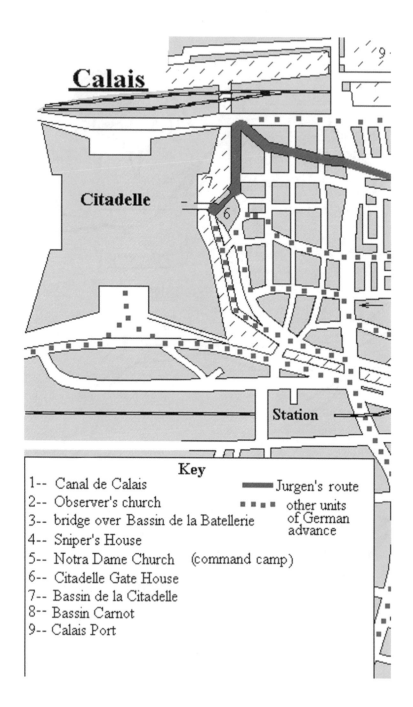

Calais

Citadelle

Station

Key

1-- Canal de Calais

2-- Observer's church

3-- bridge over Bassin de la Batellerie

4-- Sniper's House

5-- Notra Dame Church (command camp)

6-- Citadelle Gate House

7-- Bassin de la Citadelle

8-- Bassin Carnot

9-- Calais Port

━━━ Jurgen's route

■ ■ ■ ■ other units
of German
advance

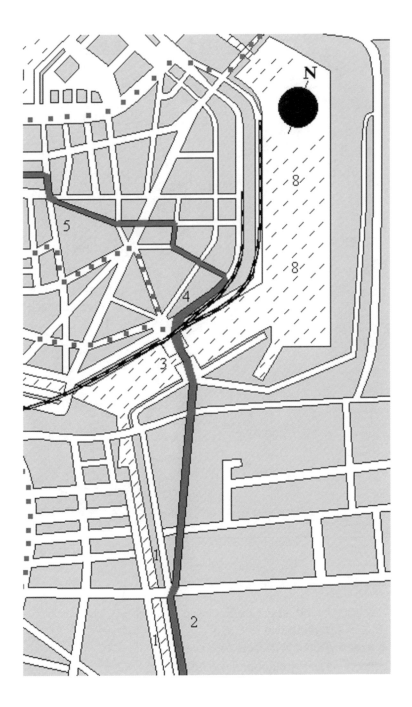

NORMANDY LANDINGS 1944

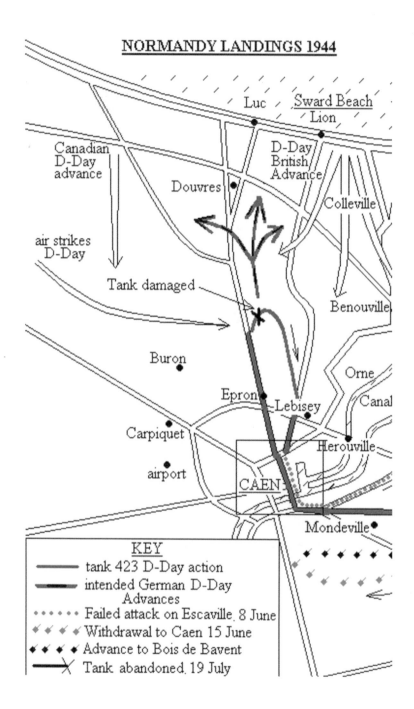

Luc · Sward Beach · Lion

Canadian D-Day advance

D-Day British Advance

Douvres

Colleville

air strikes D-Day

Tank damaged

Benouville

Buron

Orne

Epron · Lebisey

Canal

Carpiquet

Herouville

airport

CAEN

Mondeville

KEY

———— tank 423 D-Day action

━━━━ intended German D-Day Advances

· · · · · · Failed attack on Escaville. 8 June

✦ ✦ ✦ ✦ Withdrawal to Caen 15 June

✦ ✦ ✦ ✦ Advance to Bois de Bavent

———✕ Tank abandoned. 19 July

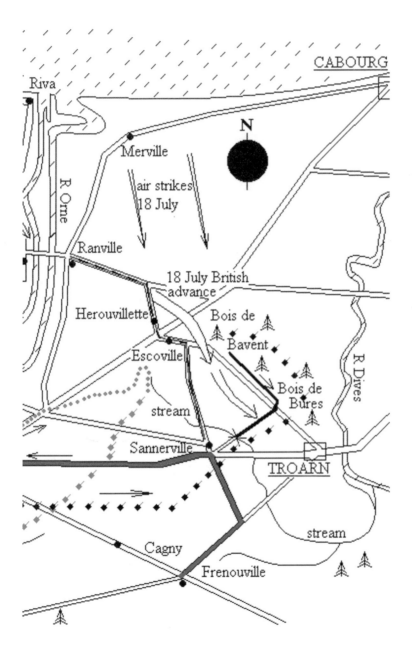

CABOURG

Riva

Merville

N

air strikes
18 July

R Orne

Ranville

18 July British
advance

Herouvillette

Bois de
Bavent

Escoville

Bois de
Bures

stream

R Dives

Sannerville

TROARN

stream

Cagny

Frenouville

Prologue

The Museum was complete. The design was intended to represent a vast row of clenched, glass teeth. An appropriate display of anger and aggression for the depiction of war. George Bailey, the designer, was happy with the effect.

Selected celebrities, dignitaries and guests gathered at the entrance. Gentlemen in dark suits escorted their ladies, brightly coloured summer dresses billowed on the warm spring day.

Robert Knight mounted the small platform to rapturous applause. A church clock chimed ten, the sound was thin and hardly noticed over the distance.

"Mr. Mayor, Ladies and Gentlemen, friends and associates, it gives me great pleasure to see you here for this opening ceremony.

"A few years ago, I didn't consider a new enterprise to be on the cards. However, an embarrassing episode forced my hand and I commissioned this building to be built here on the grounds of the old railway goods yard.

"If I may, I would like to invite our Mayor, Sir James Roach, to formally open the exhibition."

Sunlight flashed from the Mayor's Chains of as he joined Robert on the platform.

"Mr. Mayor, it is with great pleasure I present to you, and the town of Bletchington, the key to this Museum, for the enjoyment of the people." Robert handed the Mayor an extravagantly oversized, golden key. The two men shook hands while photographers recorded the event.

The Mayor waited as the tumult diminished.

"Ladies and Gentlemen, Robert, it gives me joy and encouragement to work for this town when I see some of your achievements, not least of which is this wonderful new Museum." The Mayor held the key high for all to see. "Honoured guests, it is with the greatest of pleasure that I name this centre *'The Edward Knight Military Museum.'*

Sir James inserted the token into an electronic switch. As the key turned, a fanfare sounded, the doors slid open silently and the crowd raised a huge cheer followed by more applause. "I declare the doors open." The two men stepped from the platform. The crowd strolled slowly forwards allowing Sir James and Robert Knight to precede them.

Inside, people gaped at the light and airy atmosphere surrounding the displays. The high glass roof defused the morning sun through the space. The exhibits stood like pieces set for a board game, presenting a peaceful demeanour as though it had always been their intention to be part of a display for the populace.

There were photographs, maps and diagrams of campaigns. Showcases of uniforms and badges, hand equipment and personal supplies. Exhibits ranged from field dressings to anti-aircraft guns and from military issue boot black to cut away engines.

The Mayor and Mr Knight wandered through the show, slowly making their way to the central piece. Behind them, reporters set up equipment for local television and radio.

The Mayor studied the Panzer with what he hoped was a knowing eye. He knew nothing about tanks, especially German tanks, but he did not wish to admit that in public.

"This is a Panzer IV D," Robert explained. "The two hundred and forty seventh type IV tank built and the thirty-sixth Mark D." The Mayor listened with interest.

"Really. You've done your homework. Was this the one used in the... incident?"

"Yes, but I've had the engine removed to prevent that happening again. However, the engine does make an excellent exhibit in its own right. We've cut away most of one side so the motion can be observed. If you would like to witness it."

The engine, drive shaft and gear box, freshly painted in a glossy pale green, stood in a large perspex display case. Robert indicated a red button on the information panel. The Mayor obediently pressed the device and smiled with satisfaction as the twelve pistons rose and fell in slow motion. Small LED's in the cylinders lit up as each piston came into position for the spark plugs to fire and the gears rotated in turn.

"Very impressive." He turned towards the Panzer again. "I notice you have steps to the turret."

"Indeed, this is one of the exhibits we intend the public to examine inside and out. They will be able to sit in any of the five operating positions and a group could have lots of fun pretending to take the tank into action."

The Mayor nodded. "May I?"

"Of course, be my guest, but mind your head."

The Mayor climbed the steps followed closely by Robert. At the top they dropped one after the other into the turret and vanished.

Fifteen minutes later the Mayor's head reappeared, this time from the cupola hatch. The local television-network cameraman smiled with satisfaction as he operated his equipment. He could clearly imagine the bulletin headline, 'Mayor seen in Stolen Tank'.

The Mayor looked round, smiled and waved to those who were watching. He hoisted his body and sauntered down the steps. The press gathered round thrusting microphones forward, questions barraged the Mayor.

"I am very impressed with this new show, especially this Panzer IV. I am sure we will all want to spend many hours here learning about our past." The Mayor turned to Robert. "I'm sorry I have to go now, but I have a luncheon to attend."

Later Robert's own photo opportunity arrived. He stretched with pride as he stood by the Panzer.

"Mr. Knight, can you tell us how you feel?"

"I feel immensely thrilled at being in a position to preserve all these vehicles. They have endured so much, through war and peace, and seeing them here gives me a very deep satisfaction. This tank for instance has suffered near destruction on at least three occasions, and has had many more close calls. It is only fair that she should be made comfortable for the remainder of her time. This museum will mean security and longevity for many years to come. I just wish I had more room here for other exhibits. Thank you." Robert slowly turned away from the press and mingled with his guests.

It was true, there was so much more information that could, and by rights should be explained in more detail. Between his own experience, his father's records, and the first-hand knowledge of his good friend Jürgen Klimt there was an almost complete account of the Panzer IV. Perhaps the facts could be compiled into a book. The task, he thought would at least keep him out of trouble for another couple of years.

1

KRUPP

Chief Mechanical Engineer, Wilhelm Vogel sank into the leather chair at his desk. Aged sixty-seven he could have retired but still felt the vigour and devotion for his work. His eyes were glued to two directives Director Gustav Krupp had just handed him. The Army needed more tanks. He briefly pressed a button by his phone, and waited. Almost immediately, his secretary knocked once and entered.

"Yes, *Herr Obertechnikerin?*"

"Hilda, tell Richmut Schmitt and Karl Forst to come and see me at 1.30.p.m."

"As you wish, Herr Vogel."

Wilhelm's office was not opulent, it was more utilitarian with drafting tables and high stools around the walls. He settled down to reading through the directives properly.

He was not surprised that the documents had bureaucratic statements of why such a vehicle was required interspersed amongst the list of criteria. The reasoning behind the design was controversial. These were Fast Attack Tanks, not the previously favoured slow Infantry Support Tanks of the English and French. It was only General Reichenau's prodding which had induced the German Army Ordnance to change from the outdated Great War doctrines to the new untried tactics. The development would not be an easy task, but if the company was successful the rewards would be prodigious.

When the knock came, Wilhelm had read both directives several times and was already forming a vision of what the new tanks would look like. He planted the papers firmly on his desk.

"*Herein.*"

Richmut and Karl entered and closed the door. The two men had both started work at Krupp as apprentice draftsmen directly from school. In 1914, they had been called up to the Armed Forces for the Great War. They had fought and survived. Afterwards the restrictions placed upon the Germany military by her former enemies, forbade an army of any reasonable size. Both men had been discharged and returned to the

26

company as junior draftsmen.

Karl had worked his way through promotions quite rapidly while Richmut had taken his time. Now they were both Assistant Chief Engineers under Herr Vogel.

"Gentlemen, be seated," Wilhelm paused as his assistants settled themselves. "Let us begin. The Director intends to bid for the design and construction contracts for two medium tanks as stipulated in these new Army directives," Wilhelm indicated the files on his desk. "I want you to start work on them right away."

"Yes Sir." Karl glanced at his friend Richmut. Wilhelm continued.

"As you are aware, we are not permitted as a nation to build tanks, so we must pretend for the time being that these vehicles are tractors. Therefore, these projects come under the code name *Landwirtschaftlicher Schlepper*. It is unfortunate and will mean name changes are required in the future. Individually, the two designs will be known as *Zugführerwagen* and *Begleitwagen*, but calling them 'Troop Commander car' and 'support car' is appropriate."

"The first vehicle, the Troop Commander, will from now on be referred to as ZW. It is to be a medium tank, weight not to exceed twenty-four tonnes, with a fifty mm main gun, a top speed of fifty kilometres per hour, and a range of one hundred and fifty kilometres. Frontal armour plating will be sufficient to withstand a direct hit from a gun of the same calibre at a range of a thousand metres. The task of designing this vehicle is yours, Herr Forst.

"Herr Schmitt, you will work on the second directive, the support car. It will be referred to by the letters BW. It has similar requirements to the ZW but the armament will be a seventy-five millimetre short barrelled gun, with the same specification that the armour should withstand a direct hit from a similar calibre gun at a thousand metres." Wilhelm handed the respective documents to his subordinates. "Are there any questions?"

The two younger men studied the papers. Halfway through the first page Richmut looked up. His brow furrowed with worry though generally there was little that could dampen his enthusiasm. Age forty-two he had the best position he was ever likely to attain. He had the responsibility he craved and was good at his work.

"Herr Vogel, how long do we have?"

"A basic design should be available for the Director's approval in six weeks, and a full scale wooden former in twelve."

"Yes, Sir." Richmut brightened at the prospect of what seemed a long time for a preliminary drawing.

"Herr Vogel, may we compare notes?" Karl looked hopeful. Taller than Richmut, he had an air of rebellion about him. His narrow face and pointed nose made him appear shrew-like with eyes too close together. "They are very similar in the basic design and the use of common parts would make the final build easier."

"Of course." Wilhelm hesitated. "Is there anything else?" The two assistants shook their heads. "Good, if you need anything, ask me.

"The company needs these contracts. We do not want to be on the side lines watching *Maschinenfabrik* or *Daimler-Benz* take the glory. I will not stand for another debacle like we managed while developing the 101 light tank… To work please, gentlemen." Wilhelm turned away.

"Yes, Herr Vogel." Richmut and Karl quickly left Wilhelm to his musings.

Outside the office Karl looked at Richmut.

"What do you make of it?"

Richmut considered his answer as they walked to the drafting room.

"War. One way or another, sooner or later we are going to war."

"You think so?!"

"Why else would we be building tanks?"

The large room Richmut and Karl occupied was cramped by the amount of equipment required for their two teams of draftsmen. There were twelve desks, each one over two metres long, a metre wide and furnished with a sloping draftsman's board, some tables had two. Facing their staff, Richmut and Karl occupied the two desks nearest the door. They settled together at Karl's desk and studied the new directives. Karl looked at the ZW's hull armour requirements and compared them with the BW. He made some calculations.

"Richmut, the two guns seem to have the same penetrating power at one thousand metres. We can use the same armour plating for both types. The superstructure wouldn't have to differ much so only the turret needs changing according to which gun is fitted. It means the overall weight will be similar in both vehicles, we can use the same engine and drive arrangement for both designs."

"Meaning, we only have to design one prototype between us. That sounds good."

"Better though," said Karl, "I suggest we both do a basic design and use the best parts in both of our presentations. Three days enough?"

28

"Sure, we can be flexible anyway, at least until the end of the week."

"Fine, I think we should start by basing our work on the 101 and the M.K.A. export tank. You take the 101, and I'll take the M.K.A. There's enough room for development as neither type is good enough for what we need."

"I agree."

Selecting a new piece of paper, Richmut settled down to work. Silence reigned except for the clicking of instruments and the scratching of pencils.

* * *

Friday dawned a cold and windy January day. Richmut walked into the office early, but not before Karl. Karl looked up with curiosity in his eyes.

"Good morning, Richmut. How are you managing, do you need some help?" Karl's question had become a morning ritual, as had Richmut's response.

"Good morning, Karl. I am fine, no help required thank you. How about you?"

"Everything is going to plan… So, my friend, what have you produced? Are you ready to compare?"

"I still have a little work to finish," said Richmut. " Give me an hour."

Karl was glad he wouldn't be obliged to discuss his own work quite yet, he still hadn't finished checking his last calculations.

"I think an hour will be just right, 8 o'clock then," said Karl.

Richmut settled down to work. He thought an hour to be rather tight, however, the pressure would help him concentrate. He completed the work with just moments to spare and turned to his friend. Karl was still working on his slide rule. The clock on the old head office building struck eight as Karl neatly recorded the final results of his calculation and laid down his pencil.

"Let's see your work." Richmut grinned as he looked at Karl. "You cheat, you have merely copied your M.K.A. design." He lowered his voice. "You are just a petty design thief."

"Thief!" Though Karl feigned indignation he had a broad smile on his face. "The M.K.A. is my design so why not copy it, but I tell you this much, this piece of work is completely new. I placed my whole heart and soul into it. It is much bigger than the M.K.A."

The room fell silent, even the scratching of pencils stopped. Karl looked up, several draftsmen stared back, surprised at the unfamiliar commotion.

Levity over, the two men studied each other's work more closely, comparing the differences. Richmut had proposed a smooth continuous upward curve for the hull's bow while Karl had two flat sheets. Richmut had four return rollers for the track as opposed to Karl's three. In fact the two concepts looked quite different from each other with variations in length, height, wheel size and basic turret shape.

Several hours of discussion passed before they commenced making alterations to bring the designs into line with each other. They only kept the differences where they were needed to accommodate the separate specifications.

* * *

After five weeks, Richmut finished his plans. He rolled up the design and slid it into a protective mailing tube. Later he placed the tube in the large drawings box in Herr Vogel's outer office. Karl had finished a week earlier making Richmut feel dismayed at his colleague's haste but he had been determined not to let Karl's speed influence his thoroughness.

As Wilhelm entered his office the following morning, he collected Richmut's drawings from the box. He sat to inspect them, wondering what surprises or innovations there might be. By comparison, Karl's work had been almost predictable. The paper curled at each corner as he held it open.

Wilhelm could immediately see it was an excellent design. The paper was clean, the writing was neat and even, everything was labelled clearly. The Chief Engineer studied every detail on the one-twentieth scale diagrams. The plan and left side elevation were positioned to the left of the sheet, one above the other, while the front and rear end elevations were to the right.

Underneath the end elevations, a key showed prescribed thickness and quality of metals used for various parts, the proposed power unit and type of suspension. Other sheets of paper presented information relating to weights and measures.

Herr Vogel scrutinised the proposal for several days before sending a summons for Richmut.

"Good morning, Herr Schmitt," Wilhelm greeted him. "Sit down... I am delighted with these initial drawings. However, there are items which should be changed, I will go through these with you now, before lunch."

Richmut dared not object. He listened quietly, accepting the comments while taking notes.

"I would like to see a single piece front plate on the BW superstructure," said Wilhelm, "and I also think you should expand the working compartment over the mud guards some more. This will increase the stowage space inside, while only slightly increasing the overall weight."

They discussed a range of subjects from the size of the turret to the position of defensive pistol ports for handguns. Decisions were taken covering the quality of metal used, the type of air filter, engine, gearbox and the steering system.

It was late afternoon before the meeting was concluded but Richmut quickly made his way back to the drafting room to commence the alterations.

Weeks slid by unnoticed. Richmut attended several more meetings with Herr Vogel, each one refining the design. Eventually Wilhelm was satisfied and took the drawings for the Director's signature.

After Herr Krupp's approval, Richmut was to present the drawings to the woodwork shop to organise the construction of a full scale mock-up. The model would be used later to visually experiment with the positioning of smaller external parts.

* * *

Richmut entered the works, he was immediately confronted with a strong smell of sawdust and the sound of carpenters working.

As he walked to the foreman's office he noticed the completed model of Karl's design standing a short way into the shop. It looked identical to the M.K.A. the mock up of which stood close by. Perhaps the ZW was a little larger. Richmut did not like the effect the model gave. He was glad his own work showed a marked difference.

As Richmut studied Karl's work, he slowly realised there were hardly any similarities between the two new designs. So much for using common parts, Richmut thought. This was becoming more like a contest rather than the co-operation they had agreed on initially.

The model only depicted the basic dimensions but it showed the key ideas behind turret design, the gun's position and the track width. It showed no details of wheels or suspension and had only the basic hull shape, without any of the equipment which would eventually cover the vehicle's exterior. The positions and size of hatches were marked in with black paint. The multitude of hand tools, spare parts and small items such as lights and radio equipment that would be attached to the exterior

31

were not shown at all.

Richmut considered the Commander's cupola, to his eye it looked like a dustbin.

The foreman approached him from behind.

"Good morning, Herr Schmitt. Are those your plans?"

"Good morning, Herr Runtz. I was just coming to see you," Richmut held up the roll as he spoke. "but I seem to have become engrossed in studying Herr Forst's design. I shall take great pleasure in comparing his ideas with my own. I just hope my design turns out to be the better of the two, or Herr Forst will be gloating later." He sighed loudly. "It is a good thing we are friends, he and I."

"Herr Schmitt, only time will tell, but I have seen your work before. I would consider it to be at least the equal of Herr Forst. If I were a gambling man, heaven forbid such a thing, I would place money on your design being accepted and Herr Forst's contribution being rejected. Just between you and myself, mind you."

"Really, and if you were a gambling man, how much would you be inclined to bet?"

"Oh, perhaps ten Marks, Sir."

Richmut wondered how Hermann could afford such a price on his pay, but of course he didn't have to accept when the time came.

"We have a long time to wait before any decision is made about either design," said Richmut, "but I shall remember your proposal. Shall we settle down to business?"

Leaning over a large trestle table, Richmut and Hermann ran through the plans and impending construction until Richmut was satisfied everything was in capable hands. Eventually he left intending to return that afternoon to check on progress.

Back in the drafting room Richmut took his seat. He may have finished the initial diagrams but now he had the problem of organising his team into drawing the details. Every single item from the shape of the brake pedal to the traverse and elevation system for the main gun had to be designed and made to fit, down to the last split pin. There were certain items already in existence such as the Maybach engine and the turret-hatch doors, but even these had to have fittings.

Richmut quickly produced a plan of action. He classified the different parts separately. First the engine compartment including the engine, oil and air filters, exhaust and drive shaft. Next came the gearbox, steering, braking and driver's controls. Then there was suspension, tracks, return rollers and track tensioning mechanism, followed by the fuel tanks, pumps, and fuel supply, both to the fuel tanks and the engine. This covered the actual running of the tank as a vehicle but there was also its function as a fighting machine. Gun mountings, space for ammunition, crew, radio, intercom, personal effects, food and other supplies were all essential. Also needing consideration were access and emergency exits, ventilation to the fighting compartment, vision ports and finally equipment for the defence and recovery of the tank if it were to break down or become inoperable during battle.

The work amounted to several hundred individual drawings. Richmut reckoned it was at least a year's work, and a full set would have to be produced before construction could go ahead. Realistically, he shouldn't expect the first piece of metal to take shape until February or March of 1935, well over a year after the directives had arrived.

Tackling the drawings was not a task for those with a weak constitution. Some of them would have to be full size while others would be drawn to specific scales as had his original plan.

The chore of dividing the work and allotting assignments to his team members took the whole day. He still had three tasks unassigned at the end. He would tackle one of these while the other two would be given to the team members who completed their work first.

Richmut selected the suspension and scribbled down several notes about weight distribution, the amount of play required for each wheel and the slack permitted in the loop of track the tank used in place of a road. Underneath this, he sketched several diagrams of different possible scenarios. The directive stipulated interleaved road wheels and coil spring suspension. With six wheels on each side and a gross weight of twenty-four tonnes the weight distribution would be two tonnes per wheel. This seemed rather high.

Still working on the notepad, keeping the suspension he envisaged in mind, Richmut sketched a more detailed diagram including a possible hull mounting. He selected his best slide rule and started calculating stresses, metal thickness, angles of motion, lateral and vertical play and the degree of wheel overlap for a given size. After two days work he could think of no additional calculations that might alter the final outcome. It was time to commence drawing.

He selected a clean sheet of drafting paper and started work. At the top left corner, he neatly drew up a heading using the Ordnance Departments designation, *VK 2001(K)*. Under this he wrote *Suspension*

33

and road wheel assembly, left-hand side elevation. All this was neatly underlined. He placed his T square and ruler on the paper and started marking out the initial points, full size. When being built, the proportions would be taken directly from the drawing.

The side elevation took a week to produce, after which the plan and end elevations were required. These were followed by the whole unit again duplicated as viewed from the right-hand side. Seven weeks work in all. The exercise might have passed more rapidly if he had not been interrupted by his team members who frequently consulted him. Karl also spent much time conferring with him.

* * *

Oberst Schmülling the army liaison officer for Krupp, called into the Chief Engineer's office.

"Good morning, Herr Vogel. I have just received information from the Army Ordnance Office that the specification for the BW design has changed. I realise this is a major setback but the interleaved road wheels with coil spring suspension will no longer be suitable. They must be replaced by tandem road wheels and torsion bars."

"*Herr Oberst*, they can not possibly expect us to change a major component at such a late stage in the design process."

"I am afraid, Herr Vogel, there is nothing you can do about it, objecting will only force the Ordnance Office's hand against you."

"*Herr Oberst*, you may think there is no alternative but I assure you there are always options. I have no faith in torsion bars. I will not have torsion bars on any heavy vehicle manufactured by this company. They may be cheaper to build, but rough ground, being the usual terrain for this kind of vehicle, will reduce the life expectancy of any one bar to maybe just a few hundred kilometres. The stresses involved will cause too many failures and be extremely dangerous in time of war."

"As I said, Herr Vogel, I believe there is nothing you can do except comply with the Ordnance Office's requirements. Objections will only put the company in jeopardy," Schmülling opened the door ready to leave. "It is, of course, up to you and the Director."

* * *

Wilhelm was not pleased. He paid the Director a visit.

"Herr Krupp, these changes the Army are demanding. It is outrageous. Are they suggesting our suspension is not good enough?"

"They have not said anything about our design, only that they insist on the change. They believe the interleaved wheels will present a

34

problem in thick muddy conditions and want spacing between the wheels to allow mud to fall free."

"Yes, but they insist on torsion bar suspension. They must see that such a system could be considered adequate for a lorry using graded roads, but the moment a vehicle is taken across country the level of stress acting on the suspension is increased maybe tenfold. Torsion bars are just not up to the task."

"Can you prove that to be the case?" Gustav asked.

"Easily, I can draw up some figures to show that the two systems will give vastly different life spans and performance."

"I will draft a letter insisting on our own suspension system. I would like to send your calculations as proof of our reasoning. They cannot possibly fail to see sense in the long run," Gustav rubbed his chin thoughtfully, "but we shall have to tread carefully if we are to retain the BW contract. If we push too hard they may just pass us by."

"Can they never make up their minds and stick to a system?" asked Wilhelm.

"Of course not, Wilhelm. They are bureaucrats."

* * *

Until now Richmut's design had made good progress. He was surprised to be summoned to Herr Vogel's office later that day. When he returned to his drawings, Karl seemed concerned.

"Is everything all right?"

"Yes. It is just that the Army has changed the specification for my suspension and Herr Vogel has asked me to prepare a second alternative design in addition to the new requirement."

"Oh that is hard luck my friend, I hope they never interfere with my design."

Richmut based his alternative system on eight pairs of tandem wheels fixed to an a-symmetrical leaf springs arrangement on a central pivot. Each wheel would carry a little over one and a half tonnes, making the gross capacity for each suspension unit three point one tonnes. This would give the vehicle a maximum possible weight of twenty-four point eight tonnes, easily able to cope with the directive's twenty-four tonne maximum requirement. The directive was based on the carrying capacity of European bridges.

The whole prototype, according to the current particulars would weigh less than eighteen tonnes so there was plenty of room for upgrades and additional equipment. Additionally, the weight bearing on each

35

wheel was reduced by twenty-five percent using leaf springs instead of the twelve wheel torsion bar system.

This knowledge cheered Richmut a little, though drawing the two designs together would take more time than he wanted to spend, but there was no way around the extra work.

* * *

Later Wilhelm returned to Gustav's office.

"*Herr Direktor*, I have the calculations I promised."

"Good, come in and sit down, Wilhelm."

"Torsion bars will increase breakages by forty percent. On the other hand, if we upgrade the bars to be as durable as our leaf spring system, the overall weight will increase considerably. This will in turn reduce the maximum speed and range. I am sure the Army Ordnance Office will find this unacceptable."

"Thank you, Wilhelm. I do not see how they can refuse to accept our design after I have presented our arguments in my letter with your calculations as proof."

Several weeks passed. The concerns with the suspension were still not resolved. The Ordnance Department was dragging its feet over making a decision in Krupp's favour. Wilhelm Vogel was sure that they would never make the choice other than for torsion bars. It was enough to force his hand.

When he visited the drawing office he compared Richmut's two proposals and approved the leaf spring version. He removed the completed design, rolled it up and slipped it under his arm. Later, in his office, he filed it away in a wide drawer with other spare designs.

* * *

As Christmas approached, Richmut was in good spirits. He commenced the final draft of the prototype, incorporating the main features from the different sections. All the drawings were coming along well. It would not be long before the metal workers could start on the full scale prototype. He was, therefore, shocked to be called again to Herr Vogel and this time be questioned about his team's slow progress.

"We have heard from the Ordnance Office that *Rheinmetall* has commenced construction of their prototype BW. This places us at a grave disadvantage. You can not afford to fall behind the competition. There have already been suggestions from the Department that we are too slow and old fashioned in our methods. *Oberst* Schmülling has been asking for the plans for several months now, issuing accusations of laziness and incompetence. Luckily, so far the company has been able to ward off any inconvenient investigations. You must drive your team harder. Do I have your word you will complete the task on time?"

"Yes, Herr Vogel."

"Good. That is all."

Richmut left feeling embarrassed. Numerous thoughts passed through his head. He was annoyed Karl had not shared the rebuke, even if his work was more advanced. He entered the drawing office with anguish on his face.

"What is wrong, Richmut? Do you need some help?" Karl asked.

Richmut thought about answering but decided to keep his problem to himself for the time being.

"I'll tell you at lunch," he said. It was much more important to chivvy his team members, even if the problem was not of their making. He moved between his staff ensuring there were no insurmountable problems holding them back. Richmut was not sure he wanted to discuss work with Karl anymore.

The tanks were the first projects to have been given to both Karl and himself at the same time. With this apparent competition, Karl it seemed, had changed. The development of the tanks had set them apart. Karl appeared more secretive, even devious, not in an obvious way, but his attitude had become less amicable, he was more aggressive and commanding. Somehow they had become rivals rather than colleagues! Their companionship had diminished, replaced firstly with Karl's scorn for Richmut's abilities and then with a secretive manner. Now it appeared Richmut had a real problem, he didn't want Karl gloating.

Richmut suddenly realised, the problem had started on the very first day when Karl had suggested he work from the 101 design while Karl use the much more up to date M.K.A. Why had they not both worked from the M.K.A? Richmut wondered. He felt he had been lulled into a disadvantage from the start.

When midday arrived Karl asked again.

"I want to finish this part of my drawing while I still have the ideas fresh in my head," said Richmut. "I will catch up with you in a little while."

Once the room was empty, Richmut inspected the pile of drawings constituting his design so far. He thought of it as his tank, even though there had been many different points of input from various people. He rapidly leafed through each sheet to study the various sections. He knew each page perfectly, but realised he didn't have the same familiarity with Karl's tank. He slowly looked through Karl's design.

The drawings were completely different from his own design. Different wheel arrangement, different suspension, different gun fittings, different turret. Richmut was stunned. He had expected there to be a strong resemblance to his own work with a few variations.

He took a while to study the contrast. Karl's prototype looked toy-like. The wheelbase seemed too short which made the body look top-heavy. By comparison, his own drawing looked solid and blockish, but which was better? There was no way to find out until the tanks had been built and tested. He had two months to complete the work, a short enough time, without having to change features at the last moment. He just hoped he was right and Karl, with his unpredictable temperament, was wrong.

Richmut placed the papers back in order, leaving them neatly stacked. There was little time left for lunch… Damn Karl for being so devious. He returned to his desk and continued working. He took a quick bite from his packed lunch but left the rest for the evening.

Karl returned to the office.

"You didn't come down to lunch, I was waiting for you."

"I am sorry, Karl, I was too busy with this drawing."

"Oh, let me have a look."

"No!" Richmut leaned over his drawing hiding it from Karl. "I have broken the back of it. It was just a miscalculation." Richmut hoped Karl would accept the phoney excuse.

"I could still look at it if you want, check your figures."

"No, no, I am fine now."

"You are not fine, you seem to be under a lot of stress. Was it the meeting with Herr Vogel that upset you? It must have been very bad to have you so worked up."

"It was a shock. If you must know, he told me Rheinmetall is already building their prototype BW. He gave me two months to finish and catch up with the design."

"That is a bit harsh. I hope I do not receive the same ultimatum. Do you need any help with completion? I am running a bit tight at the moment, but I could stay behind an hour or two each night and give you a hand." Karl's offer seemed genuine, but Richmut had his doubts now he had seen Karl's work.

"No, I should have this last drawing finished in two weeks. Thank you anyway." Richmut hoped he had successfully diverted his colleague and breathed a sigh of relief when Karl shifted tack.

"Well, if you need anything, just ask. After all, that is what friends are for."

The following morning Richmut arrived early. He had made his start time earlier and earlier throughout the year but Karl was always there first. They exchanged hasty greetings while Richmut organised his desk.

As Richmut settled down to work, Karl left the room with a tube of rolled drawings in his hand.

Later, when Richmut was looking at one of his completed diagrams, he noticed Karl's drawings were missing.

When Karl returned, Richmut glared at him with suspicion.

"Where are your drawings, Karl, they were here yesterday?"

"I finished them this morning, I just took them to Herr Vogel," Karl sounded smug. "I did not see much point in having them lying around collecting dust when our competitors are so far ahead of us."

"Well, you could have said you were so close to handing them in. You said yesterday your workload was tight, now I find you have nothing to do!"

"Hah! I would hardly say I have nothing to do. Herr Vogel gave me a new gun design to draw up. Something on the lines of the old twenty-eight millimetre field gun, but with increased rate of fire and better range. So you see, I am quite busy."

From then on, they worked in silence. Richmut's temperament dampened into depression. When, after three weeks, he and his team did finish the VK 2001K, he did not feel like celebrating, though he did thank each of his subordinates for their efforts.

When he dropped the design off at Herr Vogel's office, like Karl, he was given another piece of work. A new naval gun for a pocket battleship the newly self-appointed *Führer* had ordered from Bremen. The tank design left his mind as he set to work, but the betrayal by his friend lingered.

* * *

When the full set of drawings arrived on his desk, the problems with the suspension had still not been resolved. Wilhelm Vogel spread the first sheet of paper across his desk. The work was competent, clean and neat. The machine looked powerful from every angle. Even as a small drawing it seemed to exude a presence capable of pushing all resistance aside. The whole impression was better than that of the ZW. After several hours scrutiny, he had found nothing of any significance to grumble about. At last the company could vindicate itself by showing the Authorities an almost perfect set of drawings. There couldn't be any reason not to go ahead with the prototype's construction.

2

Prototype

Wilhelm was surprised and pleased when a week later, the BW drawings were returned. *Oberst* Schmülling's report was brief. He had accepted everything. It was wonderful, the BW could be built at last. He pulled the leaf spring diagram from the cabinet and placed it on his desk. Laying the signed torsion bar drawing over the top he traced over *Oberst* Schmülling's signature, pressing hard to leave an indent on the drawing below. Carefully he removed the pencil impression on the torsion bar drawing and filed the document in the cabinet. It would hopefully never be seen again.

Using the impression left on the leaf spring drawing, Wilhelm made a copy of the required signature. Once the ink had dried he filed the page with the rest of the BW drawings. He rolled the papers and slipped them into the carrying tube and sent them to the erecting hall where the prototype would be built.

* * *

A few hours later the Tank Department foreman picked up the diagrams and placed the stack on his chart table. Taking his time, he perused each drawing in turn, until he had seen them all. He made notes as he deduced from the specifications whether certain parts should be made in-house or brought in from outside the Krupp organisation.

Items such as the engine would have to come from outside suppliers. The *Maybach HL 108* had been specified, along with a *Zahnradfabrik* five speed transmission. The Wilson epicyclic steering brake could be built in-house as the same unit was already in production for the M.K.A.

There were also drawings of parts not needed for the prototype construction. Radio, guns and ammunition lockers would be represented by wooden mock-ups or even left out altogether. He would only need to consider those when the time came to finally building the product.

Reading the specification, he scribbled some notes to help him prepare the metal sheets required for the hull's exterior. Most of the metal was ten mm. thick but the front and sides were more, and there were also two bulkheads to be fitted inside. Producing the metal itself would take several hours and then to roll and press it to the required thickness would take several more hours of hot work. He checked his calculations and left his office.

Two weeks later, the hull was formed. The most difficult part to produce had been the thick bow plate, but it was a good deal easier than the curved plate originally envisaged.

The hull floor was made of three overlapping sections supporting the bulkheads. The sides were vertical but the back plate had a slight angle leaning outwards. The whole appearance was that of a very basic boat or perhaps an oversized car before it received wheels.

Slowly as the weeks passed the fuel tanks, engine, drive shaft, gearbox and controls were added. On the outside, holes were drilled and tapped for fittings such as the suspension and the final drive, but also for the towing hook and other minor parts.

Gradually the vehicle took shape. Parts arrived from other departments in the factory. The suspension units and wheels were fitted, enabling the whole unit to be taken off the blocks and set on the factory floor. There were still no tracks available so the vehicle could not be moved as yet, except by crane or tractor.

Once the steering brakes and controls were added, the final drives to the sprocket wheels were fitted outside the hull, along with the superstructure enclosing the interior. The floor over the fuel tanks went in first. There was a large hole prepared for the rotating turret deck. Fixed to the turret and resting on a spindle, the deck would turn with the turret so the three men seated within the area would not have to keep moving as the gun traversed from side to side.

* * *

Sixty-three years of age, Gustav Krupp von Bohlen und Halbach still retained the bearing and handsome Germanic looks of his former athletic self. His charisma had grown since the diplomatic position he had held under the Kaiser.

He studied the November issue of the Military Engineer's Report. It was his only obtainable source of official information on his competitors. While it did not delve into much detail concerning their work, it did give a rough idea of their progress compared with Krupp's own. It seemed, while early on Krupp had been ahead with the development of the ZW and behind with the BW, the position had now reversed.

The BW would be ready by the end of the month, well ahead of the unconfirmed test date scheduled for March 1936. Until then, the prototype would have to remain under cover and withstand considerable static tests. Secrecy was paramount.

On the other hand, the ZW was on schedule to be completed in early January, leaving barely sufficient time to complete the tests before being shipped to the official test ground, where-ever that was to be. The bureaucrats had still not released the information, or had not made up their minds.

Gustav was pleased. Both prototypes were of such high quality he couldn't see how the company could fail to be awarded the contracts.

There was a knock on the door. Gustav didn't mind the interruption. He placed the report on his desk and gently ran a hand over his balding head. He leaned forward away from the comfort of the chair. Gisal Hannemann, his secretary stood in the doorway.

"*Herr Direktor*, Herr Vogel says he is about to commence the first engine test on the BW. He assumed you would want to be present."

"Thank you, Gisal. Inform Wilhelm I shall be there shortly."

"Yes, *Herr Direktor*." Gisal retreated to her desk.

Gustav Krupp strode through the huge workshop where the two prototypes were being constructed. There was a strong smell of burned metal from welding equipment, the sound of machinery drowned his steps. At another time he would have been interested to study the numerous guns and armoured vehicles lining his route. Today he ignored his surroundings except to take note, for safety's sake, of the heavy-lift overhead crane. It hung motionless, high amongst the criss-crossed steel girders supporting the corrugated iron roof.

The BW stood turretless at the far end of the building, some seventy metres away. Except for the new matt, mid-grey undercoat, the vehicle looked no different from the last time the Director had seen it. The changes were inside where equipment had been installed to the point that most available space was now occupied. No tank had yet been built with copious amounts of room inside, or any degree of comfort.

Gustav approached Wilhelm Vogel while the project foreman supervised an engine mechanic tipping fuel into the petrol tanks. The seventy-four octane fuel shimmered above the fuel pipe as fumes evaporated in the warm workshop atmosphere. Gustav could smell the heady mixture.

Piece by piece, adjacent machinery shut down draining the area of the normally incessant noise. The unfamiliar quiet permeated the building. Suddenly voices could be heard, noises from the other end of the workshop echoed and sounded hollow.

Gustav watched as two men inserted the crank handle and waited for the foreman's signal. The engine mechanic removed the fuel funnel from the nozzle. He closed the fuel tank filler cap and signalled to the foreman. The foreman called through a hatch.

"Are you ready in there?"

A seemingly bodyless voice replied.

"All primed and ready to fire up."

"Driver?"

"Ready, Sir."

The foreman approached. "All ready to commence testing *Herr Obertechnikerin.*"

Wilhelm turned to Gustav.

"Are you ready for this?"

"I have been looking forward to it for two years," said Gustav. Carry on."

"Thank you, *Herr Direktor.*" Wilhelm turned to the foreman. "Continue."

"To begin with I was a little worried about the outcome," said Gustav, "it being such an unfamiliar area of expertise, but you seem to have pulled this one off first time."

"Thank you, Sir. I sincerely hope so. I would say we have a winning combination but I am not going to pass judgement until I am sure everything works correctly."

"Yes, considering the 101…"

"Besides which, I am not wholly responsible for the design. As you know, my assistant drew up the diagrams." Wilhelm looked around and beckoned to Richmut standing a short way away.

"Herr Vogel informs me you are responsible for this excellent piece of engineering."

"I am most appreciative of Herr Vogel's praise. I only hope my efforts do justice to the company."

"Well, we shall see in just a moment." Gustav pointed to the two men heaving on the crank handle. It seemed to be excessively hard work. "How many revolutions do they need to achieve before the engine will fire up?"

"Sixty revolutions per minute, *Herr Direktor.* It may take as much as two minutes to achieve that rate."

"Such a long time? Is there a contingency plan for starting her up quickly, in an emergency for instance?"

"There is a starter motor on board but it can only be used if the engine

44

is warm. We anticipate, and the Army agrees, the tank will be started by cranking each morning, but afterwards, the starter motor will be sufficient. There should be no long rest periods during which the engine can cool. The Army have stated, for short term rests the engine will be left ticking over, even during such tasks as refuelling."

Gustav pointed at the crank operators.

"What about when the enemy attacks at first light and the tanks are not yet running? Two minutes would seem a very long time if they were under fire."

"The Army envisages this machine will be the one attacking. The enemy will not have a chance. It was the Army Directive that specified the size of the batteries, and by default, their life span. They are just not big enough to start the engine from cold." Richmut hoped the Director would be impressed with his answers. He looked to Herr Vogel for guidance.

"It is true the initial start up is quite lengthy," said Wilhelm. "There is a second power source for providing electricity when the main engine is not running. However, that will be connected to equipment such as the radio transmitter and the firing mechanisms for the gun."

A high-pitched whine came from the prototype's engine compartment as the operators sweated at the crank handle. The foreman, using a small watch, timed the crank handle swings. He called to the driver.

"Engage the clutch." Moments later the whine dropped in pitch but was quickly drowned out as the Maybach engine turned and coughed into action. The two crank operators nearly fell over each other as the pressure from the handle eased. A cloud of smoke billowed from the barrel-sized exhaust but soon cleared as the engine picked up and ticked over at a steady rate. The engine thrummed quietly, the silencer system rendering it inaudible from just a few metres away.

Gustav turned to his companions.

"Well done, gentlemen. This is a proud day for Krupp."

"Thank you, *Herr Direktor.*" Wilhelm and Richmut replied.

"So, what is the plan?" Gustav asked. Wilhelm thought for a moment.

"For the next few days we will check through all the running gear, the brake, steering brakes and each gear setting. If everything goes to plan, we will be able to fit the tracks," Wilhelm indicated the two lines of connected track links stretching out behind the prototype. The wheels already rested on one end of the chain. "It only needs for the links to be drawn over the return rollers and be connected. Then we will be able to

45

move the BW under its own power, and fit the turret completing the work."

Gustav watched the tests for half an hour before leaving satisfied with the procedures.

Richmut stayed to watch, his excitement smouldering, as first gear was engaged. The clutch released and the two large drive sprockets at the front of the prototype rotated. Without track, the prototype remained motionless, but later, when the tracks were fitted, these two sprockets would be the wheels which hauled the track forward moving the prototype along.

The driver engaged the left steering brake followed by the right, stopping the respective drive sprockets as though making turns. The tests were repeated over and over using each gear at a variety of engine speeds.

By the time the initial tests were concluded, evening had drawn in and the light was failing. Wilhelm gave instructions to end work for the day.

The whole of the following day was spent testing and ironing out small problems. Eventually the tracks were connected to form continuous loops and the tension was taken up ready for the prototype to move under its own power.

At 16.15 hours, the driver eased his foot on the accelerator, and leaning gently into the steering levers moved the prototype forward for the first time. The vehicle edged away from its resting place and stopped in the free space between the production lines. Then with equally ponderous sluggishness it reversed back to its place.

Richmut knew this would be the full extent of any motion testing carried out before the Army tests the following year. The prototype could have been driven up and down the full length of the factory building, but all other work would have to stop each time. Equipment which was often spread over the ground would have to be cleared to avoid damage and such procedures would be too much of a disruption.

One day, in order to receive the turret, the prototype did run the length of the workshop. The ugly drum shaped piece of metal, sixty centimetres high and two metres in diameter was bolted into place on the superstructure. The only features were openings in the curved metal for the occupants to see through, and four hooks for lifting it into place. It would serve the purpose of giving an impression of a turret but without a gun or the ability to rotate, it was just a mass of metal without a proper function.

The winter months progressed. November led to December, December to the New Year and 1936 slipped into play bringing fresh snow and bitter cold. By this time the tests on the BW were complete. The machine stood in a quiet corner, out of the way, and out of sight under a protective cover.

Richmut's work on the BW was at an end. He returned to the drawing office as a full time occupation. He was buoyant with achievement.

Late in February, Karl and Richmut were called to Herr Vogel's office.

"Gentlemen," Wilhelm smiled as he greeted his two assistants. "you will be pleased to know we have at last been given the location for the Government trials. They will be at the Kummersdorf and Ulm testing ground in Wurttemburg. Both prototypes and all relevant employees will travel together. We leave by train at 19.00 hours, on Saturday the 29th. We will be there for several weeks. Have the prototypes loaded on their wagons.

The Army will be waiting for us at our destination to assist in the transfer to the testing ground. Do not be late, we must complete our journey by first light on March 1st."

3

Panzer IV

A single bright light moved forward piercing the gloom. Approaching the railway station along steel rails, the movement was resolute, accompanied by a rhythmic cough of steam and smoke belching from the double chimney. The Pacific Class locomotive came to a stop at the platform. Steam issued as the driver secured the brakes.

The train had left Essen the previous evening, shrouded in darkness, carrying the secret load and the maintenance staff. Several wooden crates had been placed on the prototypes' superstructures to alter their profiles. Covered by tarpaulins they were indistinguishable.

After releasing the coupling, the express locomotive slipped free of its charge. The wheels rumbled lightly over the frosted rails, their pressure momentarily melting the ice. Without the wagon's load, the blast of steam from the pistons was reduced to a mild wheeze like a winter cold. The engine disappeared, phantom-like, into the billowing mist leaving the body of the train headless, dead.

Silence filled the station for almost ten minutes before the replacement locomotive nudged hissing at the train, and coupled up.

Richmut felt the jolt.

A guard walked through the train compartment by compartment.

"*Guten morgen, Meine Herren*, we have arrived. *Aufwachen…*" He moved on to the next compartment, his voice becoming muffled through the glass and wood panelling. Richmut took a final look out the window. He had not slept, but had watched the dark shadows pass as the train sped along. He stood, stretched, and then woke Karl.

"Come on sleepy, we have arrived." His voice was filled with mock enthusiasm. He turned to lift his luggage from the overhead rack. "If you do not move soon, you will end up at the depot with the train."

Karl sat up and stretched. He looked at his watch.

"Five a.m. That was a damned awful night."

"I know, I could hardly see anything out the window."

They walked through the station to the street.

It was still dark outside. The small blue streetlights, like distant stars, glowed ineffectively through the mist. There was no wind but a frost had iced over the puddles in the gutters. The road was slick, a hazard waiting for unwary travellers. Buildings rose as dark shadows, enclosing spaces with malice, their weight seemed to overhang the footpaths, ready to topple and crush passers-by. The illusion was heightened by the silence. Münsingen was asleep, unaware of the activity within its confines.

A military bus waited outside. A car provided for the Director had already left. The rest of those who had made the journey with the prototypes would travel in the less stylish means provided. Richmut handed his luggage to an Army driver who loaded it roughly into an adjacent lorry. He climbed into the bus and sat. Karl selected another seat closer to the door.

Richmut felt his normally buoyant temperament sag. He was tired from the journey and now his companionship had been rejected. He wished he could have stayed at home. He sat quietly waiting for the bus to move.

* * *

The train was moved to a loading ramp. Aided by soldiers, the Krupp technicians climbed over the two vehicles removing the tarpaulins and boxes. Both prototypes were cranked into action and driven quietly from the station goods yard. The testing ground was just five kilometres away. Less than an hour after arriving at the station they were parked and locked in a large steel shed.

The sky lightened in the east as Richmut prepared for bed.

Soon after seven, as the sun crested the hills he was roused again. After breakfast he walked quickly to the parade ground outside the steel shed. Krupp's designs were not the only prototypes present. There were designs from *M.A.N.*, *Rheinmetal* and *Daimler-Benz*.

There were several men with clipboards around each vehicle taking measurements and recording statistics.

After several hours the first rolling test took place. The engine was already ticking over as members of staff climbed aboard and settled into various positions. Gustav Krupp wedged himself into the front hatch on the right side of the driving compartment. Wilhelm stood in the turret with *Oberst* Schmülling. There were others Richmut did not know, hanging on at different places.

Richmut climbed the steps provided and looked for something to hold on to. There was a hook, one of the attachments for lifting the turret off the superstructure. He crouched down on one knee and grasped the

49

fitting, he hooked his other arm through the turret hatch. He hoped he was strong enough to hang on for the duration of the exercise.

"When you are ready, *Herr Oberst*," said Gustav.

"Move off," *Oberst* Schmülling directed. Immediately the vehicle lurched forward, quickly turning off the road and heading through the trees. The machine ploughed along rutted tree-lined tracks and through open meadows. It was forced through muddy pools raising sheets of water to either side. It traversed rocky inclines, climbed steep banks and rocked wildly over fiercely uneven ground, eventually covering some fifty kilometres.

At first Richmut found it exciting. The smell of crushed grass and the fresh wind in his face. It was a joy to be in the green of the countryside.

Hanging on strained his muscles and he soon hoped the test would end. Each time the vehicle stopped, at the risk of being thrown off his perch when the machine moved off again, he quickly changed hands, stretched his legs and rubbed some of the life back into his aching muscles. By the end of the morning he was exhausted, he could hardly move. His arms and legs screamed with pain from being crouched in the same position too long.

However, the prototype had performed without fault, giving Richmut a warm feeling of satisfaction. The BW could obviously keep going long after he had reached his limit. If the Ordnance Office turned the Krupp design down it would not be due to any lack on Richmut's part. Richmut decided to decline the next offer of a ride, even if it was supposed to be a privilege.

Days dragged by. Each test was repeated several times to demonstrate the prototype's abilities. Eventually after two weeks the tests were called to a halt for a day's rest. A military driver with use of a small van offered to take Richmut into Münsingen. The driver, a very stern looking fellow in his immaculate uniform, stayed with him throughout his wanderings. The accompaniment was part of the security procedure to ensure he did not speak to anyone about the events at the local camp. Even Herr Krupp was assigned his own guard in the form of *Oberst* Schmülling. Richmut bought a number of books and a locally-made piece of lace for his wife. He missed her. Two weeks without her company each evening already seemed like an age and there was another four weeks to go before he would see her again. His heart ached.

Eventually the tests were complete. Once again, in the dead of night, the prototypes were loaded on their wagons. They were guarded at the station through the following day until it was time to leave. Richmut was grateful as he packed his clothes and in due time boarded the train. As the local clock chimed ten, they clanked into motion heading back to Essen.

* * *

At the factory, work continued as normal. Nobody mentioned the trials as though to speculate over the results might jeopardise the outcome, until one day *Oberst* Schmülling knocked loudly on Gustav's door and entered.

"*Direktor.*"

Gustav looked up, irritated at the interruption.

"*Guten morgen, Herr Oberst.*" He tried to sound friendly but an edge remained in his voice.

"I have a letter in which, I think, you will be interested." Schmülling waved an envelope in the air.

"I assume this is the decision from the Trials Board." Gustav tried not to seem too eager.

"Indeed." Schmülling looked around the ornate office with disdain while he considered his words. "I told the board I could not recommend Krupp for these contracts. You did not follow the directive provided for the BW. Also, I suspect someone even forged my signature in order to have unauthorised drawings appear as though I had approved them. I certainly do not remember the leaf spring drawing in question but I have no proof.

However, the board has seen fit to overrule my opinion, at least in part." He handed the envelope across Gustav's desk, declining to reach far enough for Gustav to receive it easily. The Director had to stand. He slit the envelope with a gold letter knife.

"It is my honour to inform you …"

"I do not need to hear you read it," Schmülling interrupted. "I have already seen the report. As I said, it is not what I would have decided." Without being invited, he sat opposite Gustav and, in an act of contempt, placed his feet on the Director's desk. He extracted a cigarette case from his pocket, selected one for himself and slipped the case back into his pocket. He lit the tip and emitted a large cloud of smoke.

"*Herr Oberst,* you may think you are the most important person in the Krupp Foundation, but I am the Director, and you would do well to give me appropriate respect. You will remove your boots, now, from my desk. It is an antique and worth a considerable amount of money, apart from its value as a family heirloom." Gustav held his anger in check.

"Humph." Schmülling slowly lifted his feet and sat upright in the chair. "Such ostentation is out of place in these surrounds. This is a factory, not some fashionable hotel on the Kurfürstendamm."

Gustav remained standing.

"Was there anything else, *Herr Oberst?*"

"Not at this moment."

"Then be so good as to leave me to my work."

With deliberate leisure Schmülling crossed to the door, slamming it behind him.

Gustav stood fuming for several minutes. His hands crushed the letter, twisting, almost rending it. As the paper in his hands gave way, he realised he was still holding the important document. He dropped it on his desk and sat down heavily.

Gustav poured himself a glass of water. His throat was dry with fury. The glass was empty before he was quenched, he filled it again and drank. The *Oberst* was altogether too full of his own importance, it was time something was done to remove him.

Gustav leaned back in his chair pulling himself together for a moment before noticing the crumpled letter on his desk. He smoothed the paper and began to read.

An hour later Gustav had regained his composure. Wilhelm was sitting with him, their discussion revolving around one aspect of the BW contract.

"They want us to proceed with the BW," said Gustav. "I cannot understand why they did not award us both contracts. Both our designs performed better than any of the others."

"Yes but they still insist on torsion bars. I suspect there have been some furtive politics involved in their decisions." Wilhelm stood up ready to leave. "I will tell Richmut Schmitt the good news."

"Thank you, Wilhelm. Do not concern yourself with the torsion bars. I still have an ace up my sleeve. As chairman of the Association of German Industrialists I have some influence with our competitors. If I can persuade them to drop their offerings I will be able to give the Ordnance Office an ultimatum, our suspension system or nothing. They will not like it, but they will have to comply or go without their precious tanks."

Wilhelm left the room.

Gustav drew out a piece of headed paper and began his letter to the

Ordnance Office.

* * *

Richmut was working on an improved design for the 231 armoured car when he heard his BW had been accepted. He needed to tell someone and celebrate in some small way. He left the design office and headed for the factory floor. He wandered round the building for a while looking at the current mock-ups of machines being developed. After a moment he was aware of a person standing at his elbow.

"Herr Schmitt, how may I be of service."

"Hello Hermann, you are just the person I wanted to see."

"You have some more drawings for me?" Hermann Runtz looked round hopefully.

"No, actually I came to pay a debt."

"A debt, you do not owe me anything that I remember."

"Yes I do, from two years ago in fact."

"That is strange, I do not remember ever lending you money. I make it a rule never to lend money, because I never get it back."

Richmut laughed.

"You do not lend money, the same way as you do not gamble."

"It is true, I do not ga…" Hermann's eyes lit up. "They accepted your tank design. Well, well! I told you so. I would like to shake your hand. Congratulations, you must be very pleased."

"Thank you, yes I am. The tank will be produced at Krupp-Grusen in Magdeburg, but they are still fighting over the suspension system."

"And what about Herr Forst's effort?"

"No, Karl's design was not accepted."

"There, you see, you see. I told you that yours would be accepted and his would not. Aha, how wonderful."

"Well, I suppose so, though actually I feel quite sad in a way." Richmut tried to keep the humour out of his voice.

"Sad! What ever is wrong with you?" Hermann looked startled.

"Well, you, though not being a gambling man, laid a bet of ten Marks, which you have now won. So I owe you ten Marks." Laughing, Richmut handed two crumpled five Mark notes to his friend.

Hermann took them eagerly. "Oh, you do not owe me anything. We never shook hands to seal the agreement." The money disappeared into Hermann's pocket as he spoke.

* * *

Several more weeks passed. Gustav was becoming worried at the delay

53

to the BW's final approval. Had he misjudged the Army's tolerance? A knock sounded.

"Enter." As the crisp military uniform came through the door Gustav thought the visitor was *Oberst* Schmülling. He stood as he realised this was another Officer.

"Good morning Herr Krupp, I am Major Manfred Gimmler, your new Army Liaison Officer."

"Good morning *Herr Major*."

"I have a letter of introduction from the *Führer* and a letter of acceptance for the changes you insist on for the BW production."

The first thought that passed through Gustav's mind was Schmülling had been removed from his factory. The second was that the ultimatum had been influential, meaning the tank could now be produced with leaf spring suspension.

"Please sit down, *Herr Major*."

Gustav read the letter noting *Major* Gimmler had been especially promoted for the position. Gimmler was much older than his predecessor, close to retirement by his appearance. "Congratulations on your recent promotion *Herr Major*. I hope you have an enjoyable stay with us."

"Thank you, *Herr* Krupp." Manfred fidgeted for a moment. "I hope too, that everything will be amicable between us."

"I am sure it will."

"I understand there was some friction between *Herr Oberst* Schmülling and the Krupp Foundation. It seems he was not being honest with either you or the Ordnance Department. We could have settled the suspension problem long ago if he had been."

"I am not surprised. No wonder *Herr Oberst* Schmülling found his position here frustrating."

"I had heard the *Oberst* was under some strain here, now I understand how he was handicapped by certain problems. I assure you I will work with the best interest of both Krupp and the Ordnance Office in mind."

"Thank you for your candour, *Herr Major*. Now, what I want to know is whether Krupp can go ahead with producing the BW." Gustav read the second letter. "It says here," Gustav waived the letter. "we may proceed with the BW according to our design. It also says the BW is now to carry the designation '*Panzerkampfwagen IV*'. At last, we are shedding the veil of secrecy that has hidden our military developments from the world. This is good."

"Yes, I agree. It is time to show the world we are not to be looked down upon as second class citizens."

"I shall ensure preparation for construction of the Panzer IV commences immediately, Major. It will take a while, of course, for us to tool up and train new staff. It may be eighteen months before the first tank comes off the production line." Gustav opened his gold cigarette case and offered it to the Major. "American," he said by way of explanation.

"Really, I have never tried an American brand." Manfred took one and held it between fore and middle finger. Gustav selected one for himself, then struck a flame for Manfred. After igniting his own cigarette, Gustav drew a deep breath and continued.

"So, by the end of next year we will be producing as many tanks as the Army could possibly require. In the meantime we will commence production of the main gun.

"Which reminds me, this low velocity seventy-five millimetre L24 is a strange stipulation on the part of the Ordnance Office. The low velocity reduces the potential range and thus the shell's striking power. I only hope it does not prove to be inadequate in battle."

Manfred had heard the argument before.

"The Authorities believe the supporting role this tank will play, means it will already be at close quarters with the enemy when action must be taken, high velocity will not be required."

"I wonder though, *Herr Major*, with such heavy armour as used on tanks like the French Char B, if more striking power may be desirable." Gustav drew another long breath on his cigarette. " In war, you can never hit too hard, but you can hit too softly."

"Possibly, but our guns are better than any produced by other nations, even the English. I am confident we will be victorious when the time comes. In any case, the *Führer* does not intend to go to war for at least ten years. We have plenty of time to rectify any problems. By that time we will have a world class Army, surpassed by none."

"Well, this is a step forward not only for the company, but for Germany. Whatever happens with the gun and this tank, I think we have something to celebrate. May I tempt you with a glass of Madeira before lunch?" Gustav opened a small drinks cabinet and selected a bottle.

"Certainly. What shall we drink to?"

Gustav chose two small crystal glasses and poured a generous amount into each.

"I propose, Military Development."

"Excellent, to Military Development."

* * *

The first Panzer IV drove off the production line in October 1937. It looked every bit the fighting machine it was supposed to be. The front view was angular and crisp but the bow plate had reverted to the original curved form. Even the short gun looked convincing despite its stubby appearance.

Accompanying the Director and Herr Vogel to the launch ceremony, Richmut considered his work's end-product to be perfect. Only the cupola detracted from the appearance. It looked like the dustbin he had so hated about Karl's ZW. He would set about correcting that for the next order.

There were, as it happened, several parts which needed re-designing. The vision ports, pistol ports and hatch handles all had to be changed. Producing the hull's curved bow plate also proved too expensive to continue. It was replaced with two thicker, angled, flat plates, and the stepped front plate on the superstructure was straightened to a single flat piece of metal. Other tests proved the Maybach engine to be inadequate.

Thirty-five model A tanks rolled off the production line. In March 1938, Richmut's altered design was implemented. The *Ausführung* B. incorporated the up graded Maybach engine with a newly designed six speed gearbox. Another forty-two were built.

In September, The Ausf. C took over with even thicker front armour. The front plate reverted to the stepped variety used on the Ausf. A. The engine was again upgraded, three hundred and twenty horsepower to keep in line with the tank's weight increase, now over 20,000 kg. Production increased from six per month to twelve.

At the end of August 1939 the design changed again. The 36th Ausf. D's hull was laid down on the 17th November. It was the two hundred and forty-seventh Panzer IV produced, carrying the chassis number 80,536. Two weeks later, it rolled off the factory floor. Loaded on to a train, the tank was taken, with others, to an open storage area near Idar-Oberstein, south-west of Mainz. Here it languished out of doors, affected by the elements as winter drifted by, waiting for a crew who would bring it to life.

4

Recruitment

A band of Hitler Youth patrolled the streets. Jürgen Klimt, blond and nearly eighteen, was the oldest and their leader. He had joined up aged thirteen and was the most experienced.

Working his way through the ranks had taken physical effort, concentration and dedication, it was work he enjoyed. Now he had a position of command, his first.

A Jew stepped off the pavement as the fifteen youths approached, he bowed as he waited for them to pass. The group did not acknowledge his presence. When on patrol, unlike some boys who would lead bands into affray at the slightest provocation, Jürgen tried to be fair to the dross living in the area.

Regular citizens caused little or no problem. Only on rare occasions did Jürgen feel inclined to punish someone for their transience. Needless to say he would not take part in the punishment himself. He had his troop to do that for him. He simply gave the order to act, and when to stop. The first sign of blood was a good indicator that punishment had reached the right level.

Jürgen enjoyed the patrols. He had power and respect, it made him feel like a man. He intended to join the Army as soon as he could after his eighteenth birthday. By then, he would be too old for the Hitler Youth.

He had heard many attractive stories about the military, he looked forward to the change, but felt a little apprehensive. It was like moving to a new home, or starting a new school where he didn't know the people or the routine.

It was dark, the sun had set at eight, leaving red streaks scattered briefly across the thinly clouded sky. A church bell chimed ten indicating the end of his duty. The band marched back to their headquarters. Jürgen dismissed the younger boys. Twenty minutes later he was walking home. The night was warm with stars shining faintly between the wispy clouds. It was beautiful. Every night was beautiful.

As he walked he thought about his military future. There were many new weapons being produced for the German *Heer* but the most impressive were the new tanks. He had heard them over the radio. The noise of their engines reverberated through the commentator's words as he described the long columns of heavy machines and their powerful guns passing the Brandenburg Gate. Yes, that was it, he would be a Tank Commander and then a Tank Battalion Commander. He went to bed with notions of heroism and medals in his head.

Three days later at his birthday breakfast, with the smell of freshly fried sausage coming from the kitchen, Jürgen's Father passed him several letters across the dining table. Most were addressed with hand writing but one was official with the Eagle and Swastika Crest stamped on the front. He opened it first.

'Jürgen Klimt, You are ordered to report to *Wehrkreisbüro V* on Sunday 7th May 1939, at 08.00 hours, for Infantry training…'

Jürgen rested the paper on the table, the remainder of his post forgotten.

Several minutes passed before Jürgen's Father broke the silence.

"Is that your enlistment order?"

"Yes, Father."

"Do not be frightened. There is nothing to worry about."

"I am not frightened, Father. I am… happy. You would not believe how happy. This is the best thing in my life. It is as though I have been granted everything I ever wanted. I am a man at last, and I will learn to protect my country, for the *Reich*, for Hitler, and for you and Mother. It is such a thrill, you would not believe."

"I know how you feel. I still have memories of when I was called up in 1917. I too was overjoyed and eager to prove myself. Even the dreadful stories coming from the front could not dampen my enthusiasm. The only advice I can give you is, do your best in everything." Ewald Klimt approached his son. "Congratulations, Jürgen, I am very proud of you." They shook hands, then clasped each other, embracing. As they parted, Jürgen's mother hugged her son tightly.

"Promise me you will be careful. I will miss you so much when you are away." There were tears on her face.

"Do not worry, Mother. I am not leaving yet, not for another two days. And I will be careful." He held her to him to comfort her. "I have to buy a few necessities in preparation. You can come with me if you like."

"I would like that, thank you."

58

"I hope you are going to finish your breakfast," Ewald interjected, "and open the rest of your post before you go shopping." Jürgen gave a start.

"I forgot! I am so excited." He sat opening the other envelopes. Cards congratulating him on his birthday soon spread across the table.

* * *

At 7.35 a.m. on the 7th, Jürgen walked alone into the local *Wehrkreis* Office. He had told his parents to stay behind, partly to prevent their seeing his nervousness, but also to impress the Recruiting Officer.

Dressed in a fresh Hitler Youth uniform, he carried a small suitcase containing the few items he would need while away, shaving kit, soap, etc. The real need for the case was to hold his current clothes which he would no longer require once in Army uniform.

The Officer behind the desk scrutinised his identity card, then directed him to a waiting room. He was the first but other youths of the same age soon joined him. They all seemed nervous as they sat quietly together, closely packed but separate in their own thoughts. None of them wanted to show their anxiety, though signing up and training for war was a daunting challenge.

An Officer entered and called them to attention. After roll call they were led outside to a canvas covered lorry. The dark-grey paint marked it as an Army vehicle, it didn't need the white crosses on the doors and tailgate.

Moments later Jürgen was sitting sideways on a bench in the back of the lorry. He listened to the gearbox whine as the lorry, moving no faster than a trotting horse, wound its way through the city streets.

Jürgen felt loneliness creep in as his former life became distanced. He looked at his fellow recruits. Each craned his neck to grasp a last glimpse of the city they called home. Like Jürgen, they wondered if they would ever see it, their parents or girlfriends again.

Eventually countryside replaced the city. Jürgen sat gripping the tailgate, he watched the road speed away from under the vehicle. Trees lined the way separating them from forested hills and open scrubland. In small towns and villages, people waved. Sometimes he waved back at the unknown, friendly faces. He studied the scenery, trying to remember the turns they had taken. The only certainty was their steady movement southwards through Schwabia.

Eventually, after several hours the journey ended outside a hut, one of many set in rows along the edge of a parade ground. The boys climbed down and lined up, this time carrying their bags. The driver stood in front of them.

"I am *Feldwebel* Adler, your training Officer, this is Geisingen Training School."

Jürgen stood in line, anxiety eating him. Much of what the officer said passed him unnoticed. "When I give an order, you will carry it out immediately, without question. Is that understood?"

Jürgen replied with the others. The sound of their voices rippled in a disorderly fashion.

"Come on, wake up. Are you all snivelling babies, or has the ride stirred your brains to pap? Answer smartly, and together. Again… Is that understood?" Adler shouted every word, his voice carrying into the distance. Soldiers on the far side watched the new group.

"Yes Sir." The second retort was more orderly but still not as Adler required.

"I can see your first lesson needs to be in discipline. Never mind, training starts tomorrow.

"When I give the order you will enter this hut and choose a bed. Some are already occupied. You are not the only trainees to arrive today, so make sure you do not take someone else's place. There are enough beds for everybody. I want you back here, lined up, in five minutes… Dismissed."

Jürgen found a lower bunk at the far end of the hut. He would have liked to be closer to the door, but all the best places had been taken by those who had arrived earlier.

He quickly noted the two grey blankets and the white sheets neatly folded under a single pillow. He was used to two pillows at home but he had been in the same situation in the camps.

He was the last to leave the hut. The officer shouted at him for his tardiness in spite of the fact he was within the five minutes and had had the farthest to go. It could have seemed unfair, but he was used to officers shouting.

When the line had reformed they were marched round the camp and shown the facilities, including the firing range and assault course. After fifteen minutes they arrived at the dining hall.

In the hut, afterwards, Jürgen watched the other recruits. Using his experience as a youth leader he assessed each of their characters. He needed a new companion, someone to train with, to share the highs and lows of army life. Lights were turned out at 21.00 hours.

The hut woke early the following morning. The recruits were forced on a five kilometre run before breakfast. At the finish, the majority of the group were too tired to eat. Jürgen ate heartily, such a short run was nothing to him.

After breakfast they were all given new training uniforms. Once changed, they had drill instruction. In the afternoon there was more drill and a lecture on rifle maintenance. By the end of the day Jürgen realised he was fitter than the rest, and more experienced in military ways. His dedication to the Hitler Youth had given him prior understanding of drill, and of how to strip, clean and re-assemble a rifle.

There was one other boy who was experienced, he came a close second in the morning run and had as much skill with a rifle. Jürgen was impressed with his stamina and knowledge.

Max Webber had also joined the Hitler Youth at age thirteen. Now he was tall, thin and muscular whereas Jürgen, being shorter, was bordering stocky. Max had dark hair and was a month older than Jürgen.

"What do you want to do when you leave here?" Jürgen asked.

"Tanks," Max replied without hesitation. "I thought about the field artillery but I also want to drive. With tanks, I can do both. You should see some of them. The new ones are wonderful. My parents took me to see the *Führer's* Spring Parade."

Jürgen liked Max. They had much in common. He was envious that Max had actually seen the parade while he had only heard it on the radio, but they both knew what they wanted.

Throughout the weeks Max and Jürgen tried constantly to beat each other. Nevertheless, when one seemed to be having unreasonable difficulty the other helped. The most daunting operation they endured was a charge across open ground while under simulated fire. Neither boy flinched at the blasts ripping the ground at their feet.

"Come on Max," Jürgen shouted, goading his friend over the din of explosions. "If you fail with this, how will you manage with flying shrapnel?"

"I shall not fail, when you trip I shall use you as a stepping stone." The exercise became a regular part of training until running through explosions and flying earth was second nature.

Weeks became months. Both Jürgen and Max qualified as marksmen on the rifle range, Max achieved top score with grenades.

As August dwindled, training came to a close.

Their next trial was Regimental selection when the trainees received a

61

new entry in their *Solbuchs*. From now on, they were regular soldiers and would be paid a full soldier's wage. It marked the end of basic training and the class would be scattered to the four corners of the nation as they transferred to new bases. Jürgen would probably never see most of his training companions again. *Feldwebel* Adler called Jürgen, Max and three others to him before the selection parade.

"It has become customary for the top recruits to be offered the posting of their choice. *Herr Major* will see you individually before the parade."

In the Major's Office, Jürgen stood smartly to attention. Major Ocklenburg looked at him, scrutinising, before speaking.

"Stand easy. Congratulations upon passing out with distinction. I might add, not many recruits reach your level of competence in so few weeks.

"You have proved your worth as a soldier and as such you are ready to immediately transfer to an Infantry Battalion. As this class's top recruit you would normally have the pick of the best. I am sure, you would pass through the ranks to become a useful officer and serve the *Reich* with excellence. This course is available if you wish to take it, but I have other options which I can offer.

"I can put your name forward for transfer to the SS, with extra training you could become part of their elite. This is not a choice I would select, I think it shameful that all the best troops are taken away from the Army.

"However, there are other options which I think you may appreciate. You can select sniper training, which will give you an element of independence when you qualify. There is the artillery, you have already shown your aptitude with guns. Or there are the Panzers. You show a powerful sense of loyalty, co-operation and leadership. These are essential in tank work."

Jürgen was cheered, he had not realised he would be offered a choice outside the Infantry, it had been his impression he would have to apply once on active duty.

"I would like to choose Panzer training, Sir."

"I see no problem with your decision. Tomorrow, you will return to your home where you will report to *Wehrkreisbüro V* Offices for civil duties. You will remain there until you receive notice of your transfer to Wunsdorf. I will send instructions directly to your new Commanding Officer.

"You will receive your transfer orders tomorrow. *Heil Hitler*, dismissed."

"*Heil Hitler*." Jürgen saluted, turned smartly and marched from the room. Outside Max stood waiting for his own interview.

"Good luck," Jürgen hissed.

Later Max joined him in the barracks.

"I have chosen the Panzers."

"So have I, Max. But then, I never doubted my future," said Jürgen.

"You liar, there must have been times when you were not sure?"

"No. I always knew I would be selected for the Panzer Divisions. My destiny demands it." Jürgen smiled reluctantly.

"Ha, ha, ha," Max laughed, "with your poker face, you had me believing you." They celebrated late into the night.

* * *

As soon as he returned to the city, Jürgen reported to the *Stuttgart Wehrkreisbüro*. The Officer scrutinised his papers.

Jürgen Klimt! I was not expecting you. However, everything seems to be in order. If I need you I will send for you. You may go, *Heil Hitler*.

"Thank you, Sir. *Heil Hitler*. Jürgen quickly left and ran home to his parents. He had not told them he was returning. They would expect him to be transferred immediately to an active unit without having the chance to visit. He knocked and tried the door. It was unlocked.

"Who is it?" his mother called.

"It is Jürgen, I am home, Mother."

"Jürgen? It is so good to see you." His mother rushed to give him a hug. "I have missed you. Wait until your father returns from work, it will be such a surprise."

The family celebrated late into the night.

During the following week Jürgen visited his old Youth group, he even went on a patrol with them, but the bond was broken. He was no longer Hitler Youth, he belonged to a higher authority. The boys felt it, and resented his presence, as though he was spying on them. He in turn, felt the group had changed, the camaraderie and his sense of belonging had vanished. His connection with these youngsters was ended.

On the last day of August he received a telegram. 'Report to Stuttgart Wehrkreis, Friday 1st September, at 07.00 hours. Bring overnight necessities.'

* * *

On September 1st, the initial Panzer IV, Ausf D. hull was laid out at

Krupp. At the same time, troops of the German *Wehrmacht* marched into Poland.

Unaware of the news, Jürgen reported to his Commanding Officer.

"Klimt, you have a civilian motorcycle licence, yes?"

"Yes, Sir."

"Give it to me."

Jürgen handed over the document. The Officer sat at his desk and typed up a form.

"I have made appropriate alterations to your *Wehrpass*. Give me your *Soldbuch* so I can record this action."

Jürgen handed over his book and watched as the Officer recorded the amendment.

"You now have a military *Führerschein* for a motorcycle." He handed the document over with the *Soldbuch*. "I have documents which must be in Berlin on Monday. You will take a motorcycle and deliver them to the *Oberkommando des Heeres* as soon as you arrive."

Jürgen repeated the instructions.

"Good. This is your letter of authority, your travel permit, petrol coupons, food coupons and hotel room requisition. This last you must have authenticated by O.K.H. in Berlin, and they will tell you at which hotel you are to stay.

"There is a motorcycle outside the back door which you will use for the journey, it is clean and full of fuel. You will return it in the same condition. You will find a map, gloves, helmet, goggles and cycle overcoat in the cloakroom. Here are the keys. Depart as soon as you are ready. Do you have any questions?"

Jürgen didn't, and left promptly. The journey was long and slow and he eventually arrived in the early hours of the following morning. Fortunately the O.K.H. building was open throughout the night. He delivered the papers and was told to return on Monday. With so much free time he spent long hours exploring the city.

In the evenings he listened to the radio. On September 3rd, while at dinner in the hotel's restaurant there was a news bulletin. Suddenly everybody was listening intently. 'Britain and France have declared war with Germany.' Instantly everyone was talking. Jürgen was shocked, he wanted to talk to someone he knew, someone who could clarify the implications.

Shortly afterwards he walked through the streets. They were just as busy as they had been during the day. Nobody seemed even a little put out by the declaration. Of course, the fighting would probably not start for several months and the British would never dare attack Berlin itself. The people felt safe.

It was late when the sirens wailed into life. Jürgen was tempted to cover his ears against the sound filling the air, it echoed from every wall. He had heard the sirens in practice, but this time they were accompanied by the threat of real enemy aircraft.

Jürgen wanted to run. The anticipation of being bombed was far worse than crossing a field under simulated fire. It was tempting to close his eyes and squash himself into the shadows, but he dare not hide. He had to set an example. His uniform represented the Army, strength in the face of adversity. He maintained his self-control among the civilians, giving advice and ordering the population into the shelters. He was proving his bravery, to himself if to nobody else.

When the populace were safely hidden in the shelters, he stared up at the night looking for the enemy high overhead. He watched, listening intently, catching glimpses of aircraft blundering into the searchlights. The planes drew away. Gradually Jürgen realised there were no bombs. Paper fell from the sky. The enemy had dropped propaganda leaflets.

Jürgen almost laughed. The dreaded threat, the devastation the city had been preparing for, had turned out to be nothing more than giant confetti. As the foe's final sounds faded into the distance Jürgen snatched up the literature and started to read.

'Your rulers have condemned you to massacre, a war they can not ever hope to win!…'

To Jürgen it was unbelievably infuriating. How could Britain, a timid pathetic nation, make threats against the *Reich*. But then, that was all they were capable of. Neither the British nor French had the strength to stand up to the *Führer*. Over the years all the European leaders had run to the beck and call. They had proved their gutless worth through the myriad treaties they had signed, each one an aid to German welfare.

As the civilians slowly emerged from their shelters an air of relief broke across the city. Britain had tried to destroy Berlin with paper, it made a fine joke. Clutching the leaflet to take home for his parents to read, Jürgen returned to his hotel.

* * *

The journey home seemed as long and slow as the ride to the capital, though he pushed the cycle to the limit. It was dark long before he entered the familiar, but it seemed subtly changed. He had always related

65

the area to his childhood. Now the atmosphere was different. He knew he had changed but the lack of people in the streets, as though everybody had gone into hiding, made the town cold and unloved.

He stopped at a roadblock. It had not been there five days before. The soldier let him pass without trouble but the encounter helped Jürgen order his thoughts. Curfew was a new and unfamiliar feature. It would probably be a permanent part of the conflict. It saddened him that people would have to lose their freedom because a foreign nation did not like the *Führer's* actions, but Stuttgart – the whole of Germany, was at war.

Arriving at the *Wehrkreis* Office Jürgen reported directly to the Duty Officer who sent him home.

Jürgen handed the flyer to his father.

"I remember this sort of thing from the last war." He spoke in a hushed voice. "The British sometimes flew over our lines, dropping their litter trying to make us surrender. It never worked. We used to shoot at them and send our pilots to drop bombs on their lines." He placed the paper on the table. "It was a vile war, that one. This time we will keep our enemies at bay and crush them one by one. Do not worry yourself about the leaflets. They mean the British are not ready to fight, which gives us time to obliterate them before they are fully equipped. We will finish this time, what we should have finished last time…

The following morning Jürgen read the newspapers. The news from the front was excellent. There were rumours already that Poland would fall within three weeks. He realised it was too late for him to join the Polish Campaign. Doubt, verging on guilt, gripped him.

"Father, have I made the right decision? Should I have joined the Infantry and fought in Poland? I am not eager to fight, but I want to play my part."

"To be keen is fine but you must be careful, not reckless. Do not make rash decisions. Do you want to join the Infantry?"

"No Father, Max and I both want to be Panzer Commanders."

"Then you have made the right decision. If you had joined the Infantry, you would have joined the reserves and not seen any fighting. And you would have missed your opportunity to join the Panzers. Now you will be better trained and more prepared when the time comes to face the enemy. There is no tank on earth that can defeat one of our Panzers."

5

Training

Jürgen boarded an early train to Hannover via Frankfurt, followed by another to Wunsdorf just twenty-five kilometres further to the west. With a heavy pack on his back, he and other recruits walked the seven kilometres from the station to the Tank Training School.

As Jürgen marched along the road, Max caught up with him.

"What do you think of the Polish campaign? It seems we have recruited too late," he said by way of greeting.

"Do not worry on that score my friend. I have been following events in the *Militär Wochenblatt* and there is still plenty going on. We keep sinking England's ships in the North Sea to show them that there is still a war to fight. It is all bound to escalate some time soon.

The area around the new camp was quite different from Geisingen. The land was flat, there were few trees and huge open spaces between the barracks, workshops and lecture halls.

There were hundreds of young men. Jürgen's hut was filled with recruits fresh from basic training. They had arrived from all over the German *Reich*. The more senior trainees, those who had already seen regular military service, were billeted in other huts.

Jürgen and Max realised they would eventually be made part of a tank crew when training concluded. It also seemed logical that the best trained recruits would be assigned the best tanks, or perhaps even be given a command.

Jürgen again was careful with whom he made friends. Gradually as the days passed he discarded those who fell behind.

The routine at Wunsdorf was very similar to that at Geisingen. Early morning runs followed by drill, physical training and more drill. There were still opportunities to fire a rifle but these were greatly reduced. To begin with, most of their time was spent in a lecture hall.

Their first lectures covered tank warfare from the Great War. They quickly moved on to tank developments of the past twenty years of peace. Their text books defined typical Panzer Division doctrine, describing everything from tactics, both offensive and defensive, to what was called 'The Panzer Lifestyle'. Jürgen was engrossed.

After a couple of weeks they commenced learning the different skills required to operate a tank. Jürgen found working on radios quite easy, it all seemed somewhat mundane once the language was mastered. Morse code was hard but using correct call signs and terminology was not demanding. There was little variation in protocols from one transmission to the next. Enigma encryptions were more interesting, but they also proved to be more difficult and very time consuming.

Jürgen also practised gunnery but as there was no local artillery range, it was restricted to loading and firing dummy rounds on 50mm anti-aircraft guns. His loader was an instructor who quickly showed it when he disliked a trainee.

Far more interesting was Jürgen's first practical driving lesson. The practice area was a vast field split into several sections, each containing a practice vehicle. At first he was dismayed by the machine, an open top caterpillar farm tractor adapted for seating two.

His instructor, *Oberleutnant* Helmet Munck, first took the vehicle round the course to demonstrate the controls. Jürgen tried to follow Munck's every move but much of the time he concentrated on where they were going. As a result, when it was his turn he was unsure how the levers and pedals functioned. He half-listened to what he was told while thinking hard about what he had read in the instruction manual. There were three levers to work and three pedals.

Two levers were identical, one on either side which were used for moving and steering. The third lever, on his right, was the gear-changer.

At his feet there was the clutch on the left and the accelerator on the right. The third pedal in the middle and positioned very much higher up, was the parking brake.

"First, you will make the tractor move forward a little way and then stop. Follow my instructions and you should find it easy." Munck was a quiet man not given to shouting, which made the instruction simple to follow. He pointed out the control positions.

"The brake is in the ON position, and the gear lever is in neutral. The driving levers are in neutral, so the first objective is to select first gear."

Jürgen studied the enamelled diagram plate, pressed his foot hard on the clutch, wiggled the lever sideways twice and pushed the gear lever away into first position.

"Good. The tractor is on flat ground so it will not roll when you release the brake. Press gently on the pedal until the ratchet lock drops down on your foot, then lift your foot in a controlled manner so the pedal does not spring back at you."

Jürgen followed the commands, breathing a sigh of relief when nothing untoward happened.

"Wonderful. Now you are ready to move. Press the accelerator until you have twelve hundred revolutions, and the needle is on the edge of the green area marked *sparbereich* on the dial."

As Jürgen pressed the accelerator, the engine behind him roared into life and the needle swung violently up beyond two thousand revolutions. A cloud of diesel fumes engulfed him. He eased off and watched the needle swing back slowly. He held it at just over twelve hundred revolutions.

"Right. Keep the accelerator there, take hold of both steering levers and push them slowly forward together. You will need to increase the revolutions as they engage. When you have moved the levers as far as they will go, count to ten, then release them, and they will spring back to vertical. Then press the foot brake to stop the tractor."

Holding his arms rigid, Jürgen leaned into the two levers, the tractor moved forward slowly. He counted for ten seconds and let go of the levers. The levers sprang back to their neutral position but the tractor did not stop.

"Put your foot on the brake, Jürgen."

Annoyed at having forgotten, Jürgen applied the brake and felt the tractor slow. Munck smiled.

"Very good. You saw how the power to the wheels was broken when you let go of the levers. Now, try it again, but this time pull back on the levers to brake. You must keep them even or you will wander off the straight line."

Each time Jürgen tried the procedure, the tractor moved forward covering about twenty metres. After the fifth effort Munck stopped him. They were close to reaching the field's edge and Jürgen was beginning to feel the joy of success.

"Now you are going to turn around and head back," Munck instructed. "Instead of pushing both levers, I want you to push the right lever but pull on the left. You will turn left and when you are facing the way you have just come, stop."

Jürgen flexed his fingers, applied the levers and pressed the accelerator.

Forgetting the delicacy required when using the foot pedal, the engine revved out of control spinning the tractor round violently in a circle. The tracks tore at the mud and tufts of grass. Shocked Jürgen released the levers. The tractor resumed a straight line and rolled to a stop at an angle from his original line.

Munck laughed. "We can do acrobatics when you have better control. Do not worry. That was only your first attempt. Next time keep the accelerator steady to produce twelve to thirteen hundred revolutions. Try it again."

This time the tractor turned slowly, pivoting on the left track. It turned in a tight circle until Jürgen applied the brakes.

"Good. Now, as we move along I want you to relax pressure on first one lever and then the other so you always have one track engaged and the other free." Munck gave a quick demonstration, punching his arms forward and back.

Jürgen, enthused by his previous experience, concentrated hard, working at the levers and pedals. The tractor moved forward, swerving gently from side to side as Jürgen worked the levers. He kept moving, growing into the thrill of the exercise until they had returned to the original starting point.

"Keep going," Munck instructed. "I want you to push the left lever and pull the right gently and then stop when we are facing the other way."

Jürgen's concentration was intent as he steered the tractor round in a wide turn. He braked gently, the tractor stopped almost exactly where he had started the lesson.

Jürgen breathed a gentle sigh of relief. His arms and shoulders were beginning to complain from the unaccustomed effort. The combination of muscles strain and the vibrations of the tractor rattled his hands. Every jolt as they moved over the uneven ground seemed to shoot through his joints.

"That went very well. I want you to repeat the exercise several times and then we will try something new."

Driving up and down the field was exhilarating, he followed his original tracks. The tractor left a clear mark on the ground. Munck urged him to drive faster, gaining a feel for how the vehicle responded to the controls.

Fifteen minutes passed before they stopped again. This time Jürgen practised moving the gear lever through the sequence from first to fourth and back.

"Now, Jürgen, you may drive wherever you want, keeping to this field and only using the first three gears. Remember to double declutching when you change gear and to press the accelerator as well if you are changing down a gear. Do not try to change gear when you are turning. If you need to turn on the spot as you did the first time, stop and use first gear. If you have a problem, just stop by using the brake."

It seemed a lot to remember all at once but Jürgen was determined to give it his best effort. The rest of the hour passed, creating an increasing pattern of muddy tracks on the grass. Jürgen drove around and around in figures of eight and wavy lines. When he finished, he was tired from the unaccustomed use of his muscles. His back, shoulders and upper arms all ached from leaning on the steering levers. At the same time, he beamed with the thrill of what he had achieved. Munck looked pleased.

"So, how do you feel now you have driven tracks?"

"Wonderful." Jürgen beamed.

"Yes, I thought you were enjoying yourself. You have taken to it very well. In fact I would say it come to you naturally. Good, I will see you at the same time tomorrow. Keep flexing your muscles or they will stiffen."

Jürgen walked back to the lecture hall to meet Max.

"How did it go?" Max asked his friend.

"It was good. I lost control of the accelerator once but I shall not make that mistake again," Jürgen smiled. "How about you?"

"Only once?" Max was envious. "I kept going off to one side all the time. My instructor was not very impressed with me. Track driving is difficult, I do not want to do it for a living, I think I will stick to gunnery."

"You have such a destructive nature, you really should try to control yourself, Max. No doubt it is because you were not allowed enough big bangs when you were little." Jürgen had to admit though, there was a certain excitement from firing a larger gun.

* * *

October changed into November and still they trained. Snow covered the ground. It was bitterly cold, the north wind biting at exposed flesh. They were given extra clothing to compensate for the lack of heating on the tractor. Jürgen enjoyed the training, but it failed to take his mind off the chill in his fingers and toes.

He advanced to driving on a road and using all the gears. Keeping the line, and staying on the proper side of the road, with all its minuscule turns, was difficult. Everything happened so much more quickly when

71

driving at speed.

He leaned forward in his seat trying to contend with other traffic and pedestrians. The tractor was almost too wide for the road he was using. It was nerve-racking but each day ended before Jürgen was ready.

As darkness fell, he drove back to the camp. It was the most tiring experience he had undertaken. Gripped by the fear of hitting something in the dark, his body strained at the controls all the way to camp. He was exhausted.

Later on he was also introduced to a Czech t38 tank. He was not permitted to drive this but learned track assembly, engine and transmission strip down and maintenance. Much of the work was messy with oil or mud for company. The work did not seem very appealing at first, but as the weeks passed, he came to appreciate the mess. He learned the necessity for repair work but also how the whole machine functioned.

After six weeks at the training school, Jürgen was given his new position. He was disappointed.

"Why was I selected to be a driver? If I can not be a Commander yet, I should be a gunner like you, Max. Even loader would be better than driver."

Max laughed. "If you were a gunner we would have ended up in different tanks. We may even have been placed in different platoons. We would not have seen very much of each other if that had happened."

When Jürgen put his grievance to his instructor, Munck had an easy counter argument.

"In many ways the driver is the second most important person in a tank. The Commander is responsible for directing the crew and hopefully he will keep you all out of trouble. You are responsible for pulling the vehicle, and crew, out of trouble if the Commander fails or is injured. If the machine breaks down, you are the first person to see if it can be repaired. If it is damaged in action, you are the one who has the best chance of returning the crew to safety. Without the driver a tank becomes a static pillbox, and an easy target."

Jürgen had not realised that he had been given such a position of responsibility. Before joining Tank School he had set his aim at commanding and nothing else would have been good enough. During training, realising the position of Commander was out of reach so early on, he had shifted his aim to either gunner or loader, thinking these were the two next-most-important positions. Now, after Munck's encouragement, he appreciated the fact that without a driver, a tank would never even leave its base, let alone accomplish required objectives. He felt greatly bolstered. He may not be firing the gun but it was he who would make sure the gunner reached his target, and returned home afterwards.

On the same day, Jürgen discovered the identity of the rest of the crew. He had always assumed Max would be gunner but had no particular person in mind as loader or radio operator.

Klaus Malcher was the first to join as Radioman.

Jürgen was not impressed. Klaus, though five months older, was in his opinion too easy-going. He accomplished each task to the necessary minimum requirement and appeared to be uncommitted. He seemed to be there only for the ride, he had no conviction. The only strong desire he expressed was, that being short, he was not forced to join the Infantry.

Not until they had worked together for a few days did Jürgen discover radio was Klaus' greatest love. He was a good driver as well.

Max had previously been selected as gunner and joined the crew with his now established loader, Alfred Rüsgen.

A little younger than Klaus, Alfred came from Aalen seventy-five kilometres from Jürgen's home. He did not seem to mind how he was trained. Competent as an athlete and always friendly, he was likeable which, though important did not necessarily make him a valued asset to a tank. It was apparent though, that Max and he worked well together but to Jürgen's eyes, he seemed a little hesitant in his manner when approaching a task. With a little more confidence perhaps he would pull through.

At last, they were a complete complement if they included an instructor as their Commander. This was the turning point, they were a team and from now on would always train together. When they had developed into a smoothly running unit, they were transferred to Putlos Gunnery School.

"I wondered when we would fire real ammunition," Alfred commented to Max as several crews travelled in a convoy of lorries northwards to Lübeck. The range was another fifty kilometres further north, on the Ostsee coast near Oldenburg.

Over the next weeks they fired a number of static field pieces utilising their previous training. They started with small calibre, twenty millimetre and thirty-seven millimetre field guns. Later they used fifty millimetre and a long seventy-five millimetre gun. Most targets were old

73

vehicles positioned at various distances and rusting in the cold north wind. Some targets were huge concrete blocks which hardly seemed to suffer from the pounding they received.

Finally the crew worked with real tanks, able at last to try hitting a target whilst on the move. They handled Panzers I and II and t38 training tanks comparing the differences between them. Jürgen did not like any of the machines, the Panzers were to small and lacked good armament while the t38 appeared too feminine.

At first he found the dark inside the driving compartment a problem. On the tractor he had always been able to see where all the controls were located, but the fact that the tank's window was only thirty millimetres high by a hundred and seventy-five millimetres wide was a big hindrance. Suddenly he had to feel for the controls, and they were not always precisely where he expected them to be.

The other thing that surprised him was the amount of adjustment required when firing a gun which bucked and jolted as the tank moved along the ground. It made him realise that the smoother he could drive, the better would be the gunner's aim.

There was a strong sense of satisfaction as shells exploded in the distance. The days went well but each one was the same, they blended like mirror images. Runs, gunnery, drill, the rifle range and lectures. The trainees seemed completely isolated from the outside world. A high earthen rampart and ditch surrounded the range preventing outsiders looking in and the trainees from looking out, except towards the sea. Only the *Militär Wochenblatt* and occasional post enabled them to keep track of time and events.

One Monday morning, Jürgen surprised Max.

"*Fröhliche Weihnachten.*" He handed his friend a card and package wrapped in brown paper. "I am sorry, it is not much."

Max was dumbfounded. "Merry Christmas to you too." He pulled the paper off to reveal a large diary. "Thank you, whatever made you think of it?"

"I thought you would like to record our– your exploits. You are always scribbling in that notebook of yours. I thought it would be nice to have a proper book with the day and date already written in for you."

"It is wonderful, thank you. When did you have time to buy it?"

"I asked my parents to send it."

"I shall of course write and thank them."

Christmas passed to New Year. A new decade. The troops moved back to Wunsdorf. Although the pace did not slacken, their training moved more towards revision.

The team still practised operating the equipment and Jürgen quickly became more competent with the controls of a t38. He soon felt ready to face his first enemy.

* * *

February loomed on the horizon, at last Jürgen felt the crew was a well oiled mechanism and it was time to move on, basic tank training was over. Munck gave them their new assignments crew by crew.

Jürgen listened intently for their names but took no notice of where the other crews were being sent. His excitement built gradually, like climbing a ladder to see a parade. Each name was another rung to the top. Eventually he heard it.

"Klimt, Malcher, Rüsgen and Webber, Seventh Panzer Regiment, Tenth Panzer Division, at Vaihingen."

Jürgen felt as though a huge warm blanket had descended over him. A glow filled his body as he joined the others in their celebration. He shook his companions' hands. At last they were ready to go to war and pitch their efforts at the destruction of the western enemy.

They moved that weekend. Travelling by train as a group with five other tank crews, they headed for the Regimental Camp. They pulled into Stuttgart station and transferred to lorries. It was still cold, possibly more so in the mountains, though the warmth of the railway carriage increased the apparent change as they stepped outside. The snow was thick on the ground. They were not looking forward to the last part of the journey. The lorry's canvas cover flapped and batted about as they moved fifty kilometres into the hills.

Despite being close to home after so long away, Jürgen did not have a chance to see his parents. He took comfort from the fact that now he was much closer to them and might have an opportunity to visit in the near future.

Once in Vaihingen they soon found training was not over after all. At their first parade they were addressed by *Major* von Wedelstadt, the camp's Commanding Officer.

"You probably think you are fully trained soldiers, and you may think you are prepared for anything. This is not true. You still have much to learn. I expect you to work hard, and in doing so, you will reap the benefits."

"You will be given live rounds and you will shoot while your tank is stationary and on the move. There will be no accidents. We are all on the same side. If you want to kill someone, save it for when you meet the French, and vent your anger against them. You will have plenty of opportunity for this in the near future."

When he had finished speaking each crew was called forward to meet their new leaders.

"I am your Tank Commander, *Oberfeldwebel* Olbermann. I am second in command of this Tank Platoon under *Oberleutnant* Heinz Lutz. You may only go to *Oberleutnant* Lutz for one reason, and that is to report my death. Is that understood?

Jürgen tried to pay close attention but was distracted by the man's twitching moustache. Dark-haired, he was muscular, several years older than the rest of the crew and had the air of authority that came with experience. It made Jürgen feel comfortable and a little more secure. Olbermann continued.

"If you have problems, whatever they may be, you bring them to me. Even if they are of great personal discomfort like boils on your buttocks, you still bring them to me, Then we can sort them out." The four men laughed. "An unsolved problem will result in a lack of concentration when it is needed most and could result in death.

"Come, I will show you our training tank." They walked to a building with a large sliding door at the front. "You may have seen one of these before, even operated one, but I will recap. This is a Panzer IV Ausf A. Built in 1937 so it is three years old. There are a number of differences between this tank and any you will operate in action. However, the basics are the same. If you can drive a Panzer I, you can drive any Panzer, including a Panzer IV." The five men climbed onto the superstructure.

Jürgen leaned into the open driver's hatch and inspected the controls, they were the familiar levers and pedals he had used on the tractor. On the right was the gear box and he could see the back of the radio above that. To the left, by where his feet and knees would be, was the round casing for the left hand steering brake. The whole space seemed so cramped.

"From now on, your instruction will include the functions of a tank within the Regiment. You have covered this in the lecture hall, now you will cover it on the ground. This is a support tank. It is used to defend the Panzer III and other vehicles against enemy tanks. It has a seventy-five millimetre L24 gun."

Jürgen listened closely though he knew L24 meant the barrel length was twenty four times the size of the calibre, in this case one point eight metres.

"It is a short gun so unofficially we call these tanks stubbies." Olbermann smiled at each of his four crew members. "In the next few weeks this machine will be your work, and you will grow to love it as your home. Any questions?"

There were none. The remainder of their training was spent manoeuvring with other units from the Regiment, linking each tank together so they operated as one.

At the end of March each soldier was granted three days leave. Jürgen went home to his parents. It was a quiet weekend and over far too quickly.

* * *

The Regimental exercises continued throughout April.

One week before the end of the month, a trainload of new tanks arrived at the base. There were some thirty small Czech t38s with five Panzer IVs behind them. The line of dark grey angular shapes looked impressive as it rolled off the train and into the camp. Jürgen longed to take possession of one, preferably a Panzer IV.

Oberfeldwebel Olbermann took his crew to take a closer look.

"One of these is ours." He looked at a piece of paper and walked up the line of machines until he reached the penultimate machine, a Panzer IV. "This is it, come on, climb aboard."

They scrambled to the hatches. Alfred was first up the steps and climbing in the turret's right-hand side. Max climbed in from the left. He noted the number stencilled on the wall behind the Commander's seat: 80,536.

Jürgen and Klaus used their personal hatches over their work places at the front. Though they took their seats side by side, they could not see each other. The radio equipment and gearbox completely blocked the space between them. Jürgen leaned forward to peer through the tiny window to the outside. He could hardly see anything through the thick glass. The opening was only forty-five centimetres wide by three centimetres high. The light outside glared at him in the dimness of the compartment. He felt around the controls finding the familiar levers and pedals. The pale green-yellow paint made everything appear tenuous and ghostlike.

Olbermann climbed down through the cupola completing the five man crew. He picked up his headset.

"So I do not have to shout all the time, put your headsets on." Each man donned his earphones and throat microphone. "This is an Ausf. D., built last year, it has never been used before, so we must take good care of it. There may be many things wrong because it has been left out in the weather for the past six months, so keep your eyes open for problems. All right Jürgen, start up and take us to our stabling point."

In the gloom, Jürgen found the key hanging on a piece of string in front of him. He snatched at it and pushed it into the ignition. The engine temperature gauge still showed warm. He pressed the starter and held it down. He was faintly aware of an electronic whirring sound came from the back, it quickly gained pitch and speed. The engine roared into life filling the tank with sound and vibrations.

Jürgen selected first gear and, steering on the left track, turned out of the line of new tanks. It suddenly reminded him of his first driving lesson when he had spun on the spot. He would make no such mistake today. Slowly he ran the machine to the front of the line and directed it towards their designated workshop. As he pulled up, he felt the thrill of control. He wanted it to continue through the day and into the night but he killed the engine. Now began the task of checking every small part to ensure the vehicle was ready for regular use.

While Jürgen investigated the oil, coolant, fuel and drive train, Max and Alfred reviewed the machine guns, the seventy-five millimetre, and loaded the tank's storage compartments with ammunition. Klaus passed a few short radio messages to other crews on the base to check he was receiving and transmitting correctly. Later Olbermann gave him a tin of yellow paint and some stencils to paint the Regimental insignia, Y^{000}, on the Panzer's front and back. He also painted the tactical formation number 326, in red, on the sides of the turret. When this was done he blacked out the white national crosses painted in readiness, but too late, for use in the Polish Campaign.

When all the tasks were accomplished, Jürgen took number 326 on its first military exercise. It was a simple matter of running the tank round for familiarisation.

April passed to May with little change. On the 5th, Max handed a package to Jürgen. "Happy Birthday!"

Jürgen carefully opened the wrapping to reveal a small pair of Leica binoculars.

"But Max, this is too much!"

"No my friend. It makes up for not giving you a Christmas present, and if you have as much joy from them, as I have with the diary, it will be money well spent."

"Thank you, it is a fine gift."

"I am glad you like them."

At dawn on the 6th of May, the Regiment lined up in their vehicles at the camp gate. They departed for a new location. It was a slow drive, Jürgen followed his Troop Leader westwards to Karlsruhe and then north to Ludwigshafen where they spent the night. The following morning, after inspecting the engine and running gear, they headed west again, towards Trier. On the 8th, they drove to within three kilometres of the Luxembourg border near Echternach. As Jürgen climbed from his Panzer IV he was overwhelmed by the mass of grey machines and black uniforms that had come together. It was a huge gathering.

6

Invasion

Jürgen stood back from the road, watching. The grey traffic had been arriving continuously for well over twenty-four hours. He watched each unit as it passed, trying to recognise insignias. Most were familiar.

Three staff cars passed. The lead car displayed a General Officer's flag. Jürgen saluted smartly, arm angled upwards, straight and stiff to his front. Staff cars had become a more common sight as Senior Officers were ferried to their posts ready for what could only be the invasion of western Europe.

Jürgen quickly returned to his tank troop ensuring he was not missed. He walked carefully through the fresh spring grass trying hard to avoid the patches of mud that would smear his boots.

The Eifel Mountains were beautiful. Oak, beech and chestnut trees were bursting into leaf with pale shades of lime and pea green. Patches of moss glowed in the dappled light as the afternoon sun shone yellow through the newly clothed branches.

Spring flowers bloomed, primrose, violets, their sweet scent battling against the smell of fuel and oil fumes. Birds sang their territorial claims, filling the air with joy, competing against the din of milling uniformed crowds on the woodland floor. The traffic rolling by proclaimed a different declaration of territory.

Jürgen took little notice of his natural surroundings. He breathed the caustic fumes and listened to the drone of machinery. The storms of winter were over, this was the beginning of a new storm.

Jürgen had been eager to escape the confines of his tank but now he was just as keen to be back. He had not realised an army could be so vast. The lines of vehicles seemed endless. They were astounding, wonderful, but intimidating. The power of any one tank or armoured car was a force to be reckoned with, but together…

In the camp, morale was high. There was nothing that could go wrong. Optimistic talk sprang from every direction.

"Hey, Jürgen," Max shouted across the clearing. "How long will it take for the west to fall? I think three weeks, Klaus says four. I have heard some claim we will be at the Atlantic in a week." Max glanced at Alfred. "That is too fast, they must be Luftwaffe, yes?"

"Max, I have no idea. But I would guess four to six weeks."

"You are not Luftwaffe! Keep your muddy feet firmly on the ground, hey?"

Jürgen looked at his boots, they would need to be cleaned in spite of his care.

Max turned to Alfred. "There, you see. One week indeed. I tell you, he knows. You will not find anyone more level-headed than my old friend Jürgen. You owe me five *Reichmarks*." Gambling was strictly forbidden but money still passed hands. Jürgen returned to his tent to remove the dirt from his boots.

The night before, the Regiment had been directed to a good camping place. The tanks had been parked in a circle under the trees. They were well hidden, camouflaged by fresh shrubbery. In spite of the rough ground they slept on, the tank crews were quite comfortable and a mobile kitchen provided plentiful food.

The sound of an aircraft engine overlaid the other noises, crackling, unsilenced.

"Take cover!" Olbermann shouted. "Quickly, move, move, move. Soldiers ran, scuttling to hide from the prying eyes. From his tent Jürgen could just make out the roundel under the wing, red and white rings with blue at the centre. Quite different from the black cross of the *Reich*. A hush filled the camp as the plane's propeller thrashed the air.

"That was not a German plane. Did you see it, was it an Engländer?" Jürgen peered through the trees at the receding intruder.

"I could not tell, I did not see it clearly," said Max . "Flying over German territory like that, it must have been one of their filthy spies."

"I think it was a Frenchman." Klaus sounded sure of himself.

"Do you think the game is up, did he see us?" asked Alfred.

"It would be difficult for him to miss the units still on the road." Max rubbed his knee where he had landed hard in his effort to hide.

"I think now, the enemy will be prepared for our coming," said Olbermann. He looked concerned.

Jürgen brightened, a smile of confidence lit his face.

"It does not matter. The might of the *Reich* is unstoppable."

"It is good to think so. We will see." Olbermann remained anxious. "I have our final confirmation. We attack tomorrow, whatever the outcome."

As darkness closed in, excitement rose to new heights. It rippled through the camp like a wave advancing on a shore line. Everyone was buoyed making the night energised and restless. For most there, sleep was elusive.

* * *

Jürgen rose at 03.30 and the whole world it seemed, moved into action with him. He yawned widely and staggered into motion. Moments later, discipline took hold, he went about his business practically without thinking. The Panzers were not going to lie in for want of rest. There was too much at stake. After months of hard and continuous training, the routine was second nature.

Jürgen checked the Panzer one final time, before climbing into his seat. The confined space closed in on him, only the hatch above his head gave access to the outside, and that too would soon be closed. He sat with his thoughts, wondering what the future would bring, but whatever the world threw at him, he knew he would triumph, the Panzers were irresistible.

The call to start engines sounded at 04.30. The bird's morning chorus was drowned by the crescendo of Maybach and Praga engines.

The first sections rolled forward promptly, others following at short intervals. Jürgen's troop moved ninety minutes later. They drove through woods before descending steeply towards a wide river, the Sauer. Suddenly the column stopped. Jürgen slammed the brake pedal. The crew slid off their seats on the incline.

"What the hell are you doing, Jürgen?" Olbermann shouted.

"We have all stopped."

"I know we have stopped, but why?"

The radio crackled in Klaus's ear. "Herr Olbermann, the bridge over the river has been damaged, it will not support us in its present condition." Klaus's report scratched over the intercom.

"So, they were forewarned." Olbermann speculated. "That is a blow. We can ill afford to languish while vital hours tick by."

The tank rested on the steep incline, nose down, engine ticking over. The crew opened their hatches to let in fresh air and reduce the growing heat.

Jürgen could hear the chatter of rifle fire in the distance.

"It sounds like fighting in the valley."

"It will not last long," Olbermann replied. "The Luxers only have a few hundred soldiers, and no tanks."

"All this sitting around." Max banged on the turret wall with his fist. "It signifies no good."

"Save your energy," snapped Olbermann. "Luxembourg is a small country. The opposition will be quickly cleared away."

Noon passed before they moved again. Slowly the line of vehicles advanced to the valley floor. Jürgen released the brake and let the tank roll down of its own accord. Speed increased as the jam cleared.

Jürgen's relief at seeing the river for the first time was palpable. He peered intently through his viewer. Already half a day had passed. All he wanted to do now was drive as fast as he could. This was supposed to be lightning war. He had moved less than a handful of kilometres and still not crossed the first border.

Though the original crossing had been made safe, it was only suitable for foot soldiers. The tank column turned upriver to the next bridge. Jürgen drove slowly, avoiding wrecked armoured cars and scattered bodies. German troops, in field grey-uniforms, waved him on. A field ambulance crew tended sundry wounded. To Jürgen, the details of his surroundings seemed distanced, as though the tank was a vast barrier protecting him from the grim reality.

In the middle of the tank troop, Jürgen crossed the river following in line of advance. Echternach was quiet. Through his vision port, it appeared clean and well maintained. The sort of place he would have liked to visit on holiday.

The streets were clear of obstructions and soon fell behind. The brakes were off at last and the column thundered along the road through dense coniferous woodland stretching up the sides of the valley like green carpet.

At first the troop drove towards Luxembourg City, but soon Jürgen was led onto minor roads to avoid the larger settlements. The way was more twisted and undulating. Their speed slowed, but this was a necessity brought about by secrecy.

The line of vehicles stretched out as they sped on through woods and small hamlets. Jürgen was just able to spot the tank in front as they twisted and turned through the forest. He raced after the leaders, the whole Company moving uniformly. The few civilians they encountered gazed open mouthed at the tanks.

Jürgen passed through another village set by a deep river. The open fields surrounding the small stone buildings and open fields provided respite from the incessant trees. Chickens cackled in alarm, scrambling out of the way. He sped over the bridge, tracks rattling.

The column slowed. The bridge at Mersch was destroyed. Olbermann searched his maps for an alternative crossing.

"Jürgen, turn right. We can try the bridges at Beringen and Moesdorf ."

Swerving off the road, Jürgen made the short detour round the outskirts of Mersch village. Avoiding the backlog of Panzers, he picked up the riverside trail to the north. The next bridge was narrow but intact. The diversion, less than a kilometre long, soon put them back on track, speeding westwards.

All of a sudden, Jürgen became leader with the whole of the division behind him. The unfamiliar position made him nervous, driving was much easier with someone to follow but he upped the pace. Leaning hard into the steering levers as though keeping a wild animal at bay, Jürgen only relaxed his grip momentarily at each turn. The ground sped beneath the tracks, gravel and dust flying behind.

At the following junction Jürgen pulled to the side. Other tanks rushed past. He pulled back into the traffic at his proper place, number six tank in his unit.

"That was a good run, Jürgen," Alfred cried. "It is a shame you cannot stay in the lead. We would definitely be at the Atlantic in a week."

The sun sank behind the hills. They would have continued but were blocked again.

"The Belgian Army has mined the road and surrounding land at the frontier," said Klaus listening to the radio again. "They almost lost the lead vehicle. Despite using full headlights, the mines were nearly invisible in the dark. They estimate several hours for the Pioneers to clear them away."

Jürgen considered his own position as leader, would he have been able to stop in time?

"Damn, this is so irritating, we are still six kilometres from the Belgian border. We were supposed to be in France by now," said Olbermann.

"Blame the bridge in Echternach," Max commiserated. "Without that problem, we would have been."

"Maybe. Secure the tank," Olbermann ordered.

They quickly ate, taking eggs from a local chicken run, and commandeered a nearby barn for sleeping and straw for bedding.

A church clock struck once. Jürgen vaguely noticed the clear chime before he descended into slumber and wondered if it was one o'clock or a half hour chime.

The night was filled with engine sounds as the slower parts of the Regiment caught up. Jürgen was sufficiently tired to sleep through the activity.

* * *

The following morning after another quickly prepared meal, Jürgen drove into Belgium. The mines had been cleared by the engineers working through the night. The boarder was deserted except for the long line of military vehicles streaming past the flattened sentry post.

Jürgen's route cut to the north of Arlon and then south to bypass the crossing over the River Semois. Keeping to the south side of the flood plain, using the smaller roads, he again motored westwards.

"Other parts of the Regiment have taken the north side of the river," Alfred called out. "It looks like they are fighting over there."

Jürgen took his foot off the accelerator.

"Keep going, do not slow down." Olbermann peered through his turret visor. "That does not concern us. I think that must be Habay. The troops there will see to it."

Jürgen powered on, touching the French border at Florenville but cutting more northwards to the Division's designated assembly area at Bouillon. He slowed a little to pass by a small armoured car. A German reconnaissance vehicle, it half rested in the roadside ditch. There was no sign of the occupants. The sight was a shock, a scene from another world. Jürgen drove on.

Some way further, where the road curved by tall trees in the hedgerow, Jürgen noted two abandoned enemy motorcycles. Close by, bodies lay like rag dolls thrown away in a fit of rage. A machine gun, ripped off it legs, pointed aimlessly across a man's severed arm. Jürgen registered the facts in passing but did not slow. Nobody passed comment, each secluded in his own private thoughts. The subject was not something to be dwelled upon but Jürgen could not resist the tug of fear.

The enemy must have fled leaving their dead and weapons in place. Run, and live to fight again? Not if he could help it, thought Jürgen. He felt no compassion for those who had fallen.

The claustrophobic atmosphere deepened at the sound of large guns firing. Bouillon was drawing nearer, now just three kilometres away. The

85

column reduced speed again as they passed more bodies, firstly a few Germans then many more Belgians, the uniform colours giving away their identities. A light tank lay on its side, abandoned. A troop lorry nosed a tree, smoke billowing from the engine.

Jürgen gritted his teeth. This had been only a skirmish, but there was more fighting ahead.

"They are almost within range." Olbermann's voice cut into Jürgen's contemplation, it was time to act.

Klaus intercepted a radio message and passed it to the Commander.

"Jürgen, turn right," Olbermann ordered. "We attack through the fields."

Double declutching, Jürgen changed into second gear. He hauled back on the right steering lever and pushed the left one forward as hard as he could. The tank spun frantically to the right. launching out over the roadside ditch, it cut a wide hole in the hedge flattening the scrub to sticks. Jürgen drove to the middle of the field before Olbermann ordered him to turn left and resume the advance against the town.

The Panzers stopped, forming into three lines abreast. Jürgen's troop composed the second line staggered behind the first.

"This is no different from training," Olbermann reminded his crew. "We advance in formation just the same as we have practised, and we keep moving until we are through the enemy. Loader – armour piercing round." Commander Olbermann shouted the order into his microphone.

"Yes Sir."

"Stand by – and remember to keep your mouths open against the percussion effect."

The order to attack came moments later. The formation moved as one. Jürgen accelerated as the lead tanks broke through another hedge. Moments later he followed wreaking total destruction to the vegetation. It was a promising start but there were more hedges and ditches to cross before they could bring their guns to bear.

A flame suddenly ballooned over the tank in front. The vehicle stopped abruptly and fell behind as Jürgen pressed forward. A tightness filled Jürgen's throat.

The longer ranged guns of the t38 tanks soon started firing. Max held back, he was just seven hundred metres from his first target before he opened fire.

From his higher position, Olbermann quickly identified the enemy position and called the coordinates. Max lined up the sights, selected the elevation and fired.

Ear-splitting thunder filled the compartment, every last vestige of the vehicle shuddered as the shell left the barrel. A pressure wave thumped simultaneously into each of their chests, momentarily preventing breath. Jürgen felt the effect as though he himself had been hit.

Alfred opened the breach. A loud clang sounded. The shell casing ejected from the breach, striking the protective rail at Olbermann's stomach before falling into the collecting bag. Smoke filled the air, a thick choking acrid stench of burning cordite. Jürgen held his breath, fear and anticipation gripped him. He could hear the others coughing. The turret fan buzzed into action extracting the noxious fumes.

"A hit, well done, second round, high explosive, same target." Olbermann called out the coordinates.

Alfred loaded a second shell and placed the spent case in a rack. Max adjusted the gun. Crash! The second shell, invisible through the smoke, flew towards the now disorganised enemy position. Clang – another spent case.

Jürgen saw the flash of explosive but took no notice, he followed his line keeping position with the rest of the formation.

"Hit, new target," Olbermann directed. The gun blasted again.

Tunk, tunk, tunk. There was a new sound, erratic, like droplets falling from a cave roof.

"Those stupid idiots," Olbermann admonished, "they are trying to stop us with rifle fire. Klaus, take care of it."

The M.G.34's rhythmic rapid fire spat forth, RDRDRDRDRD, every fifth round a beam of tracer. They curved towards the troubled adversaries, each one a beacon guiding Klaus's aim. Although the enemy tried to flee, many fell screaming. They lay moaning, or silent.

Another round flashed from Max's gun. Jürgen felt the pressure on his eardrums rather than heard the shot. Olbermann's voice came to him through a fuzz of wadding.

"Reload – Fire!"

Crash.

"Reload – Fire!"

Crash.

"Reload, new target, bearing two-two-zero, range, four-fifty, fire!"

Each call, a shorter range, four hundred, three-fifty, two-seventy-five, two-forty. Each round causing greater destruction. Enemy guns flipped into the air. Trees fell, their trunks shattered. Fires raged from smashed equipment. Jürgen drove through the enemy lines.

Abruptly, a scream shrilled from under the tank, inhuman, a sound from hell. Jürgen cringed, he had not seen the man fall beneath the tracks. It was no reason to stop.

The local firing died out.

"Halt!" Olbermann raised one side of the cupola cover. There was shooting far off to the right several hundred metres away. To the front, back and left it was quiet, save for the injured. The action was over, they had come through unscathed. Another victory for the Third *Reich*. Jürgen breathed deeply trying to calm himself. The realities of war were more frightening than the supposedly realistic war simulation of military exercises.

New orders crackled on the radio. 'Reform line abreast. Prepare to advance into Bouillon.' Klaus passed the message on.

Olbermann disliked the order. Tanks were not suited for fighting in streets. It would have been easier to shell the houses but he gave the order to prepare.

German troops in field grey moved past the tank towards the town. The first platoons hugged the hedges making short, rapid advances. These were followed by clusters of troops walking forward more openly. There was no resistance, no sign of the enemy.

Jürgen, as he waited, watched them through his viewer. He was impatient for more action. The sun ducked behind trees. Hours passed. The remaining fighting petered out.

Klaus recorded a new radio message and passed it on to Olbermann. 'Occupy the Forest of Sedan.'

The line turned south from their position overlooking Bouillon. Jürgen followed. He had survived his first engagement.

A black, yellow and red Belgian flag fluttered in the evening light. Beyond, in the distance, the red white and blue of France formed a mirror image. It was growing dark but the crew were delighted at the prospect of crossing the third and final frontier. From here the roads would be open to the Atlantic.

There were signs of resistance. Mines covered the road, just resting on the surface. Enemy weapons littered the surrounding area, abandoned by the owners who had fled at the first sign of the intruders. The lead tank fired at the mines clearing a way through.

The route between the two border posts was in good condition but the area beyond the French post was also mined. Machine gun fire sprayed the ground. The road erupted in flame. The border post cabin crumpled to matches as though a wind had swept it away. Jürgen drove through cheering as if he had won a race. Max laughed.

"You sound like this is your own personal campaign."

"Of course it is," Jürgen chuckled. "You should feel the same." Jürgen checked his gauges. "Commander, so far I have recorded one hundred and thirty-seven kilometres. It is time to refuel."

"Good," Olbermann called over the intercom. "We are stopping here to rest before descending on Sedan tomorrow. Make your checks. We do not want to break down going into battle in the morning. Then have some rest." As Jürgen pulled up behind the leading tank, Olbermann climbed out.

They took a light meal made from rations stored in the tank, simple cold fare which was quickly consumed. Until a Field Kitchen could catch up, this would have to suffice.

Later various supply lorries arrived. Max helped Alfred replace the rounds they had used. Then he made a small entry in his diary before bedding down.

Jürgen replenished the fuel from a bowser. He adjusted the idler wheel removing the slack from the tracks, and then ran a quick engine check looking for oil and water leaks. The beam from his torch formed a pool of light to work by. Midnight passed before he eventually finished.

7

Sedan

Forest of Sedan May 12th

Alfred snored loudly. Jürgen shoved him firmly to make space for his own bed. He lay huddled close to his comrades. They were protected from the weather by a tarpaulin suspended from the tank but the thick grey blankets were not sufficient to ward off the early morning cold.

At 6.00 o'clock, Olbermann nudged each of them with his foot.

"The attack on Sedan has been postponed to 16.00 hours, tomorrow. Apparently Second Panzer is having problems and we must wait for them." There was a groan from the crew. "We will use today to make sure everything is ready for our advance, and we will move camp closer to the start position on the edge of the woods this afternoon." Olbermann started to move away, but stopped. "Be alert for French counterattacks. They will not be happy we have squashed their border post."

Jürgen found no time to relax. Equipment checks, gun checks and restocking of supplies occupied him fully. There were patrols to cover, plus the move forward to the front line ready for the next day. Field Officers organised the move vehicle by vehicle. Evening darkened the camp again. After a proper meal, provided by a mobile Field Kitchen, the crew again bedded down by their tank.

* * *

May 13th dawned sunny though there were clouds drifting in small clumps across the sky. Jürgen climbed into his driving position and waited for the order to start engines. He was tense, fidgeting with the tank's ignition key as he sat wondering how long it would be before they were able to move. They were not the first wave and their deployment would depend on the success of the first echelons.

Sitting quietly Jürgen was troubled by the lack of memories he retained from the battle two days before. The noise, the destruction, the images were indistinct like darkness, or thunder without rain. He still didn't know what had actually happened. He had been cocooned in the tank, held at a distance from a world only visible through the tiny window of his viewing port. He had been protected while hell had ravaged the land. Jürgen could hear Max talking with Alfred. Klaus was fiddling with his radio. Strange electronic crackles, squeaks and whistles emanated from the earphones draped around Jürgen's neck, but he took no notice of the distractions.

Olbermann climbed into the turret. He sat in his command chair at the back of the main gun.

"I have just come from the Field H.Q. Gentlemen, I have good news. General Rommel has crossed the Meuse north of Dinant."

"Bravo to General Rommel." Jürgen snapped out of his mood. Olbermann continued.

"He has a small bridgehead, which he will consolidate today. The bridges across the river were destroyed, but once they have been rebuilt, General Rommel plans to strike westwards, as fast as possible. We must do our best not to let them reach too far ahead of us.

"In our sector, First Panzer Division have captured Sedan's fort and all resistance this side of the river has been annihilated. General Guderian expects us to be across the river tonight. So, are you ready for victory?"

"Yes Sir!" The shout filled the tank.

"Excellent. We will have some help from the Luftwaffe, in about fifteen minutes. Then we roll forward to the river and smash the French positions. Jürgen, start up." Olbermann filed his written orders. Max and Alfred climbed out to crank the engine into motion.

At precisely 07.00 hours, the first aircraft flew overhead. Jürgen couldn't see, but the droning sound indicated a large formation. Moments later explosions sounded beyond the forest, progressing away towards Sedan.

The sound of the French firing their batteries in retaliation mingled with the bombing.

The high level planes were replaced by screaming Stukas diving on individual targets. With pinpoint accuracy, they smashed bunker roofs and overturned guns in their emplacements. Distance dulled the sounds.

A new surge of high level bombs supplanted the Stukas. Wave after wave followed continuously throughout the morning.

Gradually Jürgen took his charge away from the camp and formed up with the rest of the platoon. The order 'Move Forward' came at 14.00 hours.

Jürgen inched his charge out of the trees and down towards the river, moving along tracks cleared by Assault Engineers. Jürgen's restricted view masked the craters which littered the muddy ground, houses burned furiously belching black smoke in billowing clouds. Bodies lay scattered, bloody, dismembered.

The last aircraft turned back to Germany but were replaced by artillery fire. Jürgen felt the ground tremble as the guns launched their barrage. High explosives pounded the far riverbank. Surely nothing could survive such an assault.

One by one the replies from French guns fell silent. The job was done. Relief engulfed Jürgen. The crossing would be easy. Tanks and armoured cars, like ants on a trail, moved forward with singular intent.

Despite there being only six kilometres to the river, their passage was slow. The Regiment would attack the river head-on and cross via the railway bridge straight into Novers, and on to Bulson their day's final objective. Then they would be free to turn due west, all the way to the sea.

Abruptly, earth and stone erupted before his eyes. The French were not yet beaten, their guns had resumed the defence. Violence rained down from positions across the river.

Klaus passed another radio message up through the tank to the Commander.

Jürgen heard Olbermann muttering under his breath.

"You sound troubled, Sir."

"You think so? We have another problem, our bridge has been destroyed. All the bridges in Sedan had been destroyed. We have no way to cross the river."

"What are the new plans?" Jürgen stopped just short of the levee.

"The Generals are working on them. We must wait here," said Olbermann.

"What do you think our options are, Commander?" Alfred enquired.

"We have three alternatives. We can move west to the next solid bridge, but that will entangle us with First and Second Panzer. We can move east under the guns of the Maginot line. The next bridge is twenty kilometres away but I do not think we would succeed. Finally we could build a new bridge here, but the Infantry must first cross the river and capture the far bank. They will be unprotected and it will be very dangerous."

They waited.

Night closed in and still the sound of machine guns and rifles overlaid the thrum of the Panzer's engine turning over. Towards midnight the battle slackened, but there was no chance to rest. Jürgen sat tensely as he watched for danger.

In the early hours, the radio crackled. Olbermann read the message. "Jürgen, we are moving into Sedan. The Engineers have a sixteen tonne pontoon ready for us."

Jürgen revved the engine. We may just make it, one tank at a time, he thought.

Resistance from the opposite river bank had dissolved. Only the numerous craters and wrecks told the fatal story. Jürgen queued through the town. He tried not to let his frustration show as he waited his turn to cross.

Flickering fires cast dancing shapes on shattered walls. Ghostly apparitions lurked in the shadows. The dark stench of smoke and burned flesh filled the atmosphere. It seeped into the tank's compartment through the vents.

Jürgen, creeping forward, eased the tank over piles of scree, walls fallen like mountain avalanches across the road. Behind him the sun rose slowly. The first morning rays struck, revealing shattered buildings. A town of rubble.

Jürgen was ushered onto the bridge. Moving at less than walking pace he negotiated the narrow pontoon, never stopping, never wavering, until he reached the far side. The final section, climbing onto solid ground, eased him slightly. They were across, they could rejoin the battle.

* * *

The tank troop reformed, Klaus intercepted a new order. 'Move south-east, take the Marfee Heights.'

For the past two days, the range of hills had dominated their southward view. The Regiment proceeded in line ahead following the road towards Chaumont and Bulson. They were only a day late into their original destination, but this was not to be the headlong westward attack Jürgen had anticipated. Infantry advanced ahead of them, systematically clearing the enemy, taking prisoners if they surrendered.

As Jürgen turned through Chaumont, a French machine gun, one the pioneers had missed, burst into life. Bullets sprayed off the lead tank. Alfred returned fire. The exchange was short.

The radio crackled again. 'Form line abreast, enemy tanks to the south of your position, engage'. Olbermann scrutinised the message.

"Put your foot down Jürgen, we need to move fast."

They had been moving at little more than walking pace. Jürgen plunged his foot on the accelerator. The tank thrust forward. He changed into third gear and stamped his foot on the accelerator once more. Again the tank lurched, jerking the occupants in a backbending thrust forward, gathering speed they raced to join the line on the ridge.

Before Jürgen could even see the enemy, Olbermann, from his higher vantage point, was calling directions to the gun crew.

"Tank, ten degrees right, A.P. round, six hundred metres, fire."

Max trained the sights on the distant tank's turret ring. Compensating for the rough ride and the forward momentum, he pressed the trigger. A huge cloud of smoke belched from the muzzle as the propellant ignited. Jürgen felt his controls hesitate with the detonation.

The shell struck home just underneath the enemy's main gun. A cloud of smoke and flame engulfed the target but cleared quickly in the wind.

The enemy's turret appeared lopsided. Hatches opened, men struggled to climb out. Klaus fired his machine gun. Four men fell, draped over the tank's sides like moppets.

There was no time to celebrate. Olbermann centred their focus.

"New target, twenty-three degrees right, five-twenty metres, fire."

Max pressed the trigger button, the shell struck the enemy's track, ramming the target sideways. Alfred reloaded. The gun fired. The shell struck home. Two hatches erupted open with flames.

As Jürgen advanced, enemy troops appeared from slit trenches and from behind walls. He watched them as Klaus's machine gun rattled death at them. The remaining enemy turned and fled, the attack was over. The ground was littered with wounded enemy troops.

"Well done, men." said Olbermann. "Now, we hold this front from Haraucourt, through Raucourt to Maisoncelle."

Jürgen breathed with relief. There was a strange sense of triumph, satisfaction gained from watching defeat striking the enemy down. He felt proud of his companions, they worked well together, part of the tank, a successful tank. The realisation made him feel safe.

* * *

Klaus scribbled down another radio message and passed it back to Olbermann.

"Jürgen, move south. There are more French tanks coming."

Jürgen turned towards Stonne and followed the troop as they climbed further into the hills. He watched intently for the enemy.

The French tanks appeared several kilometres away. Row upon row of them, forty, fifty, and more, moving slowly forwards. There were troops between the vehicles. A force greatly exceeding the twenty

94

Panzers.

"No wonder they are moving so slowly, just look at that crowd of Infantry." Max took aim.

"Hold it, you will hardly even reach them from here."

"I could with a longer gun!" Max complained. This one is too short. I need an eighty-eight."

The enemy crawled closer. The Panzers made the greater headway.

"Those things move like snails," Alfred observed.

At fifteen hundred metres, a German t38 fired a ranging shot. They watched the shell fall and bounce off the French armour. The enemy replied, ploughing up a pillar of soil amongst the Panzers. The earth sprinkled down on the t38 like black rain.

"Just hope their aim does not improve," Olbermann cautioned.

Max's temper flared. "Come on Jürgen, move it up."

"What!... and break formation?"

Another t38 fired with little effect.

"Wait until the range is six hundred metres." Olbermann measured the distance. "Twelve hundred, just another minute or so. Load."

"Loaded and ready," Alfred confirmed.

"Hold fire." Olbermann waited. The distance closed. "Another fifty metres... fire!"

Max pressed the trigger. Thunder filled the tank, deafening them with shock. The target stopped dead, nearby enemy troops fell to the ground.

"Reload A.P.," Olbermann shouted.

Alfred heaved on the breach handle releasing the spent shell casing from the gun barrel. He hauled another armour piercing round from the storage. Using his fist he rammed the brass casing home and shut the breach, locking the shell in place. "Loaded and ready." He dropped the old casing, still smoking, into the locker.

"Same target... fire!" Olbermann ordered. Max pressed the trigger.

"Reload."

Alfred was already removing the new round.

"Five degrees left," Olbermann instructed, "five-sixty metres."

Max pressed the electronic traverser, watching the indicator until it showed the required direction. He adjusted the elevation handle for the new range.

"Fire..." Olbermann's voice was drowned by the roar of the gun as Max pressed the firing button.

The rounds spat out one after another. Jürgen concentrated on

95

driving, hardly noticing the gradual slaughter of the more cumbersome opposition. On the receiving end of mighty German firepower, the enemy retreated back over their hill, leaving more than half their number devastated on the battlefield. The battle had finished.

"About turn, Jürgen," said Olbermann, "back to Raucourt."

"Why are we going back, Sir?" Jürgen swung the tank round and headed for their starting point.

"We must hold our south and eastern flanks while the First and Second Panzers attack westwards."

"So we are going to miss all the fun," Max observed.

"Do not complain, you have had a good couple of days so far," said Olbermann. "We only stay here until the Fourteenth Army Corps arrives. Then we move on to the new front line."

"What good will we do sitting here?"

"My dear Max. We are covering our backsides. The Maginot Line is out there," Olbermann pointed in an arbitrary direction. "We must repel any, and all attacks directed at us. The battle is not over and they have many more troops to throw at us, and they will. Unlike the Poles, they will not let us pass without a fight. But we are still better, every one of us."

Jürgen pulled up just short of the village and parked the tank in a defensive position with the rest of the unit.

"We will be here for quite a while, but no slacking please. I want a thorough check of all equipment. We will re-supply as soon as the lorries arrive. Alfred, take the first watch, I will return soon." Olbermann climbed out and walked away.

Alfred climbed onto the turret and sat astride the gun. He peered through his binoculars.

"I can see our supply lorries on the other side of the river, they should be here in a couple of hours."

"Never mind them," said Max. "You are supposed to be looking for the enemy coming from the south-east."

Alfred resumed his watch.

Jürgen opened the engine covers and checked the oil level and air filter. Then he checked the engine coolant and the twin fans. He closed the covers. After inspecting each link, he tightened the tracks.

The sound of shooting accompanied him as he worked, it was discomforting.

Olbermann returned.

"While we are here, have something to eat. It will be dark soon. I will take first watch after Alfred, then Jürgen followed by Max, Klaus and finally Alfred again at first light."

"Commander," Jürgen leaned on the front of the tank, "I had to adjust the tracks again. They are as tight as they will go. Should I remove a link now or wait until our next stop?"

"Do it now. We will be here through the night but we may have to move quickly in the morning. Better to have them adjusted than find we are in trouble later. Make sure you properly stow the links you remove." Olbermann turned to Alfred. "What is the view like up there?"

"It is good, very clear. It would be pretty if the French had not forced us to bomb it to pieces."

"Is there any movement?"

"Only our supplies."

Jürgen loosened the tank's idler wheels, then at the drive sprocket, he pulled the split pins from the connecting rods either side of a link. Using a small hammer, he slowly tapped the connecting rods out to separate the link from the rest of the track. Lifting the link free, he called to Max.

"Come and help me close this gap, here." They pulled the loose track forward over the return rollers until the space closed. While Max held the links together, Jürgen forced a bar back through the loops to rejoin the two ends, he tapped it home before refitting the split pin. "Why do they have to make these tracks so heavy? They are the worst links I have ever seen."

"Because they are fitted to the biggest and heaviest tank," Max chuckled.

"Help me with this other one," said Jürgen. "Then we can eat."

They followed the same process with the right-hand track.

"Jürgen, have you finished the job properly?" Olbermann called down to them as they settled down to eat: "did you retighten the idler wheels?"

"Hell!"

"You must remember that, or we will be stranded trackless somewhere, next time you turn a corner."

"Apologies, Herr Commander. I think I was more interested in my stomach."

"Finish the work before you eat." Olbermann turned away. "Alfred, I will take the watch now. Give me an inventory of the rounds we need, then have your meal."

Evening fell. Occasional sniper fire rang out on the hills to the south but mostly it was quiet.

Max was writing his diary as Jürgen wrapped himself up in a blanket, close by.

"You must have lots to say this evening, Max."

"A little, but I do not chatter on and on like you do," Max laughed back.

Jürgen took the watch from 22.00 hours, until midnight. When Max relieved him, he wrapped himself in the blanket Max had left. It was still warm. He slept fitfully, his dreams filled with visions of bloody corpses dancing a macabre ballet of crippled limbs and burning flesh. Cadavers, draped over guns, bounced in unison with the vibration of each exploding shell.

* * *

Alfred maintained his watch. The pre-dawn highlighted the horizon, dark-blue behind black silhouettes of trees and houses. There was no sound, but that did not mean there was nobody out there. He could smell the dust and smoke on the breeze attesting to the battle that had taken place through the night.

The sky turned blue, then golden as rays of light rose from the eastern horizon. As the sun peeked over the distant hills, new sporadic shooting drifted on the air.

Jürgen climbed up and sat next to Alfred for a moment. "Such a fine view." He turned towards Sedan, gazing through his new binoculars. The scene stretched northwards from the west, round to the south-east. The Meuse threaded its way from the hills in the south-east, through the valley, cutting Sedan in two. Closer by, picking out details of their passing, Jürgen noticed the track marks on the soil. Piles of earth and craters studded the ground. Mounds of rubble pinpointed collapsed houses. The devastation stretched northwards. Nearby, Jürgen could pick out individual soldiers. Ruined enemy guns littering the scene, their bunkers broken slabs of concrete, rested at odd angles. Dead cattle, already bloated, lay in the fields. In the distance, a pack of dogs silently ripped at a carcass.

Beyond the river were more craters and the wrecked villages they had passed through the previous day. He could see their supply lorries, mere specks, passing along the road beyond the river.

Jürgen looked east and scanned towards the famous Maginot line. The ground looked pristine, green fields with crops or roaming cattle.

98

Life there seemed to continue as though nothing unusual was happening. A farmer, leading a horse, moved slowly along a path. Maybe twelve kilometres away to the east, their motion seemed incongruous without the accompanying sound of hooves.

The countryside was still.

Jürgen climbed down from the vantage point. Moments later Alfred pointed south-east into the still shaded valley.

"I can hear engines over there."

"What do you think, more enemy tanks?" Jürgen asked.

"Possibly, we will soon know if they are. The SS will call us. *Oh, please, come and help us.*" Max used a high falsetto. "*We are the best troops in the German Reich but we cannot manage against these tanks.*"

"Just refrain from speaking like that when they are around. They will probably shoot you if they hear," Olbermann reprimanded.

"Ha, I am not that stupid."

"You think not?"

They all laughed.

"I see tanks to the south-east, about six kilometres away," Alfred pointed.

"They cannot be ours. Prepare for battle." Olbermann climbed up to the turret and searched the horizon with the glasses. "Klaus, radio the Command Post." For a long time nothing happened, then Klaus poked his head out through his hatch.

"The platoon is ordered to engage the enemy."

"Let us hope our ammunition holds out," said Olbermann. "Start her up and take your places." Olbermann watched the woods and the tops of the hill over which the enemy force was advancing. They had already started slowly down into the valley towards him. "Jürgen, drive on."

Olbermann held on tightly as the tank lurched forward. "We shall give them a nice little surprise. Alfred, load the gun, high explosive."

The troop moved east between two wooded areas, slowly they descended into the valley towards the still peaceful village of Yoncq.

In the distance, rows of enemy troops plodded in a ragged mass down the opposing slope. Behind them came a short line of high-turreted tanks.

"Hold your fire." Olbermann held them in check. Slowly they advanced, the Panzer rocked gently as it moved over the rough ground.

More enemy tanks appeared from a small wood three kilometres away, Jürgen headed directly towards them.

Two kilometres.

"Target the Infantry, wait until we are within nine hundred metres."
Olbermann cast a glance at the rest of the unit. Listening to instructions
from the Troop's Commander, he repeated the orders. "Two rounds rapid
fire. Two, one, shoot!" The whole tank troop fired together.

The simultaneous crash of eight guns discharging at the same time
was deafening. Columns of earth flew up around the enemy soldiers.
They fell– silent.

Standing head and shoulders exposed over the turret hatch,
Olbermann watched, only hearing the screams of the injured moments
later.

Jürgen watched the figures collapse like actors in a silent movie. He
wondered what the occupants of the houses in the village were thinking
as mayhem erupted so close to them. Too close for their comfort, he
thought.

Alfred loaded the second round. Instantly the gun fired again. As a
unit the timing was less precise, but the salvo was just as devastating.

By comparison the enemy shells were ill aimed. Plumes of earth
spattered the Panzers.

"Reload A.P., take the first tank on the left, fire." The range was
down to six hundred metres. The French Somua's track exploded as the
round struck. The terrified crew leapt from the hatches and ran. Other
tank crews followed suit. They seemed in disarray, as shells pounded
their positions. There was little they could do to ward off the Panzers'
fury. The remaining troops turned and fled as the last surviving tanks
retreated back to the wood.

"Come on, Jürgen," said Olbermann. "We will flatten the wood if we
have to. Max, keep firing, six rounds when you are ready."

Guns spat fire at the trees. Jürgen watched as splinters flew. Rounds
landed at the edge of the wood. The retreating French were trapped
between the exploding shells and those who fired them, they dropped
their weapons in the field and stood, horrified, waiting to die.

More soldiers shambled from the woods, hands in the air, waving
sticks with remnants of white cloth attached.

"Cease fire," Olbermann shouted. Max's gun fell silent. "They look
pitiful." Olbermann's voice was filled with contempt. "Keep going,
Jürgen, until we are upon them."

As Jürgen stopped by the closest French troops, the German troop
Commander, *Oberleutnant* Heinz Lutz, stood on his tank turret.

"Do you wish to surrender?" He addressed the dishevelled rabble but didn't try to use their native tongue. Jürgen could just make out the words through Olbermann's open hatch.

There was a mumbled reply in French.

"Lay down your weapons and equipment and walk to Bulson." Lutz seemed unsympathetic. "Do not worry, there you will be taken care of. For you, the war is over." This was a statement which would ring in Jürgen's ears many times in the future.

The men stripped off their packs and dropped them on the ground. Moving back down the slope, an imitation of their former attack, they shuffled their dejection towards imprisonment.

Lutz turned to his tank troops.

"Numbers six and eight, stay with them, make sure they do not become lost or return for their weapons."

"Yes, Sir." Olbermann's enthusiasm was non-existent. He spoke into the intercom "Gentlemen, we shall be herding cattle for a while."

Max groaned.

"It is probably just as well," Alfred reflected, "we are running dangerously low on ammunition."

"I would rather fire the gun and run out," Max retorted, "than not fire at all."

Jürgen watched the Frenchmen's actions with interest. Olbermann interrupted his musing.

"About turn, Jürgen. We are on guard duty."

"Just us! What about the rest of the unit?" Jürgen queried.

"They are going to secure the woods," Olbermann replied.

Jürgen shifted the gear and adjusted the throttle. The tank slowly swivelled round to face the way they had come.

As he turned Jürgen's sight momentarily fell on other tanks. The first, tank 328, a t38 stood out clearly as it too started to turn back. A second t38, 327 on the turret, stood a hundred metres back with one track missing. The crew seemed to be all right as they set about making repairs. With his restricted view he had not seen their misfortune.

From his side window, Jürgen could just make out another t38. Number 322 lay burning, a new and deathly reminder of his own vulnerability. He decided, that tank had been unlucky. That could not possibly happen to his own Panzer IV, it was far superior to the Czech built machines.

Jürgen kept station behind the captives. He gunned the engine gently up the hill, maintaining a slow walking pace. The process of escorting the captives across the eight kilometres to Division Headquarters took four hours. Neither verbal abuse nor the threat of being machine gunned seemed to have any effect on speeding up the demoralised prisoners.

Jürgen opened the hatch above his head letting in light and fresh air. He listened to a French Officer respond to Olbermann's badgering.

"Already today, you 'ave tried to kill us many times, we can not stop you. When we reach Bulson, you will probably kill us anyway. We are in no 'urry to die." He plodded on, not looking back.

The Regiment's headquarters was a collection of tents and armoured cars. A flag flew high overhead. Olbermann handed the prisoners to a Security Squad.

After Olbermann had spoken with a Senior Officer, Jürgen drove his companions to Raucourt, but the camp had been moved. They were redirected towards Stonne.

Jürgen parked the Panzer close behind the rest of the unit. He climbed out to stretch his legs. Max joined him.

"Are you glad it is over for the day?" Jürgen asked.

"Over!" Max seemed astonished. "It never seemed to start. All we have done is wipe up a few weak remnants. This looks like it was much more productive."

Jürgen surveyed the scene. A line of eighty-eight millimetre guns stood as though on guard duty, their grey muzzles levelled at the hill's brow. Spent shell casings lay around as testament to another battle. Clouds of smoke rose from the village. Machinery which would never work again littered the roads. Expired French tanks were strewn across the battlefield.

More French troops shuffled towards Bulson, by now there would be thousands there. 'For you, the war is over.' The words slipped into Jürgen's mind unbidden.

A number of lorries pulled up behind the tanks. The first driver stepped down and stretched, extending his tight muscles.

"You seem to have had a busy time. We have been waiting since yesterday to bring supplies."

"Oh, it was only a little skirmish." said Olbermann the *Gross-Deutschlanders* have taken care of it."

"We just sat and watched," Jürgen blurted.

"As long as you are enjoying yourselves… I have ammunition for the Tenth Panzer Division."

"That will be for us then." Olbermann pointed at the group of tanks behind him.

"Have you any fuel?" Jürgen asked.

"Or food rations?" Klaus interrupted.

"A few cans of diesel, but a lorry with petrol will be up here soon. You can fill your Panzer from that.

"Good," said Olbermann. "Max and Klaus, restock the ammunition. Alfred, Jürgen, prepare to fuel up, then we can all have dinner."

"There will be a Field Kitchen here, later," said the lorry driver.

"That is welcome information. I am growing tired of rations."

* * *

When the 29th Motorised Infantry Division arrived during the night, the *Gross-Deutschlanders* retreated to the river to recuperate. In the shadow of the Panzer, Jürgen slept deeply in spite of the noise and constant movement around him.

The morning of Thursday 16th had a chilly bite in the air. Promptly at 6.30 a.m., Jürgen drove the Panzer IV into formation with the rest of the platoon, then the whole of the Tenth Panzer Division headed west towards Bouvellemont to catch up with the First and Second Divisions. They continued onwards to Novion, Chaumont and Noircourt, heading west all the time. There was no sign of the front line.

They continued the fight, mopping up enemy units the leaders had missed. Jürgen drove on.

French civilians blocked the road, large crowds fleeing the threat of the German invasion not realising they were already being overtaken. They tumbled into the ditches, panicked by the sound of the German *"Achtung"* behind them.

Overhead, several Messerschmitts chased two Hurricanes, one of which left a thick black trail in the air. There was little hope for the British, Jürgen thought with satisfaction.

Night fell, but they maintained the pressure.

It was midday again when the tank reached La Fère. They had been on the move, non stop, for twenty-nine hours. Jürgen was exhausted, He was hungry and his body ached.

Another battle raged before him. Jürgen watched as the tank in front adjusted its turret before belching smoke at something he couldn't see. He did not stop. He kept his eyes fixed on the vehicle in front. Soon Max too was firing. They passed on through the danger before the enemy crumbled.

At Ham, members of the First Panzer Division greeted them briefly before moving on again themselves. In their place, the Tenth Division assumed the defensive positions along the banks of the Somme. They ranged northwards from Ham to Peronne and then west towards Amiens, protecting the invasion's southern flank.

"Do you think we will ever occupy the front line?" Jürgen asked Max…

8

Calais

As morning dawned, Jürgen crested the hills at Desvres. He had been driving in silence since the order to advance at 01.30 hours. Meanwhile the others slept. Suddenly he saw signs of fighting ahead. A thick column of smoke filled the air over the city forty kilometres to the north. Flames flickering against the gathering clouds left the sky red.

"It looks like someone hit Calais' fuel dump."

"Either that, or most of the city is burning," Olbermann replied. "I have been watching the smoke since first light. It will be good if we have destroyed their strongest port. The British will have no way of fleeing."

"Then Mr. Cigar will have to seek peace terms. He will have no troops left," said Klaus.

"We will be able to march right into Britain," said Alfred.

"You do not know the British," Olbermann chuckled. "I think they will fight to the last man, with cutlery if they have to."

"How can they fight us if they have lost their armies?" asked Klaus.

"Oh, they will," Jürgen interjected. "My father said, in the last war they were as determined a soldier as you would ever meet." Jürgen thought back to the conversations he had had while waiting to enlist. "He said the British are a strange nation. In peacetime you would think nothing mattered to them, but in war, even the women will fight, tooth and nail, with their babies in their arms."

"Ha, your father has a good imagination," said Olbermann, "though he may be right. We shall see when the time comes. Does anyone want to lay bets on when the British will surrender?" Olbermann offered. "I have twenty *Reichmarks* which say they will keep fighting."

"I think their fat bellied leader will cave in before we land on their shores."

"I take you up on that, Alfred." Olbermann looked at Max. "You have said nothing so far, what do you think?"

"I have no idea," Max thought hard for a moment, then brightened, "but I will hold the stakes for you if you like."

"I do not think so. We would be without a gunner before we turned the next corner, and you would be stuck up some little French skirt with our cash flowing out of your pockets like water."

"If you won't let Max hold the pot, let us keep the money until someone wins the bet," Klaus proposed. "If you win, you can always collect later and if we are dead you can collect from our possessions. You will have to return them to our families anyway, and you will send a nice letter telling them how wonderful we are."

"You think I trust you that much?" Olbermann laughed. "The way you talk, I should annul the bets right now. I am more likely to be telling your parents what a band of swindlers you are."

"You would never disappoint them," Jürgen scolded. "Surely you will at least give the impression we behaved well, even if we are the devil's own?"

"Your parents probably realise you are devils," Olbermann retorted. "I tell you what, I will tell them how good you are if you help me receive the Knight's Cross."

"Then we had better make sure you receive one," laughed Jürgen.

"With Oak Leaves!" Olbermann goaded.

"Ten times easier!"

* * *

Jürgen drove over the last hill. The flat land lay ahead with Calais, ruined, prominent on the coast.

"It looks like the First Division has defeated the *Franzosen* already. Is there nothing left for us to do here?" The thick smoke rising from the city filled the sky and stretched north-east into Belgium and Holland.

"First Panzer certainly seem to have had a field day, how could anyone survive that?" Max was dispirited.

"It looks to me like there is not much left for us," said Alfred.

"You are always on the lookout for profit," said Olbermann. "Do not despair, there are still some very strong enemy positions to defeat. First Panzer are moving against Dunkerque and we replace them against Calais. It should be easy."

Spreading round the city, Tenth Panzer Division moved into their attack positions. Jürgen followed his Company to the east side of the Canal de Calais. The advance would be along the canal's bank.

The day turned wet. Heavy rain soaked the ground. The troops moved forward slowly, thankful to be using roads as opposed to dragging their feet through muddy fields.

Jürgen squinted through the water dribbling down his viewing port, the rain was becoming worse. He followed the first line of soldiers.

Slowly the Division headed through the town. The first shots rang out, enemy snipers picked off individuals but resistance was light.

"Max, put a round through the church tower ahead of us." Olbermann stood in the cupola. Though the weather was soaking, he could see better and felt more in control. "I think the enemy have a spotter up there."

Max adjusted the gun and fired. Bricks and stone flew out scattering in all directions. In amongst the falling masonry, a human figure flopped and plummeted to the ground.

"Well done – Jürgen, pull forward."

Gradually the outer city roads were cleared of opposition. Olbermann felt confident of their success. He glimpsed the waterfront at the end of the road, the docks and basins forming the moat surrounding the old town.

The lead Panzer drove clear of the buildings to the quayside. Jürgen followed. He didn't stop but moved directly onto the bridge connecting the two sides of the canal. The area appeared quiet except for rifle fire. There was no artillery. He rode onto the heavy decking. It was only a short bridge, twenty metres. Still no substantial resistance.

* * *

Olbermann didn't hear the rifle shot, he felt a violent thrust at his left shoulder. He gasped, as a heavy weight settled on his body.

He glanced at his tunic. There were tattered threads around a hole in the chest. A growing red stain saturated the cloth. Olbermann felt slightly annoyed at the blemish on his pristine uniform. The damage would have to be darned.

Suddenly he felt dizzy, fire torched his shoulder, his body grew numb, his legs sagged, their strength drained away. Slowly he crumpled, trying desperately to support himself on the cupola. His hands skidded away on the slippery rain-wet surface. The cupola rim caught him under the arms. A grunt escaped his lips as his body impacted on the metal ring. He hung there momentarily. Realisation gradually dawned. He struggled to stand while searching for his attacker.

A second bullet ricocheted from the hatch cover by his left ear, the sound of the shot only arrived afterwards. Olbermann jerked involuntarily at the near miss. He must be a perfect target, he thought. Unable to move, trapped by his own weakness and with no cover. How long would it take the rifleman to hit him again?

107

A third shot grazed Olbermann's scalp parting his hair diagonally.

Frantically Olbermann tried to shift himself, he managed to raise his arms, freeing himself at last. He dropped into the turret and slumped on the floor gasping for breath.

Inside, Max caught sight of the strange movements from the corner of his eye. He glanced sideways to reassure himself.

"Alfred!" Max shouted, "The Commander!" He and Alfred grabbed Olbermann to make him more comfortably. "Jürgen, stop the tank. The Commander is hurt, we must go back."

"No!" Olbermann gasped the word through a sheet of pain. Teeth gritted, he tried to rise. "We must go on, I can be treated later. Kill the sniper... In the third building on the right, second floor. Then head through the town. We must clear all the enemy from the streets."

"Lie still." Max pushed the man down.

"What is happening back there?" shouted Jürgen.

"Never mind, Jürgen. Drive clear of the bridge and stop to the right." Max turned to his station. He was fuming with rage, revenge his only thought. "Alfred, load H.E."

Jürgen swerved the tank to the right and stopped.

In a single movement, Max traversed and elevated the gun. He fired, placing the shell through the adjoining wall of the second and third building. The explosion blew out the building's facade.

"Load another." The second round was lower, taking out the ground floor and completing the destruction of the upper level. A secondary detonation blasted flames through the third floor engulfing both houses.

"What was that?" Klaus exclaimed.

"Perhaps a gas pipe," Alfred mused. "Stored ammunition, who knows?"

"Load another," Max shouted. Nothing would satisfy him except the total annihilation of the offending structure.

"It is good." Alfred tried to reason with his gunner. "You have done what was needed. There will be no more trouble here."

"Load another round," Max ordered.

Jürgen listened to the building argument.

"No." Alfred sounded calm. "It would be a waste, we will need all the rounds we have... Jürgen, drive on."

"Alfred, I am the gunner, I am telling you to load another."

"No. Not until you calm down. Jürgen, drive on."

It seemed obvious Max was not thinking clearly. Jürgen pressed the accelerator leaning gently into the steering levers. The Panzer moved slowly forward, passing the burning buildings before turning along the next road through the city.

They were alone, even the support troops who should have been searching the buildings, were absent. The main Company had moved along other roads towards the church, pressing the enemy backwards. They seemed not to be aware one tank had become detached.

Jürgen listened to the argument but peered through his visor trying to spot possible enemy positions. He tried to assess the situation both inside and out. The few enemy troops he could see, seemed lightly armed with no antitank weapons but it was difficult to judge with all the civilians who blocked the road.

"Max!" Jürgen shouted, "we may be in trouble here if you do not pay attention. We are surrounded by *Franzosen*, mostly civilians but I think there are troops hiding amongst them."

Instantly Max was alert, taking control.

"Klaus, see if you can clear them out of the way."

The civilians ran in fear as Klaus raked his machine gun across the street. He fired short bursts of three or four rounds at a time. For good measure, he placed some shots through the lower windows of buildings. There would be no more attacks on this machine and its crew.

Turning a corner, Jürgen noticed a church spire come momentarily into view over the town. The tank rolled on.

"Alfred, help me with the Commander." Max grabbed the first aid kit. "We need to do something about the wound or he will bleed to death." It was a struggle to remove Olbermann's tunic and shirt but they managed eventually to dress the wound. The bullet had passed right through the shoulder, leaving a small hole under the collar bone but a much larger, ragged wound to the left of the scapula, in the back of the upper arm.

"Commander, how is the pain? Do you need morphine?"

"I can take the pain," Olbermann breathed slowly. "Just lay me on my right side, under the seating where I will be out of the way."

When Olbermann was comfortable, Max picked up the Commander's tunic and removed the notebook containing codes and objectives from the pocket. He draped the tunic back around Olbermann's body and exchanged headsets.

"At least, Commander, you will be able to hear what is happening." Max turned away. "Klaus, tell *Oberleutnant* Lutz what has happened and request orders, we need to rejoin the Company. Jürgen, take the next left,

I hope it will bring us closer to the unit." Max, using Olbermann's headset, listened in to Klaus's communications on the radio.

"Orders from *Oberleutnant* Lutz," reported Klaus. "He says continue west and meet the unit at the Citadel."

"Have you got that, Jürgen?" Max asked.

"Yes, leave it to me."

Slowly they negotiated their way through the town. The church came closer until Jürgen found himself on the square around the imposing building. The base filled Jürgen's view across the wet street. The rain was worsening.

Jürgen calculated the direction he needed to take but enemy gun emplacements blocked the route. Protected by sandbags, they looked like fifty millimetre antitank weapons but the emplacements were makeshift at best.

"Max, we have trouble."

Max glanced through his viewer and saw a puff of smoke as the first gun fired. The round exploded above and to his left. Max returned fire, blasting the antagonists. The weapon vaulted in a backward somersault crushing two of the crew.

Enemy troops appeared along the railings around the church.

As the turret traversed, Alfred fired his machine gun, raking the railings at chest level. Max took aim at the second emplacement. The target's crew were already running for cover before his shell struck. They hid in doorways and fired their rifles, before running to new hiding places.

"Jürgen, steer directly towards that third emplacement," Max ordered. "Drive over the top of it if you have to." Already deserted, the gun could give no resistance. The tank ran diagonally over the gun carriage and breach ensuring it was useless.

Jürgen caught sight of another gun on an adjacent corner of the square. "Max, to the left, another gun." The crew were already training their weapon to strike. This would be close.

Max frantically spun the traverser trying to bring his gun to bear.

"Come on, come on." Max willed the turret to move faster. Who would fire first? As the enemy came into view, Max estimated the required elevation. He pressed the trigger as the enemy's puff of smoke projected towards him. His shot blotted out the sound of the poorly aimed incoming round. Max just caught sight of his target spinning off its carriage as Jürgen entered another street.

Klaus's machine gun sprayed the pavements ahead, the short bursts of lead struck fear into the panicking crowds. Jürgen drove past French soldiers and civilian wounded lying on the pavements, some were dead.

"Jürgen, whatever happens, keep going," Max ordered, "we must find the rest of the unit."

Though only making slow headway, Jürgen continued forward, steering around fallen obstacles.

Max checked on Commander Olbermann. The man had his hand pressed against the wound, blood showed on the makeshift dressing. His eyes shut, he was breathing calmly while the others carried the war forward.

"Is there anything I can do for you, Commander? Max was concerned the wound was not being treated as it should be.

"When you have a moment I would like some water."

Max reached for a canteen and poured water onto the Commander's lips.

"Thank you. Attend to your station, I am fine for now."

Max left the canteen on the floor by the wounded man. Turning back to his duties, he scanned the map trying to assess their position.

"Where are we, Jürgen?"

Jürgen concentrated as he searched for identifying landmarks.

"I am not sure. I can see the waterfront ahead, and the sea, so we must be heading north."

"Turn left at the next street, I think it leads to the Citadel, we should find our friends somewhere that way."

Jürgen pulled into the next junction. Gradually, as he turned, another emplacement hove into view across the square.

"Max, another gun!" Jürgen shouted.

Max had already seen it. He blasted the weapon as Klaus spattered its crew with his machine gun. Many fell, the remainder ran desperately for cover.

The fleeing enemies fell back through the streets to avoid the Division's overwhelming attack. But in trying to avoid the main body of the German army, they ran into Jürgen's path. The numbers gradually increased stumbling over each other in panic. For Max they made easy pickings.

"Save your rounds, Klaus, I can deal with these idiots." Max fired at a building beyond the retreating French, it rained bricks engulfing them in masonry rubble.

Jürgen slowed as he approached the wounded soldiers.

"Do not stop, Jürgen. Just drive over them."

"But they are still alive!"

"Just keep going. It is too risky to have feeling for them." Max fired another round. It struck a tower, dropping a large portion of wall into the street. He fired again, aiming a little further along and at the other side. Max kept up the assault as they moved forward.

Jürgen reached the end of the road, he stopped before entering the junction. Ahead was a wide avenue, bordered on the far side by water and beyond that, a ten metre high wall… the Citadel.

French and British soldiers knelt firing their rifles towards Jürgen's left, others ran towards an old, block-built building.

With so many enemy troops present, Jürgen thought it safer to remain hidden in the side street. He watched the frantic activity.

"Jürgen," Max called, "pull out a little so I can bring the gun to bear."

Reluctantly Jürgen pulled forward and turned slightly towards the fort. Max scrutinised the situation through his cupola viewer, trying to identify his best target. A large group of German soldiers were pinned down at the entrance to another road. It seemed a little help was needed.

"Jürgen, swivel left to give Klaus a clear shot." Max watched with interest and satisfaction as Klaus opened up. "You have a go too, Alfred."

The machine guns rattled away, spitting lead into the enemy's flanks. Jürgen watched as he moved forward into the attack, the guns wreaking confusion as he advanced. Screams burst from the wounded. Others tried to ward off the new threat but, seeing the tank, ran for cover.

"Cease fire," Max ordered, "target those entering the building." Jürgen glanced at the huge slab-walled building, a complimentary structure to the Citadel across the canal. The enemy continued to take refuge behind the walls. Alfred opened fire on the gate and the troops running for safety.

Suddenly the seventy-five millimetre gun blasted at the walls as Max joined the attack. The first round detonated in the gateway sending the fleeing foes sprawling, many did not move again.

Enemy troops appeared on the walls firing their rifles pathetically in retaliation. Alfred returned to loading the main gun for Max. The next three shots shattered the parapet's edge, sending the defenders into hiding.

A heavy gun, positioned on the wall over the canal, fired in reply but missed widely. Max traversed again and returned the compliment. In his rush, he struck the wall a few centimetres below the embrasure, flinging rock across the opposing gunners.

Jürgen studied the building in front of him, it was some sort of Gatehouse to the Citadel. This then was the key to entering the main fort. The more troops who took refuge there, the harder it would be to defeat them, Jürgen reasoned.

"Max, we must stop them from gaining the Citadel," he shouted, "I am taking us in." Suddenly the tank lurched forward moving faster.

Max fired at the entrance, he waited for the smoke to clear before firing again. Each round ripped holes in the walls and roadway ahead. The Allied troops had been struggling to file through to the castle. As Panzer 326 drove between the gates, the enemy found their retreat denied to them.

Max fired again, aiming low to strike deep into the compound.

As the dust settled dozens of enemy troops emerged from hiding, their hands held high.

Jürgen drove slowly into the deep defences, it was a tight fit. He took no notice of the surrendering Allied soldiers but continued to the waterfront and a narrow bridge crossing the water.

The enemy stood by watching, sullen dejection masking their faces. The Panzer Troops following Jürgen took care of the rabble as they cleared the final remnants of resistance.

The Gatehouse was captured at last.

* * *

"Max, I dare not cross this bridge, I am sure it is too weak."

"All right, but I can at least open the gates for our next attack. Then we can wait for the Engineers to check the bridge before we move on."

Max took careful aim at the portal across the canal. The shot blew the wooden gates to splinters leaving the Citadel's entrance clear.

Panzer troops rushed past the tank and over the bridge. The fight was being carried forward.

The occupying defenders tried to repel the invaders. Machine guns challenged the attack but more troops replaced those who fell. With so many German troops in front, Jürgen realised the tank's usefulness was at an end.

"Max, we have done all we can here. We should find help for the Commander, it has been a long time for him."

"Yes, I agree. Turn around and go back."

Jürgen turned the tank in the wide yard at the canal's edge, and headed back through the Gatehouse to the avenue. They needed to find a Medical Officer.

Along the canal on both sides of the outpost there were arrays of t38s and armoured cars. Troops queued to join the fight. Many looked surprised as Jürgen pulled clear of the walls.

An Officer, looking miserable and wet, waved his hands in front of the machine.

"Stop. Identify yourselves."

Max stood up in the cupola, the hatch was still open from when Commander Olbermann had been shot. He saluted as smartly as the confined space permitted.

"We are Panzer 326, Seventh Panzer Regiment of the Tenth Panzer Division, Sir."

The Officer noted the lack of insignia on Max's tunic.

"Where is your Commanding Officer?"

Commander Olbermann was wounded, Sir. At his instruction, I took over command. I am *Gefreiter* Webber, Sir."

"How is it you were inside the Citadel?"

"Sir, we became separated from our troop. We were trying to relocate them but it seemed like a good idea to continue fighting while we searched."

"The forward Command Post is down there." The Officer directed Max down a side road. "You must make a full report to the Division Commander."

"We need a doctor for our Commander," Max called back.

"You will find medical help there also. What is the nature of his injury?"

Max described the shoulder wound. The Officer waved them on.

"I will inform them you are coming."

* * *

The Command Post was a collection of covered lorries and radio armoured cars. They formed a semicircle in the shadow of the Notre Dame Church, on the opposite side of the square Panzer 326 had crossed previously. Jürgen stopped the tank next to the railings.

Klaus and Alfred helped Max lift Commander Olbermann through the side hatch.

"Stretcher, stretcher!" Max shouted at the top of his voice. An Officer walked out from under an awning attached to one of the lorries.

"What is all this shouting?"

"*Herr Oberst*, our Commander has been shot. We were told to bring him here."

Recognising the tank from the recent radio message, the *Oberst* waved his hand for medics to attend. "He will be taken care of. Now come, *Generalleutnant* Schaal wants to see you."

"We only went as far as the canal, we did…"

"Do not tell me."

Max followed the Colonel to the lorry.

"*Mein General*," the *Oberst* announced, "this soldier is from the tank at the Citadel."

Max saluted as the General turned to scrutinise him.

"So, how did your Commander come to be wounded?"

"Sir, we were crossing the canal east of here." Max gave a detailed report of the action he had seen since Olbermann's wounding.

"Do I understand this correctly? While your Officer was incapacitated, the remainder of you decided to try and fight the whole of the British and French garrison on your own, without support, or instructions to do so. Do you realise in how much danger you have placed yourselves? One grenade in your cupola would have seen the end of your whole crew." The General's voice contained a stern edge. Max wondered how much trouble they were in. He did not answer.

"I can not," the General continued, "have tank crews running off and doing whatever they want without due regard for preconceived plans. My plans… Go back to your tank. You are not to leave the square."

Max saluted and left without speaking. He reported back to his three comrades, they all considered the situation to be unfavourable. They collected meals from a Field Kitchen close to the command vehicles.

"You are very lucky, you know." The cook laughed, "you are having a share of the General's own supplies. You must consider yourselves privileged."

"Either that, or we are being given the last rights before execution," Max suggested.

* * *

By dawn the four soldiers were up and tending their Panzer. Routine checks and inventories were made to confirm the vehicle was fit and ready to fight, but these were made difficult by the still heavy rain. They were short of ammunition but the tank looked in good condition and there was plenty of fuel. If they could restock with shells they would be ready for action.

It was 6.00 a.m. when a Kitchen Officer called them over.

"The General is having breakfast. He wishes you to join him."

Filled with apprehension, they marched to the General's quarters. None of them could think what was so urgent the General would wish to see them while he was still eating. How much trouble had they accumulated the day before?

They stepped into the command vehicle to find the Division's Commanding Officer sitting at a small desk with his food in front of him. Still not having had their own breakfast, the fresh eggs and hot coffee made them even more hungry as they stood waiting.

"Good morning, Gentlemen. I have had a short conversation this morning with Tank Commander Olbermann concerning your conduct. He unfortunately does not remember much. It seems he spent much of the time slumped on the floor, unable to see what was happening. He did say he is only alive because you dressed his wounds, and that you continued to fight because he ordered you to.

"I have also spoken to several others under my Command, who say the capture of the outpost at the Citadel's East Gate was largely down to your enterprise. I must inform you, by comparison, we have only just been able to come within reach of the South Gate. Perhaps if you had been there, we would have made more progress on that front as well. But even you cannot be in two places at the same time. Correct?"

"S–Sir," stammered Max.

"I can only take your word for what actually happened, there does not seem to be anyone who can corroborate the statement you made last night. On the one hand your actions were very dangerous. Being on your own, you could have caused us to loose a tank which we can ill afford to be without. However, you managed to push the enemy into their stronghold and you took our forces to their door.

"Fighting, even now, is continuing at that location and I am confident we shall have the enemy's surrender by nightfall. As such, you are to be complemented on your part in this action. You have shown the skill and determination we require from our Panzer troops. It is my intention to record your activities in my report to the *Führer*. I am sure he will have no objection to my promoting you all to *Unteroffizier*. Congratulations. All appropriate records are being adjusted as we speak."

"Thank you, Sir." Max couldn't quite comprehend the truth behind what had just been said. The General continued.

"*Oberfeldwebel* Olbermann did tell me one point of interest. In spite of your own modesty, *Unteroffizier* Webber, it seems it was you who took overall command from the moment you realised Herr Olbermann was injured. I am therefore promoting you to the position of *Unterfeldwebel*. You will take command of your tank from here on.

"I have taken the liberty of finding you a replacement gunner. He will be here some time today. Until such time as he arrives, you will make sure you are ready for battle. You will not go into action again until you are fully manned and supplied, unless there is acute need in this immediate vicinity. I shall be very grateful for your aid if we are attacked.

"There is one more item I must mention. In light of *Oberfeldwebel* Olbermann's decision to continue into the fight, even though he was seriously wounded, I am recommending him for the Knight's Cross, and he will be promoted to *Leutnant* upon his recovery and reinstatement to active duty.

"That is all, Gentlemen."

"Yes, Sir. Thank you, Sir." The four men saluted and quickly left.

Outside, the three crewmen ganged around Max.

"Congratulations, you damned lucky arse." Alfred shook Max's hand vigorously.

"Double promotion, you smooth snake." Klaus slapped Max hard on the back.

Jürgen was not so happy.

"I tell you now, so you do not do it again. It is the last time you step on my back for your own gains."

"Jürgen," Max looked chagrined, "I am sorry, you too should have had a second raise. After all, you made as many decisions as I did, and it was you who drove us into the outpost. If you had not, none of us would have been promoted."

"Do not worry yourself about it, Max. I shall remember what *Oberleutnant* Munck told me. He said the tank's driver is the second most important person in the crew, until the Commander makes a mistake. You had better not make any mistakes."

* * *

As the rain eased off towards mid afternoon, the new gunner arrived. He already displayed the rank of *Stabsgefreiter*, but this still made him the lowest rank amongst them, even though he had more experience. He was tall and spindly, about a year older than Jürgen. He approached Max and

117

Jürgen as they talked in private outside the vehicle.

"*Guten Tag*, I am Ernst Isernhagen, I am reporting for duty as gunner to Panzer 326." Across his left cheek, Ernst had a scar which disappeared as a thin white line under his ear. It must make him attractive to the ladies, thought Jürgen.

"*Willkommen*. I am Commander *Unterfeldwebel* Webber. This is our driver *Unteroffizier* Klimt. Our radioman and loader, Unteroffiziers Malcher and Rüsgen are with our last Commanding Officer in the Hospital Unit, they will return shortly."

"I am pleased to meet you. I am honoured to be assigned to such a prestigious crew. It has been reported that you single-handedly took the Citadel's East Gate."

Max glanced at Jürgen.

"We did our duty, as a well oiled crew should. I shall expect no more or less of you."

"I will not fail you, Commander."

"Come, let us show you around our stubby. How were you stationed before?"

"I was in a Panzer II at the start of the war in Poland. Most of the time we were held in reserve. Later on I was transferred to a t38. I am looking forward to working in a real Panzer."

"What do you mean, a real Panzer?" Jürgen asked.

"The Panzer II is vulnerable to shell fire and the t38 is not German built. They are both inferior machines compared with what I have heard about this type."

Max showed Ernst round the controls and described the action they had seen the day before. Alfred and Klaus joined them as 16.00 hours approached.

"Now we are a complete crew again, I must secure new orders. Please excuse me." Max turned to leave but turned back. "Start her up, we must be ready to move as soon as I return."

At the command vehicle, Max waited by the door for someone to notice him. He heard the tank cough into life and hoped he would not have to stand, unseen, for too long.

It was the General himself who beckoned him to enter.

"*Unterfeldwebel* Webber, has your new crew member arrived yet?"

"Yes, Sir. I have introduced him and we are ready to move as ordered."

"Good. You will be pleased to know we are about to take another victory on this, the twenty-sixth day of May 1940. It will be our seventh victory of this campaign. We anticipate the English will surrender at any moment. You may bring the rest of your crew here to enjoy the news as it comes fresh from the front."

"Yes, Sir." Max left and ran to collect his friends.

Back at the command lorry, they crowded into the confined space opposite the General, and listened to the radio traffic from the Citadel. Shortly before 17.00 hours, the message crackled over the airwaves.

"The Engländer have surrendered."

"You know, *Unterfeldwebel* Webber, in many ways you are responsible for this fortuitous event. I think it is time for a celebration. I have some bottles of very good French Burgundy, we shall all have a glass to toast your success." The General handed a bottle to the *Oberst.* "Open it!" When the drinks were poured the General raised his glass. "To victory!"

"To victory." Jürgen drank slowly, savouring the flavour.

"Unterfeldwebel Webber, you and your crew must rejoin your unit. They are at the south-east corner of the Citadel. Go immediately, you will carry these orders for tomorrow's campaign to your Regimental Commander." He handed the document over.

Max repeated the order to prove there was no misunderstanding, then saluted.

* * *

The following morning, before dawn, they advanced. They had had little sleep before moving south-east to their destination. The orders, 'Advance, in conjunction with the Infantry Regiment *Gross-Deutschland*, against the town of Wormhoudt.' The *Gross Deutschland* made the heading with the tanks as backup. The offensive was completed on May 28th.

"Do you think we will attack Dunkirque? It seems to be the only place we have not wiped out yet." Ernst was keen to show his mettle.

"I have heard that the *Luftwaffe* will destroy Dunkirque," Klaus replied. "We are to stay away to avoid being bombed by mistake. We just have to prevent the enemy from escaping southwards."

"I suppose, in that case, the war is over." Alfred seemed crestfallen.

"Only if you consider the rest of France to be no threat at all," said Max. "We may have destroyed a large part of their Army but there is more still. We must at least take Paris and have the French authorities surrender to us. Then if England sues for peace we will be able to go home at last."

Days slipped past with nothing more strenuous than guard duty over hundreds of wretched prisoners.

During the evening they grouped together with other crews to relax.

"Have you heard?" The voice came from a soldier Max had never seen before, "Dunkirque has fallen at last." Spontaneous celebrations erupted throughout the camp. Later they were dampened as news spread of British and French troops escaping across the Channel.

"How did they get away?" Alfred wondered.

"Ships." To Max it seemed obvious. "You remember Commander Olbermann saying we had to stop their ships making port. Obviously we failed."

"How could we have let that happen?"

"Who knows, at least they left their weapons behind. Now they have nothing to fight with." They discussed the situation for hours into the night, until more orders arrived by messenger.

Alfred was the one to break the news to Max.

"Tenth Panzer Division has been separated from the Nineteenth Army Corps. We no longer follow First and Second Panzer but must make our own way west to Brittany."

The final westward thrust made excellent time. Gradually the fighting stopped. After the final shots had faded, Jürgen, at a loss, looked at Max.

"What will happen now?" he asked.

The cease-fire became official on July 22nd.

9

Seelöwe

Max lay on his bed wondering what the day's rosters would produce. The window was still dark. He had no idea what time it was. He turned his head to look at his companions. He could just make out their vague shapes.

The room was large by normal standards. The three sets of bunk beds were simple affairs made from rough timber commandeered from the local merchant. The mattresses had been taken from a derelict hotel.

The crew from stubby 324 slept in another room in the same farmhouse. The two crews had become close during the final days of fighting. Now they shepherded prisoners of war onto trains heading for Germany. It was a demeaning task for tank crews.

Max shifted to make himself more comfortable.

Jürgen in the next bunk, turned over and looked at his friend. "Are you awake?" he whispered.

"Yes, I have things racing through my mind," Max mumbled.

"What things?" Jürgen was not exactly interested but he felt like talking. "I mean we have it easy now, no fighting, a comfortable place to sleep, good food and plenty of time off."

"I was wondering why we have not invaded England. It is two months since we left the Fatherland and a month since we fired our last shot. If we are not fighting anymore, why have we been kept here? Why not just send us home?"

"We are needed for guard duty." Jürgen thought about the past three weeks.

"Yes, but why are we being used for guard duty? The Infantry can do that."

"But what would you do instead?" asked Jürgen.

Max thought for a while.

"It is not a question of doing something else. We are a tank crew, we should work as a tank crew, not as a machine gun emplacement. We are sitting here chewing garlic when we should be invading Britain. What are we waiting for? We have not even been given extra training to

121

prepare for crossing the Channel."

Jürgen considered the matter.

"There is not much point in worrying about it. We just have to do what we are told. There must be a reason, perhaps the war is over."

"I hope so. At least in that case we will be on our way home soon. I really miss Mother's home-made *Hasenpfeffer mit Kartoffelbrei.*" Max turned over. "Go to sleep. It will soon be light."

* * *

Dawn slowly brightened the room promising another warm and sunny day. The low sun streamed through the unshuttered window, flooding Jürgen's face. He slipped out of bed and dressed, he was already thinking about breakfast. If he was quick, he could reach the chicken run before the farmer awoke.

Still in his socks, Jürgen tip-toed through the door. The farmer slept in a room downstairs but the slightest sound could wake him, or worse, his wife.

Jürgen edged his way along the landing and descended using the ends of the treads to prevent them squeaking. At the bottom he breathed a sigh of relief, the ground floor was stone and would make no noise.

Outside, Jürgen moved randomly between the hutches selecting one egg for each man and placed them in his beret. Then he crossed the open courtyard to the two tanks standing beside the house. He picked up a small pebble and threw it at their bedroom window. The impact was loud in the still air. He laid the eggs gently on the tank's mud guard before looking back at the window. There was no movement from above, he threw another pebble.

Max suddenly appeared round the corner.

"I hope you are not stealing those eggs."

"What does it matter? They are only eggs and it will save us money." Jürgen was put out by Max's attitude.

"We were told to be on our best behaviour which means no stealing." Max hoped he would not have to seriously reprimand his friend, but this was not the first infringement. Jürgen's behaviour had become an increasing problem since their respective promotions. "You will record them in the log to be paid for at the end of the week."

"Why are you making such a fuss?"

"I am only following orders and, as the Senior Rank here, it is my duty to see you do so too." Max softened his tone. "Please do not make this difficult. As you said, they are only eggs, and I do not want to spoil

122

our friendship over such a stupid business. Let the Jews Steal, let the French, British and Poles steal, but we are Aryan, we are above such behaviour... remember that."

"Yes, Commander. I will record them in the log."

"Thank you." Max turned and walked back to the farmhouse. "You may as well bring your collection and cook them indoors," he called over his shoulder.

* * *

Later Jürgen drove the tank to the railway station. He parked facing the road leading to the prisoner of war camp and waited for the next batch of P.O.Ws. to appear.

Twice a week French and British soldiers were marched to the station, crammed onto empty cattle wagons, locked in and transported east to Germany. The tank was there as a machine gun post. The two M.G. 34s provided far greater fire power and better coverage than any single ground based weapon. However, neither Klaus nor Alfred would fire unless ordered to do so by the local Commanding Officer. In this case the orders came from *Hauptmann* Helmut Ziegler.

Ziegler was an Infantry Officer. Jürgen resented the fact he was taking orders from an Infantryman. However, the Tank Battalion, being scattered across the whole of Brittany and some of the Pays De La Loire made the situation necessary, but it did not make following the orders any easier.

"Here they come." Alfred's words broke into Jürgen's brooding. "Just look at the state of their clothing, why do they always look so miserable?"

"Would you be happy, Alfred, if you had been defeated and were being removed from the Fatherland, your home and family?"

"But Max, I am removed from the Fatherland, my home and family. The only difference is, I have not been defeated. They should have fought harder, then they would not be here. This is their own fault. They should accept it and be happy they are alive."

"Huh. I think you would find it different if you were in their position."

"Perhaps, but I will never find out."

Jürgen tried to tune out the conversation. He did not have to think about the prisoners, it was unlikely he would have to drive after them even if they did try to escape. He picked up the tank's maintenance manual from beside his seat and tried to read. The tank needed a major

123

overhaul over the next weeks and it would be better if he knew exactly what he was doing.

"These ones remind me of the Jews in Warsaw," Ernst had not spoken much of his time in Poland. "They are sulky, like children just disciplined."

"Will you tell us about Poland?" asked Max.

"Oh, there is not much I can say. I was never in the fighting, I was ordered into Warsaw for crowd control when the civilians rioted. We shot many of them, Jews and non Jews alike. They soon calmed down but then the sulking started. They did what they were told most of the time but always with resentment. We made them dance so they would be happy. They liked dancing."

"Maybe we should do the same with these French," Alfred suggested.

"Why bother, we only have to see them for a while and then they will be gone," Max remarked. "Making them dance will only slow the loading process down."

"I would rather shoot them, it was an easy solution in Poland. We made them dig large holes, then shot them when the work was done. We used a bulldozer to fill in the graves."

"That sounds quick and easy, Ernst." Klaus would not have minded shooting the prisoners. "I heard though, these creatures are needed for work in the factories back home."

"Yes," said Ernst, "I heard that also, a directive for the occupied territory, men must volunteer to work in the Fatherland, in the fields and factories. It will never work, they are inferior."

"How will they know what to do if they speak French and we only speak German? Who will tell them? Alfred asked.

"There are always some who can speak both languages," Max replied, "like you, I noticed you are always talking to the girls in the village."

"I try to," said Alfred, "but they never reply. I think they do not understand me."

"Poor Alfred not being able to make a pretty girl understand him," Klaus laughed. He turned to the loader. "You could always try using signs." He made a lurid gesture.

"That is not what I was trying to say to them."

"You should stick to German girls," Max admonished.

Jürgen gave up trying to read. He didn't bother joining in the conversation but stood to watch the prisoners through his roof hatch. The defeated troops shuffled in ranks of three towards the station. German

Infantry lined the road, rifles at the ready, directing the prisoners to the platform.

Two hours passed before the last prisoner was locked into his wagon. The sun shone hot on the wagon roofs making the insides like a furnace. Jürgen could see faces at the small mesh vents on the wagon sides, wild eyed, struggling for breath, desperate, pleading. He looked away until eventually the train left.

As the locomotive progressed, pillars of steam retreating, Jürgen dropped back onto his seat.

"They have gone now, in case you had not noticed."

"Wonderful, what do we do now, Commander?" Alfred asked.

"I must see *Hauptmann* Ziegler." Max climbed from the tank and marched to the Commander's Office in the station. A few minutes later he returned. "That was the last train leaving this station. There are no further orders for today. *Hauptmann* Ziegler told me we are due some leave in Paris, next week. Then we move to a new location on August 11th."

"Leave in Paris!" Alfred blurted, "I shall go to all the restaurants and all the theatres and..."

"Then we will expect you back in three year's time," Max laughed. "The rest of us will have to be back after one week... As we have no further duties today, I want to buy some more food and maybe a bottle of wine. Does everyone agree we meet on the beach in an hour?"

"Whatever you say, Commander." Alfred saluted jokingly.

"Good. Jürgen take the tank back and secure it at the farm. Is there anything you need?" asked Max.

"Can you find me a stronger bottle? This is the first leave we have had since April, it needs a celebration," said Jürgen.

* * *

Paris was clean and bright. It seemed there were many more Germans here than French people. The hotel where they stayed even had an Axis receptionist. The French residents had fled before the invasion arrived and had not yet returned since the Armistice.

Alfred made good his intention to see every show. His friends were amazed that he always managed to extend his evenings beyond the normal NCO curfew. He would not return to the hotel until six in the morning, if he returned at all.

Max and Jürgen followed a more leisurely life but stuck together. Gradually their friendship rebuilt itself.

125

"By the looks of things we will be sent home soon. I think the war is over," Jürgen speculated.

"You may be right. With the bombing we are giving England, it would be difficult for them to invade, and if they choose peace, our invasion will be cancelled. I am sorry, you may not have another opportunity for promotion… Come on," Max punched Jürgen on the arm, "or we will miss our chance to climb the Eiffel Tower…" Max raced ahead towards the imposing metal structure towering above the adjacent buildings. Jürgen followed, laughing.

"Slow down or you will be arrested!"

That evening as they walked along the Boulevard De Clichy someone called after them.

"*Unterfeldwebel* Webber, *Unteroffizier* Klimt, how are you?"

"*Oberfeldwebel* Olbermann?" Max asked.

"*Oberfeldwebel*?… *Leutnant* Olbermann, please, and I will forgive you for not saluting."

"*Leutnant*! Of course." Max quickly saluted. "We are very well, Sir, but more important, how are you? It is good to see they stitched your brains back into your head."

"Haha, I like that… I am here on recuperation leave after my wounding. The shoulder still hurts sometimes, but if I rest it properly it gives me little trouble. And you, what are you doing here? I thought you would be in Brittany or some place on the west coast."

"We are. At the moment we are stationed at Morlaix but all the work there is complete so we are on leave, soon we move to St. Malo.

"Then I shall not see you again, perhaps." Olbermann seemed crestfallen. "I will be sent to another Company in Nantes at the end of the week, for light duties." He brightened again. "My promotion was approved two days ago, effective immediately." He pointed at his epaulets, "and the Knight's Cross has also been approved. I receive that when I join my new Company. I guess, from now on, I have to write nice things about you to your parents, even if I do have to lie."

"Surely it does not count. The agreement was the Knight's Cross and Oak Leaves," Jürgen joked.

"I shall waive that requirement… How is the new man?"

"He fits in nicely," said Max.

The three men talked long into the night. Being with *Leutnant* Olbermann, Max and Jürgen's need to observe curfew was made annulled.

* * *

The week passed quickly. Max and Jürgen soon found themselves on the train back to Brittany. Though they had not seen either Klaus or Alfred at the station, Ernst had been there, but at the other end of the platform.

The train arrived in Morlaix. During the short walk to the billet, Alfred, Ernst and Klaus caught up with them.

When they reached their billet, the farmer greeted them warmly.

"You have come to buy some more of my eggs. I like this, business is good for me when you are here."

"It will only be for a little while more, *Monsieur*. We are leaving soon." Max explained.

That is a shame. This other tank crew, they are not so friendly, you know. But you still have a little while so you will fill my pockets until then, yes."

"Probably, though I think you charge too much. We may have to go to another farmer for our food," Max replied.

"Oh *mes amis*, you will not find a better price in this village," the farmer protested.

Have you been talking to the other farmers? Agreeing the costs between you?" Jürgen asked

"No, no, no, the District tells us how much to charge!"

"I still think it is too much," Jürgen accused.

"*Monsieur*! You want to rob me, I shall die if I ask any less."

Jürgen's anger was rising. He was about to respond but Max placed a restraining hand on his shoulder.

"Let it go, we can afford what he asks."

Jürgen turned away, irritated at Max's intervention. Max tried to divert Jürgen's attention.

"What work does the stubby need?" Max asked him. Jürgen thought for a moment.

"We need to completely overhaul the engine and gearbox, oil and air filter changes, track maintenance, inspect the brakes and possibly replace the pads and clean the fuel filter. Ernst and Alfred should check the gun's load and recoil mechanism, and the operation of the traverse and elevation. Klaus should also look at his radios and ensure the batteries are sound. I think that is all."

"How long will it take?"

"It will be finished in two or three days," said Jürgen grumpily.

"Good, we will start in the morning. Make a list of everything we

127

need so I can request the parts from the stores," Max ordered.

Perhaps that was the way to keep Jürgen out of trouble, Max thought. Give him lots of responsibilities.

Jürgen trudged away to start the list. It should have taken only a few minutes but he had to consult the manual, and with his brooding the compilation took an hour. When he returned to the farmhouse he handed the list to Max.

Max approved the contents and handed it to Klaus.

"Radio this through to supply," said Max, "Everything should be readily available, after all, they have had over a month to collect parts together for the Division. If they can deliver it all tomorrow, we will have two days free at the end of the week."

The following day Jürgen walked out and patted the tank's mud guard affectionately.

"I suppose this must be your birthday or something, you will be as good as new when we have finished with you."

"Watch out," Alfred shouted, "Jürgen is talking to the tank."

"No, I am not!"

"Get to work, you two," Max ordered, cutting the level of play.

The work progressed easily. They soon found they could return to the beach for a final day of sun and sea. They talked speculatively of the impending move.

* * *

The drive to St Malo took all day. Jürgen, in the company of tank 324, had started out as the only vehicles on the road, but at almost every junction they were joined by other tanks of their unit. The road became more and more congested with armoured cars and troop lorries.

"This is like the build-up in May before we moved into France," Klaus commented.

"I do not think we are preparing to return home," Max speculated, "we would have been shipped in Companies from local stations. There is no need for everyone to come together at one place. I think this is preparation for another action."

"The invasion of England? asked Alfred.

"What else is there?" Max pointed out, "we are on the north coast of France, near a port. There is only England."

"I wish they would tell us for sure," Ernst protested.

"They will tell us, when it is time," Max interjected.

"You are the Tank Commander, Max. They are bound to tell you before they tell us. You will let us know, won't you?"

"Provided I am not ordered to keep it to myself. They will probably keep it secret until the last minute, just like in May."

"But why should they keep it secret from us? How would the *Engländer* find out with all that water between us?"

"Spies, Ernst." Max explained. "The French can not be trusted."

"So, we will not know until we board ship?" Alfred asked.

"Probably not, especially if they know how friendly you are with the French girls," Max laughed.

"Shut up, I do not know any girls here."

"That will last about five minutes, once we have arrived," Klaus joked.

At the camp, several kilometres from St. Malo, they rejoined their old unit.

"Kill the engine, Jürgen," Max instructed as he climbed to the ground. Jürgen heard a shout.

"Hey, Max, it is good to see you again. Come on, Commanders have been ordered to the *Leutnant's* tent."

Jürgen tried to recognise the voice but failed. Irritation at Max's command privileges niggled.

"So what do we do now?" Ernst asked.

"We wait for instructions," Jürgen moaned, "I am going to grab some fresh air." He climbed out and sat on the glacis plate, took a cigarette and lit it watching the smoke drift in the warm breeze. Ernst soon settled next to him.

"Are you all right, Jürgen." Ernst was soft-spoken.

Jürgen liked him, though in many ways he was still the outsider of the crew. "Oh, just frustrated."

"I know what you mean," said Ernst.

Jürgen offered him a cigarette. "Ernst, tell me about your life before you joined us."

"I was in a Panzer II, held in reserve in Poland. Then we were sent to quell the Warsaw riots."

Curiosity drew Jürgen from his brooding. "What happened?"

"Our tank caught fire. I climbed out but my friend, Johannes, he died inside, I could not get back to him."

"I am sorry to hear that, Ernst. What happened afterwards?"

"I was transferred to a t38, but that crew must have thought I was bad luck or something. I did not like them either. They were always so serious. There were never any jokes and I was not made to feel welcome. The Commander, I think, wanted to be SS. He was always shouting and giving orders. Not like now, you joke and tease each other. You are all different but you work well together, and you have been friendly to me right from the start. For that I thank you."

"Of course, we are a team and we are friends," Jürgen smiled. "Come on, let us see what the others are doing."

Walking around the tank they found Alfred and Klaus playing cards on the engine covers.

"So you have come to see what you are missing, have you?" Klaus called.

"We thought we had better come to make sure you are not plotting something," Jürgen joked.

"Well I am plotting to win Alfred's money. Soon I will have it all," Klaus laughed. "Alfred, you look like you have swallowed a lemon, such a bad loser, can you believe it?"

"Can I believe what?" Jürgen beamed at Klaus. "That you are robbing Alfred or you did not tell him you cheat? Move over so we can join you, we will play on Alfred's side."

"Ho, ho," Alfred chuckled, "I see my luck is changing. Pass the cards Klaus, my turn to deal."

Several games passed before they were interrupted.

"I have some good news and some bad news," said Max. "Which do you want first?"

"You are back from your meeting," Klaus blurted. Tell us, quickly."

"The invasion of Britain is coming very soon," said Max.

"When exactly, Tell us?" Alfred's smile split his face.

"I do not know yet, but soon. It depends on the battle between the *Luftwaffe* and the R.A.F."

"And the bad news?" Jürgen enquired.

"We have Divisional Exercises until the invasion." Max knew that would dampen their enthusiasm. The crew groaned loudly. "Cheer up, we could still be shepherding prisoners."

"But at least we would be able to lie on the beach each day," Klaus complained.

"You may still do so, once we have defeated Britain," Max assured them. "The invasion is called Operation Seelöwe. The first possible start date is next week, August 23rd."

"Sea Lion, that is a good one. I wonder who thought it up," said

Jürgen

"It is better than Plan Yellow, at least now we have something to look forward to," Alfred commented.

"So we are going to England at last," Ernst cheered, "I cannot wait."

* * *

The exercises were simple routine Company manoeuvres. Days passed. Max was called to meetings each week.

August changed to September. One day Max brought more news to the crew.

"The date for Operation Sea Lion is put back to the middle of October. I hate to say it, but if we leave it much longer we will be facing mid-winter storms."

"I thought originally the *Luftwaffe* were only going to take two weeks to defeat the R.A.F." Alfred was searching the ammunition bins to check the training rounds.

"In August, the papers were saying England only had six hundred fighter planes," said Ernst. He elevated the gun and rotated the turret checking the electric motor. "If you read today's reports, they say the *Luftwaffe* has shot down over nine hundred fighters and they are still coming up to attack."

"Someone made a mistake." Jürgen was not impressed by the numbers. He flexed his arms on the steering levers. The engine ticked over quietly.

"I think we should just go." Klaus turned the dial to the morning's frequency and listened to the radio for a moment. "If we invade when there is a raid over London, the Royal Air Force will not be able to retaliate without having their cities and factories completely wiped out."

"They would not use the fighters to attack us," Klaus pointed out, "they would use the coastal batteries, bombers and their Navy."

"The Navy? What could they do when they are docked in Scotland?" asked Jürgen.

"They would steam south and cut us off," Max explained.

"But we could live off the land," Jürgen persisted.

"That might work for food and fuel but their ammunition is not the same as ours and shells and bullets do not grow on trees," said Max.

"Soon it is not going to matter one way or the other," Alfred butted in. He opened the breach and checked the barrel. "By the time another month has passed, the storms will have set in and the Channel will be too rough to cross."

131

"That is *Leutnant* Lutz' opinion," said Max.

The manoeuvres continued. October moved in pushing the last remnants of summer into the past. The weather remained dry, clouds filled the sky more often but the routine stayed the same.

As November loomed, Max returned from another briefing with the *Leutnant*.

"I am informed Operation Seelöwe is cancelled until the spring. We move back to Brest tomorrow."

10

Barbarossa

As first light illuminated the scenery, the train ran through Dresden without stopping. The tracked elements of the Division had been loaded in France. Jürgen had expected to disembark near Stuttgart. A certain amount of apprehension had ensued within the crew when the train had continued eastwards past their old camp, but gradually they had become used to the motion and the lack of knowledge. Late in the afternoon of the third day they stopped outside Warsaw.

The troops unloaded quickly, eager to be away from their confinement. They were not given time to relax. The whole Regiment marched from Golarki station through the streets to Odolany Freight Depot. They met other Companies marching from other stations. The troops were filtered into lines and directed to their equipment.

When he found his tank, Jürgen patted the mud guard lovingly. He climbed onto the rail flat-wagon and into his beloved stubby, still numbered 326. He settled into his seat. Max's voice cut through his headphones.

"Are you ready, Jürgen?"

"Fuel on, inertia disengaged," Jürgen inserted the key, "circuits closed, gears neutral, brakes on. All ready, Max."

"Stand by to engage."

Jürgen heard Ernst and Alfred puffing and grunting as they put their backs in to the crank handle.

Jürgen looked through the windscreen and raised the blast visor. Klaus was standing centrally at the end of the wagon, ready to give guidance for driving off the train.

"Jürgen, engage." Max's order was a relief when it came. The engine started immediately. Now they could get moving, thought Jürgen.

"Take us off, Jürgen, nice and slow." Max fell silent as the tank shifted forward.

Watching Klaus's signals to keep the tank central, Jürgen moved gradually forward. At the last minute Klaus leaped aboard. Jürgen didn't even slow down for him.

On the roads surrounding the depot, the tanks, armoured cars and half-tracks formed lines before moving off in units to their destinations. They passed through the centre of battered Warsaw and over the Wisla. Jürgen followed his unit south. It was already growing dark. He cursed the need to drive through the featureless night. Using masked lamps meant virtually zero visibility.

The line of vehicles made slow progress. Jürgen consoled himself, he could calculate each turn from the sway of dim red lights on the vehicles ahead.

Eventually they turned east again towards the slowly brightening sky and the new Regimental Camp. He pulled into the compound as the first rays of sunshine cut the dark. He had no idea where he was. He didn't care as long as he could grab some sleep.

* * *

At 6.00 a.m., just two hours after lying down fully clothed on his bed, Jürgen was startled awake by the call for Reveille. Still groggy, he extracted his PT clothes from his pack. Though crumpled from their travels, he donned them anyway. He fell in line, eyes gritty, mouth dry and stale, for the first activity. A stiff reprimand for sloppy appearance pulled him together for the four kilometre run before breakfast.

Within the first few paces, Jürgen discovered just how out of condition he was. He struggled to draw the energy to place one foot in front of the other.

The exercise regime in France had been slack, just one short run per week. He had not slept well on the train, the mystery of their unknown destination keeping him awake. Now he was abruptly pulled back to reality.

Max though, had no problem with the new pace. He launched himself at a gallop as though the devil and all the hounds of hell were in his tracks. He did not wait to give encouragement to Jürgen or anyone else.

Jürgen's anger flared. He pounded the hard ground beneath his feet, eventually finishing twenty places behind his Tank Commander.

* * *

By June, the constant routine of rifle training, drill and long runs had brought Jürgen's body to optimum fitness, the whole division was ready for deployment. Eventually they were called on parade.

Jürgen stood rigidly to attention at the rear of the ranks, he could hardly see his Commanding Officer, but he could hear every word. The speech was long, but afterwards, only a few words were discussed amongst the troops. They grouped together in the dilapidated timber barrack room.

"Full alert! What for?" Klaus could not believe the news as he sat cross-legged on his bed, darning a sock. "Who is going to attack us here? Poland is ours, almost the whole of Europe is ours."

"Perhaps there are factions here still fighting against the *Führer*." Ernst reclined on the next bed looking at a magazine. "They could be Polish factions, Jews, Communists. Who can say?"

"The Jews are always a threat." Max rubbed a shine into the toe of his right boot. He took a moment to spit on the cloth before continuing to rub in small circles. "But the problem hardly needs more than a few units to quell it forever. This is something bigger. There was enough power at Odolany for a small invasion. I saw nine different Panzer Units and motorised Infantry too. They could have been just elements of Divisions, but I know ours is complete."

"But what else is there?" Alfred stood folding his freshly washed PT kit.

"The Soviet Union?" Jürgen sat behind Max brushing his tank tunic, "but the *Führer* has a ten year pact with Stalin."

"He hates the Bolsheviks," agreed Max, "remember his constant fight against Communism at home. It would seem this is the perfect time. Otherwise I can think of nothing that would require such strength."

* * *

Sunday 22nd brought confirmation and disappointment as Operation Barbarossa went into full swing.

"The army has invaded the Soviet Union and we have been left behind again," Jürgen fumed. "Every time there is action, we are sent in last. How will I ever gain another promotion?"

"Stop your whinging," said Max, trying not to be impatient. "It is a year since you told me you were over it, but you are still whining. Find something else to sing about."

"What else is there?" Jürgen blurted back. He clenched and unclenched his fists in anger.

"Nothing," Max spat back, "So shut up. Get over it."

Four days later they moved. The drive was through unfamiliar countryside, much of it damp and marshy with numerous rivers. The going was slow but steady. Initially, the hard packed mud roads provided enough support, but the tracks rapidly ripped the surface to shreds creating ruts, mud and loose gravel. Between the lower marshy valleys were wide dry grasslands. Occasionally wooded copses or low scrub dotted the scenery.

On the second day they stopped just short of Minsk. The Division encircled the enemy's sprawling positions, capturing the defeated troops left behind by General Guderian. The General had continued his advance while expecting others to clear up behind him.

Jürgen was amazed by the intensity of the fighting. It seemed every Soviet soldier had a personal vendetta against him. He kept his visor closed to prevent the frequent ricochets from blinding him. There was little cover for the vehicles but the enemy had made the most of dug out positions to hide their guns and their troops sniping from the long grass. Not only were they invisible, they were highly mobile.

It was hot inside the tank. Heat from the engine, the stench of petrol, the fetid fumes of the gun and the lack of fresh air all made the tank's interior stifling. The extractor fan battled to remove the oppressive stuffiness but was roundly defeated by its small size.

Jürgen was not the first to remove his tunic at an appropriate lull in the conflict, but even that made little difference.

"Is that dammed extractor working?" he called back to his comrades.

"Yes, are you too hot?" Albert shouted, "you can come and handle these hot shells if you want."

Jürgen's hair was matted with perspiration. Droplets, intent with irritation, trickled into his eyes and down his neck. He wiped his brow to clear his vision but the damp soon returned. The sweat ran from his body drenching his clothes, it itched down his legs soaking his socks and the inside of his boots. The only relief came from an occasional sip of tepid water, taken sparingly from his flask. It gave momentary comfort to his parched lips and tongue before his throat burned dry again. Once the sun had risen, each successive hour became more of a struggle against the heat, exhaustion, hunger and thirst.

Jürgen leaned forward against the front plate, peering through the visor's tiny slit, just another pair of eyes searching out the clusters of enemy soldiers still resisting their inevitable demise. He found concentration difficult, wondering how the others were able to continue when it was he who actually had the least work to do. Much of the time he just sat waiting for instructions.

Jürgen worried about the constant rattle of gunfire as the irregular metallic clicks of bullets struck his armoured protection. He imagined the tank going up in flames with the crew killed inside. He had seen it in

France and it seemed to happen more often now.

He started the engine using the starter motor. It was too dangerous for crew members to crank the handle from outside. Fortunately movements occurred sufficiently often for the engine to still be warm. Even the Infantry remained within their armoured transports or took refuge shielding themselves behind the open doors.

As enemy enclaves were located, Jürgen drove forward to a position for the guns to begin their slaughter.

He let the engine tick over for another few minutes to regain operating temperature, before cutting the ignition again. Then another hour would pass while he resumed squinting at the outside, his nose almost pressed against the burning metal. His tortured eyes stung from the dry air, making him blink repeatedly. Salt and dust caked his lids and lashes.

Jürgen watched a half-track advancing in front of him. A shell erupted. The half-track, engulfed in yellowish smoke, stopped abruptly.

Jürgen watched with horrified fascination as the smoke drifted in the breeze. Clods of mud, fell back to earth like black hail. As the half-track's crew pushed the vehicle's back doors open, a Soviet, his uniform the same golden yellow as the summer meadow, rose from the grass and lobbed a grenade.

"There, quickly, get him," Jürgen shouted.

The Soviet darted away throwing himself flat in the long grass, taking cover from both the resulting detonation and Alfred's machine gun fire.

Jürgen felt a rush of emotions, enraged at the Soviet for throwing the explosive. He feared for the lives of his colleagues in the half-track. Frustrated, he thumped the metal plating protecting him from the outside, but could do nothing about the situation.

"Come on, shoot the dog," Jürgen yelled.

Alfred's machine gun sprayed bullets.

Jürgen was sickened by the deaths of his anonymous comrades.

German troops appeared, searching the area, seeking retribution. Jürgen watched, keen interest building his hopes. The storm troops marched back and forth swinging their bayonetted rifles from side to side like a flock of wading marsh birds stabbing the ground for hidden grubs.

* * *

The atmosphere eased as evening brought darkness. The chill filtered through the tank's vents. It grasped Jürgen round the ankles like a manacle. Like a creeping infestation, the chill wormed upwards along his

137

legs.

The cool intensified as it drifted across Jürgen's damp skin and clothes. Evaporating perspiration turned his body heat into cold and shivers. He threw his tunic back on, hoping to warm himself in the still dry cloth. He couldn't believe the dramatic change in temperature.

The dark made fighting more difficult, it progressed more slowly. Long spells of quiet were interspersed by short bursts of vicious gunfire. The combatants awaited their opportunities. A flare of artillery fire lighting the terrain, picking out the enemy trying to steal an advance. The flash from an enemy's rifle pinpointing their snipers. Each incident drew fire from the crew.

Jürgen's night vision was constantly cut short by flashes and flames. Brilliant blue, purple and green spots danced in front of his eyes as he scanned the ground in front.

He was grateful not to have a gun at his disposal. Shadows flitted from place to place startling him into alarm. He wanted to loose off belts of ammunition, if only for reassurance rather than to quell an obvious threat. He was consumed by his constant combat against his own waking nightmares. Was he losing control, losing his edge as a trained fighting machine? He was in the middle of a battle with too much time on his hands and too much to think about. He had too little to do and had received too little sleep. He was exhausted.

Jürgen strained his eyes at the darkness. There was no chance of rest. The noise, near or far, was constant. Friendly fire, enemy fire, artillery, rifles and grenades, the distant screams of wounded, the dying, in the darkness, they all ate at Jürgen's senses, but only for a while. The nights were short so soon after the Solstice.

When the sun rose all Jürgen could think about was staying alive but he couldn't concentrate from weariness. His actions seemed poorly co-ordinated, staccato, like clockwork.

Sounds from the turret eased the boredom. Jürgen recognised the drill. Open the breach, load a round, close the breach, take aim, press the trigger. Actions he longed to experience just to break the monotony, the gloom. He was envious of his friends. He longed for some relief from the torment of watching, waiting and thinking.

In his headphones, Jürgen listened to Max identifying targets. A seemingly constant drone of bearings, ranges and target descriptions, instructions on the type of fire and how many rounds.

The different sounds blended into each other forming a constant buzz of fighting, the rhythm of hostility, the flow and crescendo of battle. The noise moved around Jürgen as though it was alive, an independent body with a will of its own.

* * *

Expunging the enemy from the battle field was not easy. For seven days the conflict pulled him about, dragging him where and when it would, he was a hostage to its whims.

At the end, there were over three hundred thousand enemy prisoners to contain.

For you, the war is over, thought Jürgen. He lay down to grab a few hours inadequate sleep.

After just a few hours he was woken up to placed the tank on guard duty, guiding the Soviets to the prisoner camps behind the fighting.

In the meantime, Field Service Units used the lull to recover the hundreds of damaged vehicles and pieces of equipment. Jürgen yearned for sleep, the longer the better, and perhaps a good meal would help. He received neither. The unit was still on full alert. Soon they moved eastwards again, towards Smolensk.

They followed the front line advancing throughout the second week of July. The clearing up process continued, stripping the land of isolated enemy units and forcing them into captivity behind the slowly advancing support enclaves. The wide open savannah with occasional woodland usually made identifying the enemy positions easy. The difficult part was preventing them retreating to strike again later.

The Tenth Panzer Division took up position at the southern end of the conflict, forcing the enemy to rethink their flanking manoeuvre. The same movement placed the Division for their own flanking action to cut off the enemy's withdrawal.

The fighting was fast and furious, though for Jürgen with his narrow field of view little seemed to happen. The days merged together, separate actions assumed the feel of one constant battle that took place somewhere beyond the gloom of his driving position. Being at the back of the advance did not render the incessant assault any easier. The leading echelons, like greedy diners at a banquet, rushed on to the next battle but always left some deadly outpost on the side of their plate, a gun emplacement, a pocket of Infantry to be purged. The whole period seemed to be spent rounding up prisoners and securing them for shipment to camps.

* * *

The last week of July commenced and a new advance with it. For the first time *Leutnant* Lutz' unit took the spearhead. Knowing the lead tank was always the most vulnerable, Lutz rotated the vehicles of his unit each day. Jürgen scratched the paint on the underside of his hatch with his knife each day, marking the position he occupied in the unit.

The third time Jürgen took the lead, the day was fine, visibility was good. The grassland seemed to stretch for miles. There was no sign of the enemy. Jürgen felt cheerful leading the way along the mud road.

The shell seemed to explode directly in front of Jürgen's face. He felt the heat through the tank's metal skin. Shock thrust him, arms and legs flailing, from the viewing port. His whole body retreated in panic from the sudden noise, flame and vibration. He bounced hard against his seat back. Terror vented from his lungs. The sounds of metal bending under pressure, burning explosive and expanding air drowned out the cry.

Just as suddenly, silence flooded Jürgen's mind, the rare silence of deafness, unconsciousness, nothingness.

Gradually Jürgen's awareness returned. He listened to the resonance in his head. The flow of breath through his mouth and throat, the blood rushing in his ears, pounding his skull. In the background he heard Max calling.

"Jürgen, Jürgen! Are you all right?" Jürgen wondered at the far away sound, perhaps Max had run to find help.

A part of his mind struggled with what had happened. Another part tried desperately to pull his thoughts together, grasping for support from his friends' movements, their struggles and cursing shouts.

Jürgen could see a light, curiously it drew his attention. The blurry impression focused the daylight probing through the viewer. The glass was dull and yellowed, the colour of thick toffee.

Jürgen's mouth filled with a taste, not toffee but blood. His vision came and went as the pain intensified.

"Jürgen, are you all right?" Max's voice called him again, that was strange if Max had left to fetch help. "Shut up all of you, I need to hear." There was anger in the words. Jürgen acknowledged the change as he would a scene change in a play. "Jürgen, Jürgen, speak to me."

Why wouldn't he just go away? Jürgen thought, he had enough problems without having to pay attention to stupid questions.

"Jürgen, answer me, are you injured, do you need help?" Max turned to Ernst. "What can you see down there? Use the torch."

Ernst pressed the switch.

"The torch is broken." He crouched down onto his hands and knees looking into the tank's front compartment. "I cannot make out if he is alive or not. If I traverse the turret, I could crawl through."

"No! If the enemy sees the gun move they will shell us again. Klaus, can you see anything?"

"He seems to be slumped in his chair."

At that moment Jürgen coughed, spitting blood. Max's voice took up a new barrage in Jürgen's ears.

"Jürgen, thank God you are alive. Are you injured?"

A groan escaped Jürgen's lips. It had not been what he wanted to say but for some reason he was unable to speak. Dam it

"Jürgen, this is Max. Please, speak to me."

Jürgen gradually regained his senses. The pain seemed to section itself into areas. There was fire in his leg. He had lesser discomfort in his back, arms and head. He tried to find out what was causing the sharp, searing pain in his left calf. It felt as though he had been stabbed with a hot knife. He adjusted his sitting position but the fire flared as he put pressure on his foot. He gave up, it was easier to stay awake if there was less pain.

"*Verdammt*! what is wrong, why do you not answer me." Max sounded frantic. Jürgen wanted to reassure him but couldn't think how. He shifted his position producing another burning stab in his leg.

"Bloody leg," Jürgen's voice rasped with dryness as he mumbled to himself, "why does it hurt so much?" Maybe it is broken, he thought.

"Your leg, Jürgen, can you move it?" Max asked.

Gingerly, Jürgen leaned forward and felt down the limb, the cloth of his trousers was wet, sticky. Something hard protruded through the cloth, unyielding metal, jagged and sharp. The leg flexed slightly as he felt the damage, a shaft of red-white torment flashed through his head. The shock momentarily galvanised his senses. His drawn breath hissed sharply through the intercom like an issue of steam.

"Max, there is something through my leg." Jürgen leaned back into his seat, his voice weak, "I cannot move it." Jürgen inspected the slick, sticky mess on his fingers. Was it oil, blood? He couldn't make out the colour in the dim light.

"All right, Jürgen, sit still, we will try to pull you out."

The voices, Jürgen recognised them now but he just wanted to sleep. If only the pain would go away, it would be so nice to sleep forever. But the voices, they would probably keep him awake.

141

"You can not pull him out, Max." Ernst's voice was a hushed whisper over the intercom but Jürgen heard every word, "if his leg is pierced by something sharp, you may rip it in shreds, then he would lose it. We need to know how bad he is before we do anything. One of us will have to open his hatch to inspect his leg."

"I do not want to lose my leg." Jürgen croaked his objection. Nobody bothered to answer.

"But that means exposing ourselves to enemy fire," said Max,

"It is the only way if we are to free him," Alfred hissed.

"What do you suggest?" Max replied.

The voices receded from Jürgen's ears. He tried to stay awake but the pain engulfed him in razor blades, slowly dragging him away. Dizziness swamped his thoughts as shock took his body. It was difficult to grasp meanings. He concentrated on the one thing that mattered to him.

"You must not take my leg, I will not let you." He repeated the words, hardly more than a choked whisper.

"We either go now or we wait until it is safe outside and then try," Alfred continued, "until then we are stuck. All of us."

"Any other ideas?" In the dim light Max watched as Alfred, then Ernst, shook their heads. "Jürgen, you will have to hold on a little while until we can move you out. Just stay still and we will be right there."

Jürgen groaned his pain through the throat microphone.

Several minutes of anguish passed as the crew looked through viewers to examine the battlefield. The fighting seemed to have moved on.

A knocking sound rang on the back of the turret. "Hey, are you all right in there?" The voice was distant, passing in through the extractor vent, the voice was German. Max recognised his friend, Hennemann.

Max opened a turret hatch. Sunlight blazed in, blinding him. He quickly ducked down out of the glare.

"Thank God you came. Jürgen is injured, but the rest of us are all right." Hennemann crawled round the structure and peered in at the faces.

"We took care of the bastard who did this, but when you did not climb out, we thought you were all dead. Can you pass Jürgen out? We have a stretcher here."

"No, we cannot reach him. You need to hurry though," Max encouraged, "I think he has blacked out."

"Do not worry, we will take him out through the front." Hennemann looked from Max to Alfred to Ernst. "You know, you all look like you need a good schnapps."

Hennemann turned to his own crew. "Jürgen is trapped, help him out, but be careful." He turned back to Max. "You may as well climb out too, the fighting is over for the time being."

It took an hour to free Jürgen from his prison ready to be transported to a Field Hospital. Something stung his thigh. Morphine? The splinter of bow plate was removed and his leg was bandaged. Fresh blood spilled red down the black uniform.

Jürgen drifted in and out of consciousness. He half recognised faces and sounds. Odd words imprinted on his mind. He listened, not understanding comments about his colour and blood loss.

Max grasped Jürgen's hand as they parted.

"I will miss you, my good friend, have a speedy recovery."

Jürgen heard the words through a thin haze. He smiled softly as the morphine took hold.

"Come on." Max called his crew together. "We need another tank as well as a replacement driver."

Tank 326 stood disabled in the now deserted battlefield south-east of Smolensk.

11

Moskau

Jürgen marched from the Field Commander's Office. He had at last passed his medical fitness examination and was ordered to rejoin his Division. He permitted a slight smile to cross his face. He might even see his friends again.

Jürgen collected his kit from his temporary lodgings, a run-down hotel close to Satalovo's Town Hall, and headed to the Transport Office. There he presented a courier with his travel orders. Giving the order suddenly reminded him of what it had felt like to have power as leader of the Hitler Youth so long ago, but this was better.

Jürgen stepped into the side car while the rider mounted the motorcycle. They sped off along the dirt track from the Field Command Post to the railhead at Jarcevo.

It seemed to Jürgen the Army had made little progress since his injury, hardly a hundred and thirty kilometres in three months. He knew the fighting had been fierce, for several weeks he had been a dispatch rider carrying reports back and forth between Military Command Posts. Being so close to the fighting, but unable to join in, had been vexing.

Now he had his chance, he could hardly wait to see his Command, he clutched his orders designating the machine and his duties.

The motorcycle pulled up in Jarcevo Freight Depot, close to five Panzers. Only one was a type IV, painted grey with the number in black on the turret. Jürgen strolled over to have a look. He noted the thicker armour on the bow plate and wondered if this was a new model. The front plate had additional shielding around the driver's viewer and across the radioman's machine gun port. As he climbed aboard he saw more armour sheeting had been added to the hull sides and along the superstructure around the fighting compartment.

He opened the turret and climbed inside. There was no sign of the crew. He decided to stow his kit before searching for them. He looked around the familiar equipment. Casually he noted the hull number painted on the back of the turret behind the command seat: 80,536. At first it didn't register, he turned back, checking he had read the number correctly. It was too improbable. He traced his finger over the digits. This is my old tank, he thought. A sudden wash of emotion swelled his heart with pride, love for an old friend. He took a moment to appreciate the significance. They had left battle together and would return together, both of them fighting fit after their injuries.

Jürgen climbed from the tank and surveyed the area looking for his crew. There were several troops in black tank uniforms grouped together by a dilapidated wooden structure. Jürgen walked slowly towards the group wondering how long it would take them to notice his presence. They were alert, while he was still several metres away they formed an inspection line and straightened to attention.

"Which of you are the crew of tank two-two-eight?" Jürgen asked.

Four soldiers stepped smartly forward. Jürgen glanced at them in turn.

"You four, attend your tank. The rest of you, dismiss." His first order to his own crew. He felt the power, the exhilaration of achievement, he was a Tank Commander.

Jürgen followed his crew as they trotted to their vehicle. They lined up waiting. Jürgen stopped a few metres away, facing them. Jürgen suddenly realised they were all young. He felt much older despite there being only a couple of years between these… Jürgen scrutinised the faces… these boys, and himself.

"I am *Stabsfeldwebel* Jürgen Klimt, your Commander… Name and rank."

The first crewman stepped forward.

"Ingwar Heitzer, *Gefreiter*, Loader." With strong muscular stature, he was a short, round-faced youth with an apparent natural inclination to smile. That would change once the lad saw real action, thought Jürgen. Ingwar quickly stepped back in line.

Jürgen studied the next man to step forward.

"Gustav Junger, *Gefreiter*, Radioman." As he spoke, his eyes drilled into Jürgen, testing, looking for weakness. His features seemed chisel-cut, like marble. Not a good-looking face, but one of determination or possibly a bully.

Jürgen moved on.

"Hubert Baumann, *Stabsgefreiter*, Driver." Tall, blond and muscular. His mouth was crisp with a slim straight nose above and clear blue eyes, this man looked to be the perfect Aryan.

"Rudolf Smets, *Gefreiter*, Gunner." Another one with muscular build and a keen eye but there was a lack of aggression in the stare. Would that change when they went into battle? Jürgen wondered.

He continued his inspection.

"You all trained together?"

"Yes, *Herr Stabsfeldwebel*," The four men replied in unison.

"And what battle experience do you have?"

There was a slight hesitance before Hubert replied.

"None, *Mein Herr*."

"How did you achieve your promotion Hubert?"

"I saved an Officer's life in a swimming accident during training."

Jürgen took a moment to consider, Hubert was obviously one able to think quickly and take action. "Very good, load your kit and start up. We move out in ten minutes. Forget nothing, we will not return until the Soviets have surrendered."

A loud cheer filled the air as the crew set to work. Hubert climbed in through the driver's hatch preventing Jürgen taking his customary position. Ingwar reversed a nearby Kubelwagen to the back of the tank. Jürgen watched with interest as Rudolf fitted a shaft between the tank's crank and some sort of gearbox fitted to the Kubelwagen's engine. Ingwar revved the car. Moments later the tank started.

"Ha! I wish that device had been invented two years ago. It would have saved a lot of effort," said Jürgen. He climbed into the turret. "Gustav, radio the Command Office, announce our readiness to depart."

"Immediately, Commander." Enthusiasm filled the man's reply. Jürgen suddenly found he had to reassess his judgement of his new crew. They may look young but they all seemed to be as well trained as he had been when he first engaged the enemy.

Moments later, with permission granted, the tank moved off towards Vyazma and Moscow.

As they travelled, suddenly the air smelled fresh. A thin waft of snow settled across the ground. Jürgen, standing in the cupola, watched as it transformed fields and trees. The weather chilled noticeably and though the sun returned as a weak white glow to the south, the snow remained.

Jürgen shivered but carried on standing, admiring the beauty of the fresh fall. The world looked clean, a thousand kilometres from the filth of battle. He looked behind and the image shattered. There were dark brown lines in the white blanket where the tank's tracks had melted the snow to mud. He felt guilty at the blemish they were leaving behind. More troubling, the sign of their passing beckoned, a sign any aircraft could follow easily. Jürgen was grateful there were so few Russian bombers.

* * *

As soon as they arrived, tank 228 was sent to the front at Vyazma. They took their position amongst their new unit and joined the fight. Jürgen recognised the type of action: advance, fight and hold the new position. He put as much effort into his unfamiliar command role as he could.

Guns blasted the air, machine guns rattled furious sprays of bullets in fans of tracer. Shells burst around them throwing mud and dirt in the air. Jürgen found the explosions distracting. Every bang and crash extracted a flinch from his muscles. His body may have recovered from his injury but his mind had not. Gripping the seat, he held himself rigid, hoping the crew would not notice his fear.

Jürgen watched with trepidation as grey tank after grey tank fell victim to incoming fire. The company was rapidly being depleted. When would his turn come? It seemed white camouflaged tanks were hit much less frequently, or was it fear boosting his imagination?

As evening fell, the fighting stopped. Jürgen organised the camp. The crew, still dressed in their summer uniforms, shivered as they worked in the subzero temperature. Though made of wool, the clothing was not thick enough to keep them warm while they were outside.

More snow settled, some blowing into drifts around the scattered bushes. There was a building, a single wooden barn, the crew searched it looking for the enemy. Satisfied the structure was safe, Jürgen gathered some broken timbers and built a fire in the centre of the earthen floor. Gustav approached.

"Look what I found, Commander." He held up two containers of whitewash powder. "There is more over there."

Jürgen breathed with relief.

"Wonderful, mix it up and paint the tank. Have Ingwar help you."

"Which parts should we cover?"

"All of it, everything that can be seen from the outside. I want a tank that can be lost in the snow. Whatever is left afterwards, pass it on to the next tank, but do not be sparing with it."

Gradually they settled down to rest. They ate their meagre rations. There were no beds, they would have to sleep on the ground. Hubert and Rudolf spread pilfered clothing and blankets over the ground as close to the fire as they dared. Several other tank crews and Infantry soldiers joined them. As they lay down, each man pulled loose straw over

147

himself. At first each man lay separately, fully clothed but embarrassed, later they huddled together conserving their warmth.

The second day was little different, though Jürgen felt less anxious.

More snow fell covering the churned ground. They advanced four hundred metres, blasting at the Soviets as though they had to totally annihilate the race. Four hundred metres! At the end of the day Jürgen could still see their starting point across the contorted snow and mud. No wonder there had been so little advance since he had been injured if it took three days to cover each kilometre.

Again as the evening fell the fighting stopped. Jürgen organised another camp. They could easily have used the same barn as the night before, but they feared the Russians would take advantage of their retreat if they fell back even ten metres.

There were no buildings. That night, and on many more to follow, Jürgen and his crew huddled together under the gun, on the turret floor. They shared their thin military blankets, running the tank's engine to keep warm.

They spent as much time as possible in the warm tank, even when not fighting. Nobody ventured out except for an essential call of nature or to find supplies.

* * *

November was cold, minus ten or fifteen degrees. How long had they been at the front, three weeks, a month? Each evening, Jürgen had written the date on the day's report but the dates no longer meant anything.

Jürgen watched the battle through the cupola viewers, directing his crew in their fight. It was hard to see through the thick frozen glass, but at least the closed hatch kept the cold at bay. Snow drifted across the turret roof, it collected around the cupola, blocking his sight. There was a momentary lull in the struggle.

"Rudolf, Ingwar, keep a look out for me, I need to clear the snow off the turret." Quickly he opened the cupola. As he worked, the wind blasted around his unprotected face. It took just a few moments but it was enough to notice one of the Infantrymen trudging alongside. The man had several scarves wrapped round his head to protect his cheeks, ears and throat, he had wrapped rags round his leather boots to keep them warm while stomping through the thick snow, head down against the stinging wind.

Jürgen ducked back down relieved for the moment at his own good fortune. He quickly closed the hatch above his head to keep the warmth in.

The day came to a close, Jürgen went through his usual ritual of organising camp. It was a simple enough task, the men knew what was required. As the cooking fire blazed into life the same soldier stepped up to warm himself. He said nothing, absorbed in his fight against the frost. After a few minutes he sat and removed his boots.

Jürgen watched as the soldier, numbed with cold, removed his socks to reveal feet, sore and blackened from caked blood and frostbite. The rags had absorbed the melted snow and soaked the leather, the wet had leeched the heat from the boots and from the soldier's feet. Bewildered by the man's wretchedness, Jürgen turned away. He was stunned into silence at the man's extreme distress. Jürgen did not want to think about it, but he knew feet like those could belong to him in the future. He said nothing to his crew…

"Hubert, make sure you fill up as soon as the fuel bowser arrives."

"Yes, Commander." Hubert left for the supply point but soon returned. "Commander, there is no fuel bowser today, supplies have not come through."

"Then we must pray we have enough to see us through tomorrow."

Fuel, as with so many supplies, was becoming a problem.

As the temperature dropped, supplies took longer to reach the front. The official policy was little and often but the trains were arriving less frequently. Three times per day had been reduced to once a day, then once every two days. Food was short, ammunition was depleted and there was still no sign of their winter clothing.

The lack of fuel forced them not to run the engine for warmth through the night. Instead they lit a fire under the hull warming the tank and preventing the engine from freezing. The fire's fuel came from the scattered ruined buildings. It burned well but someone had to tend it, lying in the snow and mud under the hull, feeding wood to the flames. They took turns, just as they took turns for guard duty and patrols. Jürgen did not shun his share.

The tiny makeshift camp now contained five tanks from the platoon, and half a dozen armoured cars. Each one had a complement of crew and soldiers sleeping on the floor and each one had a crew member on fire duty and another patrolling a section of the perimeter.

Jürgen rubbed his hands together trying to bring life into his chilled, stinging fingers. They ached, slowly turning numb as blood froze in his muscles. His rifle, slung over his shoulder, was useless to him. He knew if the enemy attacked, he might just have a chance of shouting a warning. He would never be able to unsling the gun and fire, his fingers were too cold to operate the trigger, there was little point in carrying the weapon at the ready.

He stamped his feet trying to inject some warmth into his toes. He had not wrapped cloth round his boots and could feel the warmth draining from his flesh. Perhaps the rags would help for a while, he thought as he made his camp patrol on the now hard-packed snow. Each footfall thumped loudly sending signals across the wasteland. Every movement could be observed and recorded by spies in the dark. He didn't care. If there were spies out there, they were far more hardy then he was and deserved to win the war.

He swung his arms about his body, slapping his sides, beating the warmth into his tightening muscles. He huffed into his hands to warm his gloved palms, then held them against his covered cheeks. Nothing helped. Each step was agony as frost wormed into his body.

Approaching his tank, Jürgen could see the feint glow of the fire underneath, he longed to be by the fire but averted his eyes so as not to lose his night vision.

"Are you awake under there, Ingwar?" Jürgen hissed.

"Yes, I am awake, Commander." Ingwar crawled out from under the tank. "How are you?"

"I think I left my toes back at the perimeter. I am totally frozen."

"You are not the only one. I can warm my hands, or I can warm my toes, but I cannot do both at the same time. And if I take my boots off, my fingers will be too stiff to put them back on again."

"Ingwar, you complain more than anyone I know."

"I am not complaining. It is true. Many troops have frostbite on their feet. You will see how hard it is when your turn comes."

"I know how hard it is, I have not forgotten last night." Jürgen started to leave. "I must continue, make sure you stay awake."

"Yes, Commander. Get me some more wood on your way round. There is not much left here."

"I cannot stop my patrol to pick wood for you." Jürgen turned away to continue his patrol.

"Then you will be cold, Commander, when the fire goes out."

Jürgen stomped off, limping.

Ingwar grabbed a handful of roasted acorns from a bag hanging from the back of the tank. He pounded them on a stone with a hammer. Then he dropped the crushed particles, flesh and shells alike, into a pot and filled it with snow. He hurried back and crawled under the tank placing the pot on the fire.

The drink would be bitter, thought Ingwar. There was no real coffee. There was no milk, sugar, or biscuits. At least the liquid would be hot, though it was as much the shock of the vile taste as the warmth that kept the guards awake.

The patrol normally took fifteen minutes. Jürgen had still not returned after twenty. Ingwar was beginning to wonder if something had happened. He crawled from the fire's warmth to watch for his Commander. Eventually Jürgen stomped up dragging a large bundle of planks behind him.

"Never say I do not look after you." He dropped the boards at the back of the tank.

"I was beginning to think you had been murdered or something."

"You worry too much, Ingwar. I bet the Commies are warm in their beds. It is mere prudence which makes us keep these patrols, the Ruskies are too clever to be out at night."

"You will not be thinking that when you meet one on your next round."

"I hope not, I am too frozen to fight." Jürgen fiercely rubbed his hands together.

"Here, have a cup of coffee." Ingwar held out a metal mug full of ill-smelling, grey-brown liquid.

"Thank you."

"Take it with you to thaw your hands." Ingwar collected more snow for another cup, it would be ready just about when Jürgen returned. Then there would only be another twenty or so minutes before the change of guard. He would be able to climb under his blanket in the tank, while Jürgen took over fire watch. Who was supposed to take over the patrol? Ingwar tried to think but the cold had benumbed his mind.

Ingwar scrambled back under the tank to check the fire. Time slipped by slowly, Jürgen came and went again. Eventually he heard movement from inside the tank. Moments later Hubert climbed down and called to him.

"You all right under there? Where is the Commander?"

"I am fine thank you. The commander is still not back."

"I had better set off and make sure everything is all right. If you are

151

inside when I return, sleep well."

"Thank you, good luck."

Hubert turned and plodded into the dark. "Damnation, it's colder than hell itself."

Moments later Jürgen stamped up to the tank, dragging another bundle of wood.

"Has Hubert started his duty?"

"Yes, Commander."

"Good. You can retire now, Ingwar. I think I have enough wood for the next few hours."

"Just make sure you keep the fire small or you will cook us all alive in there." Ingwar patted the tank's hull.

"At least you will be warm." Jürgen smiled.

"I do not want to be that warm. If I am dead tomorrow, I will come looking for you."

"Oooo, I am so frightened," Jürgen laughed. "Goodnight." As Ingwar climbed into the tank, Jürgen stood on one leg snapping wood across his knee. When he had a good-sized collection of shards and splinters, he bundled it into his arms and slithered under the tank. Ingwar had laid several short planks on which to lie and stay dry.

Gradually he felt the warmth from the fire. It was only a small blaze but the heat stung his exposed skin, thawing his cheeks and fingers. Pinpricks jabbed his body making him want to move, but to stay away from the fire was to invite real frostbite.

Jürgen placed another piece of wood on the flames and set to rubbing his cheeks and hands. Slowly he gained a few degrees of body warmth, enough to think about other things.

Hubert would be round soon on his patrol. Jürgen knew how much a cup of coffee was appreciated. Reluctantly he crawled out and scraped more snow into the jug Ingwar had used for the drink. At least it is warm, even if it is killing us, he thought. After placing the jug on the flames he took time to loosen his boots and pull one off. He placed the sock over the top of his boot close to the fire. Steam rose from the woollen surface

His foot was white, like a cadaver. Not a shadow of colour to be seen anywhere on his skin. He tried to wriggle his toes but could not induce movement. Placing his hands on either side, he rubbed vigorously for several minutes until the appendage looked less like dead meat. He replaced the warm but damp sock and struggled pulling the boot back on.

It was not an easy task lying on his side with little more than forty centimetres between ground and roof.

The sound of tramping feet broke his concentration.

"Hey, Hubert. You want some coffee?"

"You call that diarrhoea coffee, Commander?"

"Well it is not what I would call it personally, I am just using the common name. You can go without if you want."

"No, I will take it, and a nice cream cake if you have one."

"Sorry, all sold out."

"That is too bad," Hubert took the proffered cup. "maybe when I come back."

* * *

November moved on but little progress was made on the front. The conflict was still many kilometres short of Moscow though the intention had been to take the city before the ingress of winter. While there was little movement along the lines, the fighting intensified and many units were halved by the attrition. Tenth Division was pulled back to recuperate.

Arriving at the rest area, Jürgen wrapped rags around his hands, as much to prevent his hands sticking to the tank's super-chilled, metal exterior as to prevent frostbite. He climbed down, within moments he was shivering in minus twenty-five degrees. The chill wind found every gap in his thin uniform, stinging his skin like some evil fire. Clutching his body in his arms, he headed towards his Unit Commander. The *Oberleutnant* looked haggard from too little sleep or too much responsibility. Jürgen wondered if he himself looked the same.

"*Herr Oberleutnant*, may I have a word?"

"Of course Klimt, what is on your mind?"

"Sir, I was wondering if you would enquire after our winter uniforms?"

"It is one of my deepest concerns along with the inadequate supply of food and fuel." The platoon commander stamped his feet for warmth. "I had planned to look into it as soon as you crews have your quarters. I promise I will let you know when I have an answer. In the meantime keep your blankets around you." The Officer quickly left for the Requisition Office, part of a barn which still stood, in spite of the rest of the farm having been obliterated months before.

Jürgen rubbed his neck while wondering if anything would come of the enquiry. The town, Gagarin, still had some intact buildings though the majority had lost roofs or parts of walls.

Their billet turned out to be a small single roomed house with part of a wall missing. The wind brought in the chill. Snow flurried settling on the six bunk beds. A small stove, supposedly for keeping them warm, stood at the centre of the mud floor, a metal flue pipe was held in place by wire.

"That's good, I wonder if it works." Jürgen opened the door. The stove was full of ash and straw. He looked round for a container. An enamel washbasin lay inverted on a small stand. Jürgen placed it under the stove to riddle the ashes. The basin was full before he was satisfied. A waft of dust and ash filled the room, forcing his crew out through the door to the street.

Next Jürgen inspected the flue pipe and pulled out a bundle of straw and feathers.

"Look at this, a blasted bird's nest."

"Any birds or eggs in it?" Rudolf, shivering, called through the door.

"Stupid, at this time of year? Though I fancy a nice omelette myself." Jürgen rubbed his hands together before continuing his work.

"Oh, please Commander, no talk about food." Ingwar held his stomach. "If you start, it will never end, and we will all die of longing."

"No talk of food then, but I still have to get this stove fixed if we are to avoid dying of cold." Jürgen pushed his arm up the chimney and extracted a mass of leaves. "Nobody has used this thing since last winter. I only hope it does not smoke too much or we will all be asphyxiated."

"I could not care less, as long as I am warm when I die."

"Shut up about dying," Gustav exploded. "Ingwar, all of you, think about something happy to pass the time. Anyway, Commander, how long are you going to be? I am perishing."

"A while yet. You would be better off looking for fuel to burn in this contraption." Jürgen said as he pulled out another handful of leaves. He took the curtain rail, a thin wooden rod and poked it up the chimney. More leaves and soot fell into the room, then the pole moved easily. "Right, I think it is clear. Let us start with those leaves for kindling but I will want something more substantial in a minute."

The others scattered through the room looking for wood or coal. Rudolf picked up the only stool in the room and smashed it against the wall. Dust settled from the rafters as he pounded the seat.

"Careful you will bring the house down around us," said Jürgen.

Soon there were several small piles of wood from the few pieces of inessential furniture. Jürgen struck a match, holding it to the dried leaves in the grate. They caught quickly, shrivelling and crackling as the flames advanced. He added the bird's nest and placed a few small splinters of wood on top. Smoke rose easily up the flue. Soon there was a good fire. Jürgen left the fire door open for a while, letting the heat into the room.

"We will need more fuel if we are to be warm. Remember, we stay here a whole week."

"We can look for more when we have warmed up some." Rudolf pulled a bed close to the fire, and sat holding his hands towards the flames. The rest quickly joined him.

* * *

There were no proper facilities in the makeshift camp, no canteen, no shower or latrine block, and no real procedure for collecting supplies. To begin with the crew made do with the equipment from the tank, cooking their rations on the stove and collecting supplies by scavenging the area. Two days passed.

Hubert rushed into the room.

"A supply train has arrived." He was nearly knocked flat as his friends stormed out to scrounge what they could. They grouped by the railway wagons, shouting for their share.

"Do you have any clothes?"

"Where is the fuel?"

"What food do you have?"

"There is one crate of knitted winter coats," came a reply, "but they are not for you… You are tank crew, you have a tank to keep you warm. These are for the Infantry."

Troops pushed and shoved towards the open crate. Gustav pushed with them. As the crowd cleared in front of him, he looked into an empty container. A voice called from two wagons down the train.

"I have one case of boots, good leather boots." There was a stampede as troops flooded towards the sound. Gustav reached in, desperately fighting forward to claim a prize. His hand came away bloody, holding one boot, size small, a woman's size. Bursting with anger he threw it on the icy ground.

As he pushed out of the throng he saw crates being loaded onto lorries at the far end of the train. There must be more coats and boots there, he thought. He grabbed at a crate not caring what it contained. He was fiercely repelled by the working troops.

"These things are for the front line. You do not need them while you

155

are on leave."

"I want a coat, I am cold, my friends are cold." Gustav pleaded, his energy and anger draining away in the freeze.

"Go back to your billet, sit in front of your fire." The Supervisor turned away. "Come on, load these crates. I want you out of here in an hour."

Gustav searched for a friendly face. Hubert stood a short way away, listening.

"There is no petrol until the day you move out; wood, we do not have." The speaker turned to the next in line.

"What about food? There must be food," Hubert begged.

"Only your Commander can collect food, there, at the front of the train."

Hubert headed towards the engine. Gustav joined him.

"This is pitiful. How do they expect us to live on such short rations?"

"I do not know. We just have to try. The two men tramped over the hard icy ground until they found Ingwar and Rudolf carrying a small box."

"There you are, Gustav, Hubert. Did you get anything?" Ingwar called.

"A big fat NICHTS. What have you got there, Ingwar?"

"Commander Klimt has collected two boxes of food. You two can carry the other one.

"Well, at least we have something to eat now," Gustav said as he carried the supplies to the room. "I nearly had a knitted coat."

"Nearly? What happened?"

"The crate was empty before I got there."

"My grandmother said Hitler has told everyone to knit coats for us," said Rudolf. "She was going to send me one direct but the authorities came and took it, and told her to start another one. I thought she was joking."

They made a meal of dark bread and hard cheese.

"Go easy with that food," Jürgen cautioned. "It must last all week."

"*Ja, ja.*" Gustav stuffed his mouth full, "I still want a good coat though. I am going to look around the derelict houses again." He left the room and walked into the street.

"We already did that," Hubert called after him.

Gustav wandered across the road to where several Infantry Troops stood milling around. They were watching a short line of perhaps fifty

Soviets being escorted to the railhead.

"W–Where are they going?" Gustav shivered, pointing at the captives.

"For them, the war is over. They are invited to enjoy the *Führer's* hospitality in a Prisoner of War Camp." The soldier looked at his companions, smiling. "They will probably never see their Motherland again."

"That is true, the *Führer* has plans for them." The second soldier ran his finger across his throat and laughed.

"They look so warm?" Gustav observed.

"They have the right clothes for this weather. Here, look." The soldier opened his field-grey coat to reveal another, underneath. It was green like the Russian's uniform, a rust coloured stain around tattered threads blemished the cloth. "I took it off a dead Soviet. It is very warm but it must be worn under the uniform or I would be shot as a Soviet escapee."

"Where can I get one?" Gustav could almost imagine the warmth.

"There." The soldier nodded pointing at the Russian column. "Boots too, they are fur lined, very good if you do not mind the smell."

Gustav rushed into the house.

"Come on, you lot. There are coats outside, come quickly before they are all gone."

"What are you talking about?" Rudolf called after Gustav, but there was no hesitation as the rest of the crew dashed to follow. Jürgen started forward but stopped at the doorway. Suddenly he was aware of Gustav's intentions and wondered if he should join them or intervene.

Gustav marched swiftly across the street drawing his Walther P38.

"Halt, halt, or I will shoot." He aimed at a prisoner's head. The man shuffled to a stop. The rest of the line stopped behind him looking sullen and dejected. They seemed to have little hope for their future, whatever happened.

"What are you doing?" A guard ran up brandishing his rifle. "You must not stop the prisoners."

"I want a warm coat"" Gustav paid the guard little heed but carefully studied the line of Soviets looking for someone who was about his size and weight.

"You cannot stop the prisoners." The guard turned to the line waving his rifle at them. "Move on."

"No! Halt," shouted Gustav. "I want a coat, and boots."

"What do you mean, you want a coat and boots. There are no coats to

157

be had here." The guard was becoming angry.

"There are!" Gustav turned to the guard, fury in his eyes, and took aim. His hand shook with cold.

Gustav scrutinised the guard. Judging the amount of padding the man had, his uniform was more than the regular German issue. "You have one." Gustav reached out and turned back the guard's coat lapel revealing green under the grey. "Why should I freeze when you are warm?" The guard recoiled but remained silent.

Gustav turned back to the prisoners and slowly walked past each man.

Jürgen breathed more easily.

Gustav stopped by a tall Communist and placed his foot next to the prisoner's.

"Take off your coat and boots."

The soldier didn't move.

"Take off your coat and boots, or I will shoot you and take them anyway."

"What are you doing, Gustav." Hubert stood watching the scene from a short way off.

"You are not very bright? I am getting myself a warm coat and boots."

"But not like this?"

"Why not? He did," Gustav casually waved his gun at the guard before turning back to the prisoner. "I will not tell you again." He cocked and levelled the pistol.

"*Da, da.*" The prisoner, frozen hands trembling, unfastened his garment.

"Thank you. And the boots." Gustav pointed. He removed his tank tunic and quickly fitted the heavy waterproof over his shirt. The inside was warm from the prisoner's body. He replaced his tunic over the top. It was a tight fit but better than the tunic on its own. He breathed a sigh of comfort.

The prisoner had by now removed one boot. Gustav yanked it from his hand and tried it on. It was too small.

"Hey, Ingwar. Your feet are smaller than mine, try these for size." Gustav did not wait for Ingwar's response. He dropped the boot by the owner. The Russian bent to replace it on his foot.

"No!" Gustav screamed. The man straightened, standing docile like a cow at the abattoir, one bare foot in the icy snow, waiting to see if he would lose his second boot.

Gustav limped along the line wearing one sock, one boot and carrying his other boot, he found another suitable supplier.

"Take off your boots," he shouted. "Take off your boots."

The gun pressed against his head, the prisoner crouched down unfastening the leather, his stiff fingers fumbling the laces.

Gustav's fury boiled, this should not have been necessary, but he was not about to let the opportunity slip by.

The second set of footwear fitted. Gustav relaxed. "These are lovely, now I might keep my toes." Gustav grasped the prisoner's cheek and pinched it like he might a child's. The man recoiled, staggering into his neighbour. Gustav's gun was suddenly there, inches away from the fellow's face, ready to ward off any threat. There was no threat, only reluctant charity. Gustav regained his calm.

"Thank you." He spun, set to return to the billet but stopped short. His friends were still testing for good fits. Other Panzer Troops had joined the inspection. He waited and watched to make sure the enemy did not resist.

At the back three prisoners stood wearing short quilted jackets. Gustav was intrigued. He wandered forwards to inspect the attire.

"Why have you got these jackets, they are not proper Russian uniform."

"Yes, Russian tank uniform." The prisoner replied in broken German.

"Very nice, this will do for our Commander, take it off." Gustav again used his pistol to intimidate. The prisoner, grim-faced, hurried to comply.

"Imperialist thief."

"War and peace, my friend. War and peace. You have read Tolstoy, I presume." Gustav snatched the jacket and walked back to the head of the line. The others seemed to be kitted out at last. Gustav turned to the guard.

"You can move them on now. Thank you for your assistance." Returning to the billet, he scanned the room for Jürgen but the commander was not there. Then he sat by the fire, his hands in his new coat's pockets. He felt very comfortable.

"Why did you make us take these things, Gustav. We can not wear them outside, they are all too long." Rudolf carried his coat over his arm.

"If you try thinking instead of moaning all the time, you would realise you can cut it just below your tunic and tuck it in your trousers,

159

you can use the rest as linings for your legs. It will keep you warm whichever way you wear it." Gustav pulled his coat off, pulled a knife and hacked at the material. He left the edges ragged.

An hour later, Jürgen returned.

"I am sorry, I visited the supply depot again but there are still no uniforms but I did pick up some boxes for fire wood."

"Do not worry, Commander. We have solved the problem and I have a present for you." Gustav handed the quilted jacket over. "I took it off a Commy."

"Hum." Jürgen reluctantly accepted the gift but scrutinised the material. "Very nice, and with *Leutnant* pips." It was a gift, a bonding with his crew. He had not looked to steal a coat for himself but they had provided for him. It showed their respect for him, his heart swelled. "Thank you, that is very generous of you."

"I would have got you boots too, but I do not know your size."

* * *

Tank 228 went back to the front. The new initiative, Operation Typhoon, was supposed to have ended with the capture of Moscow. However, at each attempt, they were blocked by superior forces. The Soviets dug in with huge numbers of fresh troops. Jürgen couldn't make out where they had come from.

Blizzards raged. Much of the time targets couldn't be seen through the blowing snow. The weather deepened, minus thirty degrees. If touched, the Panzer's frozen body stuck to the skin. The fuel froze. By the end of January it was too cold to fight. Many troops died, frostbitten, malnourished and demoralised from the conditions, the Division's numbers dwindled.

February was just as cold, March seemed less so. One morning in late April, Jürgen rose from his bed on the turret floor. Something felt different. He opened the hatch to look around. The snow was melting. He had known for several days the thaw was due. Recently they had not needed the usual fire under the hull, now the fields and trees showed the evidence. He climbed out. The ground seemed higher than normal. He studied the tracks. During the night his command had sunk into the thawing waterlogged soil. It would be difficult extracting the vehicle.

Jürgen paced to the tank's rear. He had intended to relieve himself but stopped abruptly. The hull rested firmly on the ground with two booted feet protruding from underneath.

Jürgen was struck with horror. Someone had taken refuge for the night under the tank, and the habit had cost him his life. Was this the only such casualty? The thought was agonising. The soldier had somehow survived the hardships of winter to die now, pointlessly, as the warmth greeted them once again. Jürgen wanted to cry. How many more friends and unknown companions would die in this bleak and pointless wasteland?

* * *

In May, the Russians gained the upper hand, but the Tenth Panzer Division, by then, had moved to Northern France to re-equip. Jürgen was promoted *Leutnant* producing a spontaneous celebration, though he felt he had only achieved the rank over the backs of fallen comrades.

In November, with a full compliment of personnel and all new equipment, the Division headed south to invade Vichy Free France. The Panzer IV with hull number 80,536 remained in the north.

Part two

12

D-Day

On arrival at the new camp *Unteroffizier* Nicholaus von Rosen was assigned as driver to tank 423. Aged 26, he was a veteran of the war having seen battle in Poland, France and finally Russia. He looked older than his years.

In November 1942, his Panther had been crippled outside Stalingrad. He had escaped the wreck and rolled in the snow to extinguish the flames but not before it had caused irreparable damage. On one side of his head, his hair refused to grow and his skin would not tan.

As he had run from the scene, his leg had been shot from under him by rifle fire. The bullet had fractured his left femur but he had continued to struggle for three kilometres before being picked up by medics. Though the bone had healed adequately, it was a weakness and he would always limp. After hospitalisation he had been sent to France to recuperate.

He thought he would never be assigned front line duty again, but declared fit for secondary duties, Nicholaus had worked on the Normandy coastal defences. He had dug foundations and constructed wooden formers for the reinforced concrete walls of the huge defensive gun emplacements. He had dug pits for shoreline defences all along the beach from Riva-Bella to Luc-sur-Mer. Nicholaus hated the Atlantic Wall but at least he had not been forced to stand knee deep in the sea erecting Belgian gates and *Hemmbalk*. At last the majority of work was complete and all ex-tank crewmen had suddenly been assigned to the twenty-first Panzer Division, at Frenouville camp, east of Caen.

Nicholaus knew the twenty-first was not the original and prestigious Division of North Africa. Though the name had a good reputation, the new units were formed of older or injured second-rate troops, gathered together from formations like his own company, who were all veterans unfit for front line duty.

As he approached the Panzer IV, he dabbed his hand over his scar as though testing the integrity of the skin. He was dismayed to see the tank was an older version. The paintwork was the new multicolour camouflage but it looked dull and weather-worn. Nicholaus was glad to see the L43 gun but even that was old by comparison with the latest L48 which had been fitted to the Panzer IV Ausf H.

The tank had secondary armour, bolt-on plates fitted to the hull and superstructure. The turret had a storage bin attached to the back, and thin metal sheet round the back and sides, held in place, thirty centimetres from the main skin by long brackets. The bow plate and glacis had spare track links bolted in place to act as additional armour. There were brackets along the mud guards for fitting armour over the sprockets, wheels and suspension, but the actual armour had not been put in place yet.

Nicholaus climbed into the turret and noted the hull number: 80,536. This was an old machine. He ran his hand over his scar again in an unconscious nervous reaction before wriggling through the small opening between the gunners position and the driver's seat. There were the usual levers and pedals. It was a relief to see them, he had never been in a Panzer IV before.

He opened the overhead hatch to let more light in. As he worked checking the linkages between the controls and the machinery, three other soldiers joined him. He had spoken to each on many occasions but had never built a proper friendship.

"Hello, von Rosen." Pascha Derichs had a broad smile on his tanned face as he leaned down through the hatch and shook Nicholaus' hand.

"Pascha, and it's Nicholaus, not VON Rosen. How many more times do I have to tell you?"

Nicholaus suddenly heard greetings shouted at him from inside the turret. He turned to see two faces peering at him through the space he had just crawled through.

"Boris Kirchmeier and Siegfried Feisel. Who would have guessed? So you are all together, see no evil, hear no evil and speak no evil."

"That is not very nice. You will have to show better manners if you are crewing with us." said Siegfried. "Besides, now we are four. You will have to find a new nickname."

"Yes, It looks like I am your driver, but I doubt I shall be driving this thing very far."

"True, what is there to fight here in France? Or are they planning to send us back to the Eastern Front?" asked Boris

"I have no idea. I would rather not think about it until I have to." Nicholaus ran his hand over his scarred head again.

"Oh, I forgot," said Pascha, "you only just managed to escape from your last tank. But this time, you will have Boris, Siegfried and me to look after you."

"I find that very encouraging," said Nicholaus, scowling. "So how are you positioned, and where is our Commander?

"I am your radioman," said Pascha. "The moment we are in trouble, just tell me and I will call for help. Siegfried is loader, Boris is gunner and I think *Feldwebel* Hillbrunner is our Commander. We shall probably never see him, I heard he is shell shock crazy," Pascha laughed.

"Most reassuring," said Nicholaus. "Are you going to carry out inspections. I do not want to go into battle with only half the equipment working."

"What are you worrying about?" asked Boris. "We will not be sent into battle. We are too far away from the front and none of us are battle fit."

"Then tell me, why have we just been told to take charge of this old heap?" Nicholaus patted the bulkhead between himself and his companions.

"How am I supposed to know?" Boris shrugged his shoulders. "It is probably some Officer's joke, or maybe they just assign the tank so they can fill in some paperwork."

"I still want to check everything, just in case. I heard the British will land here."

"The British!" Boris was derisory. "You waste your time if you want, I am going for a drink. Are you coming Pascha, Siegfried? Why not come with us, VON Rosen, we will take care of you." Boris scrambled from the turret but stopped dead before he could drop to the ground.

Feldwebel Hillbrunner stood by the Panzer.

"Stay where you are, *Herr* Kirchmeier. You must check your equipment. Feisel, load up with practice rounds. In one hour we go on manoeuvres and we shall have manoeuvres every day until I say otherwise."

* * *

Tuesday 6th June 1944 00.15

Their rest was shattered again, low flying aircraft thundered overhead.

"Hell! They are almost on the ground," said Boris. Lying in bed, he rolled over to look out the window.

"Probably trying to stay below the clouds to see where they are going," said Pascha.

"I wonder where they are headed." Nicholaus leaned on his elbow, listening.

"Could be anywhere."

The sound of the aircraft continued, sometimes close by, more often at a distance. Explosions could be heard far away. A continuous barrage of bombing.

"Sounds like Caen again."

Towards 2.00 a.m. an Orderly stormed into their quarters. "*Aufstehen, schnell.*" The troops shifted reluctantly. "Man your tanks. You will leave as soon as your orders come. Move it, *schnell.*" Within minutes, the building was empty. Tank 423, one of five in the group, was quickly loaded with fuel and ammunition and ready to move. The crew waited for instructions.

"One thing is for sure now," said Hillbrunner, "we will not have any more sleep tonight."

Bombs were still dropping on Caen six kilometres to the west. The flashes of explosives lit the night's sky in colours of red and orange. Clouds of smoke, mixed with the smell of brick and cement dust, drifted swiftly on the west wind. Even after the bombing stopped, the sky still flickered orange from the burning city. The respite was short-lived. Bombing restarted half an hour later. Hours passed.

"What is the point in telling us to prepare to move," asked Siegfried, "and then make us sit here."

"It's just one of those things they do to see if we will snap," said Hillbrunner.

"Well I wish they would let me 'snap' in my bed. At least I would have been warm. Bloody war!" Siegfried objected.

The wind and intermittent rain swept the village streets. The tank's engine ticked over monotonously. Pre-dawn lightened the sky, turning the black of the windswept night into an almost as impenetrable grey.

Hours later the Orderly returned. "Move out, the *Engländer* are coming." It was only as they moved off that anyone realised what the Orderly had said.

"*Engländer*! Not possible," Boris objected. The church clock struck nine.

"It seems the English have parachuted into Bonouville and Ranville," said Hillbrunner, reading from the official report handed to him by Pascha. "They have captured the bridges over the Orne. We are to attack at Escoville to prevent them reaching further inland. It is probably just another Dieppe type raid, but it has taken them long enough to try it."

"Yes they really had their noses blooded last time."

"Do our generals think there are enough for a whole tank company to have to intervene?" asked Boris.

"Probably not, but it is better to be on top of the matter," said the Commander. "Even a small group, if left to their own devices, could cause a huge amount of trouble."

Nicholaus shifted the tank into third gear and continued accelerating. "I thought last night's manoeuvres were in Escoville?"

"Yes," Hillbrunner confirmed.

"Well, the units who took part in those should take on the enemy."

"Impossible, they only have practice rounds."

"Try not to worry so much, Von Rosen," Pascha called through the space by the radio. "It will be over by lunch time."

Hours later, as they approached the Caen-Troarn road, they were redirected.

"It seems we are needed elsewhere more urgently," said Hillbrunner. "Nicholaus, turn left at the main road."

"Yes, Sir." Tank 423 turned due west in the direction of Caen.

"Commander, I thought the English had landed at Bonouville."

"They have, Siegfried. But a much stronger force has landed from ships at Luc-sur-Mer. We can come back for these others later."

"Heaven help us."

The column continued into the already seriously battered city. Many buildings had dissolved into rubble. Huge explosions burst on either side as five hundred pound bombs detonated around them. The B24 bombers were already flying away, out of sight behind the broken masonry.

Approaching the river, the column slowed to a crawl as other fighting vehicles joined them. Gradually the whole assembly ground to a halt.

"What is causing the hold-up?" frustration sounded in Nicholaus' voice.

Using the advantage of height in the cupola, Hillbrunner peered through his vision ports. "It looks like we are queuing to cross the Orne. There are Panzers everywhere but it should not take long."

"Time will not matter if one of those bombs lands on us," Nicholaus replied.

"Has anyone got some drink?" Boris asked. His voice trembled.

"Where is your water?" Generally frustrated with the day,

167

Hillbrunner was ready to lose his temper.

"I want something stronger, like schnapps."

"I am sure we could all do with some. Now, pull yourself together."

"Sorry, Commander."

As the afternoon settled in, they drove clear of Caen and rolling towards the coast. They advanced at walking pace so the Panzer Grenadiers could keep up. Many soldiers hitched rides on the armour for the first few kilometres.

At 17.00 hours, the Brigade formed line-abreast ready for their attack.

They moved forward again. The ground around them was ripped apart as Allied Flights passed overhead dropping bombs and firing rockets. Slowly, one by one, vehicles dropped out, crippled by the enemy's attacks.

Metal rattled off the tank's side as bullets ricocheted from the roof.

"Thank God for secondary armour plating," said Boris.

The constant attack churned the ground, turning it from green to brown. There was no manoeuvre they could make that could take them quickly out of danger.

To the right, an armoured car burst into flames. It ground to a stop, peeled open like a tin of ham. The crew spilled on the ground, their uniforms burning about their bodies. Loud detonations erupted from inside as the stored shells ignited.

Abruptly tank 423 lifted and lurched sideways, almost tipping on its side. The hull rang like a bell as it slewed to a stop and landed righting itself. Outside flames spread across the track and hull. Nicholaus was momentarily blinded by the flash. There had been no warning.

"What the hell was that!" shouted Boris.

"A message from Churchill," said Hillbrunner. "Thank God it missed. Everyone out, now."

"How do you know it missed?" The hatches flew open disgorging the five crew onto the ground.

"We would be dead if it had hit us."

They gathered on the right-hand side of the tank away from the hull and the incoming aircraft. Hillbrunner called for his four comrades' attention. "Any injuries?"

The crew stood looking at the Infantry fatalities and mutilated survivors. Nobody answered.

"Come on men, are any of you injured?"

Slowly the crew pulled their thoughts away from the carnage around them.

"No, Commander," said Nicholaus.

"Good, check the tank over. I need a damage report."

"What was that, Commander?" asked Pascha.

"A shell… three hundred millimetre, maybe three-fifty" Hillbrunner watched the rest of the line continue forward as though nothing had happened. Was it a blessing, drawing the fire away from them, or did their static position make them more vulnerable? "Where is that damage report, Nicholaus."

"Yes, yes, I am on it… Boris, come with me." Nicholaus led his friend round to the other side of the tank.

A large crater, five metres deep, smoked where the weapon had struck. Someone's leg lay severed on the edge. All about, bodies lay mangled, bloody, covered in clods of earth, smouldering from fire. Someone groaned in pain. Neither man cared to inspect the casualties.

"That must be the closest they can come without actually hitting us," said Boris.

Nicholaus said nothing.

Loose soil covered the superstructure as though someone had tried to bury the vehicle. Smoke drifted casually from where something still burned under the Panzer. Fragments of wheel, twisted track links and other pieces of metal were scattered amongst the debris. There were holes in the secondary armour where bullets or shrapnel had penetrated to the turret.

"We were lucky there," observed Boris, looking at the shattered track. Two wheels and several leaf springs were missing.

"The whole suspension unit will have to be replaced," said Nicholaus. "It will take some effort to mend."

"If we clear the debris and replace the track, we can at least move, but only slowly or we will roll the track off. If we tighten the track as much as possible, I think we could get away with it until we are out of the firing zone…" Suddenly Boris stopped. He turned towards a noise coming from behind him. "More planes," he shouted. "Take cover." The two men scrambled back to the rest of the crew, placing the Panzer between themselves and the incoming fighters. "At least we are out of sight here."

Two Hawker Tempest rocket launchers passed forward of their position, firing at the advancing German line five hundred metres further on. Trails of white smoke homed in on one of the advancing vehicles.

The first explosion lifted the tank clear of the ground, the second sheared the turret off. Flames belched from the open top while additional explosions blasted from inside. The fireworks lasted several minutes, the sounds from the blasts scattering across the countryside. The turret landed on its side leaning against the pyrotechnic vehicle.

"Jesus! poor wretches," Pascha sighed.

"Incinerated!" agreed Boris.

"That is the worst I have seen," said Hillbrunner. "Even on the Eastern Front there was never anything like that."

"Where is our *Luftwaffe*?"

"*Luftwaffe*! Nicholaus shouted. "What *Luft*-bloody-*waffe*?"

"I do not want to be in the firing line anymore." Pascha trembled as he spoke.

"We will not to be walking into battle again just yet," said Hillbrunner.

"Nicholaus, how bad is it, and how long to repair?"

"One of the suspension units is destroyed, Commander. To make us mobile will take an hour, fixing the problem completely will take two to three hours more."

Hillbrunner thought for a moment as he watched the burning tank a short distance away. He needed a safe place to hide until dark and somewhere to find a replacement suspension and wheel arrangement. Gradually it dawned on him.

"We will stay here for a while, let the rest of the line advance away drawing the enemy fire with them. Then we will try to fix the damage, before getting out of here. Our replacement is over there." Hillbrunner pointed at the stricken tank five hundred metres away. "We fix the track, pull up alongside that wreck and transfer the necessary parts. We will set to work as soon as dark hides us."

Another tank, a Panther, exploded. Distance dulled the effect.

The crew crouched on the tank's east side, taking cover from the enemy aircraft attacking from the west. Hours passed as the sun slowly dropped dragging night into place. Hillbrunner only waited until dusk.

"We need to get out of here as quickly as possible. Nicholaus, Boris, Siegfried, fix this tank so we can move it. Do not use any lights… Pascha, come with me and help salvage the spares." The two teams set about their tasks. Hillbrunner and Pascha made a dash for the stricken tank half a kilometre away.

Nicholaus led Boris and Siegfried round to 423's damaged side. To their surprise, they found several medical orderlies still attending the wounded and removing bodies.

Nicholaus set his friends to work clearing the piled earth from the side of the tank.

"Siegfried, you remove the side bolts on the suspension unit. Boris, count the track links. We need one hundred and six. I will take out the underside bolts."

Nicholaus wriggled under the tank.

Within half an hour the remains of the old suspension unit was cleared away. It took another fifteen minutes to repair the damaged section of track. The sky turned through crimson to purple.

Nicholaus climbed from under the tank and brushed himself off. "Right, let's go. Shout if the track starts to ride off."

Nicholaus drove slowly forward for about five hundred metres then made a gentle U-turn to bring the vehicle up next to its stricken sister. Nicholaus parked beside the other vehicle but left the engine ticking over.

"Well done, that did not take long at all," said Hillbrunner.

"No, but one of the bolts sheared off, it will have to be drilled out later," said Nicholaus.

The five men removed the suspension from the derelict tank and fitted it part by part to their own machine. Two hours elapsed. It was pitch dark long before they had finished.

"Everyone, it is time to leave." Hillbrunner took command again. "Nicholaus, head into Caen." The vehicle pulled away, accelerating quickly, lifting clods as it ploughed across the fields towards the city. It took far less time to make the retreat than it had to advance the same distance.

In the city they were joined by other battle-worn and damaged vehicles who managed to limp in behind them. Only half of the initial force returned. They had an uneasy night.

* * *

June 7th dawned slowly. Nicholaus heard reports on the enemy's beachhead but tried to ignore the increasingly bad news. They had been woken again by the sound of gunfire to the north and knew it was no exercise. A few of the twenty-first's Panzers had been wiped out near Buron, early that morning. Added to the fifty lost the day before, the Division had taken a mauling.

In the makeshift camp the previous day's survivors performed repairs

171

and maintenance. Tank 423 was one of those in better condition. Boris volunteered to drill the sheared bolt and replace it. Other crew members set about helping with repairs on other equipment.

At noon, selected vehicles were ordered to form a defensive line at Lebisey. Most units were dug in by the end of the day. Tank 423 lingered in Caen with a few others as reserve.

During the afternoon they received instructions to form a small force for a new action against the British at Escoville and Ranville.

Through the evening, ten tanks prepared for battle. Hillbrunner returned from a Commander's meeting to explain the command signals to Pascha and Nicholaus. "There will be complete radio silence during the operation. The attack will be a straightforward advance with Grenadier support."

At midnight the short column moved forward. They crossed the Orne and turned north-east towards Cuverville. Nothing marked their movement except the sound of their engines, and the tracks on the road. Once they reached fields they could not be heard from more than a few metres away. The action was to commence at 03.00 hours, on the 8th, before daylight could reveal them to the enemy.

On a ridge half a kilometre to the south of Escoville, the lead tank flashed his taillights. Nicholaus had expected it, this was the signal to take up attack formation.

Each tank, spaced fifty metres apart, turned simultaneously forming a wedge with the command tank in the lead. Nicholaus didn't stop as he turned and took position on the formation's right flank.

The Panzer freewheeled down the slope towards the village, almost silent in the dark. No one spoke. Just shadows in the dark, the buildings were almost impossible to make out. Nicholaus felt confident. Wide eyed, staring into the night, he held his breath in anticipation. They would smash through the enemy and drive them back.

Within moments, huge detonations erupted around the tanks. Barely a second passed between the blasts. Nicholaus was shocked as ten metre deep craters appeared in his path, showering his advance with thick clods of mud.

"Where the hell did that come from, have they mined the ground?" shouted Nicholaus.

"They are shells from their Navy. I can see the guns firing in the dark," said Hillbrunner.

In less than five minutes, four of the tanks were flaming wrecks flood- the scenery and the attack with light.

Nicholaus could see the rest of the line to his left. Forty percent of their task force had been instantly put out of action. "We hardly stand a chance against this."

"Hold your tongue and concentrate."

The radio crackled.

"Fall back. Fall back to the start line."

Nicholaus plunged his foot on the accelerator.

The Maybach thundered into life, the vehicle swung wildly to the right as Nicholaus steered away from the danger. Breathing quickly he tried to guide the Panzer away from the destruction. The tank clawed its way back up the hill. Time dragged by, the pitch black of night covering the trees he sought for sanctuary. As his Panzer crested the hill, he sighed in relief. It seemed to speak for everyone. This had been their second violent defeat, but they were not going to die today.

The disarray of retreating Panzers stopped over the ridge and formed a defensive position. Just four tanks dug in.

As dawn broke they were able to see the battlefield and the sea beyond. In the distance British battleships lined the horizon.

For two days the tanks held the line against the enemy's probing. Enemy troops advanced several times each day, testing the strength of the emplacement. Each time, the four Panzers retaliated with rapid machine gun fire. Even though the enemy fell back at the slightest sign of resistance, the Panzers' supporting Grenadiers were quickly whittled down.

On the 10th, a larger attack erupted. With heavy artillery in support of troops, the British forced their way up the hill and into the camp. The Panzers pulled back to Cuverville two and a half kilometres further south. The attacking force did not immediately follow.

After the move, Nicholaus left the Panzer's engine ticking over. He took a moment to rest before preparing a small meal. He didn't manage to cut a slice of bread before shells started landing on the village. Houses erupted in all directions forcing him to move again.

Was there anywhere, Nicholaus wondered, that couldn't be reached by the Royal Navy's heavy guns?

On the evening of June 14th, the three remaining tanks retreated again and reformed on the eastern side of the Orne, south of Caen.

* * *

The next day, Tank 423 was assigned to a new unit with a number of

173

other tanks and Eighty-Eights. The new defensive position was situated in the Bois de Bavent which would provide excellent cover for harassing fire when the enemy's inevitable attack came from Ranville.

Nicholaus helped restock the Panzer. Then he took the opportunity to freshen up. There would be little chance for comforts such as baths and a latrine in the woods. He and the crew would have to sleep in, by or under the tank, and any comforts such as shaving or a wash would be in the open air with cold water.

The column, a mix of seven Panzer IVs, a Panther, two Tigers and two eighty-eight millimetre antitank guns, moved out during the dead of night. Travelling east along the Troarn road to Sannerville, they turned north to enter the Bois de Bavent.

Nicholaus detached from the line of vehicles to take his position along the wood's western edge. As he turned, the front of the tank whipped across several spindly saplings snapping them off at ground level. The bow pressed against a small tree, bending it over until it too snapped under the hull. He cleared a path to his allocated position just inside the boundary. When he cut the engine the crew baled out. The sky was already lightening to the east.

The morning meal the five men prepared was scanty. When they had finished, they dug a pit a metre deep and wide enough for the tank to drive into. It was heavy work with the thick clay soil and the tree roots threading their way through every spade-full of soil.

July had become hot after the cool wet of June. Mosquitoes sang in Nicholaus' ears, they bit incessantly at his face and arms in their search for blood. There was no escape. He slapped erratically trying to drive the annoyance away but only succeeded in making his skin even more red and angry.

The digging lasted into the following night with only brief stops for food. Eventually Nicholaus was able to manoeuvre the Panzer into the excavation, leaving just the superstructure and turret above ground.

Exhausted, the five men settled down to sleep but were soon roused again when additional supplies arrived. They laboured into the early hours unloading shells, water and fuel but the supply lorries were long gone by the morning. As the day bloomed Nicholaus sat in his driver position waiting for instructions.

The warm wind dried the land and a smell of rot filled the air. It had been there for several days but had steadily worsened with the increasing heat. Nicholaus wrinkled his nose.

"What is that stench? It smells like a rat died in here."

"Not in here. The smell is outside as well," said Boris.

"I think it is all the dead Englishmen across the river," said Pascha. "We must be giving them a pounding somewhere."

"It is not just the English, the Americans are out there somewhere, and the Canadians," said Siegfried.

"Do not forget," said Hillbrunner, "the fields are littered with dead cattle. They are too stupid to get out of the way. I have seen half-wild dogs scavenging the carcasses."

"I suppose every town and village has witnessed a battle and they all have bodies lying amongst the rubble," said Pascha. "no one has had a chance to clear them up yet. I bet the streets are full of vermin taking advantage of the feast and spreading filth and disease to the water supply."

"I am glad we are away from all that. – Where did this water come from?" Boris asked, holding out a metal cup."

"With any luck it will be from south of the battle area. Otherwise it will have been filtered from the river…"

the Panzer IVs engine ticked over gently as Nicholaus watched the British troop numbers swell. They were grouping just over the Orne Bridge. Then under air protection they flooded across the river towards Ranville. Tanks, heavy artillery and hundreds of soldiers, in orderly fashion, headed closer to the waiting Panzers. Nicholaus felt frustrated as they hid, but even a single shot would give their positions away, voiding the benefit of the trap they had set.

"I am glad they are not heading directly at us," said Pascha.

"Do not worry," said Hillbrunner. "As soon as we open fire they will, make no mistake,"

"Just make sure the hatches are clear so we can get out if it gets too hot inside," said Boris.

"All you have to worry about is firing that gun," said Hillbrunner.

The build-up of British forces continued through the evening. Nicholaus gave up watching as the dark took away his vision but the movement from heavy vehicles could still be heard well into the night. Hillbrunner advised him to sleep while he could.

The action started at 05.30hours, the next morning. British guns pounded the villages and open ground alike. There seemed to be no discrimination of targets. The fall of shot started just to the north of the hidden positions and worked steadily south towards them, through, and

175

beyond. Boris and Siegfried attended the gun while Nicholaus and Pascha brought up extra ammo from the stockpile deep in the woods. The majority of British positions were still out of range and would be until they started their advance. The barrage continued for half an hour. "Is this the start of the forward push?" asked Pascha.

"I hope so, I want to get back at those *Engländer*," said Boris. "I want to give them a taste of their own medicine. All this sitting around is getting to me."

"Just hold on until we are sure," said Hillbrunner.

To their dismay the sound of aircraft flying low overhead, filled the air. More explosions erupted around them as bombs fell like rain. One of the Tigers spun over. The turret flipped off and landed metres away from the stricken hull. Flames engulfed the machine, nobody escaped.

Huge plumes of soil shot into the air in front of Boris's sights. Nearby, another explosion ripped the air. A stately oak tottered slightly before tilting headlong across an Eight-Eight, bending the barrel with its dead weight. Bombs exploded all around. Within minutes five tanks were out of action, they hadn't fired a shot. In the distance Siegfried could see thick swarms of aircraft bombing Colombelles and Guberville. The sky was filled.

"Come on Nicholaus, get us out of here. They are killing us before we have even opened fire," said Siegfried.

"You cannot just pull out," Hillbrunner argued.

"I would rather pull out now and live to fight another day than stay here and be pulverised," Siegfried shouted back. "I reckon it is just luck we are still alive."

"Sure" said Pascha. "I am not staying in this place any longer than I have to."

"Then you had better get the engine started," said Boris.

Moments later Nicholaus reversed away from their dug-in emplacement. Suddenly there was a shout from the trees.

"Hey, what are you doing?" An Officer came running from nearby shrubbery.

"We are leaving, and quick. I advise you to do the same," Hillbrunner shouted.

"You can not leave, you must wait for orders. Stop, or I will…" The final sound was ear-splitting as a bomb detonated. Hillbrunner's antagonist was engulfed in flames. Earth showered down. An arm dropped through a hatch landing on Pasha's lap. His involuntary jerk threw it out moments before he heaved his stomach's content onto the floor.

"Sorry," said Pascha, "it caught me by surprise."

Slowly the tank moved through the trees, the tiny slitted viewer hardly showing Nicholaus the way. Saplings and brush collapsed under the Panzer's hull as it headed away from the destruction.

They headed south-east towards the Bois de Bures. The tank gave a series of lurches. The engine spluttered but seemed to pick up again as they drove into the welcome shelter.

"It looks as though we will make it," relief sounded in Nicholaus' voice. "I thought we were going to run out of fuel just then." Twenty metres into the wood, he pulled up and waited, the engine ticked over quietly. "They seem to be avoiding this section."

"Yes, it should be a good place to hide for a while," said Hillbrunner. "We will wait here until it is safe to move again."

They watched nervously as, to their west friendly tanks, gun emplacements and troops were relentlessly ripped to pieces. Anti-aircraft guns and smaller field guns put up a thick curtain of flak but only a handful of the huge American bombers were brought down.

One by one, the bombing put the flak guns out of action. The last plane drew away at 06.40 hours, abandoning the battered recipients with their ringing ears. Hillbrunner took a few minutes to recover and pull himself together.

"Right, it is time to get out of here."

"Which way?" asked Nicholaus.

"I was going to say Troarn but looking at Sannerville I think we should head there. It is closer."

Nicholaus gunned the engine and headed out of the wood and down the hill towards the village. They quickly joined a road headed in the right direction. The tank rolled easily down the slope; as the road levelled at the bottom of the valley the engine spluttered again more insistently.

"Come on you old oilcan, keep going," Boris shouted.

"Ha, it will look after us, there is only one more kilometre and we will be safe," said Nicholaus.

"Come on then, put your foot down, get us up there quickly."

A narrow bridge took the road across a stream.

The last of the fuel ran through the carburettor. The weight of the tank kept them moving. Splutter, roll, splutter, the engine died.

Nicholaus applied the clutch to keep the tank moving but on the flat she lost momentum rapidly. They rolled slowly onto the bridge stopping a fraction past the span's centre.

"What the hell?"

"Come on, start her up again."

Nicholaus pressed the starter. The engine turned but there was no ignition. Nicholaus tried again with the same result but slower. Again he tried. Each time, the engine turned more slowly. Eventually nothing happened.

"What is the matter?" Hillbrunner enquired.

"We are out of fuel, and now the battery is dead too. We are stuck until we find more fuel. Someone will have to walk to the dump and bring a fuel bowser."

"I will go, but not on my own." Pascha seemed eager to leave.

"I am coming with you," said Siegfried.

"Me too," said Boris.

"Someone must stay, we must have at least two people to fire the gun." Hillbrunner was furious at his crew's behaviour. To leave a position for a better location was one thing but to abandon the tank altogether was not acceptable.

"I am not staying here, with what they just threw at us, coming over that hill. I want to get out of here and come back when it is safe. Besides, there is not enough battery power to fire the gun," Boris pointed out, "stupid electric machine."

"I agree, we should all go." Siegfried's eyes seemed to plead.

Without the sound of the tank's engine to cover it, they slowly became aware of a new droning vibration.

"Sounds like more planes. Come on, let's get out of here." They scrambled from the machine and ran for the village. At the edge of Sannerville, they stopped, taking cover from the wave of explosions.

"I am not coming back here, fuel or no fuel," Pascha gasped as he dropped behind a wall in the hope it would protect him.

"Well, the dump is at Soumont just north of Falaise, about forty kilometres away," said Nicholaus.

"And I suppose we will have to walk all the way." The sound of the aeroplanes reached a crescendo. All around them huge explosions erupted showering them with mud and stone.

"Do not worry about that, we still have to live through this air raid." said Siegfried wiping dust from his mouth.

The five men stumbled into the narrow rubble-strewn lane. Bombs dropped all around lifting dirt and rubble high into the air as they bunched up against the wall, the cracked stones standing precariously.

13

Captured

Operation Goodwood, Day 2 19th July 1944

Sgt. Reed took his platoon through the fields to the shallow stream. Earlier, the troops had pulled back as soon as they had seen the Panzer IV. They had reported the position and skirted round to their next objective. Now Reed had been ordered to take the tank to prevent it menacing their backs.

Their approach was slow and cautious. He and his platoon had doubled back, using the hedgerows for cover. They had managed to advance, unseen, until they were within a few yards. The remaining distance was open and was where people could be killed. The tank stood on a bridge over a shallow stream which flowed deep in a ditch.

Reed had already set a plan of attack and assigned tasks. He waited until the team members were in position. The wind was in their favour, blowing gently from the troops to the tank.

Sgt. Reed crouched in the shrubbery and pulled out his binoculars. He inched forward under the foliage until he had a clear view. The vehicle was huge in the lenses but that was good, he could pick out details which might give away enemy intentions.

Nothing. The area looked deserted. The Panzer was parked square in the middle of the bridge. Why hadn't it been used in defence during his original advance an hour previously? Reed was puzzled. Maybe it was an obsolete model, using to block access. He was sure it hadn't been knocked out, it was in too good a condition.

It was too quiet, like a trap about to be sprung. Sgt. Reed wondered at the duplicity of it all, was the tank abandoned, or an ambush? There was only one way to find out.

Reed signalled for action.

Two smoke bombs ignited filling the air with a thick white stink. The wind drifted the smoky blanket towards the tank, shielding the men.

Lance-Corporal Filch, second in command, sprang forward. Even if the tank crew opened their viewers now, they would be blinded by smoke. He felt safe even though loose gravel crunched under his boots.

Crouching low, Filch reached the front of the tank. He pulled the pin from a grenade, leaped and grasped the end of the barrel. Hanging free by one hand, he let the handle fly from his explosive and rammed the now live charge into the mouth of the seventy-five millimetre gun. He prayed the grenade wouldn't stick in the muzzle-brake.

The explosive slid down the barrel towards the breach. With relief, Filch dropped to the ground and took cover under the hull between the sprocket wheels.

Seconds ticked by until a muffled detonation sounded. Smoke and a small flame, hardly noticed in the sunlight, issued from the muzzle.

Filch crawled out and climbed onto the left side of the glacis. He hoped his mates were in position to give him cover.

Straddling the main gun, Filch strapped a grenade to the turret machine gun. Private Watts joined him and strapped another explosive to the forward machine gun. Filch glanced at his friend. "Ready?"

"Ready."

"Two, one, pull." The two men pulled the pins and leapt for cover. Moments later the two explosions detonated almost simultaneously, buckling the machine gun barrels into useless scrap.

Filch crawled back out. The smoke still drifted across the scene. Why hadn't the enemy retaliated?

Filch recovered his rifle and cocked it ready to fire. He covered the tank as the rest of the platoon came forward, rifles at the ready. Filch and Watts climbed onto the superstructure. Watts climbed onto the turret. He stood with his rifle cocked and aimed at the cupola hatch. Filch knelt to one side of the cupola, crowbar in hand, ready to lever the cupola hatch open.

"Ready?"

"Ready," came the reply. The cupola hatch flew open, it wasn't locked. Instantly Watts fired into the opening. The men ducked down to avoid the ricochet.

Watts took a grenade and prepared to arm it and drop it into the opening. He knew he shouldn't delay but he held back. Nothing had stirred. There was no motion, no sound from inside the tank. Was it possible the shot had killed the tank crew? He released his hold on the grenade's pin.

Carefully Filch peered down into the turret hatch. There were three seats, none of them occupied. There didn't seem to be any bodies, dead or alive. He leaned down into the cupola, supporting himself on the edge of the turret ring. "There's nobody here." He pulled himself out and looked at Watts. "Keep guard here." He turned to the front of the tank. "The turret's clear, Sergeant."

"Move in the rest of you." Reed shouted.

Suddenly the front of the tank was awash with troops. It took less than a minute to have the whole tank secured.

"All clear, Lance Corporal." The shout rang out bringing with it a huge sense of relief.

Filch turned to Sgt. Reed. "All clear, Sergeant. There's no one here."

"Well done, lads. Now get the rest of those hatches open. Filch, Watts, you can take care of that. I don't care if it rains in there but we need to show the thing's abandoned. Check there's nobody hiding in the engine compartment. Follow as soon as you're done. Five minutes I'd say... The rest of you, fall in." He hesitated a moment. "Left turn. Quick march." He turned and started away. "Signals, request a heavy to move that bloody thing. You've got the map ref.?"

"Yes, Sarge."

The platoon headed south across fields towards Sannerville.

Filch looked at Watts.

"Mark, stand guard. I'll open the hatches and check the engine compartment."

"Right oh, Corp."

Filch dropped into the cupola. "It don't half stink in here. Needs a bloody good airing I'd say." Moments later he hoisted himself out and scrambled to the ground. "All right let's go."

"Can't we have a smoke before we move on."

"Reed said five minutes, so we'd better get moving."

"I suppose you're right." The two men walked off following the path of bent grass indicating the direction the squad had taken. For the second time in two days Panzer 423 was left abandoned.

* * *

Towards evening, a large American built M32 recovery vehicle approached from the north. It stopped several yards short of the bridge and the six crew piled out of the heavily armour plated body. They looked appraisingly at their next job. Roy Murrey turned to the driver.

"What are we supposed to do here, Charlie?"

"Just move the thing out the way so we can get traffic over the bridge. I wasn't told to do anything more. I suppose the nearest place we can leave it is in the field here." Charlie looked around the area with little interest. "All right, hook her up." Charlie climbed back into the cab. Roy attached a towing cable to the Panzer.

"All set."

Charlie didn't wait for the gate to be opened but drove into the thin wooded structure taking the two posts with him. The gate crumpled into splinters. The M32's tracks pressed the remnants firmly into the soft ground. The Panzer followed obediently crushing more of the fence and hedgerow. The recovery vehicle inched slowly into the field where the tank was abandoned for a third time.

* * *

August the 6th saw some villagers return to Sannerville. Madam Pascalle was one of the first to venture back to the village where she was born. She brought her son, Frederic, and her neighbour's young daughter, Giselle, with her. Charlotte Pascalle hardly noticed the tank as she trudged past. It was Frederic who observed the abandoned vehicle and the wide open hatches. The three people walked on towards their village, but Frederic was keen to investigate the new landmark.

The home they had loved was a crumbled pile of debris. The roof and two walls were completely destroyed but one room at the back was still intact, albeit with the window blasted away. With a little work it could be made habitable, at least until it rained.

Charlotte sifted through the rubble looking for items which might still be of use. Frederic cleared stones from the door to the one remaining room. A dented cooking pot made a useful receptacle for carrying the debris to the street. He only cleared enough for a space to sleep. It would have taken a long time to remove all the wreckage. Giselle helped, picking up odd fragments and throwing them into the road.

Charlotte watched them as they laboured. For a seven year old, Frederic had a much older head on his shoulders, she thought, but occupation and war could do that. She just hoped he could have his childhood back when this was all over.

They worked for long hours. Giselle grew tired and lay down in a corner and curled into sleep. Frederic eventually finished and sat down beside his surrogate sister. He was tired but didn't want to rest. He felt thirsty, the dust had dried his throat making it raw. He picked up the pan and went to look for water. There had been a well in the back garden but like everything else the hand pump was flattened. It lay on its side several metres away with the up-down handle snapped off. There was no sign of the pipe the pump had been attached to. He would have to look elsewhere for a drink.

183

Frederic scrambled over the fallen fence into the next garden. There the pump was still in place but the revolving handle was missing. He looked towards the next garden but the story was the same, destruction everywhere. Turning round he wandered back to his own house. He stood in the yard where vegetables and flowers had grown two months before. He could see through other gardens to the edge of the village; beyond lay the stream near where the tank stood. The stream, thought Frederic, it always had water. Looking round to find his mother, he saw Giselle standing where the back door had been.

"Are you thirsty, Giselle?" he asked. She nodded. "The well is broken but we can drink from the stream." He knew times were difficult, his mother had been hard put to provide them with meals. He didn't know if his mother would find any food for a meal today, but he hoped. He waved the pan. "We'll bring some water back to cook with." He knew that any help he could give would make it a little easier for his mother.

Giselle trotted forward and took his hand. Together they walked through the craters and piles of bare earth to the edge of the ditch.

"Stay here," he said, "I'll bring some back to you. There's no point us both getting wet." Giselle nodded and watched as her friend scrambled through the stinging nettles and tall grass to the stream. He slipped off the bank into shin deep water. He didn't grumble as the nettles turned his bare legs and arms into red welts. The water cooled the angry affliction; he stood for a moment enjoying the comfort before scooping the water and scrambling up the bank again. He handed the girl the pan, supporting it so she could sip at the liquid. Then he drank his fill before offering her again. It was a large pan and still held more than enough for both of them. They sat together for a while on the grass at the side of the field. He had remembered the water but that was not the most important subject on his mind. He was so close. He offered the pan to Giselle.

"Take this back to Mother. I'm going to look at the tank."

Giselle put her hands behind her back, shaking her head.

"Why not? Do you want to come with me?"

Giselle nodded.

"All right, but you can't climb in, you're too small."

Giselle shrugged her shoulders.

Holding hands, the children walked slowly to the field. They had both seen tanks before but had always run away to hide from the soldiers. Here, there were no soldiers, no roaring engines, no rattling tracks tearing up the dirt roads. All seemed calm, nothing to be frightened of.

184

A few metres from the tank, Giselle slipped her hand from Frederic's. He stopped and looked at her.

"Don't you want to go any closer, Giselle?" She shook her head. "All right, stay here, I'll go on my own." He placed the pan of water at the girl's feet.

He stood in front of the tank for several moments before tentatively pressing a finger against the mud strewn body. Nothing happened. With intent concentration, he walked round touching the various parts he could reach. The glacis plate, wheels, track, mudguards, exhaust box, then he walked back along the other side. He looked at the girl again.

"It's all right, it won't do anything, look." He gave the metal a slap with his flat hand. Giselle started as though ready to flee. "Come on, it's fine. Here, take my hand, I'll show you." Giselle reluctantly permitted herself to be led round the Panzer. "See, it's dead, it can't hurt you." Frederic reassured. "You can even climb on it if you want, I'll help you."

He grasped the track and hauled himself onto the glacis. He turned round and sat next to the machine gun sticking from the front plate. He folded his arms and looked smugly at Giselle.

"There, nothing to it. Do you want to come up?" he asked.

Giselle took a step back shaking her head. She looked ready to run. Frederic could see a tear in her eye.

"All right, I'll come down." He stood up and jumped to the ground. "Come on, we better take the water to Mother." He picked up the pan and, with Giselle clutching his other hand, returned home.

* * *

"Where have you been?" Charlotte cried when they returned. "You can't go wondering off just anywhere, there are soldiers all over the place, not to mention bombs which could kill you. I'd never see you again. I don't know what I'd do if anything happened to either of you."

"It's all right, *Maman*. The well in the garden was broken so we went to get water in the stream. We were only gone a little while. We had a drink and brought you some, and you need some for cooking."

"You're a wonderful boy..." She struggled to hold back tears. "Thank you..." She took a sip of water and then a deeper drink. "I've only been able to find a few old potatoes and an onion in the cellar."

"There's still some bread from the journey," Frederic announced happily.

"Yes dear, but I was going to save that for breakfast tomorrow."

185

"Onion and potatoes sounds fine," Frederic turned to the girl, "doesn't it *Sorcière*? Let's go and gather some wood to make the fire." It was not a difficult task. There were pieces of beams and floorboards strewn throughout the house and the streets were full of such litter. Most pieces were too big for the small fire they wanted, but there were enough fragments to build a cooking hearth including some kindling. Charlotte had some matches in the pack they had used for travelling. Frederic soon had a small fire burning in what was left of the cast-iron stove. It stood precariously on three legs with a stack of stones as the fourth. It would be enough to heat a pan of water to boil potatoes and onion. Mashed together with a touch of vinegar and oil they would make a tasty and filling meal.

The potatoes were wrinkled and scabbed. Chits sprouted from the eyes. Charlotte didn't bother pealing them, she cut them into quarters and dropped them in the water, noticing a lot of the flesh had gone grey with age. She peeled the onion and quartered that as well. She drained some of the water into a jug for use in the morning. It would be good for soaking the bread which, now a week old, was hard and stale.

When they sat to eat, the sky was already red. The meal didn't last very long but they were grateful for something in their stomachs. Tomorrow would be more difficult. Frederic looked at his mother, concerned.

"Don't worry, it will be all right, something will happen to make it good. I'll go and get some more water in the morning and I'll look in the fields, there may be berries."

"You're going to feed us on wild berries, are you? I wish I had your confidence. I don't know how you do it." As her tears started, she stood and took the empty cooking pan to the garden. She yanked frantically at some tufts of grass and wiped the inside. Then sitting on a pile of earth she let her emotions take over.

A while later Frederic came and sat beside her, placing his arms around her as best he could.

"Don't worry, Mother, it will be all right, I promise."

"It's easy for you, you can promise the moon and believe it's true. I can't do that." She stroked his hair and tried to smile at him. "Where's Giselle?"

"She's sleeping, I covered her in a curtain."

"You're a good and brave boy, I wish I could be as strong as you." Charlotte looked at the sky for a moment, its blood red already fading to purple as the night deepened. "Come on, it's time we went to bed as well. We'll work something out tomorrow."

* * *

Frederic woke first. It was still early but he was hungry. He found the knife his mother had used to cut the vegetables the previous evening and sliced the bread into three almost equal parts. He took the smallest and after soaking it in the little bit of water that was left, he ate ravenously. It was time for him to fulfil his promise to feed the family. He picked up two pots. The larger one he had used for water the previous day, the other was for the berries. He was about to leave when Giselle slipped out the room into the old kitchen area. She saw the bread and picked up the smaller of the two remaining slices. Frederic looked at her, wondering how he was going to make her stay behind.

"Good morning, I'm going to look for food. You must stay here."

Giselle shook her head. Frederic continued.

"I can't take you with me, it's dangerous and Mother will worry."

Giselle nodded as he spoke. Frederic persisted.

"You can't come, I won't let you."

Giselle continued to nod and stepped towards him, indicating Frederic should give up and let her come.

"Oh, all right, but don't get into any trouble, I've got work to do." He didn't care. She was pretty much an enigma. She only ever did what he told her when it suited her. How could you argue with someone who refused to talk, he wondered.

Frederic stepped into the lane and turned towards the village centre. There was a horse trough which should be full. He didn't know why he hadn't thought of it before, was it because he had wanted to look at the tank so very much?

Giselle followed a few paces behind, chewing her bread. She was carrying a small piece of rag which Frederic hadn't noticed before. A doll she had found?

In the village square he found the horse trough. It had been knocked off its stand. There was a large hole in the side, there was no water, only a wedge of dry silty mud in the corner.

He looked around the square. The church had lost its spire and the windows were glassless and gaping. A piece of paper spun in circles on the ground as the wind funnelled through different banks of rubble. There were no shops, no houses and no people. He quickly turned and headed back the way he had come.

187

"Come on, we'll have to go back to the river for water. I can look for berries on the way."

There were few berries to be had. The hedges, which the locals had always nurtured to provide wild crops, were in disarray. Even the brambles which usually gave copious blackberries were fruitless and those which did have a few weak offerings were still unripe. He would have to go much further if he was to find what he was looking for, somewhere where the war hadn't destroyed everything. Perhaps the Bois de Bures would be all right.

The children crossed the bridge and headed up the hill to the woods. The ground was less torn here, the hedges were green and lush. There was certainly some fruit, they picked rapidly as they walked from bush to bush, redcurrants, wild gooseberries and even a few early blackberries. They managed to half fill the small pot only leaving the hips because of the thorns. When he looked at the quantity, he realised it would only be a small meal. Better than nothing though.

"Come on Giselle, let's get some more water from the stream and then we can head back home." As they passed the tank, Frederic looked with longing. He wanted to investigate some more, he hadn't even climbed inside yet. He pulled Giselle into the field. Then, letting go of her hand, he placed the pans on the ground and ran to the vehicle. He quickly climbed onto the superstructure and peered into the driver's hatch. There was nothing to be frightened of here. He scrambled onto the seat and started pulling levers. His legs were too short to reach the pedals and he couldn't see through the visor, but that didn't matter. He notched the gear lever back and forth, not understanding the meaning of the numbers written on the side panel. Some of the letters were nothing like the letters he had learned in school.

After a while, he stopped and looked around. He had completely forgotten about Giselle. Behind the seat he found a rack of shells. He tried to lift one but it was too heavy for his small hands.

Frederic scrambled over the seat and the shells into the turret compartment. Here there were wheels to turn and more levers to pull. He found the wheel which made the gun move up and down, and another close by which made the turret turn. Both were heavy but he managed to start the turret rotating – once in motion, the handle was easier. He turned it as fast as he could, watching the rest of the tank swivel about him as he stood on the turret floor. Briefly he looked out of the side hatch, the sky was moving. It all seemed very peculiar. How could the sky be moving. He stopped and watched the sky slowly come to a stop. Suddenly he realised, the sky was not moving, only he and the turret had turned. He wound the handle back.

Giselle walked slowly towards the Panzer, listening. Her need to see Frederic was stronger than her fear. She stopped a metre from the front. She could hear her playmate moving around inside, he hadn't screamed or anything so he must be all right. She watched with trepidation as the turret swung to the left. There was no sound. It just moved, all by itself as though by magic. Frederic was inside the tank, did he know the gun was moving? She wondered how she was going to tell him. Would she have to say something to draw his attention. She didn't want to talk, she wasn't even sure she could any more. Her indecision was taken away by another distraction.

The sound of an engine softly thrumming in the distance crept into her awareness. Another threat. She recognised the noise and turned to meet it. The sound grew closer. It was coming from the woods where they had just been fruit picking. She trembled, holding her breath as the volume increased.

A dark green thing hove into view over the hedgerows. It grew bigger until Giselle was able to make out the shape of a lorry. It had a white star on the side. She had never seen markings like that before.

The lorry turned from the wood down the road towards her village. It wasn't just one lorry, there were lots of them in a long line following each other. There were soldiers inside. They would pass the gate cutting off her escape. The troops were coming to get her just as they had her mother.

Petrified, she could feel the terror building inside her. She wanted to run but couldn't make her legs move. There was Frederic to think of. He didn't know, and the gun was still moving. Suddenly she let the tightly held air from her lungs.

She didn't know how it happened. The high-pitched scream filled her ears. Like a brake being released Giselle was able to move. She turned from the lorry and ran to hide beside the tank. It was the only hiding place in the whole field. She stood there trembling, squashed up against the tracks, her scream renewed with each breath.

In panic Frederic released the handle. Something had happened to Giselle. Guilt flooded his mind. He scrambled to the gunners seat and leaned out the hatch. He couldn't see the girl. It seemed as though the sound was coming from under him. How could she be inside the tank?

189

He had to find her and save her. He climbed out and jumped to the ground. The scream was louder and directly behind him. He turned to find the little girl he loved, standing on the track in between the Panzer's wheels. Her mouth was wide, emitting the unbearable noise. He couldn't see what was wrong.

"Stop! Stop!" he shouted. "It's all right. Did I frighten you?"

Giselle stopped screaming, shook her head and pointed to the gate. Frederic turned to look as a lorry pulled up. The engines' rumbling and the sight of several troops climbing from vehicles confronted him. This would be the end for both Giselle and himself.

* * *

Graham Hunt drove the lead in the thirty-two lorry convoy. Destined for the British troops fighting in Falaise, they had crossed the Orne and its neighbouring canal just after first light, heading towards Troarn. Graham approached the junction where the road to Sannerville split away past a derelict tank and over a bridge. There would have been nothing extraordinary about the abandoned Panzer IV except Graham saw the turret move. He didn't believe his eyes. Lifting his foot off the accelerator he turned to his passenger.

"Hey Mick, that tank's got someone in it."

"What!" Corporal Mick Ash hadn't been paying attention to the road. A copy of Playboy cadged off a Canadian held his attention. Tearing his eyes away from the centrefold he stared at the tank. The main gun was slowly turning away from them. "Christ, I was sure they said this area was all cleared. We better check it out. I hope the others can see why we're turning down here."

The tank's turret stopped, moments later it turned in reverse towards them. "They've seen us, we'd better get there bloody quick or we'll all be gonners."

The lorry pulled up at the gateway. Mick dropped out the passenger door signalling the others to prepare to attack. There was hardly time for the other trucks to stop before soldiers were dropping from the convoy, cramming helmets on their heads and diving for the hedge, rifles at the ready. Should they open fire or wait for the tank to start the offensive. The tank turret stopped moving. There was a high pitched screaming sound.

Mick crouched where the gate post had been. He couldn't make sense of the situation.

He cocked his rifle ready to fire. There was movement to the side of

190

the enemy vehicle. Basic training kicked in. Take out the bad guy. He aimed the riffle, his finger slipped into the trigger-guard and squeezed. He had the first target in sight, a figure standing facing the Panzer. He passed first pressure.

"Bloody hell! It's kids," someone shouted beside him.

Instinctively, Mick threw his rifle to one side. The shot he could no longer prevent cracked out and flew away high over the boy's head.

"Hold your fire. Hold your fire." Mick's shouts came just in time preventing others making the same mistake. He had only just avoided putting a 303 calibre bullet through the boy's heart.

At the sound of the shot someone screamed again, high pitched, piercing. Mick watched, amazed as a little girl ducked out from under the mudguard and ran to the back of the tank.

There were two kids! The boy seemed to have become frozen. Mick stayed crouching behind the broken gate post and thought hard. How was he to tackle this. Just because there were kids here, didn't necessarily mean there weren't any Germans.

The kids would be French not German. He didn't speak French but there was a lad, his mother was French or something.

"Get Reg Innis down here quick."

Precious seconds ticked by while the order passed up the line of men.

"What's up, Corp.?" Innis was not happy at having been singled out.

"Innis, you're half French, aren't you?"

"No! My mother's half French."

"You speak the lingo?"

"I can understand some."

"In that case Private Innis, you can go over to that tank and bring those French kids over here." Mick pointed towards the boy who stood beside the tank.

"I didn't say I could speak French!"

"No, but understanding is better than any of the rest of us can do." Mick turned to the nearest soldier hiding behind the hedge. "Keep the tank in your sights. Pass it on." He turned back to Reg. "Keep well to the right, they'll cover you just in case. Ready?"

"I suppose so."

"Good, off you go, I'm right behind you." Mick scrambled up, recovered his rifle and prepared to follow Reg into the field. "We're going in," he called back to the rest of the troops.

Reg, holding his rifle casually, started slowly forward. How could he make himself look friendly? He didn't want to frighten the children more than they already were. He stopped, drew a cigarette from a pack and lit it before setting off again blowing small clouds of smoke as he went. Mick stayed several paces behind, moving at the same pace. The area was still.

The little girl had had enough. She broke from her hiding place running as hard as she could to the other side of the field.

Reg stopped about thirty feet away from the boy. The lad seemed to have turned to stone, the only way to break the ice was to talk. Reg drummed up his best accent and uttered a poor version of French etiquette.

"Bon jooar," he called, "er, voolay voo earn per de chocolate?" The language flooded back.

The boy looked nervously at him before glancing quickly at the girl.

She would have to stop at the far hedge, Reg thought as the boy turned back to the more immediate danger of his assailants.

Reg crouched down on one knee and drew a bar of chocolate from his breast pocket. The outer wrapping was crumpled but inside the dark brown bar was dry and fragrant. The chocolate snapped in half easily.

"What's your name?" he asked in French. He offered a section of chocolate to the boy, holding it at arm's length. The child looked nervously at Reg. It was easy for the man to see the desire in the kid's eyes. Long seconds passed but gradually the chocolate broke the ice. The boy took slow steps forward until the sweet was in reach. He took it and bit. It was good. He smiled and a torrent of words broke from his lips

"Merci, Je m'appelle Frederic. J'ai sept ans."

"Are you going to call your sister so she can have some too?"

"She is not my sister. She is the *Petite Sorcière*, she used to live across the road."

"Is there anyone else in the tank?" Reg asked.

"No." Frederic took another bite of chocolate.

Reg turned to Mick. "It's all right, Corp. It's just the boy and his girlfriend."

"He's a bit young for a girlfriend, isn't he?" Mick observed.

"Not that sort of a girlfriend, you idiot, more a companion." Reg turned back to Frederic. "Your friend, she doesn't look like a witch. Call her over."

"She is not really a witch, I call her Witch because she doesn't talk but she still gets her own way all the time." Frederic turned to the girl.

"Giselle, *viens ici.*"

The little girl, standing pressed into the bushes, as far from the soldiers as she could get, shook her head slowly.

"Hey, Giselle, I have some chocolate for you." Reg held the piece out to the girl.

"She won't come. She doesn't like soldiers. The last ones took her father away and killed her mother. That was in the spring. That is why she doesn't talk."

"I'll take the chocolate to her," Reg suggested.

"She'll only run away from you if you do, but if I take you to her, she may let you come closer." They started across the field, Giselle seemed to shrink even deeper into the hedge.

"It's all right, these soldiers aren't like the others, I don't think so anyway."

She didn't look at him. She only had eyes for the huge and terrifying uniform.

The boy turned back to Reg. "May I give her the chocolate?"

The boy took the small brown square and approached the girl.

"Here Giselle, this is for you, I've had my piece." There was no acknowledgement. "It's quite nice, better than the German stuff." There was no reaction, her eyes darted between Reg and the Panzer behind him.

Troops were climbing over the derelict, checking it was indeed empty.

Frederic tried again to catch the girl's attention.

"If you don't want it, I'll have to give it back. The man might not want to offer it again if you're not going to be nice."

"Hey, Reg," someone shouted from beside the tank. "We're done, find out where they live so we can take them home. I'm going to radio for the M.P.s to sort this beast out. It's got live rounds in it."

Reg turned away from the children.

"Right oh." He turned back to Frederic. "Where do you live Frederic?"

"In the village over there." Frederic pointed over the river. "We came here to get water. The wells in the town are all broken. Even the horse trough is broken. I was collecting berries too."

"Where are your Mum and Dad?" Reg asked.

"Father was taken away by the Germans. Mother is in the village trying to make our home good. There's not much left so she has a lot of

193

work to do. I thought if I found some food she wouldn't have to worry so much."

"Well Frederic, I have to take you back to your mother. If you can get your little friend to come with us, we can be back there nice and quick. You can't stay here, it's very dangerous, and we don't want you to blow yourself up."

"If we go back to the village, will you kill my mother?"

"Of course not. Why do you think I would do that?"

"That's what the Germans did. They either took people away or they killed them. I don't want you to kill my mother. If that is what you are going to do, I do not want to go."

"It's all right, I'm not going to kill anyone except the Germans."

"You have to promise. I won't believe you otherwise."

"All right, Frederic." Reg knelt down and placed his rifle on the ground pointing the barrel away from the children. "I promise, and swear by almighty God, that neither I nor any of these troops will kill your mother." His halting French was not the most clear but Frederic seemed relieved.

"I think Giselle will believe you too, now."

"Come on then, we need to go." Reg stood up and slung his rifle over his shoulder. The boy turned to the girl one more time.

"Do you want this, or should I give it back to the man." The chocolate was beginning to melt in his hand. As he turned back towards Reg, Giselle stepped from the hedge and held out her hand. Reg breathed a sigh of relief, perhaps this wouldn't be too difficult after all.

"Frederic handed the morsel over. He took hold of Reg's hand and the two started to walk away.

"Come on Giselle, it's time to go. Mother will be worried about us.

Giselle ran to take Frederic's free hand and the three walked slowly across the field to the gate. Frederic stopped abruptly to retrieve the pan of berries. Reg looked at the two receptacles.

"So you were collecting berries. Nothing poisonous I hope!"

"No. But I didn't get the water."

"I'll do that for you." They turned onto the track and headed over the bridge. Reg took the pot, quickly made his way down the bank, scooped up what he could, and handed the pot to the boy. The three headed towards the small collection of battered houses.

* * *

As they walked up the hill, the boy chattered first to the girl, reassuring

194

her, then to Reg. He talked about their return to the village the day before.

In the village Frederic ran past some piles of bricks into an area which still had standing walls.

"*Maman*, we have a visitor. An English soldier." He ran through the house with Giselle close behind. Reg stopped in what would have been the doorway and waited. There was no sound except the excitement of the boy calling his mother.

The house was a wreck. The only thing to do would be to pull it down and rebuild. He was about to turn away when a woman entered the back. She stood looking at him, fear in her eyes. She stared at Reg but made no attempt to come closer. Reg tried to break the tension.

"I gave Frederic and Giselle some chocolate. They were playing on a tank."

"Yes, that is what the Germans did. They gave the children chocolate before they came into our houses to rape and kill. They stole our food, our men and anything else they wanted. They gave nothing in return, except chocolate." The woman's English was faltering. Reg tried to reply but nothing came out. Charlotte continued.

"I am sorry, I should not have said this. I know you did not do it. But look. The English and American bombers have destroyed our homes... We have nothing left... How can we live like this?" She turned, arms spread as though displaying her wealth. A wealth of shattered stones and broken beams.

"I'm sorry."

"Why? Why are you sorry?..." She sounded angry but her voice quickly became tearful. "The Germans, I tried to hide what they did from Frederic, but Giselle knows, she saw. She has never seen the village without soldiers. They killed her mother, she saw them do it."

"That is why I am sorry. I'll go now. I hope it'll be better for you from now on." Reg turned and walked to the edge of the village. He stopped at the last pile of rubble and lit a cigarette. As he looked back sadness drained his will away. He thought of the evil which must have made the woman feel so helpless, and angry. Was it like this throughout the whole of France? Deep in thought, he started back along the track towards the river. He didn't notice the column of trucks advancing until they were nearly on him.

When they stopped Reg sat back in the passenger seat and lit another cigarette. He didn't want to talk but could feel the Corporal and his driver looking at him.

"They have nothing. A quarter of a house, that's all. No food, no water, nothing. I don't know how they're going to live more than a few days. We should help them if we can."

Mick nodded his response.

"There's a contingency plan for refugees. I'll get on to Supply to come and help them. It's like this over most of our sector, we've had to fight so hard everything has been wiped out. You saw the fields of dead cows. We haven't even had time to clear them up. The only good thing that's happened to these people in the past four years is this total destruction. It may help them wipe away the misery of their occupation more easily. You know, starting from scratch, putting the past behind them and getting on with a whole new life… Which is their house?"

"The third pile of rubble on the left. They still have a room intact at the back."

"Stop there, Graham." Mick pointed. "I'll give them a case of rations to tide them over. I can write it off our inventory somehow." He climbed from the cab and went to the back of the lorry. After rummaging around he found what he wanted. The case was not very heavy. Mick placed it on his shoulder and picked up a jerry can of water. Carrying them into the house, he stopped just inside the threshold. The woman stood washing herself in the back garden. She had been hidden by the debris before he entered. Standing sideways, naked to her waist, her smoothness seemed out of place, contradictory to the ragged surroundings. She was good-looking, handsome even, though very thin from lack of food. Mick turned his back, but not before he had observed her curves, shapely, but showing evidence of past childbirth and breast-feeding. He coughed loudly.

"Sorry to trouble you Ma'am, I brought you some food and water. It's not much but it should carry you over until we can bring some proper stuff."

Charlotte looked up, startled, but took her time covering herself. She didn't care who saw her or how long they looked. There was nothing bad they could do to her that she wasn't already expecting. She buttoned her blouse and walked into the remains of her house.

"Thank you for turning your back, *Monsieur.*" She knew he had let his eyes linger. "Please put the food on the floor over here. It is very kind of you to think of us." She stepped back as Mick turned, this was not the same man who had brought her children back earlier. "I'm sorry!

196

I thought you were the other soldier who came before."

"No I'm not, he's here though. You want to talk to him?"

"No. It's not necessary. Did he ask you to give me these things?"

"In a manner of speaking, yes Ma'am. He told me you were in difficulty, so I decided to drop you this stuff. As I say, it's not much and it may not taste too good, but it will keep you alive until proper supplies can be brought in a couple of days.

"Thank you, it was very... thoughtful. Please thank the other man. I'm sorry, I was not very nice to him."

"Sure, I'll tell him. I have to go now, we still have a war to fight." Mick turned to leave.

Charlotte took a step towards him but stopped short. "Thank you."

When the stranger had gone Charlotte called to the children.

"Come and see what we've been given."

The two children bounded into the building as the lorries slowly inched their way passed the rubble in the street. They were distracted momentarily by all the traffic and waved frantically. The woman opened the box. Seeing the food, Frederic realised he would not have to look for berries anymore.

Later that afternoon Giselle drew Frederic to the edge of the village, her frantic tugging the only indication of what she wanted.

Standing in the middle of the road looking towards the river he could see another vehicle, and soldiers moving around the tank. As he watched, the boy wondered what the men were doing.

Slowly the tank was dragged from the field. Over the next three months it made a slow and tedious way to England.

14

Stripped and Searched

Towards the end of November, after severe winter storms, long delays in port, the Panzer IV arrived at Chislehurst Camp. It was parked in a rusty corrugate iron Nissen hut out of the weather for the first time in five years. A few days later Private Ben Whipping was ordered to check the vehicle and store all the loose equipment.

Whipping took a quick look at the vehicle and called his mates to help. Nineteen years old, he was already balding. He resented being stuck in England when he could have been fighting on the continent. His lack of hair had denied him A1 fitness as the army doctor had suspected some sort of infection. However, tests had always come up negative.

Outside, the wind howled and rain battered at the hut's metal sheeting. Dribbles of water spattered on the floor under the leaking roof bolts.

"Why'd you pick on us?" asked Private Beckett. He was an older soldier, originally recruited into the Home Guard. With the invasion of France he had been drafted into the Service Corps.

"I thought it would free you from the Sergeant, and you'll be out of the weather," said Whipping, "but if you don't want to... Come on, let's have a look."

"You expect to find something special in there, do you?" asked Private Halland.

"I just want to see what the Kraut stuff is like," Whipping explained.

"You're bloody nosy, you are. All right, I don't mind a bit of messing about."

The three climbed onto the superstructure using the folding steps at the side.

"They stuck enough blooming junk on it, didn't they?" said Beckett as they looked round.

"Maybe they thought, with all this around them, our shells would never get through." Halland dropped a bundle of three rods on the ground. "I wonder what they are for?"

"Who knows," said Beckett, "could be anything."

"I don't believe this," said Halland. "They even have a crank handle."

"I don't know, maybe ours do too," said Whipping, "can't say I ever looked, but it must be bloody hard work starting this with the crank."

"Easier than pushing the damn thing." Halland threw another tool on the floor.

"If they got so much stuff on the outside I wonder what they put inside," said Whipping.

"Don't know. Bags I get the first find."

"No you don't, Beckett. It goes to the person who finds it. Which will be me, 'cause I'll be first inside." Halland unclipped a hammer and wrench from the deck and clambered round the turret. "I'll soon have this hatch open," he said.

Whipping stood at the back by the large turret storage bin.

"I wonder what's in here." He picked up some bolt cutters and snapped the padlocks.

"Phoo. It's full of mouldy clothes," Whipping turned away from the stench. He took a deep breath and held it before turning back to reach in. "There's equipment, food. Yuck, some of this is disgusting. It must have been rotting here for weeks." Whipping started pulling out odd garments and packets and threw them on the ground. "Hey, look at this." He lifted out a machine gun belt full of rounds and held it high for the others to see. "They use canvas on their ammo belts."

"How many you got there, can we share them between us? They'll fetch a packet on the black market." Halland leaned over to have a better look. "Damn, it stinks like a pit, you can keep them."

"You and the bloody black market. You'll be an a charge again, ain't you learned your lesson yet?" asked Beckett. Halland grimaced at him.

"I can't help the stink, but we got to clear the bin out," said Whipping.

"You found the stuff," said Halland. "You clean it out."

Whipping stacked the rounds on the tank's back deck.

Halland made one last heave on the turret hatch, the latch inside dropped free, releasing the cover.

"Come on, let's look inside. I want to see if their tanks are better than ours." Halland prised the heavy hatch with his fingers.

"Of course they're not better. We wouldn't be winning the war if they were." said Beckett grabbing hold and heaving it open. "It's bloody heavy."

"Out the way, let's have a look." Halland leaned into the opening. "It stinks in here too, doesn't Jerry ever wash. An' it's dark, I can't see a thing. One of you get us a light."

"Get your own light." Beckett walked round to the other side and worked on the second hatch. It opened easily. "There, is that better?"

"Yes, much." Halland strained to look round inside but it grew dark again. "Hey, what you doing? Get out the light."

"I'm climbing in, that's what," said Beckett.

"No you're not!" shouted Halland.

"Will you two stop arguing? Whipping asked. "Just pass the stuff out and I'll stack it ready to take to the stores."

"Right." Beckett looked around in the dim light and opened a stowage box holding the damp mildewed canvas cover to one side. "There's more live ammo in here, shells." He looked in other boxes. "There must be thirty of the bloody things, and spent cases, I'll hand them out. Are you ready?"

"Ready," Halland called back.

Clearing out the shells took time, not because of the amount to be cleared but from the care required in the handling. As Halland passed the last shell to Whipping, a cry came from inside the tank.

"Hey, I found a pair of binoculars, I'm keepin' these."

"You'd better climb out then and let us have a look," said Halland. "It's not fair if you nab everything."

It's all right, I'll tell you when I find stuff and we can share it all when we finish," Beckett called out.

"Ha, you think I trust you?" Halland was getting annoyed. "Come out now or I'll come and get you out."

"Why don't you climb in, there's room enough for at least three, and the job will go quicker," said Whipping.

"We don't want that, we should do it nice and slow, take our time, make sure we do it thorough, nothing missed, nothing left behind." Halland climbed in with Beckett. "Come on Whipping, or you'll miss out."

Halland found a camera stuffed in a corner. He slipped it in his tunic.

Whipping crawled through to the driver's area and opened the overhead hatch. There were more shells behind the driver's seat. He lifted them out through the hatch and stood them on the superstructure. The only things he found worth keeping were the instruction manuals stuffed down the side of the driver's seat. They were written in German but that didn't matter, he just wanted something as a keepsake.

Sgt. Bates strode into the workshop just as Whipping was climbing out. Whipping checked he had hidden the books properly under his uniform.

"How are you ladies doing?" Bates asked. They formed a line on Whipping and snapped to attention. "All right, all right, you're not on the parade ground now, stand easy. Are you finished yet?"

Whipping looked at his companions. The Sergeant was not usually this jovial, it seemed like a trap, though Bates for once, had a smile on his face.

"We've finished removing all the loose fittings and equipment, Sergeant. What should we do with the ammo?"

Bates looked at the collection of shells and machine gun belts.

"Take the ammo to the Armoury. – Next week we have a team of tank experts coming from Leyland to assess this beast. We don't want them getting hurt on high explosives, do we? Stack the rest of the stuff by the tank." Sgt. Bates turned away. "Carry on, you're doing a fine job."

"Sarge, what about this stuff what's rotting?" Whipping didn't want to touch the things again but something had to be done to stop them stinking out the workshop.

"Rotting you say. Burn it. Use a brazier outside, we don't want the whole camp going up." Sgt. Bates marched out.

Beckett turned to Whipping. "Burn it all? And the ammo belts?"

"I don't think the ammo belts will need burning," said Whipping. "We'll let the Armourer deal with them."

"Thank God for that, I didn't fancy having to remove all them bullets," said Beckett.

"Oh, that's all right," said Whipping, "I wouldn't have bothered, I was thinking of having a fireworks display, you know like the 5th of November. Haven't seen fireworks for years."

After the inspection the hatches were closed, the tank was removed from the workshop and left in the rain. The loose parts however, remained in a pile in the corner of the workshop floor. Months passed. Slowly one by one, the loose items disappeared as soldiers found things they fancied or thought they could sell on.

* * *

V. E. Day filled the camp with excitement as the news of victory spread. There was a feeling of relief, a lightness of foot entered everyone's step. The rush was quite different from the desperation of the past six years. Reluctance vanished replaced by cheer and joviality. For Whipping it was a double celebration as his A1 fitness was granted at the same time. The good cheer lasted a few weeks.

Forces started returning from Germany, whole Companies were de-mobbed. Private Whipping's enthusiasm waned as he watched troops pass into camp and almost immediately pass out again as civilians. He knew the end of the war meant the Army would downsize, but he didn't want to be de-mobbed. Whipping enjoyed military life, the fixed routine.

When his guard duty finished, he crossed the parade ground and caught his Sergeant.

"Sgt. Bates, may I have a word?"

"Keep pace with me, laddie, and you can have as many words as you like. There's nothing you can say will concern me in the slightest in two days' time." Sgt. Bates did not stop in his march towards the Mess Hall. Whipping fell into step.

"How's that then, Sarge?"

"I'm going back to Civvy Street, at last, after eighteen years."

"Oh, C-Congratulations." Whipping stammered. "I thought you would always be in the Army, that you would never retire unless you were forced to. That's why I wanted to ask you my question."

"That's just it, I don't have a choice. Too many Chiefs and not enough Indians, but I'm determined to make the most of my new life. Anyway, enough about me. Ask your question, I'm still your Mother and Mother always knows best."

"I don't want to leave the Army, how can I make sure I'm not demobbed like all the others?"

Bates stopped abruptly.

"I can see as how this way of life suits you, having no family and all. My advice is, make yourself indispensable. If you're indispensable, they won't want to lose you. Being in the Army is like a jigsaw puzzle."

"A jigsaw puzzle?"

"Yes." Bates headed towards the Mess again. "For the past six years the Army has been a big jigsaw puzzle with lots of sky, people doing things which aren't necessary in peacetime. But the sky is difficult and boring and some people don't bother with it. You have to make sure you are in the main picture. You don't have enough experience to be an instructor, so if I was you, I'd transfer to the Engineers. The Army will always have things that need fixing, especially now so much is being scrapped. What they keep will have to be maintained in good working order... *Join the Engineers, and be part of the main picture...* Good slogan that, if I say so myself."

"Yes Sergeant, thank you."

"You better go to Admin. and sign your transfer request before they write out your discharge. Watch how you go, make your choices carefully."

* * *

Whipping's first day as an Engineer was spent cleaning. The parade ground, the billet, the Mess Hall, the list seemed endless.

Next day, Corporal Wane set his small group of twelve Engineers on separate tasks.

"Dibben, Mitchem, Whipping. Strip that Panzer down."

Dibben and Mitchem quickly broke ranks to survey the task ahead. Whipping, having worked on the tank before, was less speedy as he took in the enormity of the task. He caught up with his two new companions.

"Either of you done something like this before? he asked.

"No, mate," said Mitchem. "But how hard can it be. It's just undoing nuts and bolts."

"Are you sure, what about when the Corp. wants us to put it together again?"

"I don't care about putting it back together," said Dibben, "but I know he'll want everything clean and shiny. I been with him for a while and he's fussy about clean, like having us sweep the parade ground till it's spotless.

"I heard say," Dibben continued, "his fuss is a result of the war, some form of shell shock. He'll want the thing spotless like his glorious playground out there, so we better wash the beast first, then get it in the shop before we strip her down. He'll be over any minute wanting to know why we ain't working yet."

"Oi, you three, I didn't say you could stand around talking all day." Corporal Wane's voice bellowed at them as if he had been reading Dibben's mind.

"Yes, Corporal," Dibben shouted back. He turned back to his friends. "See what I mean? You two had better get the hose and brushes while I clear a space in the workshop." He turned and headed into the Nissen hut.

Whipping handed the hose and a brush to Mitchem.

"Here, wet her down, then brush her off. I'll wash the tracks." They set to, hoping Corporal Wane would not come to inspect their progress.

Dibben emerged from the shop. "You done there, I've cleared a space ready to bring her in."

"How we going to move her?" Mitchem asked.

Dibben looked around him. "Start her up, an' we can drive her in."

"Can you drive a tank then?"

"No, but I can try."

"Don't be stupid you two," said Whipping. "It won't be like one of our tanks, and the controls'll be written in Bosch. You won't be able to tell your handbrake from your elbow. If you can drive them, use those Bren-Gun carriers to drag her in." Whipping pointed at two machines standing outside another workshop.

Dibben marched off to get one. "Come an' help, Mitchem, and Whipping, I saw some chains in the shop, you can hook her up for us."

"Who bloody said he was in charge?" Mitchem asked Whipping.

"Who cares? As long as we get the job done without Wane killing us first."

Trying to pull the twenty ton Panzer with two vehicles less than a fifth its weight was an adventure. The carrier's tracks skidded on the parade ground ripping up the surface. They pulled the tank off the grass, yanking repeatedly on one side to line it up.

Whipping went to unhook the chains.

"Oh hell."

"What's up mate?" asked Mitchem.

"The towing points have been ripped off the carrier, here," said Whipping pointing.

"Shit! How the hell are we to fix that?" Dibben yelled.

"Don't know," said Mitchem. "Bloody good thing we didn't have to pull that thing all the way across the square."

"Look, stop fussing about it," said Dibben. "connect up at the other end and tow this thing in the workshop. Then we'll park them back exactly where they were before. Maybe nobody will notice."

"What do you mean nobody will notice?"

"Shut up Mitch, and get on with it."

They linked the carriers to the tank's other end and pulled it backwards into the workshop.

"Remember to walk back after you park up. If you run, it will look suspicious." Whipping turned back to the tank. "I'll start removing the tracks."

Dibben and Mitchem soon returned.

"All done?" asked Whipping.

"Yep. No problem."

"Good… When the Corp. says strip the tank, how far does he mean?" asked Whipping.

"Down to the last nut and bolt I would think," said Dibben.

"I'll start with these lights here." Mitchem pointed. He reached for a set of spanners from the workbench and climbed on the tank's front.

"Don't remove the steps, then we can climb up on top easy," said Whipping.

"Steps, now you tell me," Mitchem grumbled. He tested the spanners for size. "None of these fit."

"There used to be tools to fit this thing but they all seem to have gone now. You'll have to use an adjustable," said Whipping.

"Fancy the Krauts using different size nuts and bolts," said Mitchem. "I bet they did it just so we couldn't repair their stuff when we captured it. Hey, Dibbs, bring us a couple of adjustables, I don't want to climb down again."

"Lazy Sod." Dibben searched the bench for the tools.

Whipping finished with the tracks and climbed on the tank to remove the brackets and trims at the back.

Corporal Wane entered the workshop.

"Don't forget, you three, I want everything spotless and I want it all labelled in order to make it easy to put back together later."

"Yes Corp.," said Whipping. He turned to Mitchem. "I told you we'd end up putting it back together afterwards, didn't I."

"Quite right, Whipping," said Wane, standing behind the soldier. "Nuts and bolts as Dibben so aptly put it earlier. The best way to learn about something is to pull it apart. Better you work on this Kraut shit and mess it up, than one of our own pieces." Corporal Wane walked out, leaving them stymied.

"He was bloody standing there listening to us. Bloody spy," Dibben whispered. "I bet he's still there."

"Probably, but more importantly, where the hell do we start?" asked Mitchem. "It's easy removing things like lights and number plates but what comes next?"

"No idea," said Dibben. "Whipping did the easy bit removing the tracks."

"Suppose we remove the hatches and let some light in first," said Whipping. "Then we just undo nuts and bolts until they're all done. Come on, we can take turns, two of us removing parts, the other one can

205

label and set them aside."

"I'll do the labelling," said Mitchem.

"Right!" Dibben turned to Whipping. "I said he was lazy. Here, you hold, I'll undo the bolts." Dibben climbed in the turret to remove the hatch fixtures.

"How long have you and Mitch known each other?" Whipping asked Dibben.

"We were together in France and then in Holland, Catering Corps. We transferred to the Engineers when it all ended. Didn't fancy being behind a hot stove through another summer, but I bet I'll miss the warmth in winter. What about you?"

"I never got to the Continent," Whipping replied. "I spent a year doing guard duty here for the Army Service Corps. I transferred because I didn't want to leave the Army, I've got nobody to go home to, see."

"What! No girl waiting for you?" Dibben asked.

"No, not anymore." Whipping hesitated. "A V2 got her... got her and her whole family. It happened just up the road here, in Eltham. My Mum and Dad caught it one night in forty-one."

"That's tough. You should have dropped out to go find yourself another girl. I bet there's hundreds of them who lost their blokes in the fighting."

"I don't have the heart for it. Sue meant the world to me, I couldn't betray her. You know, I was so glad when I was told I wouldn't be going over there. I thought we'd always be close, then she goes and gets it just as if I'd been shot. It's not bloody fair."

"Snap out of it, she's gone, you're still here, you've got to move on. She wouldn't want you being miserable and I bet she'd have found another bloke if it had happened the other way round." Dibben removed the bolts holding the left-hand turret hatch. "You don't want to be stuck here for the rest of your life. They probably won't want you anyhow, you'll have to go back to civvies some time."

"But what if I don't find someone?"

"Come off it, you should look in the Dance Halls and Night Clubs. There'll be loads of Wrens and the like looking for someone just like you."

"Perhaps... How come you stayed in, Dibbs?"

"I got married in a rush a few months before D-Day. I don't want to go back to her though, I mean, she's just not my type. I have to see her sometimes, what with leave and so on, but if I didn't have to, well, you know…"

"Back of a bus is she? One of those lovely Wrens you were talking about."

"I must have been three sheets to the wind when I tied the knot, I swear her face got scrambled when she was born."

"Ha! And you're giving me advice," said Whipping, "My advice to you is, if you don't like her, cut the tie. – What about you, Mitch, why did you stay enlisted?"

"What me? Don't know. Suppose I thought I could make something of myself, more than outside anyway. I'm hoping I can get myself some sort of education… You got the first bit loose yet?"

"It's just coming," said Whipping. "Stick the handles, nuts and bolts back on, just loose like. Oil them first."

"All right." Mitchem took the iron hatch from Whipping and laid it on the ground in the corner. "Weighs a bloomin' ton. I suppose it's all going to be like this."

"Probably." Dibben scrambled through the turret and started work on the second hatch.

Part by part, the Panzer came to pieces. They took turns at stripping, carrying and labelling.

"You know what," said Whipping, "if we remove the gun and then the turret, we'll have a lot more light to work by."

"How we going to lift it?" asked Beckett.

"We'll use that winch," said Whipping pointing to an engine lift.

By the end of the week the tank was a shell, the superstructure was still attached to the hull which rested on blocks, the turret was to one side. There were parts strewn everywhere across the floor with hardly any place to walk.

Corporal Wane inspected the results.

"Now, you can start putting it together again. When you refit the gun, leave out the firing pin. Do the same to the machine guns and take the pins to the Armoury. Mind you, those M.G.s will never fire again with the damage they've got. The radio equipment can go to the Stores, it's no good to us over here. Otherwise, I want the thing put back together just as it was. If it works I'll let you loose on something else, but you keep at it until it does work."

"Can't some of the others put it together, Corporal?" Mitchem asked. "We worked on it all week, we want a change now.

"They will work on it, when you have it all put back together. Then

207

you can replace them sweeping the parade ground or cleaning the billets… Or stripping and repairing damaged Bren-Gun carriers." He emphasised the last words. "All right, get to it." Wane turned and quietly left.

"He bloody knows about the carriers," hissed Dibben.

"Well, we may have to fix them later, at least we're not up on charges for the damage," said Whipping.

"Damn this for a lark. It's just like being on a charge," said Mitchem.

"You think so? I quite enjoy it," said Whipping.

"I hate it, all this mess and oil," Mitchem complained.

"Why'd you join the Engineers then?"

"Explosives."

"At least we're dry if it starts raining," Dibben chipped in. "I think it's quite a good little number."

"Yes, well, let's get started," said Whipping. "We should assemble the engine first, then the gearbox and drive chain. Then we can add the petrol tanks and work our way up from there. We can leave the gun until everything else is in and the turret is on."

"All right so we start with the engine." Mitchem reached for a push rod and slid it into the cylinder block. Whipping watched him.

"Make sure you put those in the right way up, Mitch."

Mitchem looked up. "What, is there a wrong way?"

* * *

They worked for two weeks before the engine started. Each time they tried, they filled the carburettor with fuel, gravity fed from a jerry can resting on the tank's back deck. If it didn't work they made adjustments and then tried again. They were under strict instructions not to put fuel into the main fuel tanks. Eventually they breathed sighs of relief as the engine's roar filled the workshop. Corporal Wane watched as smoke surged from the exhaust.

"Well done, chaps. Will it move?"

Whipping was sitting in the driver's seat. He slipped the gear stick into first and leaned into the steering levers. The tank jolted forward.

"All right, all right, stop there," Wane shouted. "Syphon the exhaust fumes into the fuel tanks to make sure there's no fuel gasses left in them. Run her until the jerry can is empty. Then I've got another little job for you."

Within ten minutes the engine stopped, starved of fuel.

"Come along now. This'll give you a nice rest from tinkering with machinery." Wane beckoned. They walked out of the workshop into brilliant afternoon sunshine. "You can sweep the parade ground. I want every leaf, every speck of dirt removed. Brushes are over there." Wane pointed to the storehouse. "You have three hours, then everyone will parade in full kit. At the double now."

It was late when the camp fell in. The C.O.'s announcement was short. The grounds were to be returned to their original function as a golf course and the compliment split apart and sent their separate ways.

Whipping was shocked to learn the camp was to close.

"Here, look at that," Mitchem whispered. "Bastard Wane has a new stripe."

"Bloody hell, so he has," said Dibben.

"Silence in the ranks." Wane's voice cut through the rising chatter.

"You heard the Major. Everything must go. Sounds like the bloody January sales, but it does not mean things can just disappear into your pockets and kitbags. Any thieving will be dealt with severely…

"Every-bloody-thing must go. Not one round, bootlace, tin of Blanco or canteen will be left to mar the new greens.

"Tomorrow, at 07.00 hours, you start with the vacant buildings and work through the camp. You have two weeks, so no slacking. Dismissed."

The following day the rush commenced. Buildings rapidly developed huge piles of furniture and equipment outside the doors. Lorries arrived to take the equipment away.

On the second day the first of the huts was dismantled. The floorboards, doors and windows were removed before the wooden walls were carefully dismantled. Finally the concrete base was hacked to pieces by workmen from a local Civil Engineers.

As the first week ended Sgt. Wane called Whipping.

"I've got a special number for you and your two mates. There will be a transporter here tomorrow. As you know how the German tank works, you three will be responsible for taking it down to West Lulworth. Make sure you have all your kit with you, because you won't be coming back here. When you're done, you'll report to the Royal Engineers at Brompton Camp. I'll see you there in a week's time… Oh, and one last thing, when you find time tonight, stitch that on your sleeve." Wane handed over a Lance Corporal stripe. "Well done."

"Thank you, Sergeant." Whipping wanted to jump for joy. After a whole year on guard duty he had his first stripe, at last. Dibben and

Mitchem were not so pleased.

"Ha-ha, look at him, he's bloody sprouting feathers." Dibben was feeling cocky. "So what do we call you now? Lance Corporal Muck." He laughed at his own joke.

"Give over, I don't know why I got it," said Whipping. "It just means more work and I'll have to look after you two for the next few days."

"I don't need looking after," Mitchem grumbled.

"You know best. But don't let some stupid bit of cloth mess up our friendship."

"Friends, I don't make friends with zebras!" Mitchem growled.

"Pack it in Mitch," Dibben snapped. "We should see how it goes."

"Oh I suppose, but he started it, sewing on that stripe."

"No, Wane started it by giving me this stripe." Whipping tied off the thread and lay on his bed looking at the ceiling. "You'll get yours soon if you keep your heads." He turned to look at his friends. "You better pack all your stuff. Tomorrow we're taking the *Fräulein* to Lulworth. We're not coming back here."

"What! Who said?" Dibben asked.

"Wane told me when he gave me the stripe." Whipping closed his eyes ready for sleep.

* * *

The following day dawned cloudy though it was still warm. The threat of September rain did not spoil the excitement of the journey.

At 9.00 a.m., a huge lorry drove onto the base. Oversized white stars proclaimed it an Allied ex-war vehicle.

"Just look at that thing, it's a bloody Dragon-Wagon," said Mitchem. He, Dibben and Whipping stood outside the Panzer's workshop.

"So tell me again where we're moving this thing to?" asked Dibben.

"West Lulworth, it's a tank firing range on the south coast. Seems like a good place for a tank, even for the *Fräulein* here," said Whipping. He raised his hand and waved at the driver.

The lorry slowly carved a wide turn on the parade ground, and rolled towards them.

"Bloody Americans, always showing off how big their things are." Mitchem turned his back and walked into the workshop. The driver climbed from his cab and shook hands with Whipping.

"Hello, Sergeant Dan Riding. Are you the boss here?" He had a Yorkshire accent.

Whipping looked at Riding's three stripes.

"Lance Corporal Ben Whipping, Sergeant. I was until you arrived."

"That's all right, you can stay in charge until we're all loaded. Is this the tank we're moving?"

"Yes," said Whipping.

"All right, let's have a look." Riding approached the Panzer. "Never thought I would see one of these over here. I saw plenty in France, mostly blown up of course. This one looks in pretty good nick."

It took an hour to load the tank and secure it. Then slowly they drove to the gate. A military police jeep took the lead and another followed as they moved onto the main road.

"We won't be going any more than about fifteen miles per hour," said Rider.

"What! All the way to Lulworth?" Mitchem blurted.

"Well, yes. This thing is designed for American highways, and it goes well on the German Autobahns. It's too big for most of our roads. We'll stop on Salisbury Plain at Bulford Camp tonight, we'll move on to West Lulworth tomorrow.

The tank carrier crawled along the narrow roads straddling both lanes much of the way. Whipping was glad to climb down at the end of the day.

The following morning they finished the slow drag across the country arriving at a narrow lane in the early afternoon. Rider reduced speed until they were moving at little more than walking pace. The road was just wide enough for the lorry, it scraped the grass verges on either side when taking the tight bends.

The gate Security Guard waved them on.

"Follow the road through the camp, it'll lead you directly to the range. I'll get someone over there to tell you where to unload."

The range was a huge green area between the camp buildings and the coast. As they entered the area, a Sergeant waved them down.

"Unload over there on the far hill. You'll find a small prepared plateau at the right position."

The unloading took the whole of the afternoon. Eventually the Panzer stood a short way up the slope facing along the contours.

The tank carrier returned to Bulford. Whipping, Mitchem and Dibben left to catch a train to London.

"Nice little touch that, I thought," said Mitchem, pointing at the Panzer.

"You daft bastard, they won't like it when they see," said Dibben.

211

"You know, I shall miss the *Fräulein*, "said Whipping.

"You're mad," said Dibben, laughing. "You'd find her a poor replacement for a real woman."

A huge angular bovine creature, the Panzer had been put to grass. The gentle slopes of the green Dorset hills complemented the vehicle's mottled camouflage. – Except for the gun aimed directly at the Officers'- Mess.

15

Ruddington

For the past six months, the range had been inactive. Nothing was permitted to interfere with the birds during their nesting season. There had been the usual complement of troops at the camp but activities had been centred on the ranges around Blandford Forum and on the Salisbury Plains. The hills had seemed quiet through the summer months, except for the sound of the gulls' incessant squawks. Once all the chicks had fledged, the range resumed its military usage.

Every day shots crashed out and echoed round the valley. Burning cordite stuck to the projectiles, left trails of smoke as the round arced through the air to strike home. The blue dummy rounds bounced on the far slope before finally sliding downhill for a few feet and coming to rest. After the practice session, the dummy missiles would be collected to be used again in another session.

The soil was thin over the chalk hills meaning the projectiles were often damaged against the rock. The hills were of the same chalk which made the Isle of Wight just thirty miles away. But while The Needles' white cliffs were famous, the local cliffs were hardly ever seen due to the range and the embargo on public access.

Occasionally, shots flew over the hill a mile away from the shooters. If a gunner did manage to miss the slope the rounds ended up in the sea. There was no danger of sinking ships. The exclusion zone, which was well marked on all recent nautical charts, extended well beyond the maximum range of any tank.

Week after week, dummy shells soared across the valley and bounced in numerous different ways on the far side. Sometimes, small priming charges were fitted to the nose cones of rounds. They were not strong enough to cause damage but the resulting flash could give a better indication of the strike's position in poor weather.

Captain Goddard scrutinised his range schedule. He had received a request for permission to test a new antitank rifle. The Ministry had granted the use of military grounds for the test but had not specified the location yet. Goddard was keen to have the test at his range. It would bring in additional funds. There were not that many ranges that had heavy armour in situ, and Goddard had a good chance his range would be the chosen location.

He had seen the old armour piercing rifles in use during the war. They had been heavy and unwieldy in battle to the point of being a liability, once a shot had been taken. Moving to a new location was almost impossible without the enemy spotting the sniper and killing him first.

From what Goddard had heard, this new weapon was no different, but it had to be tested, and Lulworth was the perfect place. However, the scheduling was proving difficult. There was only one solution, the gun would have to be tested at the weekend.

There were four tanks on the slope, the Panzer was the closest to the firing position with an M4 Sherman and two Churchills providing increasing ranges. Normally these tanks were only there to give a guide to the distance. The practice shots were supposed to be aimed to avoid hitting the four targets, but this was going to be different.

* * *

The rifles and test personnel arrived earl one Saturday morning. Roy Benson, the designer, walked the range with Goddard, deciding where to position the rifle.

"This little baby is going to be the new weapon against tanks," Benson explained. "It's lighter than the old Solothurm and the like, and it's more accurate than the M2, M7 and M8 rifle-fitted grenade launchers." Benson inspected each target.

"It's a shame they're all side-on to the direction of fire. It will do, but ideally we want to be shooting at the thickest armour in the front. Would it be all right to have the tanks turned so we can attack the front plates?"

Goddard thought for a moment.

"I can have the targets turned, but I'm not sure the brakes will hold. None of them have had any maintenance since they arrived. If the brakes fail, they'll just come trundling down towards us."

"Oh! I see." Benson looked around again. "Well, we appear to have quite a wide front here, perhaps we could fire at a more oblique angle which would be equivalent to hitting thicker armour. It wouldn't put the village in danger from stray rounds or ricochets, would it?"

Goddard did some quick estimations.

"Apart from recalculating the ranges, I think that'll be all right. I'll have to clear it with the C.O. but I don't think there will be a problem as far as the village is concerned.

There are boats at sea to consider. There will be a limit to the angle we can use. I shall have to get the precise details from the Coast Guard. We don't want you firing anything into the shipping lanes. Lulworth Cove is popular with pleasure craft you know."

"Yes, I've run in there a couple of times myself to get out of storms in the Channel. It's quite pretty."

"Quite popular with birders and fishermen too. There's some good crab to be had… Have you seen all you need to see? I was just thinking the sooner I get these queries off, the sooner we'll have our answers."

"Oh yes, certainly. I'm quite satisfied," said Benson. The two men turned and headed back towards the camp. "I'll go and brief Gerald, my gunner. I suppose I'll be able to watch from a safe distance?"

"Certainly," said Goddard, "there's an old pillbox, you can watch from there."

"Oh good. We'll need to check each round after firing, of course. We will be able to see inside the tanks, won't we?"

"I believe they are all open if you don't mind the rust and cobwebs."

"Excellent, in that case we just have to wait for confirmation on the angles. It should be a good day tomorrow."

Sunday was clear and sunny. A perfect day for testing a rifle. Before dawn, the gunner set up the rifle ready for the first shots. The two-man camera crew rigged their equipment to record the action. Captain Goddard had field telephones installed between the three locations for Benson to co-ordinate the action. After breakfast Benson crawled into hiding in the pillbox and picked up the phones.

"Take your first three shots at the Panzer, one shot each into the turret, superstructure and hull. Your range is three-fifty yards." Benson instructed the gunner. He changed handsets. "Camera crew, are you ready?"

"Ready," came the reply.

"Good, roll camera. Make sure you catch it all." Benson changed handsets again. "The cameras are rolling, we're ready when you are."

The first shot rang out, aimed directly at the side of the Panzer. At the point of impact the Panzer's upper hull armour plate glowed red hot and liquefied. The entry hole was less than half an inch across. Inside the molten metal burst inwards under pressure leaving a four inch wide funnel shape, the edges of which had rolled outwards and back. The glowing metal spattered the inside of the turret, landing on all the

215

surfaces. It burned holes in the seating and solidified in globs on the cold metal fittings of the interior. Two more shots followed about thirty seconds apart.

"Try the same thing with the closer of the two Churchills."

The shots cracked out. They moved on, firing at the Sherman and finally the more distant Churchill. When the last round was expended, Benson called again.

"That's fine. Let's go and inspect the results, then we'll do it again."

After making the gun safe, the men walked slowly down the range. At the Panzer, the tiny holes were not easy to find on the huge expanse of dull paintwork. The rifleman circled and numbered each hit with white chalk, while the photographer snapped the holes.

Inside, the gaping wounds were easy to spot, their shiny silver metallic surface reflecting the dim light filtering in through the open hatches. Again the gunner ringed the perforations with chalk, subsequent holes would be recognisable by their lack of chalk identifiers. The group moved on to the next tank, and on up the hill until all twelve shots had been photographed inside and out.

"This seems to be working beautifully. If we can get the same sort of result on the front plates, I shall be very happy."

Several more rounds were fired at each tank before the gun was moved to a more easterly position. Each time, though all the targets suffered, the Panzer came off worst from the shorter range and its thinner protection. By the end of the day, there were over a hundred holes of varying dimensions. The whole of the Panzer's forward and left-hand armour plating had been targeted and now looked more like a strange pepper pot rather than a tank. The inside resembled some sort of oversized modernist beehive. The tank, which had survived six years of war, finally succumbed in peacetime. From now on, when it rained, the Panzer IV would leak.

* * *

February 1955

"I say, Goddard. Have you seen this notice from Bovington?" Major Withington held up an official Edict.

"No, Sir, I can't say I have."

"They're extending their Museum and want to inspect our targets to see if there's anything suitable. Damned cheek. If they take one, I hope they're going to replace it with something appropriate. They probably think they can just take what they want and leave us with a hole in our range. I suppose we could always use your car, Captain, to fill the hole."

"My car, Sir?" Goddard frowned for a moment then laughed. "Yes, might as well, I haven't been able to start her for a week."

"Call these people and find out when they want to do their damned inspection. I suppose we'll have to accommodate them, they seem to have backing from The Ministry."

"Yes, Sir, I'll do it right away."

A week later the Inspector arrived. He took a few minutes to look at each tank on the range.

"No, there's nothing here we can use. I had rather hoped we could do something with your Panzer but it's too far gone, shame! Though I may take it later to show the effect of AP rounds. We could cut out a part of one panel and hang it on the wall with all those cone shapes showing. What we actually want at the moment is a working examples to run round our demonstration field. Never mind, if I don't find something better, I may come back for it. Thank you for your assistance, I'll keep in touch."

Several months passed before another notice arrived from Bovington. Major Withington scanned the missive.

"Well I'm blowed. Bovington is offering six tanks with our range if we want to take delivery. What do you think, Goddard? Should we replace our old rust heaps for some newer stuff?"

"Absolutely, Sir. If they are being provided for free." Goddard replied.

"That's what I think. The other thing is, the War Department is selecting old machinery to be sold off at auction at Ruddington, something to do with boosting funds. If we're having new targets for our range and moving things about, they may as well take our old stuff and try and sell that as well. Let them know they can have that little lot, will you." Withington handed the papers to his deputy.

The Panzer left several months later, shortly after the new tanks arrived from Bovington.

* * *

Early June 1955

On the outskirts of Nottingham, Ruddington camp sprawled over several acres of derelict land, occupied originally during the war for bomb and shell manufacture. The land was flat with several Nissen huts and

217

prefabricated, concrete office buildings. The parade ground was covered corner to corner with ex-army equipment, much of it dating from World War II. Soldiers worked on several vehicles removing written signs, washing, painting, polishing, or fixing parts which were easy and cost-effective to mend. No major overhauls or repair work was to be undertaken. If a piece of equipment did not work, it would still be sold, as seen, with a chalked sign across it saying 'Not Serviceable'.

The four lorries carrying the tanks from Bovington, parked up on the edge of the parade ground. Several troops moved to help unload and park the new arrivals.

"Come on, get those tanks moving." Sergeant Major Whipping bellowed at the top of his voice. His shouts were more for the Officers' benefits than to make the troops work harder. At least it sounded as though he was taking control.

An ageing and rusty M32 recovery vehicle towed each tank into place.

Whipping took a close look at the Panzer IV.

"You know what, lads? I think this is the very same tank I worked on when I was training. She may be a Kraut but she became a blooming good friend to me. I've fond memories of this little baby, I owe her a lot." He walked along the right-hand side and round the back. When he saw the left side he stopped dead.

"Strike me down!" He blanched as he saw the holes. Thank God I was never in the Tank Corps." He fingered one of the holes made by A.P. rounds. "What have they been doing to you?"

He walked on to look at the other new arrivals. "Don't bother doing any work on these, they're too badly damaged. Just wash them down so they're clean. On second thoughts, see if you can make the Panzer look a bit better. Fill those holes with something."

"What with, Sergeant Major?" one of the lads asked.

"Oh, anything. Earwax if you have to. It breaks my heart to see it like this." He quickly left, a comment from one of the chaps followed him.

"I think the Sergeant Major's taken a funny turn. He's changed sides, he has."

Whipping took no notice. He entered his office to collect the paperwork he was obliged to fill out for each new item. He returned to the Panzer and wrote the first form.

Panzer mark 4, complete, non serviceable. Considerable bodywork damage. Price:-

Whipping left the price blank. The C.O would fill that in later after the auction, if the Panzer was sold. He walked along the other new arrivals filling in a different form for each one, then he headed back to the office. Though the next auction was a month away he liked to have all the paperwork finished as soon as possible.

* * *

Early July 1955

When the gates opened, customers flooded the parade ground to inspect the vehicles. The majority of visitors were auto dealers looking for good lorries and cars in working order to be passed on to Joe Bloggs as fast as possible. Only a few came for other reasons, mainly enthusiasts looking to expand their collections.

S.M. Whipping was amazed at what people would buy. A thousand packets of outdated flea powder, five hundred tins of Blanco or a gross of webbing belts. Who on earth could want these things, and how did they pass them on? It was a mystery.

Sentries patrolled on a random schedule to keep the visitors away from forbidden areas. Whipping patrolled separately keeping an eye on both civilians and troops. As he approached the Panzer, he heard voices. They were lowered, coming from round the corner. Whipping stopped to listen.

"Call me Nipper, all I want is a couple of good lorries for a good price," said the first voice.

"They're all there, mate. Just select the one and bid for it. It couldn't be simpler," came the reply.

Whipping recognised Private Cook's tones.

"But other people will be bidding, I want lorries what are in good nick but nobody else will bid for 'em," said Nipper.

"How the hell am I supposed to work that for you. You want me to evacuate the hall so there's only you and the auctioneer in there?" Cook hissed.

"No, dummy. You select a good lorry, find the paperwork and mark it as unserviceable. Then tell me the Lot number. No one else will bid because they'll think it's no good, see."

"Oh, so what's in it for me?" Cook asked.

"I'll give you half of what I think I saved on the deal."

"How much will that be?"

"I don't know, do I?" Nipper exclaimed "It's like, if I buy a lorry for

219

sixty quid, and I reckon I would have spent a hundred, well, the difference is forty so I give you twenty. What about it?"

"I don't know, it sounds awful dodgy to me." Cook sounded nervous.

"Of course it's dodgy," said Nipper, "but you don't win the stakes if you ain't put a little something down. Think about it, I'll see you later." Nipper walked off.

Cook lent against the German tank, thinking about the proposition. It didn't sound too bad provided he wasn't caught, he had no doubt that Nipper would turn him in if anything went wrong but twenty was worth the risk. He'd do it, he thought. Cook straightened himself out, walked round the Panzer and almost bounced off Whipping standing just feet away.

"I just heard a very interesting conversation."

"It weren't nothing, Sergeant Major, honest." Cook was startled.

"Really. You call twenty pounds nothing do you? I would have said it was quite a lot for a soldier on basic pay."

"I don't know what you're talking about." Cook's voice shook.

"No? I tell you what, you tell your friend you want two thirds the difference, and I'll split it with you fifty, fifty."

"What, you'd do that? All right, you're on."

"No, I won't." said Whipping, "But I'll tell you what I will do. I want to catch this swindler. So I want you to meet him later and tell him you want a bigger cut, – after all, you're the one taking the risk. – When the deal is struck, I'll step in with the M.Ps. Do that, and I won't put you on a charge with possible Court Martial to follow. How does that sound?"

"Y-Yes, Sergeant Major. Thank you."

"I'm watching you, make sure the deal happens… Dismissed." Cook turned away, relieved to be off the hook for a while. Whipping watched him leave. There was too much of this kind of thing and he intended to put a stop to it, an example had to be made.

Whipping found an M.P. in the office and warned him of the arrangement.

"Make sure you have your civvy friends ready to hand because I can't carry out an interrogation without them being present," Whipping warned.

"Yes, Sergeant Major." The M.P. picked up his phone.

Whipping left to find Cook, and set a tail on him until the following meeting took place.

Cook eventually met his accomplice shortly before closing time.

220

Nipper walked up brazenly and opened the conversation, in full view of everyone.

"Where can a man get a cup of tea around here?"

"There's the canteen along the road there, but I'll have to escort you, Sir," Cook suggested.

"Well, come on then, let's go have one." Cook led Nipper along the concrete road towards the NAFI. The tail signalled to the nearest M.P. who alerted Whipping.

As the two men entered the NAFI, a soldier followed them in. He bought himself a drink before sitting down behind Nipper. The soldier removed a black M.P. armband from his pocket and slipped it on his arm, he looked up at Cook and nodded. Cook was distracted, he quickly turned aside so as not to give himself away. He tried to think. It was obvious the police were ready to move, all he had to do was clinch the deal, but not too quickly, that would look suspicious. Two more M.P.s joined the first.

Cook tried to concentrate. "I want two thirds."

"Two thirds, you're having a laugh."

"It'll be me taking all the risk, two thirds or nothing doing."

"How about sixty percent?"

Cook pretended to think about it. "Sixty percent's not bad. All right, it's a deal." Cook held out his hand to seal the contract. Nipper reached out to accept but was distracted by a loud scraping of chairs behind him. The three military police stood up and grasped his arms.

"Sir, we would like you to accompany us to the Commander's Office please," said the first M.P.

"You can't hold me, I'm a civilian, I ain't done nothing."

Whipping opened the door and held it for two civilians. He stepped in behind them.

"Conspiracy to commit a crime, conspiracy to defraud a Government Department," said the civilian police officer, holding out his warrant card. "For the past ten minutes, we've been listening at the window. There are at least seven witnesses. You could get five years. At the moment you are just being held for questioning, the C.O. will have to decide whether to press charges. Come along now." The little group filed out quietly.

Whipping stood by Cook.

"Well done. We'll need you to give evidence. I already spoke to the C.O. about the matter, so don't worry. Nothing will reflect on you, but

221

I'm still watching you."

"Yes Sergeant Major." Cook was only just able to respond.

"It was you," Nipper bellowed. "You turned me in, you filthy stinking turncoat, you wait, I'll get you for this, I will." He lunged at Cook but an M.P. grabbed his collar.

"Ah. Now I can add threatening behaviour," said the civilian officer. You know, it is not the words that matter so much as the way they are said. I took that to be threatening, didn't you Sgt. Major?"

"Definitely, Sir."

* * *

There were still a few members of the public about, inspecting the machinery before the sale in two week's time. Edward Knight glanced at the group of soldiers and civilians passing by. He'd been talking with an engineer but held up their conversation until the group were out of hearing.

As Sergeant Major Whipping and Cook rounded another corner, Edward led the engineer to a less exposed area behind a lorry and continued the chat.

"Lot eighty-two. Just remove the ignition coil, place it in the cab under the driver's seat, then mark the papers as unserviceable." He pulled an envelope from his pocket. "Here, there's five in there," Edward pressed the package into the soldier's hand, "and if I get the bid for less than a hundred there'll be more for you. I'll send the extra by post. The letter will be marked E.J. Finds on the back, so make sure you open it carefully when nobody's about." He made a note of the guard's name.

"Thanks, mate. I'll see what I can do." The engineer quickly left.

Edward turned the other way. He would know if the trick had come off when the auctioneer described the lot as serviceable, or not. Edward soon found another soldier who seemed willing to make a deal and a sly penny or two. Within minutes he was negotiating for a second lorry.

16

The Casting Couch

Late July 1955

Jeremy Shepherd sat comfortably in one of the deeply-padded, green leather armchairs of the Smoking Room. Of all the seating arrangements in the room, Jeremy preferred this particular one, if he could get it. Its location, close to the fire, provided warmth and a view of the heavy oak door. He could watch the comings and goings of the members and staff without appearing to show any interest.

An ex-RAF Flight Lieutenant from World War II, Jeremy still enjoyed the comforts of the Club when he wasn't directing films. He found it a very peaceful location to mull over crusty problems that bothered him on odd occasions. He gazed at the door as though he was sleeping with his eyes open. There was no activity at the entrance hall. Most members were either on duty, at work, or just hadn't bothered to get up yet. This was of course, why he had the chair to himself.

His forearms rested on the padded horsehair arms, a cigarette fixed vertically between the first two fingers of his right hand. He had lit it several minutes ago, taking one draw with the lighted match at the other end. The smouldering filter tip had rested motionless in his grasp ever since. The red-hot ember had burned to the last of the tobacco, leaving a vertical stack of grey ash tentatively balanced and ready to fall. A thin coil of smoke rose in blue-grey paisley until it dissipated close to the ceiling.

So deep were Jeremy's ruminations, that he didn't register his friend, Flight Lieutenant Alex Wood, as he entered the room.

Alex observed the silent thinker. He walked round the edge of the room picking up an ashtray en route and came to stand at Jeremy's right elbow. Alex nudged Jeremy's hand with the ashtray. The ash collapsed. Jeremy looked up at the intrusion.

"Hu! Oh, thanks." He stubbed out the remainder, even though by this time the fiery glow had expired.

"What ho, Sheepy, nearly took you for a gonner then, eyes staring, and that pillar of Hades. If you keep staring into space like that, they'll be carrying you of in a box. Buried alive, I dread to think of it."

223

"What, yes, I suppose so, thanks Knotty."

"So come on, who is she?" Alex asked. "Tell all, I want to know every detail right down to the dimples on her… well, you know."

"Actually I wasn't thinking about that," said Jeremy. "I was trying to work out how to find a tank for this film I've taken on."

"Ha, not very nice to call her a tank," Alex jibed, he took the seat facing his friend, "bit old with a hard exterior, is she, difficult to get at? You're all right though, your secret's safe with me. So what's this film about?"

"War film," explained Jeremy, "about the second Alamein and driving Rommel out of Africa. I need military equipment. The War Department says I've got to buy the equipment, but I don't want to buy the stuff. What would I do with it after the film's complete? Besides, I can't have all my capital used up by machinery when I need it for acting fees and sets."

"It just so happens I know a chap, Edward Knight, who may be able to help."

"Really!"

"Decent sort of fellow. He was a World War One pilot, flew a few sorties from 1917 onwards. He actually changed his Birth Certificate so as not to miss the action. Anyway, I understand he's a dab hand at dealing with the War Department. He's been collecting material since the end of 1945 and has certainly supplied other film companies."

"Then he's a rival." Jeremy was taken aback.

"No! He's strictly freelance."

"Mercenary you mean?"

"You should be nice. It was he who designed and built the two replica motor sleds for the *Scott of the Antarctic* film. He made them from Bren-Gun carriers, you know."

"What, the 1948 Film Festival, John Mills' *Scott*?"

"Yes. Anyway, how about I look him up, and steer him your way?"

"You really think he could help?" Jeremy rubbed his thirty-three year old chin as though he had just been struck.

"Sure," said Alex. "He doesn't come up here very often but I can dig out his number."

"Yes, you may as well give him a try," said Jeremy. "Thank you."

"I'd lay a bet, if he hasn't got what you want, he can get it within two weeks," said Alex.

"You're on, five bob all right?"

"Come on Sheepy, try being a wolf for once and make it ten."

"Oh, all right. Two weeks from today."

Alex Wood, hastily left the room to find the number.

* * *

"Good morning, E. Knight and Company. How may I help you?"

"Good morning to you young lady, may I speak with E.J. please?"

"Certainly Sir, who should I say is calling?"

"Oh, tell him it's Knotty Wood."

There was a loud click as Edward Knight picked up his receiver.

"Knotty, how good to hear from you. Is this business or pleasure?"

"Bit of both really. Thought I'd look you up as it's been a year since we last spoke, and I have a friend who needs your help. You've heard of Jeremy Shepherd, the film director?" Edward grunted. "Well, he's making a film of the North Africa Campaign and needs military equipment suitable for the time. I told him you could help."

"Did you now?" Edward sounded surprised.

"Well I jolly well hope you can," said Alex. "I've got ten bob riding on the outcome."

"And I suppose you'll want me to bail you out if you lose? What does Mr. Shepherd need?"

"I don't actually know," said Jeremy, "but I said you could get anything he needs within two weeks." Wood sounded quite proud of his boast.

"That was foolish of you. I can probably find what he wants, but within two weeks, that's a tall order." Edward thought about his coming trip. "Mind you, it just so happens I'm going up to Ruddington tomorrow for an auction. Is he staying at the club?"

"Yes."

"In that case, I could leave tonight, stop over this evening, have a chat with him and carry on to Ruddington in the morning."

"Whacko, that sounds brilliant. He said he'll get me some autographs if this all works out." Alex's enthusiasm came bubbling out of Edward's telephone.

"Steady now, Alex. Why on earth can't you be a normal person and collect stamps or something?" Edward jested.

"Stamps cost too much. Autographs don't cost a thing and I only have to wait for the stars and badger them a bit. They nearly always cave in."

"I believe you. Are you in the Club now? and will you be around this evening?"

"Yes, to both questions."

"Then I'll book my room for tonight. I'll meet you in the Cocktail Bar about eight. We can catch up with each other and you can introduce me to Shepherd. Pass me to the concierge, will you?" Edward was already quite taken with the idea of stopping for the night at the Club. He'd been a member from its inception in 1918 and liked the comfortable opulence.

"Right-oh." Alex waved at the concierge to pick up the phone.

* * *

With one arm stretched out the window, Edward waved to his wife as he eased his car away from Froghole Farm and along the narrow tree-lined drive to the road. He drove through Bletchington, then he headed north towards London.

There was only slight traffic as he drove through the countryside. In Redhill, he stopped for a bite of tea. Later, he passed Clapham Common, drove over Chelsea Bridge and turned towards Victoria station. The short distance to Piccadilly via Hyde Park Corner took another five minutes. He parked at the back of the club in Yarmouth Place. Moments later he was being issued his room key.

Precisely at eight, Edward descended the stairs to the first floor. The Cocktail Bar was located to the back of the building. There was now a single bar, a miniature reflection of the former drinking house, *The Running Horse*, of 1872. As he walked through he was enveloped by a low murmur of voices. He closed the door, looked around slowly and noticed Alex waving frantically from one corner.

"Hello old chap, come and join us." Alex stood to introduce Jeremy Shepherd. The two strangers greeted each other, Edward settled into one of the comfortable chairs close to the wall. Alex went to order drinks.

"So, what line of work are you in?" asked Jeremy.

"Civil engineering. Roads, flat surfaces, drainage, some demolition, that sort of thing. The conversation quickly took full swing around the finer points of flow rates, pipe bores, and filtration. I also deal in scrap metal, I had a couple of clearance contracts with the War Department so now I can supply ex-military equipment."

All Alex could do was listen and fidget as the conversation moved to other subjects. Eventually Alex's frustration got the better of him.

"Come on chaps, I introduced you so you could talk films not bloody road construction and sewerage works.

Jeremy grinned at Edward.

226

"Sorry, Alex. It seems we're both interested in the same things. Didn't realise you were bored with our chitchat."

"Come on Knotty, it's your own fault." Edward's rejoinder was full of humour.

"What do you mean, my fault? I've hardly had a chance to say a thing since you arrived."

"No, but you've let your vested interest in the outcome of a certain bet sway your mind somewhat. Naturally, we steered the conversation, quite skilfully, if I may say so, away from your desired topic."

"Oh you swines, you've been playing me on a bloody hook."

"Well, yes, we sort of made the agreement while you were ordering our drinks. Which makes me think, would anyone like another?" Edward raised his hand to call the waiter.

They placed their order and settled down again.

"Right, down to business Jeremy. What have you got so far?"

"Well at the moment, I have an M3 armoured scout car and a six-pounder field gun, both supposedly in working order."

"Goodness," said Edward. "I think you'd better tell me what you would like and how you're going to show them in your film. Then I can tell you what I can provide and how much more I can acquire."

The discussion extended into the night with Jeremy pointing out what would be ideal and Edward making suggestions to suit. The bar closed at 10.30 and they moved into the Smoking Room. It was early morning before they retired to their rooms.

* * *

At 7.30 a.m. Edward placed his overnight bag in the back of his car. A standard 1938 Rolls Royce Phantom III but with Bentley trims, the car looked immaculate in its freshly restored condition. He and his brother James had spent the last three years, working weekends, to bring the vehicle back to perfect condition. Painted black with mid-grey panels and gold lining. Edward considered it an excellent symbol of his Managing Directorship, proof of prosperity. With a press of a button, the engine purring into life as the three hundred and eighty-four cubic inches of power turned over.

The comforts were as splendid as the arrangements at the Club with deep, red leather seats and walnut-burr surrounds. The heavy angled radiator grill with the prominent filler cap topped with a chromed 'B' and wings, nosed along the road as though guiding the driver.

Edward joined Park Lane at the Dorchester Hotel and cruised north.

At 11.20 a.m. Edward pulled up at the gate of the War Department Compound. He was late but he knew from the Lot numbers he hadn't missed what he was most interested in. He would have an easy task, he thought, with little competition bidding for most of what Jeremy wanted. At breakfast, Edward had picked out an eighty-eight millimetre flak gun, an armoured car or two and a VW Kubelwagen type 82 but none of them would be put under the hammer until about midday.

The guard at the gate waved Edward to the car park.

As Edward entered the Auction Hall, the sound of the gavel hitting the block filled the room. Edward took a seat along the wall and readied himself for the next Lot number.

Mr. David Ringer, the auctioneer was in full flow.

"Next on the Agenda is Lot number sixty-three, a K2 ambulance from the Italian campaign, in mediocre condition. With this Lot are six stretchers, forty-two boxes of field dressings, sixteen grey blankets and a hundred and sixty pads of medical report forms. May I start the bidding at forty pounds? Forty, thank you sir, I have forty, forty-five? Forty-five, fifty, fifty, thank you, and five?" The tempo slowed. "Fifty-five pounds I have. Sixty anyone? I have sixty pounds, and five, do I hear seventy? Any offers for seventy? Seventy anyone? No, do I hear sixty-six? Sixty-six anyone? No, any more offers? So at sixty-five pounds, going once, twice…" Again the gavel's sound clacked out across the room. "Sold for sixty-five pounds to bidder one-seven-two." David Ringer conferred with one of the stewards before continuing.

Edward wondered what the buyer would do with over two thousand field dressings, or a hundred and sixty pads of Army Medical Forms for that matter. Originally he had not wanted to bid for anything before Lot eighty-two but now, with Jeremy's interest he would bid for number seventy-four, a war damaged German 222 armoured car. He looked at his watch, there was still an hour before he had to concentrate.

He took a printed sheet of paper from his inside pocket. The list of Lot numbers with a brief description of each had numerous scribbles and underlines marked all over it. Perusing the catalogue he noticed item one-six-one, a Panzer IV, the last item of the day. The description just said *Considerable body damage.*

Robert remembered seeing the tank two weeks before but had taken no notice of its condition. He wondered what kind of damage was involved. Was it worth bidding for? Whatever the condition, it was a once in a life time chance and perfect for Jeremy's film.

228

With his own engineering expertise and James' mechanical knowledge they could probably fix any problem the tank might have, unless it had been blown apart. After some deliberation he decided to try for it. It could be a real boon in the film industry even if Jeremy didn't want it, but Edward had an inkling the Director would be keen.

The bidding for Lot seventy-four went well. Starting at thirty-five pounds, the price rose in fives to fifty and then in ones to fifty-six where Edward finally beat off his competition. Lot eighty-two, a canvas covered Bedford lorry in unserviceable condition, went equally well, but at ninety pounds, it cost more than Edward had hoped. He planned to load the Bentley on the back and drive it straight home. He had trade plates to cover tax and insurance.

Lot eighty-nine was a one point eight metre trailer searchlight, Edward paid thirty-four pounds. Lot ninety-two was the second of his wrongly labelled Bedford lorries. Lot by Lot, he gathered everything he needed.

Through the afternoon the crowd thinned slowly, most of the seats were vacant by 7.00 p.m. when Lot one-six-one came under the hammer. David Ringer seemed to breath a sigh of relief.

"Ladies and Gentlemen, thank you all for being so patient during what has been a very long day. We have had some exciting bidding and I hope you have all secured what you came for. You will be pleased to hear we are now on the final Lot, number one-six-one, a Mark IV Panzer Tank of the German Wehrmacht. It stands alone. The catalogue says there is some damage, unfortunately I have no additional information. If we are ready, I'll start the bidding at fifty pounds." Edward nodded, accepting the price. David Ringer continued. "Thank you, Sir. Fifty-five? Anyone? Fifty-five pounds for a Panzer IV, no, fifty-four; fifty-three; fifty-two;" The pauses between each number seemed to lengthen. "I'm down to fifty-one pounds, fifty-one anybody, no, then at fifty pounds, going once, last call of the day, sold for fifty pounds to bidder four-fifteen. Thank you very much Sir.– Gentlemen, that concludes the business for the day, thank you all for attending. Goodnight."

Edward settled up with the cashier. Then he booked into a small hotel for the night, in the centre of Nottingham. He called home and arranged for his son Robert to come by train to be a second driver to move the acquisitions.

The Government allowed a week for bidders to remove their purchases from Ministry Grounds. Edward reasoned if the majority of items could be driven home the next day, he and Robert could return over the weekend to collect the Panzer.

Robert's train arrived at eleven the next morning.

"I'm sorry I'm late, Father. I swear the trains are becoming worse by the day."

"At least you made it. We can leave as soon as we've eaten, unless you want to go now and eat on the way."

"No, whatever you want to do, Father, is fine by me."

The journey home was long. Robert in one lorry, with the Kubelwagen on the back and pulling the searchlight, made good progress. Edward driving the second lorry with the Bentley on the back and towing a flak gun, eventually arrived home in the early hours of the following day. He slept in late.

When he awoke he phoned Jeremy at the RAF Club.

"I say, you'll never guess what I found, I'm sure you'll be impressed."

"I'd be surprised if you had found anything yet," said Jeremy.

"Well I did find some things, like an Eighty-eight, a type 82 Volkswagen, and a 222 armoured car. But I found something else which could lend real 'weight' to your film." Edward goaded his client.

"What do you mean, real weight? You found some heavy equipment?" Jeremy asked.

"Yes, just what you need for an authentic desert battle. What do you say to a Panzer IV?"

"You're joking!"

"No, not at all. It's damaged, but nothing that can't be fixed and I actually think the damage can be put to good use for your special effects like bullet ricochets and explosions. She will need a coat of paint of course but that's a small matter. She also needs two machine guns."

"You went and bought a tank?" Jeremy could still not fathom the enormity of the offer.

"Yes," said Edward, "I was wondering if you would like to take a train to Nottingham tomorrow, I could show you what she's like. I'm going down today with a low loader. It will probably take all day so I'll return tomorrow, once I've loaded up. I could collect you from the station and bring you back to London, we can discuss the loan on the way."

"Definitely, I want to see this miracle. Look, the first train down leaves St. Pancras at about seven and arrives at about nine."

230

"Fine, I'll see you then, outside Nottingham station. Have a good journey." Edward replaced the receiver.

* * *

Back at Ruddington again, Edward walked Jeremy to the Panzer and showed him the damage. They climbed inside and inspected the cone shaped entry wounds where the armour piercing rounds had crippled the working area.

"I see what you mean, this is wonderful," said Jeremy.

"I thought you'd be impressed," said Edward.

"I wonder, do you suppose she's still a runner?" asked Jeremy.

"I have no idea, but I can fix her if she's not. Come on, let's ask." Edward climbed out and called to a nearby soldier. "Excuse me Sergeant, can you help me a moment?"

Whipping turned and halted by the Panzer.

"Sergeant Major Whipping, Royal Engineers, Sir. What can I do for you, Gentlemen."

"Er, Sergeant Major, we're collecting, after the last auction. I was just wondering if this tank still runs."

"I have no idea, Sir," said Whipping seeing a chance for a little fun, "but I can find out for you if you will bear with me awhile." He turned and collared the first soldier who passed. "You lad, fetch me a jerry can of petrol, a funnel, and a syphoning hose."

"Right away Sar' Major." The soldier darted away.

Whipping turned back to Edward and Jeremy.

"Actually, I know this tank quite well." Whipping smiled. "After the war, I transferred to the Engineers, and it was on this machine I did most of my early mechanical training. Bit of luck you asking me, because as far as I know, only two other people in the British Army ever worked on her, and they were both discharged years ago." He climbed up the steps and opened the driver's hatch. "You are indeed lucky because when I noticed parts going missing back in 1945, I placed the most important items, such as the crank handle, under the driver's seat. With a bit of luck it will still be there." He disappeared inside. Moments later, after some rattling around, he reappeared. "Will you look at this." He held up the crank handle. "It was right where I left it."

"You do know this machine," Jeremy said.

"Yes, Sir," said Whipping. "But I doubt she will run at present. She's been stuck in the open down at West Lulworth Range for ten years and as far as I know, nothing has been touched since I dropped her off."

231

The soldier came running up with the fuel and hose.

"Thank you lad, now fetch another good strong lad to help start this thing." Whipping turned back to his audience. "As I was saying, I had to work on the *Fräulein* here, when I first started as an Engineer. My Corporal made me strip her down. Once that was done he told me to put her together again. I had to keep at it until it worked properly. Well, this is how I eventually got her started."

Whipping opened the engine compartment and spent some time fiddling. Then he opened the jerry can and poured some fuel down the hose into the carburettor. The soldier returned with a buddy.

"You two, take this and fit it in the hole under the exhaust down there." Whipping handed the men the crank handle. "When I say, you turn that thing as fast as you can until it starts. Make sure you put your backs into it." Whipping took the driver's seat and released the brakes and clutch so the fly wheel rotated freely.

"Right you two, start turning that handle."

The first motion was imperceptible. Gradually the soldiers got to grips with the task.

Eventually Whipping engaged the clutch. Nothing happened. He climbed out and tinkered for a while, then set the two boys to work again.

"Well, it was ten years ago, but we must remember Robert the Bruce."

At the fourth try, the engine spluttered slightly and roared into life. The noise was phenomenal. With several rust holes in the silencer there was little to dampen the engine's true volume. Whipping disconnected the jerry can. The engine quickly sputtered and died.

Edward stood with his fingers in his ears, when he unplugged them, his ears still rang.

Whipping looked down at him.

"It may have taken a couple of hours, but now she is a runner. The wonder of German craftsmanship. You have to give them that... Actually Sir, I have something else that will interest you. It's the maintenance and operating manual from when I first cleared the junk out of her. If you load her up on your wagen, I will go and find it for you." Whipping turned and marched off at a smart pace. Edward and Jeremy were almost finished when he returned forty minutes later.

"Here you are, Sir," He held up an ageing manual. "My mates and I each nicked something when we worked on her. At the time I thought

232

they had the better deals, one had binoculars, the other a camera, and I came away with this. I was a mite disgruntled at the time, I must say. But it's stood me in good stead, when I was posted to Germany I set to translating it into English. I was still a Lance Corporal then. I shall be sorry to let it go, but I think you have more need than I ever will. You can have my translation too, for all it's worth. Good luck."

17

Film Star

Angus McKenzie watched as the Panzer IV was hoisted off the old Liberty ship's deck. As Edward Knight's foreman, the forty-year old was in charge of the various vehicles that had been transported and would be held responsible if anything was damaged. The voyage had been long but uneventful, however, for the last few days the sun had been blistering.

The harbour area looked like a scene from 1943 and could have been authentic in Tripoli with a mass of German uniforms milling around.

The tank had been one of three vehicles transported on the deck. As it settled on the quay, local dock workers strolled forward to untie the lifting gear. The men seemed in no hurry and Angus had no inclination to chivvy them in the heat. He noted their lips moving and the obvious signs made to ward off evil.

Eventually a dock foreman turned and waved Angus over. It was obvious the man remembered the same sort of equipment from during the war. The expression on his face spoke volumes about what he thought of the situation. Anyone who had survived the war would have difficulty forgetting, as he did himself. His experiences of El Alamein were the reason he had been instructed to accompany the cargo. As engineer and driver of the Panzer, he would be available to advise on making the shots look realistic. The film was called *Rommel's Defeat*. He wondered why Jeremy had insisted on filming in Africa, surely there was somewhere in England that was sandy like the desert.

"It ready, you go."

The brevity of the foreman's statement left nothing in doubt.

"Thank you." Angus hoped the man understood.

"Pah." The local turned and walked away, robes billowing in the wind.

Angus put on some leather gloves, the tank was too hot to touch with bare hands. He climbed up the tank's left hand drive sprocket, onto the glacis. He reached for the driver's hatch and pulled. Baking heat rose from the compartment like the breath of the devil. Angus broke into a sweat as it engulfed his face. Thank God I don't have to do anything physical, he thought as he climbed down into the small space.

One of the many alterations which had been made to the tank was the starter motor which now ran from a secondary engine driving a generator. Why the original designers hadn't thought of this when they had first built the tank, Angus couldn't understand. At least it avoided anyone having to labour under the intense African sun.

Once the key was slotted between the contact terminals, Angus started the generator. As soon as it was running at speed, he pressed the starter for the main engine. It took less than a minute.

Angus slipped the lever into first gear and pulled away from the ship. At the end of the quay, out of the way, he stopped to watch the rest of the unloading. Armoured cars and a Kubelwagen followed. They each drove past him and turned into the town along the dusty streets to the assembly point. The last two vehicles out of the ship were both Bedford lorries containing all the equipment necessary for filming. When they drove past, Angus followed them into the town. After a few minutes the lorries pulled up at the back of the convoy. Angus drove carefully along the side to take the lead ready for the drive to the film location in the desert.

In spite of the fan's best efforts, the inside of the driving compartment was still stifling. There seemed to be little chance of it cooling down even when the Panzer was moving fast. Angus stood on his seat with his body out the hatch to try and cool off a little. He could feel the sweat running down his body and legs, he longed for a cool drink and wondered how long it would be before the convoy left. The only bonus was that once they were moving, the location was not far away.

As he looked around waiting for the off, Angus noticed locals, mainly women, peering through their doorways at the convoy. They called their children and herded them inside to hide, then slammed the door. Hardly surprising considering what had gone on just a decade ago, thought Angus.

Suddenly a Libyan police car sped past to the front of the convoy. Their guide, and to ward off attack from the town's folk, it would remain with them until they were clear of the town.

* * *

Angus sat in a dedicated director's chair, located a discrete distance from Jeremy and out of view of the cameras. He drank chilled beers. Every member of the team had been warned to drink at every opportunity. It was not just the high sun that was the problem, the parching wind didn't help. An umbrella stood overhead to keep the sun from burning while he watched the crew and actors record several static shots.

Angus himself was not required during the shoots but was called upon to move the sand-coloured tank into new positions close to buildings or on sand dunes, in readiness for each take.

They were expecting to film here for the next three or four weeks depending on the number of retakes required but much of the film was already in the can. Most of the indoors scenes had already been finished in studios in England while Jeremy Shepherd had waited for the Panzer and other equipment to be serviced and brought up to a suitable standard for the location work.

Three days passed before Angus was required to be in the Panzer for a take. It was early morning. He had made a point of requesting the scenes involving the tank in motion be shot as soon after first light as possible, before the sun started to bake everything. It was the only way he could see of being able to drive without floods of perspiration filling his eyes. Fortunately Jeremy had agreed, though not all the actors were so keen to be up and working before they had had their breakfast.

"Listen up, everybody," Along with twelve actors and seven crew, Angus turned his attention to Jeremy. He stood on his driver's seat in the Panzer and had a clear view of the director over the heads of the others.

"This next set of scenes is of the Huns sneaking through the Qattara Depression in an attempt to surprise us in Cairo. They never actually tried this because the depression will only support the lightest of equipment. But what the hell, this is the flicks."

For the shot, we have made our own little patch of quicksand here in Gazala. About half of you are going to be sucked in, and will come to a sticky end, at least that is the effect we want on film.

"The props team have been experimenting with all sorts of media from waterlogged sand to a new sort of waterbased glue. The best thing they could come up with, which looks and acts like quicksand, is porridge." The gathering burst into laughter.

"Okay, but I have seen the stuff and it really is convincing. With a thin covering of sand it looks solid and will even support a couple of stone in weight. But, if you stand on it, the surface splits and you slowly sink. If you stir it about, you sink more quickly, which is precisely what I want those of you who are going in, to do, as though you are struggling against its suction."

236

"Is it real porridge?" one of the extras asked.

"Yes, oats, salt and water."

"That'll be all right for Scotty's breakfast, if it's cold," said another.

"Shut up you Sassenach." Several people giggled at Scott Mc Cloud's discomfort.

"How much porridge are we talking about?" the first extra asked.

"The container is twelve feet wide and ten feet across."

That's a lot of porridge, even Scotty couldn't eat it all in one sitting."

"You can eat it if you want," Jeremy joked, "but I ask that you hold off until we finish filming… Right, you will be treading carefully so as to find the safe path. We'll have three or four takes before you find the quicksand and then we'll go through the process of being sucked under and the subsequent attempted rescue. Any questions?"

"Which side of the track is the porridge going to be?"

"I'm not going to tell you. Hopefully, the people going in will be caught by surprise making their reactions more realistic… I want you troops spaced two feet apart with you, Scott, directly in front of the tank. All right, places, please."

The slow advance across the makeshift depression was shot five times. Some takes showed the Panzer's front with the troops to either side, shot with a wide field of view. Others were taken from the tank looking forward. The troops advanced with the minutest care as though looking for mines, though there was no danger from mines or quicksand.

Scott followed a line of green stone markers leading the tank in the right direction. The odd-coloured rocks would not look any different from the rest of the desert when viewed on black and white film. Angus ran the tank at a slow crawl keeping Scott almost directly under the gun's muzzle. Two other actors were visible through his viewer, both to Scott's left.

For the last takes, camera one was mounted on the Panzer's turret. The view included a small section of gun and front armour with Scott directly in front of the tank and an extra to his left.

Camera two was on a rail truck to the Panzer's right hand side viewing the actors and the front of the Panzer using a long lens. When the actors fell into the porridge the camera would be pushed round until it was opposite the tank to zoom in on the struggle.

"Sound, cameras." Jeremy's voice just reached him through the air vents.

"Rommel's Defeat. Scene one-four-six, take one." The clapper boy snapped the clapper before the camera lens and stepped to one side off the tank.

"Action."

Angus knew there was at least thirty feet to the porridge but he could not tell exactly where the change from sand to porridge took place, it was too well camouflaged.

Scott stepped out. Angus gently advanced the steering levers. The Panzer lurched forward momentarily before smoothing off. Angus knew the tank's initial sway could easily be removed from the final cut.

Scott had slowed a little and seemed to be dragging his feet. The extras were pulling ahead slightly. Angus eased the levers off wondering what was wrong. He watched intently as the actor stepped carefully along the approved line.

Scott seemed to hesitate for a moment. Had he detected a slight softness? Angus wondered.

Camera two started to move round to the front of the tank.

The extra to Scott's left stumbled and pitched into the porridge giving a cry of surprise. Scott stepped but stopped short. He tried to turn and save himself. The surface of the porridge broke. He quickly sank to the top of his boots, lost his balance and slowly tipped forward sprawling into the mash. The porridge gave way under his weight making him sink. Trying to push himself up, he paddled with his arms, but his hands just sank deeper into the pulp.

He had been instructed not to speak unless it was in German. He couldn't help himself.

"Oh my God!" A string of vile words flowed from his mouth. The soundman sitting behind camera two listened intently but could not make out their meaning.

Jeremy, standing by the camera, leaned over to the cameraman. "Let it run," he said. He was convinced Scott's tirade would not matter in the final cut and it could always be dubbed.

Scott kept trying to raise himself. He thrashed desperately but each time he pressed down, the corresponding shoulder sank a little further. The crud smeared onto his cheek. He strained his head back trying to avoid the mess. His legs flailed, gradually sinking. The glutinous mix covered his body. Gradually consumed by the pulp, fear set in.

"Help. Help me, I'm sinking." The thick Scottish accent covered the clarity of his words. "I'm going down, somebody do something please!" He wriggled himself onto his back and suddenly caught sight of camera

238

one – so close, yet no one was doing anything to save him. The goo reached his chin. "Are y' jus' going to let me die?" The porridge entered his mouth.

"Cut." Jeremy would have liked to continue but those last words had been too clear. "All right, haul him up."

Two assistants, dressed in waders, stepped in up to their hips and hauled on Scott's arms standing him up. "There you go."

Scott stood waist deep looking bemused at the muck covering his German uniform.

"Y'bloody tricked me. I tell you I never want to see another mouthful of porridge in my life, even if I live to ninety."

"Don't worry Scott, you won't live that long." Jeremy smiled broadly as he spoke. "You die in the next shot."

"That's what I'm afraid of."

"I want you to do the final part of that last shot again. Take it from where you turned over but this time try not to do all that tartan shouting. Then I want you to duck your head under, and just stir your hand about over the surface as though you're writhing in your death throes. We'll shoot it in close-up. When you stop moving we'll shoot for another five seconds before we heave you out again. While you're under, just count nice and slow because you won't here me call 'cut'. Mind you take a deep breath."

"Pardon?! I can-na hear you, I think ma ears a' full of porridge."

"I can tell you in sign language if you want," Jeremy shouted through cupped hands.

"Na. Don't bother, but I think I should have a bonus for doin' this twice."

"You Scots are all the same." Jeremy turned away. "Are you ready cameras, sound?"

"Ready."

"Fine. Scott are you ready?"

"As I'll ever be."

"Places everyone... Sound, roll cameras."

"Rommel's Defeat. Scene one-forty-seven, take one."

"Action."

* * *

Once the set of scenes were in the can, Jeremy called a halt for the morning. The sun was already high and the heat was building.

With Scott riding on the front, Angus drove the Panzer back to the camp where the next shots were to be filmed, well away from the makeshift quicksand.

Scott looked like a desert ghost, an apparition of terror. His whole uniform was caked and gooey, the muck covered him from tip to toe.

Angus pulled up by the camp tents so Scott could quickly go and shower. Jeremy arrived just behind them.

Local children lingered nearby sitting in a small group, watching for something of interest. Scott shifted his perch. The kids' faces immediately changed from boredom to shock. Scott noticed the change and not being one to miss the chance for a prank, he slid off the glacis plate onto the ground. As he dropped from the Panzer's front the children stood up ready to flee. Slowly Scott straightened and turned to face them. Alarm seemed to fill every face. Scott gradually raised his arms out in front of him and stepped towards the group. "Gaarrr." he shouted. The children instantly fled screaming. Angus climbed from the tank laughing.

"Very funny Scott, they'll be having nightmares for weeks."

"But it made me feel a lot better after what happened back there."

"You had better go and clean yourself off," said Jeremy, "before their parents come round with pitchforks and rifles, besides, you don't want that stuff to dry and turn into concrete."

"Yes," said Angus, "and I've got to clean your breakfast off the front of my tank."

"What about my uniform, who's going to clean that?"

"Take it in the shower with you," said Jeremy. "Most of the stuff should just rinse off but we don't need it again unless you want to be an extra later on."

"I wouldn't mind if I get extra pay."

"I'll think about it. Now get going or I won't be responsible for what those parents do to you."

* * *

London March 1959

Four years later, Jeremy once again embarked on a war film and needed Edward Knight's equipment. *Maquis* was the fifth war film in a row he had undertaken.

The Panzer was parked outside a Victorian Seaman's Registry Office in the docks area of East London. The building was supposed to represent a German headquarters in a French port. The huge red flags

240

with black cross and encircled Swastika rippled gently in the wind as they hung from the roof. The condemned building awaited the shooting of the next scene in the film. Though cordoned off because of war damage, Jeremy had been able to persuade the local authority to let him film during the demolition.

Angus, again included as driver, had parked the Panzer across the road from the German Headquarters. Inside the vehicle, camera one was set up to film the building through the partially open turret hatch, only a sheet of glass protected the lens. The camera crew were happy to use the Panzer's armour as protection.

Camera two was further away, well back from the scene, ready to film with the tank clearly displayed in the foreground.

The explosion, when it happened, filled the street with clouds of dust and flying masonry. The sound was deafening making the film crew's ears ring. The tank was momentarily engulfed.

Camera one rolled, catching the whole effect until a piece of stone smacked against the glass shield. The second camera continued to roll as gradually the tank loomed from the fog of dust. The building had vanished.

"Cut," shouted Jeremy. "Fine, is everybody all right, no injuries from the demolition?" Jeremy looked at each person to check they were fine. "Good, get ready for the next shot. This is the one showing the Panzer under attack. Come on, let's get this camera out of here and on the street…" It took over an hour to remove the equipment and set it up again in the right position with the correct angle. Jeremy fidgeted while Angus twiddled his thumbs waiting for his part in the action.

"Are we all ready?"

Angus gave a thumbs up gesture through the driver's hatch. Looking through the visor he could just make out the cameraman, as he also held his thumb high.

"Sound, cameras…" Jeremy called. Angus closed the hatch and waited. "Action."

Several actors dressed as French resistance fighters ran into view from behind one of the cameras. They threw makeshift petrol bombs made from paraffin, before they turned again and fled into a side street. As flames burst across the Panzer, Angus shifted into first gear, pressed the accelerator and thrust the steering levers forward. The tank lurched after the escaping villains, towards the camera. The camera panned the shot as the tank passed by, until Jeremy called again.

241

"Cut. Good, let's get in position for the next shot. Quickly please, we'll lose the light soon and we have to have this one done today. I wish we still had double summertime, we'd still have well over an hour of light left."

For the next shot the same actors joined the running battle against the Panzer but they always made a retreat away from the headquarters. The tank followed eagerly trying to capture the French resistance troops. The final shot of the day was taken from the tank's roof as it chased the French soldiers onto the quayside of the Millwall Outer Dock.

As the Panzer cleared the buildings, Jeremy called a halt to the shoot. Satisfied the cameraman and sound crew were happy, he ordered the tank secured for the night.

"Remember, everyone, tomorrow we only get one shot at this, so make sure everything is absolutely as it should be." He turned to the cameraman. "You'll have the camera bolted to the van's floor, won't you."

"Yes, Jeremy. I'll put sound in there too with the mike on a boom out the back. We should be able to hear Marcus panting as he runs from the tank."

"Good, I look forward to it. Goodnight."

Angus pulled the key from the contacts and climbed from the tank. He carefully closed the hatch and turned the handle locking it.

* * *

The following morning the day was cloudy again.

"Thank God there's no sun," said Jeremy, as he and Angus approached the scene.

"Yes, makes for easy continuity if there's no sun or rain," said Angus.

"Right everybody, positions. This is the important one. We can't afford any mistakes. There will be no retakes. Are you happy with the arrangements, Angus?"

"Yes, just get me out of there quickly." Angus climbed into his position and helped the technicians seal the hatch. All the other openings had been sealed, stopped or bunged up the previous evening after filming had finished. The Panzer should be watertight.

Once everything was secured Angus sat in his driver's seat, fitted his restraining harness and waited. The engine had to be as cold as possible for this shot. He could not start up until the very last moment before *Action* was called. Then he had less than five minutes to the end of the shot before he had to cut the engine again. It would be a close call.

242

Angus inspected the machine gun trigger, a small three way switch that had been taped to the top of the right steering lever. Centre was off, left fired a sequence of squibs and right fired a second sequence, it was important not to mix them up. The switch was another gadget that had not been tested for the shot.

The Panzer was standing just a short way up the road, away from the quay. This shot was one long take of the tank exiting the road onto the quayside, turning towards the camera to run along the quay until the *Cut.* Such a long take was a risk in itself but this one was even more difficult. There were so many variables.

The only people Angus could see were the actors playing the parts of the French Resistance. He had no way of hearing the call for action so had to rely on the actors for his cue. He gazed through the viewer hoping the signal would come soon. He had been told the air in the Panzer would last an hour, perhaps ninety minutes, but he didn't like the idea of sitting doing nothing while he used up the air. His anticipation and enthusiasm was high but his anxiety was growing too. The sooner he could get moving the better. What was keeping them?

All of a sudden one of the actors turned to him and waved, the signal at last. Angus started the generator and then the main engine. Once it was running steadily he flashed his lights at the actors. It was time to go.

The five actors dashed forward to the end of the street and round the corner to the right. Angus pressed the accelerator to the floor. As he passed the end of the last building he heaved back on the right lever swinging the Panzer round to follow the actors. The tank skidded across the concrete surface but quickly regained its grip to rapidly catch the foes.

The camera van was directly in front. Angus could see the camera crew inside filming the action. The van moved off slowly. Four of the actors run past, out of shot. Only Marcus, the fifth man stayed behind the camera being filmed in close-up.

They must be able to pick up his every freckle, thought Angus. But this was not the time for him to have such musings. He had to catch up with Marcus ready for the next part of the shot, and the quay was rapidly running out of space.

As the tank closed the gap, Angus flipped the switch on the steering lever. The first batch of squibs ignited in the dummy machine gun, he heard the small detonations as they fired off in a rapid sequence. He was practically on top of Marcus before the actor took a glance behind him.

In that moment, Angus saw the effort in the actor's straining features and with glee flipped the switch again. The second run of squibs rattled off.

Marcus snatched a grenade from his belt. He pulled the pin and with another quick glance, dropped the charge. An expression of excitement crossed his face as the dummy weapon bounced on the ground. He fled out of camera shot leaving the tank to fill the frame.

Strapped to the underside of the tank, a small pack of explosives erupted in a loud detonation. Smoke belched from under the hull.

It was time for the final play and Angus had to get it exactly right. He hauled back on the steering lever while accelerating hard. The Panzer veered dramatically to the left as though a track had broken. There were seconds left. The quayside was fast approaching. Three, two, one, the tank leapt out over the water. Angus had pressed both levers hard forward to provide as much speed as possible. For a split second the tank seemed to fly. Angus disengaged the flywheel and pulled the key from the ignition contacts. The flywheel would continue to turn while the engine died, but it was not quick enough. Seconds seemed like hours as Angus waited to hear the engine stop turning. It had to stop to prevent the dock water reaching into the cylinders or else the cylinder block would crack from the cold.

The Panzer landed nose first into the water. Angus was jolted out of his seat hanging from the harness straps. He hung helpless, unable to move but grateful not to be falling to the front of the hull next to the drive shaft and brake equipment.

The Panzer did not wallow on the surface but sank nose first, wheels still turning, to the bottom of the dock twenty feet below.

I hope the cameras caught all that Angus thought to himself as the tank settled. He shifted himself back into his seat and glanced at the viewer. Murky brown water filled his sight.

Angus considered the situation. Jeremy would watch the tank go over the side keeping the cameras rolling as the water swallowed the Panzer. He would film the ripples spreading and bubbles rising from where the tank had disappeared. How long would he let the bubbles rise? A few seconds, or longer?

Water spurted in through the overhead hatch. It was only a fine spray but it soaked his clothes. Angus wonder how many other places hadn't been sealed properly and how much less time his air would last as a result.

He had intended to just wait for the team to lift the tank out of the water, but now, rather than sit in the cold spray, it seemed prudent to crawl to the highest point in the vehicle so he could use all the air available as the water level rose inside.

He picked up the breathing equipment and thrust it through the gap into the turret compartment. Thank God she settled the right way up, he thought. It would have been so easy for the old girl to land on her side or upside down. He slipped the key in his pocket and engaged the parking brake, pressing the pedal as hard as possible and kicked the retaining clip into place. It seemed a ludicrous thing to do in the murky depths of the harbour but it was better than rolling down some aquatic slope and never be seen again. Then he felt around the cab for anything he had forgotten. Satisfied, he wriggled through under the gun controls to the turret. When he straightened up he remembered the torch he had installed in the front so he could see his way around.

"Damn!" but he didn't think it was worth the effort of going back for it.

After a while, he became aware of clanking sounds like something metal striking the outside of the hull. The rescue crew must be in place already. They had practised the recovery plan several times on the quayside but never in the water. However, the frogmen were professionals, experienced in underwater salvage. Edward Knight had insisted on the best.

He picked up a spanner from a tool box in the side of the turret and tapped three times on the roof. He waited for a while and repeated the signal. Moments later he heard a reply. At least they knew he was still alive. It might give them incentive to work faster.

Angus had thought about opening a hatch and just floating to the surface until he had realised that all the hatches opened outwards against the water pressure. There had been one hatch down at the radioman's feet that he could have escaped from, but that had been welded shut. He just had to sit it out and hope for the best.

He wondered how long it would take to lift him clear. He tried to think through the process of rescue. The divers would come down to locate him while the crane moved into position, that would take ten minutes. Then the hook would be lowered while the other lifting gear was fitted to the tank, another ten minutes at least. Finally the whole thing would be raised, with him inside, and returned to the quayside. So, how much time had passed already? Minutes or tens of minutes, the dark and claustrophobia began to take its toll on his nerves.

Three taps sounded on the outside of the hull. Angus tapped back in response. The tank jolted, suddenly there was movement, it made the whole world seem unstable. He was being lifted, at last. He released his breath and took another. No matter how much they paid him he did not ever want to do that stunt again.

* * *

Minutes slipped by, Jeremy had to assume the frogmen had hooked the tank to the crane and it would be lifted soon. The water seemed even more murky from where the tank and frogmen had stirred up the muddy harbour bottom. The bubbles had stopped rising, there was no more air escaping. Whether it also meant there was no more air in the tank, was a question that could not be answered yet. Jeremy waited.

Eventually a frogman surfaced and held his hand up with thumb extended. The crane driver took the slack. Inch by inch the cable rose from the water. Another frogman appeared some way off from the cable, he sculled keeping himself on station.

The hook appeared with four chains attached. They slowly separated outwards as they lifted free of the depths. The cupola broke the surface spilling water from the top. Slowly the turret and gun rose clear. A frogman climbed onto the superstructure, removed his face mask and opened the turret hatch. He called into the tank.

"Hey, you all right in there?"

Jeremy heard the call but not the reply. A tense moment passed until the frogman turned and shouted.

"He's all right, Mr. Shepherd."

Jeremy exhaled in relief.

"I think we can all celebrate a good job done. And that man in there deserves a bonus."

Suddenly everything seemed to run more quickly. Before Jeremy even realised, the tank was secure on the quayside and Angus was climbing out, a big smile on his face. He didn't seem too steady at first but clutched at one of the bystanders for a little support.

"Angus, come and have a whisky," Jeremy called. "You deserve it."

Angus sauntered over, wet up to his ankles from the leakage in the tank.

"I'll have a double if I may, Mr. Shepherd."

"After what you have been through, you can have the whole bottle."

18

Show time

Bletchington 1966

Edward was unhappy about the gradual deterioration of his military vehicle collection. War films were no longer the vogue. Producers had moved on, gone were the days of *Ice Cold in Alex*, *The Heroes of Telemark* or *Mr. Drake's Duck* – films that told true stories. Those were the films that reminded the people who had been at the front what they had been through, and how they had survived. Now it was all spies, James Bond and the battle against Communism.

The vehicles had gradually become impossible to maintain. Finding spare parts had become too difficult and costly, and with only a slight possibility of a film contract, the incentives were no longer there. Edward had heard rumour of a film based on The Battle of Britain, but it was a story of flying, not of a ground battle.

He looked out of his kitchen window at the fallow field beyond the garden. Most of the collection was there, stored on the farm, derelict. The pieces had been moved out of the workshops to make way for more important commercial equipment. The company was expanding. He had been aiming higher and the new contracts reflected this, but he still mourned the decline in the Film Supply Industry.

The closest vehicle to the window was the German 222 armoured car. It had been the first to move into the open, three years ago. With one door missing and the turret open to the sky, it was overgrown with brambles and bindweed spreading rampant both inside and out. During the height of summer he could hardly believe there was a vehicle hidden under the thick foliage.

There were two half-tracks in similar condition. They had not been out for quite so long but with their rotted canvas roofs, it would not be long before plants took root in the moss growing on their floors. One vehicle already had a small silver birch growing in the air-vent in front of the shattered windscreen. It had taken root in last year's leaflitter.

Tyres were flat and cracked, the wheels rusty and tracks were thick with mud where they had sunk into the ground during the wet winter months. The paint was flaking away, with rust picking away at the thick armour.

The Panzer IV, one of the last to enter the field, still appeared pristine in the distance. When it had first joined the collection, Edward's brother James had been the one to repair the damage and look after it. He had adjusted the engine and fitted new piston heads and cylinder sleeves to accept ordinary two-star petrol instead of the seventy-four octane fuel it was designed for.

When it had been dunked in London Docks, James had again lovingly restored it to working order. He had even had the engine running for a few minutes before shutting it down for what would probably be the last time.

Edward missed his brother. There was nobody else who could coax a last hour of work from a seeming pile of scrap. James had sealed the Panzer's engine and gearbox in plastic film to prevent corrosion. He had fastened the hatch doors closed, and even fitted a wooden tampon to the gun's barrel to prevent birds nesting in the muzzle. Even so, nettles and brambles were starting to climb the tracks, they penetrated the fuel filler pipes and worked their way through the engine compartment. The gun and turret still pointed aggressively towards the valley but soon even these details would be hidden by greenery.

Edward wondered what would happen to the vehicles. Neither he nor his son, Robert, had time to look after them. The company had to take precedence, until he retired. Maybe then he would be able to dabble in the workshop and set about some restoration, maybe he could even build a museum for them so they would be safe and dry, protected from the weather.

* * *

1974

Robert Knight was forty-seven years old. He pulled back the old hangar doors and stepped inside. The collection of military vehicles looked forlorn and abandoned in the gloom but for all their rundown condition, Robert loved and admired every one of them. He had watched the collection grow through his teenage years and had been to film locations with many of them.

Then the collection had almost been lost to the elements but he had persuaded his father to have the hangar moved from the company's grounds and re-erected in the corner of the top field at the farm. Once the building had been completed, Robert had spent each weekend removing the scrub and hauling the dead vehicles inside. He looked forward to carrying out the restoration his father had always intended for them.

For all that Edward had said he would retire, he never had. He had never felt it was time to relinquish his hold on the company and as a result he had never found the time to fulfil his desire.

Robert had no intention of following in his father's footsteps. After just three years in full control, he had passed some of the business management to his own son who was now making vast changes in favour of modernisation. Robert had known the changes were necessary but did not have the heart to wipe out the old ways, his father's ways, while his father was still around.

Robert stepped across the threshold and wandered amongst the vehicles to the workbench. He rummaged through several drawers until he found the hand lamp and extension lead. He plugged the lamp into a socket and carried it to the back corner where the Panzer stood.

On the wall there was a stack of shelves with books, documents and manuals, mostly translations of German originals. He selected several and stacked them on the back of the tank, but the one he was most interested in was not in its proper place. Robert looked around, the book didn't seem to be anywhere obvious. He turned to the Panzer.

"So, old girl, what did Father do with your instructions?" he looked on the workbench where the lamp had been, but there was no sign. Various notes were pinned to a board above the workbench, among them was a photograph of Edward holding the German document and the translation written by an army Sergeant Major. Suddenly Robert remembered, Whipping had said that he found the book stuffed down the side of the driver's seat.

He walked round the Panzer and climbed onto the front. He heaved the driver's hatch open, and lowered the lamp down inside. The yellow-green interior shone back at him. It was a sickly colour, perhaps when he restored the tank he would use something different – something more friendly.

Robert searched either side of the seat but saw nothing obvious. He was about to pull the lamp out again when he noticed a small triangle of black poking out from under the front of the chair. He lowered himself through the hatch and reached down. There it was, the original, still in good condition with the handwritten translation tucked inside. He settled himself as comfortably as he could in the disintegrating chair and started to thumb through the pages.

It was amazing, such a well thought-out set of instructions. It started with all the technical data. Then each piece of equipment was described, with full instructions on how to maintain and operate that unit even going so far as to give warnings on things not to do. At the back there were diagrams of the various parts including a full wiring plan.

Robert looked at some of the wiring around him. The old cloth-bound cables had survived well considering the conditions they had been forced to endure. However there were patches where the material had rotted and some of the metal wires were showing through. A complete rewire was probably a sensible place to start the tank's restoration, but not today. He would need help for such a big project though most of the mechanical side was still in excellent working order.

The Kubelwagen seemed a more likely project to start with. It was simple in its design and easy to repair. In the meantime he could study the schematics of the other vehicles until he was ready to tackle them.

* * *

July 1985

Robert enjoyed reading military enthusiasts magazines, a throwback from his father's enthusiasm. In one issue he found an advertisement for a show being held by a small Kent group called the Invicta Military-Vehicle Preservation Society. Located in Tenterden, the two day event did not seem to be too far away for him to attend. He marked the dates on the calendar and informed his wife.

On the day, he wandered the rows of trade stands, taking in the diversity of interests, and chatted to the exhibitors. He looked at several stalls selling vehicle parts, before moving on past uniforms and models, books and hand weaponry. Slowly he realised just how widespread the interest in military memorabilia was. There were thousands of people who had the same interests as he and his late father.

Walking round the vehicles on display he stopped by a young man sitting in a half-track.

"Excuse me, is this yours?"

"Yes, good isn't she. I did all the work myself." The man must have been about thirty but he was like a boy seeking approval from a parent.

"How do you get around the problem of spare parts?" Robert asked.

"That is the hardest part of all in this game, sometimes you just can't find what you're looking for. You know, last year I spent nearly all of my holiday looking for an alternator for this heap, do you think I could find one? No. In the end I had to use parts from a Ford Grenada and make other parts myself. The only original piece in there now is the alternator casing."

"Do you have to make many parts?"

"A fair number. Anything that needs work, if it can't be fixed using the original, you have to make it from scratch. Sometimes you can substitute parts, like if you have one of those VW. Kubelwagens, you may find parts from an old Beetle will fit, but that doesn't work for things like this." The man patted the steering wheel of his SdKfz. 250/1. "Jack Briars by the way."

"Nice to meet you Jack, I'm Robert Knight."

"Knight? You're not the Knight who supplied all that equipment for war films in the fifties are you?"

"No, that was my father."

"Oh – I thought you were a bit too young to be him. Anyway, what happened to all those armoured cars of your dad's?"

"I still have them stored away. I'm dealing with them slowly, bringing them back to working order, but you know how it is, it takes time."

"I'll say. Now wouldn't that be one for the show if you could bring them all here. I bet you'd use up almost half the show by yourself."

"Yes, it would be something, but I hate to think what it would take to bringing them all over here. It would look like World War Two had started again."

"Ha, don't say that, it fills me with shivers… It's a shame but I reckon this'll be the last time I'll be coming here. I was made redundant a few weeks back. Unless I can find something pretty quick, I think I'll have to sell this thing to make ends meet. At best I'll have to park her up and let her grow old, there's no way I can afford to keep her going. I almost dropped out this year but as I had already paid for my stand, I thought I might as well use it."

"Where do you have to come from?" Robert asked.

"Worthing, not too far from your place really."

"No. And if you don't mind me asking, what did you do before you were laid off?"

"I worked on the railways as a trackman."

"Very interesting. How keen are you on war time vehicles et cetera?"

"Until this latest setback I used to spend all my spare time fiddling with this old girl, even my wife Sally joins in. She loves it." He looked

251

around the showground. "She should be back here soon, she went to powder her nose."

Robert looked around thinking.

"I've just had an idea which I think would solve both our problems. You have no job and a vehicle which you are afraid you may have to sell, while I have all my vehicles and no time to restore them. It would probably be a full time occupation, how would you feel about working for me as a vehicle restorer?"

"You are joking!"

"No, but you don't have to of course, I just thought it might work out to both our benefits."

"I can't believe it."

"Why don't you think it over, talk with your wife and give me a call sometime next week – here, take my card."

"Thank you very much, I'm sure Sally will be pleased... Funny how things work out, isn't it?"

* * *

Robert was surprised when his secretary informed him that Jack Briars was on the line. He had to think hard to connect the name with the man he had met at the show.

"Jack, so glad you called. So what is your decision?"

"I would love to take you up on your offer."

"Good. If we start with a month's trial period, see how it goes and take it from there. How does that sound?"

"Wonderful." They talked briefly about hours and pay before agreeing Jack could start the next Monday. They would meet at the hanger at nine. Robert gave directions before hanging up.

* * *

There was only one short road beyond the church before the scenery broke into a quilt of crops and grazing cattle. Robert Knight owned most of the land between the town and the river at the bottom of the hill, some two hundred acres split evenly between grazing and arable.

Jack stopped his car at the end of the paved road outside the hangar. He was early but Robert had said he could have a look round until he turned up himself.

Jack stepped up to the hanger door and slid it open just enough to permit access. It was dark inside. The sun, fighting a losing battle with the dirty windows, failed to illuminate the deeper recesses and the light from the doorway seemed to diminish quickly over the mass of grey. He shivered involuntarily from the sudden drop in temperature as he stepped inside.

Fortunately he had a torch in his pocket. Jack swung the beam of light around the hangar catching glimpses of several different vehicles. The beam made a set of dim concentric rings on the far wall as he passed it over the collection. Closer to, it made a small bright circular patch of yellow. The deep shadows of the hangar gave a ghost-like appearance to the vaguely discernible shapes, each one illuminated momentarily by the wandering torch beam. The light seemed to have a will of its own. Shapes flashed into sudden clear reality and faded again as his hand shook with nerves. Long-barrelled guns loomed at him and angled sheets of heavy metal were picked out in green and grey.

Jack's fascination led him to the back of the building. The Panzer brooded menacingly in the dark, the long gun pointing towards the corner of the building just above the door. Jack was overcome with awe. He made his way carefully towards the tank, excitement building in his chest.

Standing in front of the machine, Jack wondered at the almost perceptible weight as he played light slowly over the front armour. Gradually in the dimness, rivets, hatches and track links built up an impression of the heavy mass. It was big, seemingly a solid metal block able to withstand any force, the crushing power slightly tainted by rust and a thin layer of dirt. Slowly he walked round the narrow space desperately trying not to disturb the haunting dust as he moved.

Returning to the front, he pondered for a moment. Should he climb up and try to find a way in or should he wait for Robert Knight? He grabbed hold of the drive sprocket, placed his foot in the middle of the wheel and heaved himself up. It proved easier than he had thought it would. He stood in the shadows balancing precariously. He grasped the gun barrel, stepped onto the superstructure and then onto the turret.

He looked at the cupola's hatch and wondered if he could climb inside. The gap between the two halves of the hatch was hidden by a quarter inch wide strip of metal. There was no handle to pull. As he looked for a way into the machine he noticed none of the hatches had handles. He bent down to prize a hatch cover open with his fingers.

Suddenly the hangar door slid open making him jump. The beam of light illuminated the area, Jack looked round, startled. Robert's silhouette filled the gap in the doorway.

"Good morning. Why the hell are you looking around in the dark?"

said Robert. "You should have at least turned the lights on." He reached across to the wall and flicked a switch. Strip lights flickered round the building and burst into life. "The light switch is on the wall here, just inside the door, I suppose I should have told you on the phone." Robert pushed the door. "Might as well have the door open and let some warmth in. It will be a different matter in the winter, though I do have a small stove which works quite well."

Jack recovered from his shock and climbed down from the top of the tank.

"It's all right, I was finding my way round with the help of my torch. Lucky I thought of bringing it along."

"Yes. Well, you don't need it now but you'll need something of the sort when you climb inside the tank or one of the armoured cars. Most of the other vehicles have windows big enough to let light in. Actually I use a mechanic's lamp, the sort with a hook, when I work inside them.

"Supposing I take you round and tell you how my father came to buy these treasures and the films they were in? – Ask any questions you want. God, that doesn't half sound like I'm about to give a lecture or something."

Robert spent twenty minutes explaining a little about each item in the collection. He ended up by a British Humber armoured car.

"This is the one I'm working on at the moment, she's got a leaky water pump. You know, I would have had all this lot up and running years ago, but these old girls have a knack of making a job five times more difficult than it should be, that's why I need your help."

They set to work. The hours ticked by slowly. Eventually Robert tightened the last nut.

"Well I reckon that's that, and for once it was quite easy. I hope I haven't bored you too much with my chatter. I guess it's lunch time. – If you're happy to continue, I think we'll start on the 222 armoured car this afternoon. We'll clean her out first and then strip the engine down. I have been thinking about the Panzer IV but it's a pretty big job, that one."

"It sounds to me, Mr. Knight, like you have been avoiding it for some time. You know what they say, never put off till tomorrow what you can do today. Why don't we start on the Panzer now. Just think about the crowd it will pull."

"You sound like you have already made up your mind. You're right of course. I have put it off for far too long and I don't have an excuse anymore. All right, we'll start on the Panzer.

When they had finished eating, Robert picked up a spanner and led Jack to the Panzer IV. He fitted the spanner to a bolt head on the turret hatch and turned. Jack saw the hatch door spring free slightly. Robert opened the hatch and climbed in.

"Mind your head when you climb in. Mechanically she is in good running order, we just have to remove the protective coverings and take out the mothballs. But as you can see, the wiring is shot, so we will have to refit the whole system, right down to the last contact. It will be a long and tedious job but once it's done we should be able to start her up."

"Let's set to it then."

"Ha! I hope, you're this eager in a few week's time."

"I don't see why not, to me this is a dream come true.

"Good. I have a wiring plan so we can check up if anything goes wrong, I think the easiest way is to run the new wire alongside the old and then exchange the connections before pulling the old one out. If we do that systematically throughout, I can't see we will have many problems. I've got the new wire here."

"That's what I did with my 250."

The job was not as simple as Robert had made out. Much of the wiring ran under the turret floor so they first had to remove the floor to gain access. Then it became a matter of locating a cable end and following it through bulkheads and behind equipment, placing the new cable alongside until they found the other end. It was slow backbreaking work, done on hands and knees much of the time.

At four-thirty Robert called a halt.

"It's getting late, tea time I think." Robert looked at his watch. "This gives us enough time to clean up before heading home. – It makes a big change having somebody to help me. I thought about taking one of my men off a contract, but which one would I choose? And then there would be the problem of being a man short on that project and having to find someone new."

"I'm glad I have been of help to you, honestly I feel like a kid in a sweet factory."

"Really. Most people who find out about the collection come round because they think I'll let them drive something, or they just want to nick bits. It's nice to see someone who is genuinely interested. Do you think you could stick it a couple of years?"

"Definitely."

"Good. Come on, let's get cleaned up." After removing most of the dust and grime they left the building. Robert shut the door. "My wife, Dorothy, will be making tea, can I offer you a cup before you leave?"

"That's very kind of you, but Sally will be cooking for me, I'd better head home, but It's been a great day."

* * *

Several weeks passed and Robert was reassured to find that Jack continued to turn up. He decided to offer Jack a treat.

"I was thinking, I don't want to make this all work and no play, perhaps tomorrow I could show you some of the smaller items in the collection. Photographs, stills of film action shots, autographs, that sort of thing. Would you be interested to see them?"

"Sounds great, I look forward to it."

"Just come down to the house and I'll dig them out of the attic.

Next day, Robert led Jack into the living room, to a large settee by a low table. The table was stacked high with shoe boxes and ageing box files. "This is just some of the memorabilia Father collected over the years. There's a lot more upstairs, I don't even know what half of it is." Robert opened the first box. "This was my father's most prized possession," he said picking up a badge. It's his Royal Flying Corps wings. He received them in 1917. He flew several sorties until the end of war. Take a look." Robert offered the embroidered patch to Jack. "He used to tell the story about how he was given the wings, went out to celebrate and had to sew them on when he returned from the pub. Except, he was so over the top he stitched them on upside down. The following morning he had to unpick the stitching and do it again before the morning parade. He missed his breakfast as a result. He used to say he'd never had so much trouble with something so small before or since.

"And this is his R.F.C. tie. He wore one like this every day from 1918 onwards. You know, it was through membership of the RAF club that he got on so well later in life. That was how he made many of his contacts for the business, and how he got into film supply. From there he became a member of the Royal Antediluvian Order of Buffaloes, that's a stage or film workers club not related to acting."

"Here, this is his flying log, and a photograph of him with his aeroplane at Croydon in 1917. He used to say *'Never call it a plane, it's an aeroplane'*. Of course they were still quite novel then. They had only been invented for sixteen years when the First World War came to an end, not like now when one flies overhead every two minutes."

256

"What sort of plane, sorry, aeroplane was it?"

"Oh, a Sopwith Camel. He bought one when they became obsolete and were sold off by the Ministry in about 1925. There's a picture of him with an Auster Autocrat Aircraft somewhere, parked outside our offices." Robert started to rummage through the pieces of paper and photographs in one of the boxes. "I remember it quite well, I was about twenty five when he sold that one...

Oh this will interest you, it's a photo of Father with the Panzer IV at Gazala, just west of Tobruk. It was taken during the fifties when they were making one of the numerous films about Rommel and his Africa corps."

The two men worked their way slowly through the pile of memorabilia.

* * *

1996

Each year, Robert took one of his collection pieces to the military show, at first in Tenterden but later at The Whitbread Hop Farm in Beltring where four hundred acres of available land allowed for the show's expansion.

He always intended taking the Panzer but it never seemed to reach the point of being finished. Instead he settled for showing either the 222 armoured car, the Kubelwagen or either of the two half-tracks. The show had grown each year but Robert just didn't feel capable of taking more than one vehicle at a time and Jack had his own half-track to exhibit.

Recently there had been the *Back to the Beaches Show* in 1994 to celebrate the 50th anniversary of D-Day, and then there had been the *Victory Show* in 1995 to celebrate the 50th anniversary of the German defeat. Robert wished he had contributed more to both of them. He had only ever shown four of his twenty or so vehicles.

He made his decision as he and Jack finished the Panzer's last coat of paint and started her up. The next show would be different. The tank roared into life and with Jack to guide him, Robert pulled the old girl slowly out of her corner onto the track leading past the house.

"Jump on," he called. Jack climbed onto the superstructure and Robert revved the engine feeling the thrum of power. "Here, take this," Robert handed Jack a toy walkie-talkie, "then we can talk to each other as we go. I thought we'd need something like this since they took all the radio equipment out. Hang on." They rolled down the hill to the river. It was only a narrow bridge that crossed the water so Robert had to stop and turn round. They roared back up the hill but when they reached a vacant field Robert stopped.

"Open the gate, will you," he called.

Jack jumped down, opened the gate and Robert drove through. Once Jack was back on board, Robert drove round the field several times ploughing deep ruts and furrows in the soft ground. Both of them loved the game. Eventually Robert drove slowly back to the hangar and parked the tank back in its place.

As he secured the hanger Robert suddenly stopped. "Hang on Jack, there's still one thing we have to do. He pulled the original maintenance manual from the book shelf and placed it down the side of the driver's seat, in its original position. At last the Panzer's preservation work was complete. Robert wanted to celebrate.

"This year, I will show the Panzer IV at the *War and Peace Show*," he told Jack. He also decided that as the show lasted three days this time, he would camp on site. He hoped Dorothy wouldn't mind too much.

On the Wednesday before the show, Robert moved the tank to the show ground. The load was just narrow enough not to require police escort. When he arrived at the Hop Farm, he was escorted to his pre-booked pitch. He parked the transporter across the track and winched the tank into the parking place leaving enough room to one side for the transporter. He hoped to set up his camp behind the tank.

Robert made the second run the next day so as to be ready for Friday's launch. He parked the transporter, nose in, with the 222 armoured car and the Kubelwagen on the deck. There was just enough room to pitch his tent on the ground between the vehicles. He was looking forward to three days of rough living.

That evening he wandered the campsite admiring the various vehicles already in place, he didn't return to his tent until dark.

The following morning Robert rose early to queue at the wash facilities. There was only the one wash block and he knew it would be a long wait if he didn't arrive early. There were already three people waiting. He joined the line planning to bide his time in silence.

"Same old thing every year." The American accent jarred on Robert's early morning senses. "I bin comin' here for the past three years and it never gets better. You'd-a-thought they'd provide more facilities with so many people an' all."

Robert could not help but comment. He half turned to look at the malcontent. The man was dressed in combat trousers and a green shirt topped off with a cream Stetson.

"If you don't like it, why do you keep coming here?" Robert asked.

"Are you kiddin? I couldn't miss this show for the world."

"No, maybe not, but there are hotels around where you could have proper facilities."

"No way. The beer tent here is too darn good. Chuck Hesinger by the way." Chuck held out his hand to be shaken. Robert took it reluctantly.

"Robert Knight."

"Hi Rob, nice to meet you."

"No. My name is Robert. Rob is what villains do."

"Well sor-ree. I didn't mean to ruffle your feathers none. I should have remembered, you Brits are sensitive about those things," Robert winced at the term 'Brits'. Chuck continued, changing the subject. "You bring any equipment or are you just here to look?" The queue moved on.

"I brought a few items, German artefacts."

"I'll have to come over and see what you got, where you at?"

"I'm over that way somewhere," he replied with a wave of his hand.

"Hey, I know what you mean. It's kind-a-hard finding your way around to begin with. Don't worry, I'll find you."

I hope not, thought Robert, as the queue moved forward again.

"I brought with me a big-old, Second World War Dodge staff car," said Chuck. "You know, I spent the last three years makin' it look like new. And I brought a U.S. half-track."

The queue moved again and Robert finally had his shower. In spite of the running water and other noises he could still hear Chuck going on about his exhibits to anyone who would listen.

Back at his little camp, Robert quickly had breakfast and then left to investigate the rest of the show. Many stalls were not open to begin with but Robert walked round until he thought he had seen everything.

He moved to the main arena, selected a shady spot to sit, and watched the displays, *The Noon Day Gun*, then *Military Oddities* followed by the *Gathering Storm*. There were six events through the afternoon, Robert watched them all.

As the show progressed Robert realised he could run his vehicles in the arena just like anyone else. He headed towards the nearest official.

"I would like to show my Panzer IV in the Axis show tomorrow. How do I go about it?"

"Just bring it along and queue out there," said the official, pointing

259

through the arena entrance. "You need to be here about fifteen minutes before the event."

"Would there be anyone available to help me drive her over? I don't want to cause any accidents."

"If you call the Organisers ten minutes before you're ready to go, we'll see if we can find someone. It shouldn't be a problem. Look forward to seeing you tomorrow."

Robert bought a quick evening meal from one of the vendors before returning to his camp. He hadn't planned to leave again before retiring to bed, but found the continuous line of gawping people too irritating.

"Cooor look at that gun, Dad…"

"Of course the Tiger was the best World War Two tank…"

"The paint scheme's not authentic for a start…"

"Those machine guns look fake…"

Robert wandered round for an hour eventually ending up at the beer tent. He didn't mind having one drink before settling down to sleep. He placed his order, but as he paid, the American accent invaded his space.

"Hey, Rob… Robert I mean, where've you been, I've been looking for you all day. I still want to see your stuff."

Robert grimaced at the interruption.

"Hello Chuck, I've been roaming through the show, taking in the sights."

"I guessed that was what you were doing. Shame it's too dark out there now, I'll come by your place tomorrow morning before things get going, what's your plot number?"

Robert realised he would never be able to avoid the American all day every day. He gave in.

"All right," he tried to sound cheery. "I'm at A76. Come round tomorrow morning and I'll introduce you to my collection."

"Well thanks Rob-ert, I look forward to it. You have a goodnight, you hear."

"Yes, thank you Chuck. You too."

* * *

Chuck turned up at eight the next morning. Robert had just finished eating.

"Hey, Robert, good morning. You never said you had a Panzer, can I have a look-see?"

"Certainly. Give me a few minutes and I'll open her up for you."

Robert cleared away his breakfast, climbed onto the superstructure and opened the tank's hatches. "There you go. Just don't bang your head on anything, it's a little tight in places."

"You goin' to show me round? I ain't never been in one of these things before."

"If you like. It's probably better if I do, you'll be less likely to lose a part of your anatomy." Robert, standing on the glacis plate, held out a hand for Chuck. "Up you come then."

Chuck climbed into the driver's compartment. Robert eased himself into the radio operator's seat beside him. Without the radio equipment in place, there was a clear view between the positions. Robert explained the steering levers and the gears, taking Chuck through a full tour of driving a tank. They moved to the turret. Chuck tried each seat, turning handles and adjusting levers for half an hour. Eventually Robert left him to it.

Chuck emerged a while later with a broad grin on his face.

"This is by far the best bit of equipment I have seen in a long time. I'd like to take it back home, how much do you want for it?"

"She's not for sale, Chuck. Not for any price."

"Oh come on, Robert, every man has his price. I'll give you fifteen thou'."

"You don't have to believe me when I say she's not for sale but it would save a lot of aggravation if you did."

"Sixteen thou', pounds?"

"No, and I'll not even bother acknowledging your next offer."

"Too bad. Can you imagine what folks back home would have said if I had turned up with one of these?"

"I dread to think," said Robert. "However, I have an idea, by way of compensation for not selling her to you, if you're interested."

"I'm listening." Chuck sounded eager.

"I'm planning to show her in the main arena this afternoon, in the Axis show. Would you like to help guide me through the camp as I drive?"

"Sure, sounds like fun. What time?"

"The event starts at two-fifteen, we need to be there about a quarter of an hour before that. If you get here at one-forty-five, that will give us plenty of time."

"Sure thing. I'll be here, you can count on me."

"Thanks, in the meantime I had better get some fuel for her. I'll see you later."

The fuel tanker turned up just before midday.

261

"Hey, look at this. I've never supplied fuel to a German tank before."
The tanker driver mopped his brow. "Do you mind if I take a photo?"

"No, I don't mind. Should I take it for you, with you pumping the fuel?"

"Yes, that would be great. Imagine my wife's face when she sees it."

"Say cheese." Robert aimed, snapped the shutter and handed the disposable camera back.

"Brilliant, thanks a lot." The driver walked back to the lorry to start pumping. Robert crouched by the tank listening for the gurgle of fuel backing up the filler pipe. The delivery of four hundred litres took just over five minutes.

* * *

Chuck was true to his word. The tank purred into life and Robert handed Chuck the little walkie-talkie.

"We won't have to shout at each other with these."

The show started a few minutes late. The presenter gave a short account of each unit as they drove into the arena, and all the way around before parking up along the edges. When all the vehicles were in place, they were asked again to drive round one by one. As Robert took his turn, Chuck operated the turret and elevated the gun to add extra effect. The fact there was no way to fire a round didn't matter.

Eventually Robert was directed out of the arena. The audience applauded loudly as they drove away. An elderly man struggled to his feet and followed the tank.

At the campsite, Chuck directed Robert back into the parking place beside his transporter. As Robert cut the engine the old man limped up and stopped. Chuck turned to him.

"Hi there. If you're going to ask how much he wants for the tank, don't bother. I already asked and it's not for sale."

"No, that is not why I am here." The man replied, his German accent was very pronounced. "I am wanting to see a Panzer IV again. I am hoping I might be permit to see inside."

"I don't know Buddy, I ain't the owner. You'll have to wait for Mr. Knight, he's inside at the moment but he won't be long."

Robert stuck his head out the driver's hatch.

"Did I hear my name mentioned?"

"Sure did, Robert. This guy wants to look inside your tank."

Robert looked at the German, taking in the stick and his crooked stance.

"Are you sure you can manage all right climbing up here."

"Yes, I can do this."

"Well then, come up and I'll tell you all about my tank. Chuck, would you give him a hand, please." Robert climbed out and stood ready to assist while Chuck stood by on the ground.

The old man leaned his stick against the tank's bow plate chuckling to himself.

"That is quite funny. I think it is more right to say I will tell you, about your tank. My name is Jürgen Klimt, I am driver of a Panzer IV during 1940 and 1941, then I am Commander in 1941 until 1943." Jürgen moved round to the tank's left-hand side, lowered the steps and climbed up. "At the arena they said this was a Panzer IV *Ausführung* D, but the armour at the front is a little thicker which means this is a Panzer IV *Ausführung* E."

"Well spotted" said Robert, "but this is definitely a IV D, I looked up the hull number in the records."

"What is the hull number, I would be interested to know this." Jürgen prepared to climb inside the driver's compartment.

"Eight-zero-five-three-six. It's painted inside the back of the turret."

"No, that can not be correct." Jürgen stopped in his tracks. "The number must have been changed, perhaps when you are restoring."

"All I did was repaint the number already there."

"I must see it. If this is true, this is my tank, the one I am driving in 1940 and my first Command in 1941." Jürgen suddenly seemed to exude enthusiasm.

Robert moved to the turret and helped the old man inside. Jürgen inspected the number. "This is not possible!" Tracing his finger over the digits, a faint memory of a similar action long ago caught him by surprise. "*Unmöglich!*" He looked round the rest of the turret. "I would like to see the driver's position now please."

"Of course," Robert helped Jürgen round to the front.

The German climbed down and sat in the refurbished seat. Everything seemed so familiar. He ran his finger over the new paintwork, there were grooves in the surface. Could they be those he had made all those years ago in Russia? He felt down the side of the seat where the maintenance instruction book had always been kept. There was something there, he pulled it out. The book looked the same but older. He opened the front cover. The words flashed at him. *Jürgen Klimt, Dienstag 23 April 1940.* That had been the day he had first inserted the key in the ignition. This

263

was his book! He had been the first to drive this tank in battle.

There were other names under his. *Hubert Baumann, 1941* and *Nicholaus von Rosen, 1944.* Jürgen sat quite still for a minute, memories flooding through his mind. The book clinched it, this was his tank.

"Are you all right in there?" Robert sounded concerned, he knew it would be difficult to pull the German out if he was too tired to manage by himself and Chuck had left to see to his own collection.

"I apologise, I am very well, thank you. I am just thinking so many situations I have in this tank. Look, this is my name." Jürgen held up the open manual through the hatch for Robert to see. "I am not thinking ever to see this Panzer again when I am sent to Tunisia in 1942. There I am captured by Americans and am prisoner of war until 1945."

"That's you is it? I always wondered about the people that those names belonged to, now I have met one at last."

Jürgen replaced the book and climbed from the tank. "This is truly... *wunderbar.*"

The two men settled down in Robert's camp. Jürgen told Robert about his life in the Second World War and Robert recounted how the tank had come to be in his possession. They talked through the evening and into the night, gradually building the tank's history between them.

* * *

Bletchington 2003

Every year Robert took vehicles to the show, and always included the Panzer IV, it was after all the biggest crowd puller. Often he had neighbouring stands with Jack and Sally with Jack's half-track parked next to Robert's own vehicles. There had also been a full diary of work changing the look of vehicles with a new coat of paint and a new number, or fixing parts that had broken from natural usage.

The Panzer had been decorated in several different paint schemes representing tanks from all over the German theatre of war.

Robert had made numerous acquaintances at the show and it had become a major event for meeting friends. But now at seventy-six it was becoming tiring. It was too much effort for what was becoming the same old same old. As Robert and Jack worked together one autumn afternoon on yet another repair job, Robert stopped to have a break.

"Look Jack, I don't know what you'll think about this but I've a suggestion."

"Oh yes, what's that."

"Well, I'm getting too old to do all the shows and stuff on my own. I was thinking we should join forces and take our pieces to the show together next year. We could take say the Panzer and an armoured car, amongst other things, including your 150 if you want, and you could drive them for me. What do you think?"

Jack hardly had to think.

"Yes, why not?"

"They're not easy. I know you have moved things around and parked them but that's not like real driving. It's quite hard work doing it properly, especially the Panzer, she's really physically demanding. But if you are willing to learn the intricacies, I can teach you. It would be an enormous bit of fun during the show. What do you think?"

"I'd love to."

"Good, that's settled then, we can start next week if it's not too cold and wet."

"I look forward to it."

After that, Jack took the controls of the tank every day for an hour or so. He had driven a JCB for the railways and quickly picked up the technique of driving the Panzer. His biggest problem was remembering to double declutch the six speed gearbox during each gear change, that and remembering what he had learned the previous day.

As time passed, Jack became more confident, he seemed to have the knack and was competent by early spring. The days warmed, the trees burst into leaf and flowers bloomed. Summer arrived and instruction was reduced to once a week as maintenance took precedence. Robert had put every conceivable procedure in front of Jack and Jack had accomplished them all with ease, even loading and unloading the big M26 Dragon Wagon transporter. One hot day in July, Robert stopped Jack's practice.

"Well, you look ready for the show next week, how do you feel?"

I'm as ready as I'll ever be."

"I reckon you are." They replaced the vehicles in the hangar.

The following Sunday they strapped the Kubelwagen crossways on the front of the trailer with the Panzer loaded behind. This time the extra wide load did require a police escort. Robert drove the M26 to The Hop Farm while Jack drove behind with the Humber armoured car. Robert had hurriedly provided an MOT, insurance and tax for the occasion. On their arrival, even though they were regulars, they were shown how to find their designated static location. A small Landrover with *The Hop*

Farm written along the sides, guided them through the maze of other exhibitors. Eventually Robert pulled the laden transporter into a large area located about as far away from the entrance as was possible.

They set about arranging the vehicles on the plot. As the work progressed a small crowd of spectators gathered round, all of them fellow owners. A man in his sixties walked up.

"Hello Robert." His Texan accent was immediately recognisable in the international throng. "I thought you weren't coming back here any more."

"Hello, Chuck. I wasn't, but I've persuaded young Jack here to help me out at the show, as well as at the farm. He's been driving the Panzer since the beginning of the year."

Jack and Chuck had met before. They shook hands in greeting. Robert chatted on.

"With a bit of luck we should be able to keep coming for another few years now… So what have you brought this year, Chuck?"

"Oh just a couple of pieces to run around the Main Arena."

As Robert and Chuck chatted, Jack reversed the Panzer into the plot. Once parked, he let the engine idle for a few minutes before shutting down for the day. He wouldn't have to drive the tank again until the show opened when he would perform his first demonstration. He breathed a sigh of relief. It would be a cinch.

He and Robert joined Chuck and discussed the coming show. It was a while before Dorothy arrived to take Robert home. They dropped Jack off at his door.

The next day they loaded a twelve tonne low-loader with Jack's half-track. On the Tuesday Robert again drove the lorry while Jack drove the 222 armoured car.

On Wednesday, the first day of the show, Jack and Sally arrived a little before Robert in his Bentley. There were twice as many people milling around and most of the camping places were full.

The Panzer's only event that day, was *Tanks at Play* at three o'clock so Jack was free to see the other exhibitors. He and Sally wandered round the various tents and stands. At lunch time they returned to the pitch and took advantage of an awning Robert had erected. It was a little more tolerable in the shade, but not much.

As Jack sat sipping a cool lemonade, trying to relax before his run, he looked at the schedule of events he was participating in. Apart from today's one event, he had *Tanks, Tanks, Tanks* tomorrow and on Friday he had two events, *Gathering of the Storm* at 11.00 a.m., and *The Axis Display* at 14.45, both of which were specifically for German World War Two vehicles. These were both repeated on Saturday and Sunday with slight time changes.

When the time came to move, Jack, directed by the show officials, drove the Panzer to the arena, with Sally as Commander in the cupola. Once in place he waited for his turn to put the vehicle through its paces. Robert drove the Kubelwagen to the same event. After forty minutes, they returned to their pitch and parked up for the night. Jack was feeling hugely buoyed up after his experience.

Later, when the show drew to a close, Jack and Sally drove home. Robert, like many exhibitors, stayed in a small tent at the side of his plot.

As the days passed Jack became more confident in showing the Panzer off. He was surprised when he found groups of people following the tank between the camp and the arena. Some even called him, begging for a ride. He found it exhilarating to have all that attention. He even drove his own half-track to one event *The Tracked Finale* on the Friday and had a good reception from the spectators.

While the crowds on the first three days had been good, they were nothing compared with those at the week end. Some parts of the grounds were so thick with people, it was almost impossible to move, let alone drive a tank through. During both afternoons he needed official escorts to clear a path through the mass. All the events were well attended and at the end, on Sunday evening Jack was completely overwhelmed. He was sorry it was all over.

The throng dispersed Robert and Jack reloaded the M26 ready to depart. The police escort was waiting for them at the gate as Robert pulled onto the road. Jack trailed behind, already thinking about next year's show.

They would collect the other vehicles the next day.

19

Theft

Jack sat in a quiet corner of the *Dun Cow*, nursing the remains of his cider as though it were pure gold. He liked to have just one drink, alone, before going home to watch telly, it was a sort of nightly ritual.

Slowly the bar door opened, a middle aged man stepped into the room. He took a keen look around before stepping up to the bar. In those brief moments he didn't acknowledge Jack though Oliver had kept in touch since school.

Jack on the other hand, guessed Oliver would be a problem for his planned departure, now due in just a few minutes. He gulped his drink and stood, hoping to exit the pub before Oliver had paid. He was too slow and too deeply wedged in his alcove. Oliver picked up his drink and change from the bar, and made straight for Jack.

The two men were of an similar age, Jack thin and tall while Oliver was now thicker set, a heavy drinker.

"Good evening Jack, I thought I might find you here at this time of the night."

"Hello. It's been a while, Oliver." Jack's greeting was hesitant, like passing a ghost on a dark night.

"Have you got a minute? It's just that I want to run something by you."

"I'm listening." Jack mumbled reluctantly, keeping low over his glass as he settled back into his place.

Oliver's face split with a wide grin, he slipped into the seat next to Jack blocking him in, and leaned over conspiratorially. Jack could feel Oliver's insincere charm almost dripping onto the table. Oliver's voice was a harsh whisper only just audible over the hum of the other patrons.

"You know, Jack, how you're always short of a ready bob or two."

Jack nodded. "It's just the way life is. I suppose I was never destined to be wealthy."

"Well I reckon I found a way to help you out, both of us actually. A few months ago I started working part time at BankBase Securities."

Jack looked puzzled. Oliver had been made redundant but with a huge pay off and pension, there was no way he could possibly need to work again so soon. A crease of fear winced across Jack's face as he realised this would probably be another ridiculous, crooked brainchild. They had been a feature of Oliver's school life when Jack had been the one who received the ensuing punishment for Oliver's frequent misdemeanours.

An incident one weekend, came to Jack's mind, when Oliver, then aged thirteen, had set the school science block on fire. Jack however, two years Oliver's junior, had been the one who spent the night in a police cell, his parents had been alerted and called to fetch him the next morning. He had been suspended from classes for a month while Oliver had got away with it.

"It's a cash recycling centre," said Oliver. "The banks and shops send us money, mixed up quantities of notes and coins. We sort it into denominations, count it and send it back, millions of it. I reckon we could make ourselves quite wealthy if you're interested."

Jack groaned. His first hunch had been right. This would be a stupid plan which would just end in trouble, and about fifteen years in prison. On the other hand, Jack didn't want to upset Oliver who had a violent streak.

"Oliver, I would jump at the idea but it doesn't sound legal to me."

"Well, strictly speaking of course it isn't, but they'll never notice a few notes go missing, and we'll be quids in."

"How much do you think you can get?" Jack's tone was dull, he hated the idea of stealing though he was interested to a point in having more money.

"Oh, about twenty million…"

"Twenty million!" Jack leaped from his seat drawing glances from the other customers. "You just said a few notes, twenty million isn't a few notes. Now let me out."

"Shush, do you want everyone to hear? Lower your voice, you idiot, and sit down."

Jack settled back into his place, his stomach churning with shock.

"Are you mad? Twenty million's a bloody truck load, not a few notes. I'll have nothing to do with it." Jack's whisper could be heard across the room. But few people seemed to take notice now his shouting had stopped.

"Too late, I've told you now. You're in. – Look Jack, no hard feelings. Come round tomorrow at about seven and I'll tell you my plan.

Mary plays badminton until 9.30 so we can talk as loud as we want without anybody listening." Oliver stood up, acknowledged Jack's grunt and walked to the bar for a refill. Jack quickly left the pub with Oliver's eyes on his back.

The barman looked at Oliver suspiciously.

"What was all the shouting about then?"

"Oh, Jack's going to help me distribute a few Neighbourhood Watch leaflets but he didn't like the idea of doing twenty million. A good joke though, it's really only two thousand."

"Ha, nice one. With two million you could post one through every door on the British Isles." The barman passed the refilled glass towards Oliver and collected his cash off the bar. "I wouldn't have taken you for a Neighbourhood Watch man, Oliver, more the opposite really."

"Thanks a lot!"

* * *

The next evening Jack didn't go to the pub. He wandered the promenade watching the seagulls swoop over the surf and thought about Oliver's proposal. Ten mill each. How far could ten million pounds in sterling take you. Cash that could be spent without trace. What would he do with it? He only wanted a decent place to live.

But the whole idea was impossible. There would be cameras, infrared sensors, and all kinds of security. It was stupid, but then, the possibility of taking a beating, as had happened in school when he had refused Oliver's ideas, also crossed his mind.

It was the fear of being left in the gutter somewhere, that eventually made Jack walk to Olive's house. It was a huge place. What was Oliver thinking of putting this kind of luxury at stake.

Jack knew that Oliver had not had a bad life. He had worked his way up through the Bank becoming one of London's West End Branch Managers, After five years at the top, he had been made redundant at fifty but with a huge pay off and pension. Now at fifty-four, he had taken a low paying job at a cash centre, but why? Jack didn't understand. Was it purely for the chance to case the place? Doubtless the company had taken him on instantly, with his career background he would have seemed perfect.

With this in mind Jack walked up the drive and stopped at the plastic double glazed front door. It looked common for an entrance to such a nice house. Why hadn't Oliver had a proper handmade oak door fitted? Something classy, but that was Oliver through and through. He would

270

buy something expensive and ruin it with cheap fittings. It was ten minutes to eight, Jack knocked, the sound echoed weakly inside.

"Jack, I was beginning to think you weren't coming." Oliver smiled pleased that Jack's desire had bettered him. It seemed the cat was in the bag. "Come in, come in, we can have a couple of beers and talk about the job."

"Sorry I'm late, I was in two minds about coming. Jack stammered.

"You're not late."

"I was thinking about the trouble we'd be in if we're caught."

"We won't be caught. Here, hang your coat up and we can go in and have a beer."

The two men were soon seated in the comfortable living room. Oliver placed an atlas on a shelf. "I was just looking to see where I'd settle when we're done. I'm thinking the Far East – Thailand, with all those pretty girls you hear about."

"You weren't thinking of taking Mary with you then?"

"No way, she uses money as though I am already a millionaire. I hate to think what she'd be like if I really was that wealthy."

Jack looked around the spacious room. For all that the house was a status symbol, the decorations were rubbish. Stuff even Jack wouldn't have had in his small terrace house "I think if we do make a few million, I'd head for South America. Sally has always said she fancied Peru, and she speaks a little Spanish.

"Why not? You'd pick the language up quick enough. Here, have a beer?"

"Thanks. So what's your plan?"

"A ram raid." Oliver pulled the ring on another can.

"What? You want to grab a hole-in-the-wall, or do you aim to ram a security truck?"

"No, it's better than that, we're going to ram the vault at work." Oliver briefly outlined his plan for breaking into the building. "The money moves in and out of the building via those reinforced security vans. The indoor working area is all at truck level so they just have to open the back and run the pallets in and out the vans."

"Pallets! The cash comes on pallets!"

"Well, it comes in security cages on pallets actually. We don't work with small amounts. A cage of Tens holds one million pounds, if it's Twenties then you get three and a half million. They usually stack two cages together to save space. They never mix denominations going out

271

but anything may come in, in any mix of denominations. We have to take the cash after it's been sorted, but before it goes out."

"Why does it have to be sorted first?"

"If we take unsorted money we'd have to separate it ourselves. There will be coins mixed in with the notes, ripped notes, unreadable notes that have gone through the washing machine, and counterfeits. And it'll be much too bulky because it gets thrown in the bags like so much rubbish. Much better to have it sorted and take it when it's nice and neat.

"The biggest amounts come in during the evening and night. It gets sorted the next day and goes out the following night. However, nothing goes in or out between about 11 o'clock, Friday night and two or three, Monday morning and security gets transferred directly to the police via a telephone line.

"Now, if any of the hundred and sixty infrared motion detectors is disrupted the alarm goes off and the police only have to come round the corner, about five hundred yards. The wonderful thing is these security points are all on doors and work points. The vault is closed and airtight most of the time and at night the air is sucked out so anyone hiding in there would die. There's no way anyone could hide inside and then knock the place off. You have to come from outside, through the wall at the side of the vault."

"You mean you won't trip an alarm if you don't use the doors or walk around inside?"

"Right. The infrared sensor will be set off when we start moving cages around but hopefully that will mean we are almost ready to leave. Now we'll need a substantial vehicle to break through, and because the floor level inside is about three feet high we need a vehicle that can climb walls, to do the breaching. Once there's a hole, we can reverse a ten tonner up, trolley what we want on board, and drive off. If we can take eight cages of Twenties, that's four double pallet loads, we get well over our twenty million. We should be able to do it in the five minutes between the alarm going off and the police turning up."

"It sounds good, but I can see a huge problem. How are we going to find a vehicle to climb three foot of wall and still knock a big enough hole in it?"

"That's where you come in. I figure the only thing capable of doing it would be one of Knight's tanks."

"You're joking. Robert Knight? He'd never do it."

"You're wrong there, I don't want him, I want the Panzer. I know it

272

works and that you can drive it 'cause I saw you at the show in Beltring. It'll be a piece of cake."

"Yes, may be, but I can't abuse his trust.

"Look Jack, you can either go along with me nice and easy or I'll bloody have you and give you something you'll never forget."

"All right, all right," Jack's mouth was suddenly dry. He went to take another drink but his can was empty.

"You want another?" said Oliver. "I could do with one, myself. All this talking is making my throat dry."

"I suppose, if you've got one."

"No problem." Oliver went to the kitchen to retrieve another couple of cans. Jack thought about leaving quickly but decided he would never make it.

Oliver returned. "There, that should keep us going a little longer." He passed one to Jack.

Jack pulled the ring and took a deep draught to give himself time to think. "So what's your plan?"

"The way I see it, we strike during a weekend. I thought the best time would be to go in on the penultimate weekend before Christmas on Saturday December 17th. Everyone'll be going to the cash points so they can have fun at parties and buy presents. The company will be collecting cash ready for the ATMs. So there'll be a greater chance of getting Twenties and maybe some Fifties. If we get three cages of Fifties we won't need any more."

"Maybe, but they are easier to trace. Anyone spending large quantities of Fifties will automatically get the shop assistant's attention and raise suspicion."

"I'm afraid it'll be pot luck as to what we get, but we'll have a better chance of a good haul on the seventeenth than any other day. It gives us a few months to find a lorry, and to plot our escape. We'll have to scarper as quick as possible, get to the Continent and head for Spain or Portugal for our first stop. Then Morocco, and the world's our oyster."

"It all sounds fine but we still have a small problem of how we get the tank. You don't just walk up to a Panzer and drive it off. You need people to start them. Two to crank the starter and the driver to engage the engine." Jack hoped that Oliver was not acquainted with the alterations that had been made. "So who else are you going to ask to join us?"

"Nobody you idiot. I've seen you start it and it doesn't need a second person. Don't you try and worm out of this, you're in for the ride now."

Jack was crushed, he had used his final opt out card. He reached for his drink but Oliver's heavy hand grabbed his wrist.

"And don't you go sneaking to the police either. I'll be watching you." Oliver released him. Jack picked up his drink and emptied the can for his nerves.

"All right... but we still have to work out how we're actually going to take the Panzer without Robert knowing."

"You work for Knight and you have access any time you want?"

"Yes, but Robert is bound to smell a rat."

"Of course he won't, he's just a doddery old man. Go about your business as though nothing has changed and he'll never guess. Besides, it won't matter after we've done the job. – You, Jack, have two tasks to complete before the day. Make sure the Panzer's full of fuel and make sure it's at the front of that hangar on the day in question. In the meantime, I'll find us a good ten tonner and form a get-away plan."

Jack thought for several minutes. He could see a few problems with grabbing the tank, but it was probably better not to mention them just now. With a bit of luck, one of them would prove to be insurmountable and the job would collapse altogether.

"And if any unforeseen problems crop up, let me know so I can deal with them. I don't want any surprises putting a block on the job," said Oliver, as if he had read Jack's mind.

"And you think we can take twenty million?" To Jack, the money was the only plus side and it was a very small plus compared with the minus.

"I think that's the minimum we will take. We should be able to double it if we play the game right. In fact, I think it'll be a cinch."

"OK, but if it proves too difficult, we call it off, right?"

"I don't reckon I can do it without you, mate."

* * *

On Thursday, December 15th, Jack and Oliver took leave from work. Oliver hired a white transit, a trailer and a mini-digger from a commercial hire company in Worthing. Jack drove to Oliver's garage where they sprayed the van to look like a Transco Emergency Gas Service vehicle. The waterbased paint wouldn't last very long in the rain but the weather was supposed to be good for the next few days.

Early on the sixteenth they drove to Bletchington, to the far end of the road away from BankBase Securities. They excavated a ditch three feet wide and five feet deep across the junction. At the end of the day they covered their work with thick steel sheets which Oliver had taken from a

274

railway supply yard. With a cordon of red and white striped construction fencing and a set of roadworks lights to control traffic, the hole would create little suspicion over the weekend.

They drove back to Oliver's garage and hosed the paint and mud from the van and digger. By 6 p.m. the equipment had been returned to the hire company, their escape plan was set. There was twenty-four hours to go.

On Saturday Jack sat at home fretting, irritating his wife. She in turn irritated him by repeatedly asking what was wrong and if there was anything she could do. Finally she gave up. He had been like this for months but today was by far the worst she had seen him. She hoped he would pull through eventually.

Early that afternoon Jack left the house and walked along the seafront. At five he entered the *Dun Cow* and ordered his usual drink. At quarter past he had a second followed by a third a while later. It was nearly six when Oliver came in and found him.

"What the hell are you doing drinking now, you idiot." Oliver hissed. "The last thing we need is you being stopped on the road for being under the influence. How many have you had anyway?"

"This is my fourth."

"Get out and sober yourself up." If you don't get it right tonight, you won't bloody see Christmas. Do you understand?"

Jack left and headed home, unaware that Oliver was following him. He didn't eat the meal Sally had cooked for him and during the evening he sat brooding. Sally watched him but didn't try to make him talk. At eleven-thirty Jack got up to leave.

"I'm going for a walk, I'll be back later, don't wait up."

"I wish you'd tell me what is troubling you, I can't help if you don't tell me what's wrong." Sally burst into tears but Jack didn't stop. In his car he slowly made his way to Bletchington, parking at the edge of town a short way from the lane to Froghole farm. He walked along the lane to the hangar, slid the door open and stepped inside closing it behind him.

It was dark inside but he didn't turn on the light. He flicked the switch on his torch and followed the tiny glow to the workbench. He picked up a cloth and carefully cleaned the Panzer's tiny windows, then he raised the end flaps on the mud guards. The work was finished within minutes. He sat on the floor behind the tank and waited while the seconds ticked by one by one. Slowly, dread built up inside him.

Eventually the door rattled open and a dark shadow slipped in. Jack leapt to his feet.

"Who's that?"

"Who do you think it is? The three Wise Men?" The sound of Oliver's voice was not what Jack had wanted to hear. For a moment he had hoped it was the police, or Robert come to check on a noise he'd heard. At least that way he would have had a way out of this mess. He was too afraid of Oliver to actually call for help himself.

"I just came to make sure you're all right."

"I'm all done except starting her up." Jack's voice shook.

"Good, I'll stay with you until it's time to leave."

This was exactly what Jack didn't want.

At 1.15 a.m. Jack climbed into the driver's seat again. The Panzer purred into life, Oliver opened the door. Jack eased the tank out of its place and accelerated down the track away from the town. Oliver stayed to close the hangar, he donned a kitted mask before making his own way to BankBase in the stolen lorry.

Jack made good time along the farm trail. Apart from the tank tracks thrashing at the winter hedge rows, there was nothing much to indicate anything out of the ordinary was happening. The tank's hooded lights provided just enough visibility to see by. He turned his charge onto the single width Cornfield Lane heading back towards Bletchington. Jack was worried. The metal tracks made a lot more noise on the paved road, but there was unlikely to be any traffic at this time of night. He had chosen this route because it was isolated and safer than going through the middle of town, where he would probably have met up with a squad car on patrol.

Just before the end of the lane Jack stopped and looked at his watch. He didn't want to arrive too early. He turned into the ditch and waited deep in the shadows of the overhanging trees. Filled with fear and anticipation, he felt as though he were setting a trap ready to spring on some passer-by. This must be how it had felt during the war, waiting for the call to attack. Fear and anxiety.

After ten minutes he moved on. At the end of the lane he turned onto the Old Pulborough Road and accelerated. Entering Bletchington he turned to pass over the excavations they had dug on Friday. He arrived outside the security company moments before Oliver.

Oliver parked his lorry and walked across the road to the security fence and indicated the place Jack was to go in. Jack swung the tank across the road and rammed the fence, flattening the railings. He didn't stop, but continued accelerating the extra few yards until he was brought to an abrupt halt by the building's thick walls. The L43 gun barrel breached the wall crushing the muzzle brake in the process.

Bricks fell on the front of the tank. Jack reversed away letting more bricks fall to the ground as the outer wall gave way. The pile of rubble would raise the front of the tank enough to climb the wall.

Jack rammed the wall for the second time and had the satisfaction of seeing a large hole as he reversed away again.

Oliver climbed up into the opening and started clearing the fallen debris. Every brick on the ground would help the tank climb. Jack made his third run at the wall causing a dent in the inner wall, but no bricks fell.

As the tank pulled away, Oliver started levering at the bricks with a crowbar until Jack started his next approach. This time a substantial quantity of wall fell leaving a large hole high up. The streetlights illuminated metal cages showing through the breach.

Oliver hacked at the wall with the crowbar until gradually he was able to open it up. It took longer than he had wanted but at last he would be able to walk through into the vault.

They had no time to waste. Jack drove the tank back to the middle of the road effectively blocking both lanes. He cut the engine, pocketed the key and climbed out.

Oliver slowly reversed the lorry over the flattened railings until he was within a few feet of the damaged wall. Jack lowered the loading ramp to cover the gap.

"Start with the ones in yellow or pink bags then take blue if we still have time, but don't waste time shifting cages just to get better ones at the back. We've got to be away from here as quick as possible."

Oliver pulled a pair of cages on a pump-trolley, into the waiting vehicle. He turned it round and dropped the load, then removed the trolley and went for a second pallet. Jack followed suit selecting the next cages in line. It was surprising just how heavy money could be.

It took just under a minute to move each pallet load. They wouldn't manage more than four pairs of cages before their time was up, but it would still be a good haul. Split between them, they would be able to retire to any place they wanted.

"Four minutes," said Oliver. "Make that your last one then stow the ramp. I'm going to jump in the cab so I'm ready to go when you climb in." Oliver dropped his pallet off the trolley-Jack and climbed down from the trailer. Jack pulled hard to drag his last pallet over the ramp. He didn't bother removing the trolley.

Jumping down, Jack lifted the tailgate into place until the latch clicked down. The lorry's engine started. Jack raised the gate on the hydraulics, locking it in place. Though the lights were off the lorry started to move.

Terrified that Oliver would leave without him, Jack dashed to the front and climbed to the cab.

He almost lost his hold as Oliver put his foot on the accelerator. Jack managed to pull himself into the seat as Oliver made the sharp turn onto the road, accelerating away from the crime scene.

"Steady on there Oliver, you nearly threw me off."

"Sorry mate, got to move quick. The cops will be on their way by now."

They had just four hundred metres to go before stopping to uncover the trench they had dug. Now the effort of digging the hole would pay off itself. The lorry rolled over the sheet metal covers and stopped. The two men quickly dropped from the cab and using improvised hooks, dragged the sheet metal away from the trench.

Oliver suddenly noticed flashing blue lights appear at the other end of the road behind the Panzer. He quickly ran to the cab and drove on.

20

Crime Scene

Police cars screeched to a halt. Sgt. Rawlins rubbed his eyes momentarily trying to remove the hallucination blocking the road. He had come to a stop just inches away from the heavy armour.

The two following squad cars slewed across the road behind him looking as though they had been thrown like dice.

Sgt. Rawlins stared through the windows in astonishment.

"Jesus Christ, what the hell's that doing here?"

His partner gawped. They didn't see the lorry departing at the other end of the road a quarter of a mile away.

Sgt. Rawlins stepped from the car. He decided there was no need to set a cordon yet, the three cars were sufficient. He took his hat and high visibility jacket from the back seat and walked along the road past the tank towards the security company.

The site at BankBase Securities was just as astonishing. The perimeter fence had been flattened for twenty feet along its length. Beyond that, there was a yawning eight foot hole in the building's wall.

Rawlins put on his hat and slowly pulled the jacket over his uniform. The other five officers joined him one by one, each in his own private world of awe.

"Come on you lot, let's get moving. We're here to catch the criminals, not watch them get away. One of you get back to the cars and stop the public coming through."

Suddenly there was a crash. The grouped officers turned towards the sound. Two police cars had stopped at the other end of the road, their blue lights flashing like Christmas trees.

"Go and make sure they're OK," Rawlins instructed.

PC Aimes, trotted towards the accident. As he approached the scene he called to the officers gaping at their car.

"What happened to you?"

"There's a bloody trench here!"

Aimes peered at the darkened scene, the flashing blue lights didn't help, but he could see the lead car was nose down as though it was sinking into the ground.

"Is anyone hurt?"

"No, I'm fine. Mick, you OK?"

"I bruised my arm on the door but otherwise I'm good."

The two officers from the second car came to take a look.

"Looks like you need another eye test," one jested. "You can teach bats to drive better than that."

Aimes butted in.

"All right, never mind the jokes. Rawlins will want a cordon across this end of the street. No one's to pass for any reason until the Inspector's say so, except forensics of course, though I don't see how they'll get their van past this. Two of you come up and help us at BankBase. It's a right mess." He walked back towards the security company.

At the crime scene, yellow and black striped ribbons were being used to cordon off the area. Aimes found Rawlins and reported.

"Thanks Mark," said Rawlins. "The car's a right off?"

"Definitely."

"Oh well, it's not the first, and it won't be the last. Tell me what you make of that." Rawlins thumbed over his shoulder at the tank.

"You should get Robert Knight over here. It may be one of his. He lives over Forest Road way. If it is his, I'd say it makes him the prime suspect."

"Do you know him?"

"We've talked tanks a couple of times. He's got quite a collection, you know."

"Take your partner and bring Knight here. If this is his work, we don't want him leaving for anywhere exotic. Any other suggestions?"

"Not at the moment."

"Carry on then."

Inspector Abbott drew up and parked in his car on the double yellow line. He ducked under the cordon and grunted an acknowledgement to the Bobby on duty. He passed the tank, not quite believing that he saw a real Panzer IV with German markings, he rubbed his eyes briefly before taking a second look.

"Good morning, Inspector. This is another fine mess you've got to sort out." Rawlins' greeting was, for Abbott's taste, much too cheery so early in the morning.

"All right, Oliver bloody Hardy, good morning to you too. Tell me, is

280

that thing back there real, or am I still under the influence?" Abbott's voice held an edge of sarcasm as though he expected the whole crime to have been solved by now. In fact it was just irritation at being hauled out of bed at two in the morning.

"It's real, Sir."

"All right, I believe you. So, what's the situation?"

Rawlins put him in the picture including the incident with the excavation at the other end of the road.

"Would you say it was a professional job?"

"I don't know, Sir. However, I would say it's probably an inside job and very well planned."

"What evidence have we got so far?"

"The tank should give some fingerprint indication of who was driving it. There are tyre tracks on the grass between the pavement and the fence but they superimpose the tank's tracks which are much more prominent. I don't know if forensics will be able to get anything definite, the grass is quite long and the ground has been churned up quite badly by the tank."

"Yes tracks can do that, what else."

"There are footprints from at least two different types of shoe. There's the trench which was dug on Friday, apparently by Transco staff, I saw the van when the work was being done. We haven't had Transco confirm that they are responsible yet. Other than that, there's not a lot here except a pile of rubble."

"OK. What was your response time when the alarm went off?"

"Five, six minutes. No more, though we did lose time when we all nearly piled into that thing." Rawlins pointed aimlessly in the Panzer's direction. "It was a bit of a surprise, Sir, took me a moment to recover."

"Yes. I bet it did, just like they had a surprise down the other end of the road. I'm going down and have a look. Let me know as soon as forensics arrive." Abbott took his time walking the distance. He stopped in front of the patrol car. The grill and headlights were pressed firmly into the edge of the trench, glass was scattered across the road. The front wheels hung in mid air over the five foot drop. The wings and bonnet were crumpled with the front of the wheel arches pressing against the tyres.

"So what happened here?" He called to the nearest officer.

"Not a lot, Sir. Someone pulled the metal sheets away from the excavation leaving the roadworks wide open. The covers were dumped on the road by the hole. Bloody stupid thing to do, anyone could have fallen in."

"Someone did fall in, at least they drove their car into it, you ass. It's exactly what the crooks wanted. – Have you noticed, for all this was supposed to be a gas excavation, there are no gas pipes down there?"

"No gas pipes! Then why is the hole here?

"It was put here by the crooks to stop us chasing them. A fine detective you'll make if you can't fathom that out... Is there any other evidence?"

"There are some deep scratch marks in the road there."

"Do a thorough sweep for anything suspicious and identify it for forensics. We need to have everything here looked at before the traffic starts later on." Abbott turned away but quickly turned back. "Another thing, we don't want anyone falling down there and making a claim against us, see if you can pull some of these covers back over the hole, but don't spoil any evidence."

"Right, Sir."

Inspector Abbott walked back to the main crime scene. The forensics team had just arrived. They each looked quizzically at the tank as they passed. "Makes a bit of a change from your usual investigation, Inspector."

"I have to admit it's not your everyday evidence but there's other stuff which will make you feel right at home." Abbott pointed out the obvious items found so far. "It should be enough to be getting on with. I'll leave you to find out the rest. We'll have to wait for the company staff to arrive before we can look around inside, and while you're waiting, check the other end of the road as soon as possible."

"Fine, we'll get right on it." The team spread out and started measuring, photographing, bagging and taking plaster impressions.

Twenty minutes later the company's Head of Security arrived. He was stopped at the cordon while an officer fetched Abbott.

"Good morning, Sir. I'm Inspector Abbott, head of this investigation. I need to ask you a few questions, and I'd like to wait for your boss before we go in. We'll start with your full name and address and how you were contacted, land line or mobile?"

"Yes, of course. Michael James Clerkin... I assume I was a suspect."

"You still are. Until we have a little more information everyone connected with the company is a suspect. But, with your co-operation, I hope we will soon be able to eliminate you from our list."

Rawlins stopped beside the Inspector.

"Sir, Mr. Larkman has arrived, he's being held at the other end of the road."

"Oh good, thanks, Pat." Abbott turned to Michael Clerkin. "Would you come with me please."

"Inspector, what do you think happened here?" Michael Clerkin enquired as he followed Abbott.

"It looks quite simple. Persons unknown have used the tank to flatten the perimeter fence and breach the wall of your premises. I presume, they have then removed an amount of money in a second vehicle and left for destinations unknown."

"Well, you must realise I had nothing to do with it?"

"Why? Just because you weren't here at the time doesn't mean you're not the instigator, after all, who else would have the knowledge of the building's security. The crooks went in through the wall rather than the door. From that I would assume all the doors are alarmed, and that knowledge says it has to be an inside job, don't you think?"

"Yes, I suppose so."

They stopped by the crashed police car. "Please wait here with the Constable, while I speak privately with Mr. Larkman, I won't be a moment."

"Of course."

Abbott left Michael and greeted the Branch Manager. He quickly asked the same questions taking the answers down in his notebook. They rejoined Michael Clerkin and walked back to the crime scene. First they inspected the damage from a distance.

"My God, that puts us out of business for a while." Matthew Larkman pulled a mobile phone from his pocket. "We'll have to arrange for the stock to be transferred to another branch and I have to phone the staff and tell them not to come in tomorrow." Abbott stopped him before he dialled.

"Mr. Larkman, can I ask you to refrain from that until we have a few other things sorted out. I need to see inside the building, I want to know exactly how much has been taken and I want a list of every member of staff, including temps and part-timers."

"Yes of course, I was only going to call the numbers I have here."

"Later – shall we go in?"

Inside the building, Matthew Larkman asked the Inspector and the three accompanying officers to sign the guest book while he and Michael signed the staff register.

"I take it every person entering the building signs in and out, without exception?" Abbott scrawled his signature next to his printed name and the time of entry.

"Yes, just as you have done. We don't ask drivers and their assistants to sign in, but they never actually enter the work area. The money is transferred through an airlock."

"I shall want a full list of staff and all the visitors you've had over the past three months. We may need to go back further but this will do to start with." Abbott held out his hand as though expecting the list immediately.

"No problem, the personnel and visitor clocking times are all kept on file on the computer. We can have them printed off in a few minutes. Working out how much is supposed to be in the vault will take a little longer, maybe an hour or two."

"Well the sooner we find out, the sooner we'll know exactly what we're looking for."

"I'll need some other staff. The Vault Supervisor and the Dispatch Supervisor."

"Get me the personnel list first, then call them. How far have they got to come?"

"They're both locals, they should be here in about ten minutes."

* * *

On the other side of town, two police officers were pounding on Robert Knight's front door, other officers were at the back to prevent any escape. Reluctantly, Robert opened the door giving a big yawn as he did so.

"Good morning gentlemen, I assume I must be on fire or something for you to make so much noise at such an ungodly hour."

"Mr Robert Knight?"

"Yes."

"PC Aimes and PC Cummings, Bletchington Police. We think you can help us with our inquiries, would you come with us please."

"What, right now, or can it wait until I'm dressed?"

"You can dress, Sir."

"Thank you. What's this all about anyway? Am I under arrest?"

"No Sir, not yet."

"Not yet, hey. Perhaps there's some question as to whether sleeping in one's own bed is a crime?"

"There was an incident early this morning, Sir. I was told to collect

284

you and take you to Inspector Abbott who is investigating a crime."

"Early this morning," Robert looked at the grandfather clock standing in the hall. "It's twenty-five to three, you can't get much earlier can you?"

"You'd be surprised, Sir."

"Who is it, Robert?" Dorothy called from the top of the stairs.

"It's all right, Dorothy. It's the police, they want me to go with them to answer questions or something. I'm sure it won't take very long." Robert climbed the stairs to his bedroom. PC Aimes followed him to the landing.

"But can't they ask their questions here, instead of dragging you all the way to the station at this hour."

"I don't know, dear, they must have their reasons. Don't worry, I'm sure it will all be sorted out in a short while and I'll be back before you know it."

Twenty minutes later the police car returned to BankBase. Robert Knight was escorted to Sgt. Rawlins.

"Mr. Knight! Good morning. I'm sorry to haul you down here at this time of night, I think you probably realise now why you had to come."

"Do I? Oh, yes, I suppose I do, that's my Panzer, at least it looks like mine. What's it doing here?"

"That's what we'd like to ask you."

"I can't give you an explanation. It was in the hangar where it's kept, last time I saw it."

"When was that?"

"Well, it would have been, um, Tuesday afternoon, about 3.15 p.m. I had to go to the hangar to use my lathe for a bit. I have one in a workshop lorry, it's very useful when I have little jobs in the field, as it were."

"Yes Sir, little jobs in the field? Hum, but you haven't seen the tank since then?"

"It could have been a little later but it was definitely before it got dark at four."

"And you didn't know the tank had been taken until you saw it here just now?"

"No, never had an inkling. Jack Briars, my helper would know better when it was last in the workshop."

"How many people do you think know how to drive a tank?"

"Oh, there must be hundreds, anyone who has ever driven a tank

285

would be able to jump in and take it, if they knew how to start the thing. Anyone who can drive a tracked vehicle of any sort could learn quite quickly."

"I shall rephrase the question. How many people do YOU know who could start it and drive it?"

"Five or six. Myself, and a few of my staff, past and present."

"Can you give me their names please?" Rawlins wrote the information in his notebook.

"Sergeant, how did my tank get here?"

"I'll let the Inspector answer your questions in a minute. Would you wait here please." Rawlins opened the back door to one of the squad cars. Robert sat obediently. Rawlins shut the door so the childproof locks prevented Robert opening the door from inside.

* * *

Inside the BankBase building, Inspector Abbott held a list of one hundred and twenty-seven employees' names and addresses along with the security duty rosters, shift details and a list of recent visitors.

"So Mr. Larkman, the majority of your people work one of two shifts, six till two or ten till six during the day, and… only the loading bay is covered at night."

"And the main security station, Inspector. They control the loading bay doors and crash barriers from in there."

"And you have no personnel on duty at weekends?"

"Not between midnight Friday and midnight Sunday."

"So these thieves chose the best time to break in. In the middle of the unmanned period at a weekend." Abbott smiled. "Ironic, isn't it?"

"Bloody irritating."

"Yes. OK, call your people in to check the vault, you can call the rest of the staff this afternoon to tell them not to come into work until further notice. Don't give any reasons."

Another officer approached the Inspector.

"Sir, Sgt. Rawlins says he has a Robert Knight in custody outside. Do you want to talk to him?"

"Ah, the tank owner. Tell Rawlins I'll be there in a minute.

"Yes Sir."

"Er, Inspector," Matthew Larkman called after him. "You'll have to sign out, and in again later, if you're leaving the premises."

The Inspector left quickly. He found Robert Knight sitting patiently in the back of the police car.

"Good morning Mr. Knight. I'm sorry you had to be dragged out so early in the morning but there is a little matter of a Panzer which I believe may be yours. Am I right?"

"Yes, it's mine, though it's been damaged since I last saw it."

"Really? Well, it seems to have been used to break into this building. Any ideas?"

"I can only repeat what I told the other officer. The only person I know who can drive it, apart from myself that is, is Jack Briars. Some of my earlier staff would have been able to, but they are mostly dead now."

Abbott looked down the list of BankBase employees but none of the names Robert gave him tallied up.

"Would you have Mr. Briars' address, please?" He scribbled the information onto a piece of paper. "Thank you, you've been very helpful. Will you excuse me please, I'll be back in a moment." Abbott turned to an officer standing a short distance away. "Tell the dispatcher to send a car to this address and take Jack Briars into custody, right away. Don't let him talk to anyone and keep him under observation. Also send some officers back to Robert Knight's place to investigate the suspected theft of this tank and interview Mrs. Knight about her husband's whereabouts over the past couple of hours." He returned to Robert Knight and continued questioning him for another ten minutes.

"Thank you for your time, I'm sorry to have caused you so much inconvenience. You're free to go now, I'll have one of my officers drive you home. Um, you're not planning on going anywhere out of the ordinary, in say, the next week or so, are you? We may want you for additional questioning. You are still a suspect in this matter."

"I understand Inspector, I'll be home or at the office as usual. Inspector, before you go, when can I have my tank back?"

"It will be some time yet, probably weeks. We'll call you when you can collect it."

* * *

At 4.20 a.m. two additional employees arrived. Lawrence Ribbings, the Vault Supervisor, and Brian Titchner, the Dispatch Supervisor, were escorted into the building together. After preliminary questioning, Abbott permitted them to check the vault. The doors were still securely locked. Lawrence looked a little worried.

"I can't access the vault until the security timer switches itself off at six tomorrow morning. Once that's cleared, it takes half an hour before we can open the vault door. I won't be able to start checking the contents until after six thirty tomorrow."

"What! You don't have an emergency plan for accessing the money?"

"No, once the vault is locked and the timer is set, it stays that way until the timer clicks off on its own."

"You know there's a huge hole in the side of the building, don't you? You can enter the vault from there. It just means going out in the cold, first." The two men collected various papers and printed report sheets and made their way outside. The police officers followed.

* * *

At 6 a.m. Inspector Abbott drove to the police station. He had seen the night's video coverage of the area. There was clear screening of the Panzer first flattening the fence and then ramming the wall. Afterwards the tank had moved away and a seven and a half tonne lorry had reversed up to the hole. Four minutes and twenty-seven seconds elapsed while other activities took place before the lorry was driven away.

By now, Abbott also knew Jack Briars was missing from home and had not been seen since the previous evening. The police officers who had attended his property had been met by the worried wife claiming to have no idea of her husband's whereabouts.

In addition, the two officers investigating the Panzer's theft had reported the probable path to the crime scene. Transco had confirmed they were not responsible for the work done at the other end of the road. It was all coming together very nicely.

Abbott set in motion a search for abandoned lorries. He also instigated an Apprehend On Sight Notification for Customs and Excise at both air and sea ports. It would take a couple of hours for the message to reach the appropriate authorities, he just wished he'd been able to implement it earlier. If the crooks were headed for the tunnel at Folkestone it was possible they were already on a train to France.

Abbott's phone rang.

"Rawlins here, Sir. The thieves took twenty-four million."

"What denominations?"

"Seventeen and a half million in Twenties, four million in Fifties and three million in Tens."

"That makes twenty-four and a half million, not twenty-four. Is the amount exact?"

"Yes, Sir."

Abbott rung off. He wondered how many people had been involved in the plot. Twenty-four million was a fair haul and would be a good sum to have split even five or six ways. It wasn't possible anyone could have done this alone. Two at a pinch maybe, it was much more likely three or more, though the cameras only showed two.

At 07.30 a.m. Abbott's concentration was broken when a constable entered his room.

"Sir, an abandoned lorry has been spotted a couple of miles away just off the Old Pulborough Road near Marehill. forensics is headed there now."

Abbott drove to the location, it was still dark when he arrived. The forensics team were well into their work, dusting the cab. He watched them for a while, hoping something would come up but his impatience took over.

"So what have you found?"

"Not a lot. A print on each of the buttons on the tail lift, a few partials around the sides of the shutter guides. Partials here on the steering wheel and other controls. I hope that will be enough for you?"

"It may be, thank you. But there is one thing I am sure of… this is the lorry used at the crime scene. The writing on the side panel and that very distinct scratch mark along the side were clearly visible on the BankBase video tapes."

"One other thing, Inspector. The keys were left in the ignition."

"Really? That's interesting. Make sure you get a photo of those side panels so I can compare them properly with the crime scene CCTV." The forensic photographer nodded.

"Yes, Sir."

"So what do you think? Did they head for Gatwick, or make for a port?"

"They wouldn't be so stupid as to try and push the money through Airport Security, would they?"

"We can always hope."

Satisfied, the Inspector left. He was halfway back to the station when his mobile rang.

"Abbott."

"PC Young, Sir. We've just received a phone call from Shoreham Police investigating a theft at the Lady Bee Marina. One of their cruisers has gone missing."

"Really! The crafty rascals, they did a Uee. Get on to Shoreham Police and tell them I'm on my way. I'll bet the missing boat is connected to our little incident." He drove into Bletchington and then

289

turned towards Worthing, unknowingly following the same route his quarry had taken hours before. His blue light flashing, he arrived at the Marina in just twenty minutes. It was nearly 08.30. He was greeted by a local officer.

"Good morning, Constable, I'm Inspector Abbott, Bletchington Police. What can you tell me about the boat?"

"It was reported missing at 07.30 by a marina staff member when he arrived for work. I asked the Port Authority about the departure. Apparently it cleared the lock at 07.28 hours."

Abbott swept the area with his eyes. Three people were standing around a lorry parked further along the car park. They seemed to be arguing.

"That seems suspicious, have you looked into it yet?"

"No, Sir."

"Well why not, come on." Abbott walked to the lorry, holding his warrant card for inspection. "Police! what's the trouble here?"

The three men looked up. The older one spoke first.

"Some idiot has left this truck parked against our doors and we can't get into work. We need someone to move it. I was just about to phone the police so it's a good thing you're here. They shouldn't be allowed to do this sort of thing."

"True, they shouldn't. Why didn't you just move it?" The lorry was parked nose in to the building. Abbott took out his handkerchief and opened the cab door. "See, the keys are still in the ignition."

Abbott went to the back of the lorry. The shutter was open but the tail-lift was up.

"Someone find me something to stand on?" He looked around. There was a low wall at the water's edge. "It's all right, I'll stand on this," he pointed.

Once balanced, he pulled a small pair of theatre glasses from his pocket. He could just see into the lorry's hold. There were several metal cages inside. Abbott immediately recognised them as the same sort he had seen in the BankBase vault. The difference being, these were empty. He called the local constable.

"Set up a cordon around this lorry and get your forensics down here right away. I'm pretty certain this is another vehicle used in the crime I'm investigating. And I'm sure there will be lots of prints, the gang have been none too clever about covering their tracks so far. Tell your people I want a copy of the report as soon as possible."

"I'll call them right away." The officer turned away, punching furiously on his mobile. Moments later he turned back. "They've put it on their to-do list."

"How very reassuring. Oh well, I'll go back and talk to the marina staff." Abbott turned to the three disgruntled employees. "You missed your chance. I can't let you move it now, not until forensics have dealt with it. You may as well go home. Sorry."

Abbott left the lorry. At the marina office he introduced himself.

"So, are you the chandler, what time did you report the boat missing?"

"Evely, my name's John Evely. I noticed it was gone as soon as I arrived this morning at 7.15. Well I was a bit late actually, ten minutes or so. I'm not expecting any customers down here today. Anyway, it's our biggest boat and it sort of fills my view when I look through the window. It was covered with a blue tarpaulin. I found the tarp floating in the water."

"What's the name of the boat?"

"*Sea Queen*, she's a forty-five foot, motor cruiser. Nice lines, about a million's worth. Top speed of about twenty to twenty-five knots, range about a thousand nautical miles." Abbott thought the chandler seemed to admire the vessel. "She's probably got enough fuel for two or three hundred at the moment so she'll have to come into port soon or end up adrift."

"Who is the owner?"

"Ronald Lancaster. I've told him she is missing."

"And he was at home when you phoned him?"

"Yes, well I suppose so, we only have his mobile number. He was really pissed-off when I told him, said he'd booked in to have her careened tomorrow."

"So, in theory he wouldn't have been expecting her to go anywhere in the near future. What's the furthest port she could reach with the current fuel on board?"

"Falmouth, maybe St Ives going west. Great Yarmouth or Skegness going east. Anywhere between about Amsterdam and Brest on the Continent."

"And what would be the shortest crossing to the Continent?"

"From here, Dieppe. She could manage that in about three hours at full speed."

"Do you know if the Coast Guard could track her?"

"I would think so, but you'd have to check with them to find out the details. This area's covered by the Solent Radar station."

Abbott drew out his mobile and dialled his office. The line was picked up after three rings. "Is that PC Young? Patch me through to the Solent Coast Guard station. The line went dead for a moment then it rang again.

"H. M. Coast Guard, Operations Solent, Lieutenant Keegan speaking."

"Good morning Lieutenant Keegan. I'm Inspector Abbott, Bletchington Police. Would you be able to track a vessel from Shoreham to say Dieppe on your radar, and would you keep a record of such a crossing?" Abbott gave all the information he had so far.

"I assume this is not just some hypothetical query?"

"You've hit it on the head first time."

"It'll take me about ten minutes to look through the radar contacts for this morning, can I call you back when I've got an answer?"

Abbott passed his mobile number and hung up. He addressed himself to the chandler again, "While I'm waiting for his call, Mr. Evely, I'm going to take a closer look at where the *Sea Queen* was moored. You haven't touched anything out there since you arrived this morning, have you?"

"No, I just pulled the tarp out the water before it sank or fouled one of the other boats. It would have been hell to retrieve it if it had drifted under a boat and fouled a prop."

"Yes, I suppose it would."

Along the concrete waterfront, faint tracks in the wet dust indicated a heavy vehicle with double wheels on one of its axles had been there recently. Abbott took notes and walked back to the cordoned off lorry. The four treads on the back axle were identical to the imprint, confirming the lorry had probably made the tracks. He returned to the jetty to the now vacant mooring but found nothing to point the finger. The blue plastic tarpaulin lay crumpled on the walkway. His phone rang.

"Abbott."

"Lieutenant Keegan, Solent Coast Guard, Sir. I've had a thorough look at the data and there is just one observed departure from Shoreham this morning. Our first contact when she left the shore was at 07.37 hours, and headed on a bearing of one-seven-zero degrees. Judging by her headway she should make landfall west of Dieppe around Fécamp, Falaise or Le Havre some time after 10.15. She's not keeping a very steady line and our contact is a little intermittent because of the deep swell. That's not surprising with such a small vessel."

"That's wonderful news. She's the *Sea Queen,* would it be possible for one of your vessels to haul her in and place the occupants under arrest? She is believed stolen along with a quantity of cash which I think will be found on board."

"Sorry, Inspector. We don't have anything to overhaul her with. You'll need to call Customs and Excise to contact the French Port Authorities."

Abbott called the office.

"Young? draw up a request for French International Co-operation and have them stop the motor cruiser *Sea Queen* off the Normandy coast. They should concentrate their search around Dieppe, Fécamp and Le Havre. If Jack Briars is found on board with other people and a large amount of cash, they should apprehend them and return them to Britain as soon as. Otherwise they should just hold anyone found on board for theft of the vessel. Get it sent to Customs Head Office for immediate action. Follow it up with extradition orders in case the boat arrives in Port. Tell the Super what it's about and have him sign the orders. I expect all this to be completed by the time I return to the station. No mistakes mind, we want this to go as smooth as a well-greased ball race, got that?"

"Yes Sir." The call was disconnected.

All Abbott could do now was wait to see if the boat was stopped. Would the cash be found on board? Had the cash thieves taken the boat or was this a separate incident? If they had, how long would it be before the money and the crooks were returned for criminal proceedings? He returned to the Marina Office for Lancaster's address.

It was a short drive to the boat owner's house. Mr. Lancaster was a retired businessman who spent long periods each summer, cruising European waters. He seemed particularly upset about his vessel. Abbott wondered if the emotion was a front. After half an hour of questioning, he left convinced Lancaster really was that upset about his pride and joy.

Abbott drove back to Bletchington. Now it was just a case of linking the persons on the boat with the two lorries, and the BankBase Securities camera footage.

21

The Return

Inspector Abbott found several reports on his desk. He filed each to the appropriate investigation mulling over the robbery's known facts as he worked.

Earlier, he had arranged a mobile crane and a transporter to move the tank, at a cost of eight hundred and eighty pounds. It seemed ridiculous to go to such expense to move the vehicle just half a mile but it had to take place, Forensic evidence had to be preserved so driving the tank was out of the question and the costs would probably be charged to Robert knight anyway.

The transporter eventually arrived at the police station just after 1.00 p.m. with the Panzer on the back. Five minutes later the crane arrived. The crane carefully lifted the tank over the wall into the police car park and set it down close to the forensics laboratory.

Abbott watched from his office window as the operation proceeded. The tank ended up occupying two parking places. That would not please the Super, he thought. Rawlins entered the office as Abbott turned away from the window.

"Ah, here you are, Sir. I just had a phone call from the police in Fécamp, *Sea Queen* has moored in the local marina but there's no sign of the crew."

"What! how the hell did they get away? The French authorities had hours of notice."

"I don't know Sir, and the French didn't offer any explanation."

"I suppose this is going to end up as another Continental balls up. Thanks for letting me know, anyway." Abbott turned back to the window and stared at the tank. "Are you the only part of this monumental fiasco we are ever going to recover?"

Two forensic technicians climbed onto the tank and disappeared inside. Abbott watched for a while, waiting for the investigators to re-emerge. All he saw was the occasional hand reach out and place an evidence bag on the mudguard.

A police clerk entered Abbott's office.

"Preliminary reports on the two lorries found dumped this morning, and another about Shoreham harbour, Sir."

"Thank you."

The local lorry report gave no real evidence, Abbott could see he would have to wait until other reports showed print matches, or not, as the case may be. The Shoreham report was much more interesting. The cages found at the marina had definitely come from BankBase. The remains of several cut padlocks had been found, each with markings peculiar to the Bletchington Branch. There were also remains of some pink, yellow and blue plastic cash bags as used for bagging freshly counted money, but not enough to account for twenty-four million's worth. Local forensics had also managed to match the Shoreham lorry fingerprints with the Bletchington lorry prints but there were still no names.

Abbott threw the pages onto his desk. This is totally useless, he thought. I can collect as many reports as I want, but unless the French pick up the culprits before they become properly mobile, the case will never be solved. He stormed out of his office, a constable was passing in the hallway.

"Young, tell anyone who asks, I've gone home. It's been a long day and I need some peace and quiet to think things over."

"Yes, Sir."

"If anything important crops up, call me, otherwise leave it all on my desk, and I'll sort it through in the morning."

"Yes, Sir."

* * *

Inspector Abbott walked into his office promptly at eight the following day. There were several folders on his desk. Abbott smiled as he read the first dossier.

Rawlins entered.

"Have you seen the French fax, Gov? They caught the two who did it."

"Yes, I've got the report here. Why do you assume there were only two. I still find Larkman and Clerkin suspicious, especially Clerkin. He was far too keen to be removed from the suspect list… and Knight's not off the hook yet either."

"If you say so, Sir."

"You know, Rawlins, someone planned this well. The tank, the ditch, the timing. It says here these two men each went and changed a thousand into Euros and then they hired two vans. They were loading the vans with the cash when the French Port Authority stepped in. If that missing boat hadn't been noticed, we wouldn't have found the second lorry and they would have been off and away."

"And I don't suppose it would be difficult to pick up false papers over there, especially when you have twenty-four million to hand. They could have had completely new identities within the week."

"Apparently! Incidentally, they were stopped for entering the country without valid passports, would you believe it.?"

"I believe it, Sir. Shoreham found two passports behind the dash in the lorry, it wasn't in the pre-lim. They must have slipped down the air vents as they were driving. Jack Briars and Oliver Golding, Sir.

"Oliver Golding, now that name is on my list of BankBase employees, so there's your insider.

"The two men are also being charged with possession of stolen property, laundering stolen moneys, importing excessive amounts of cash without a licence and trying to evade lawful police arrest."

"Sounds like a good line-up to me, there must be five to eight years for the lot."

"True. But if the French make it all stick, you'll have to delay your retirement before you see justice served."

"Come off it, I'm not that bloomin' old."

"At least we know it was Jack Briars and Oliver Golding, Sir. The French Authorities faxed copies of their driving licences, with their photos and a set of fingerprints for each of them. We should be able to clinch this pretty quickly now. And we'll get the money back eventually, that will be a feather in your cap."

* * *

Wednesday, December 21st dawned grey, wet and cold. The winter Solstice, the shortest day of the year in the Northern Hemisphere. Abbott wondered why people said it was the shortest day. Every day was twenty-four hours long. Just because it grew dark early, and light later, didn't mean he worked less than eighteen hours per day.

His 'IN' tray held a new stack of papers. He cursed quietly to himself as he settled down.

"A job is never finished until the paperwork is done." As a young PC, he had had a poster depicting a baby on a potty with that caption over the top. At first it had been stuck to the inside of his locker door. When he had moved into an office job, he had wanted to move the poster to his wall but had been told it was not considered professional. The caption still applied, as did the potty's contents, sometimes.

Abbott took a while to arrange the paperwork into the respective files, only responding to those items needing immediate follow up.

As he worked, he glanced out the window at the tarp covered Panzer. All the forensic evidence had been taken from that quarter. It would be better if the machine was returned, so long as Knight made it secure. Even a lockable cabinet for the keys would be better than nothing. Perhaps the man had learned his lesson.

The tank certainly couldn't stay in the courtyard for years while the case went to Court. A car would simply have been signed back to the legal owner, but the nature of the tank meant certain security factors had to be looked into first. The weapons required various licences and certificates before they could be handed back. Then there was the problem of removing the tank from the yard. With no road tax, insurance or MOT, the Panzer could not be legally driven beyond the police gates. The metal tracks also prohibited its use on the road, and there was the matter that Robert Knight was responsible for the removal and any fee the operation may involve.

Abbott fixed himself up with another coffee and picked up the phone. "Hello."

"Robert Knight? Inspector Abbott."

" Inspector. So nice of you to call, how's the investigation coming? Can I have my tank back yet?"

"As a matter of fact, that is exactly what I want to talk to you about. There are a number of problems to be sorted before I can release your property." Abbott recounted the list.

"Oh, you don't need to worry. I have all the paperwork from when my father bought her. You don't need worry about transporting her either, tell me when, and I can come and collect. I have the necessary equipment to lift and transport her."

"I wish it were that simple, but unfortunately fifty year-old certificates are a little out of date for my department. I shall have to have the weapons checked and reclassified. It will probably take about three weeks to a month."

"Oh well, if you must. I presume I will hear from you when you are ready.

"The problem is not so much your vehicle but Christmas and the New Year. We should be able to have things moving again after that. In the

297

meantime you have a wonderful holiday season and I'll call you when I've received the certificates."

"Thank you. Merry Christmas to you too."

The case slowed dramatically for Christmas. Tackling shoplifting and drunk and disorderly behaviour took priority. Christmas Day itself, however, proved to be quiet. New Year brought work dealing with drunks, drink-drivers and public order offences. Abbott's 'IN' box filled steadily from the additional paperwork.

* * *

Soon after New Year the results of the Panzers Forensic tests arrive on Abbott's desk. He scrutinised the pages detailing numerous samples of fluids, powders, fabric, leather, rubber and gum. Photographs had been taken of dusty footprints, each with a measure for size comparison. After thirty-seven man-hours, the investigation team had made a nice little collection of evidence which might or might not be incriminating. There were details of seventeen hair samples, fourteen sets of fingerprints, one hundred and twenty-eight cloth fibre types and two aged blood samples.

Two sets of fingerprints belonged to Robert Knight and Sally Briars. Another set, matched prints found on the stolen money cages, the two abandoned lorries and a trolley-jack. A twelve point match proved the first set were definitely those of Briars and a thirteen point match between the lorries and the French fax proved Golding was the second man.

The blood samples proved to be too old to be of any use for identification by DNA. Their condition suggested they were many years old, if not decades.

The fabric samples dated from between the 1930s to the present day and were of mixed origins. Some proved to be of World War II German uniforms, others were of British uniforms from the same time. More came from civilian clothes from the Fifties and Sixties. Only those which were of recent manufacture had been studied in any depth. Some of these might lead to a match with the suspect's clothing. Every little link helped the case.

He gazed out of his window. The tank had been covered with a large green tarpaulin to await its release back to the owner. Abbott wondered speculatively if the cash would be returned to BankBase before he had to take the culprits to Court. The French Police were bound to keep the money as evidence, at least until the French trial proceedings were concluded. The big question was, what would they do, prosecute or deport? Time would tell.

Now Abbott had to try and obtain permission to question the two crooks. He had to find out who they had been working with, or the other members of the gang would have split before he found them.

Abbott considered this for a while. The probability was that any accomplices would have already left the country, but now the plan had failed, there was no reward for them to pick up. Would they come sneaking back and pretend they were not involved or would they lie low and hope the case would blow over without their being incriminated by Briars and Golding.

The fact that only these two were found with the money also suggested that maybe Briars and Golding had worked the crime alone. It was becoming evident they had not needed a third person. Abbott considered the two men, particularly Golding who had been a bank manager for some time. He would know his way around security and he certainly had the brains to come up with the plan. Working in the company, he would have had inside information, anything he didn't know he could probably have surmised. The company didn't seem to hide their security from the employees, in fact they seemed to flaunt it. A sort of, *try something if you dare, we're watching you*, attitude.

Obviously Golding had taken the dare, thought Abbott, and almost got away with it.

By the second week in January, Abbott had still not heard from either the French or from the Firearms Inspectors. Irritated at the delay he made several phone calls. By the end of the day he had received permission to travel to France. Sgt. Lane, the Weapons Inspector from London, had promised to be there the following week.

* * *

Abbott was in Fécamp when Sgt Lane removed the tarpaulin and scrutinised the main gun's barrel. At first it looked bent. Lane wondered if it was an optical illusion. Looking along the barrel's length, it was clear there was significant curvature and a slight bulge about a third of the way along its length, either of which would prevent the gun from ever firing safely again.

Lane climbed into the turret and studied the breach. The barrel was stuck in the recoil position with the breach block open. Lane had difficulty closing the breach, the mechanism hadn't been lubricated for a long time. When he succeeded, a three-quarter inch hole through the breach block showed where the firing pin arrangement had been removed. There was no way the gun, in its present condition, could be fired. He inspected the turret's M.G.34. It was a fake, the barrel protruding from the front of the tank was not connected to any real mechanism inside.

Sgt. Lane slipped easily into the Radio Operator's position to inspect the lower machine gun. Reaching up, he opened the overhead hatch to let in some light. Apparently both Machine Guns had been treated the same way. It would be easy to write his report and issue the certificates. He stood on the radio man's seat and climbed out. He closed the hatches and with help from a couple of officers, hauled the tarp back over the vehicle. He walked to the police station to fill out his paperwork before returning to his own station later that afternoon. Abbot found the certificates on his desk when he arrived back from France, two days later.

Robert Knight was overjoyed when he answered the phone.

"You mean I can have my Panzer back?"

"Yes, Mr. Knight. There is just the small matter of security."

"I've had all new roller doors and locks fitted to prevent this kind of thing happening again. My dear lady suggested I should put the collection in a museum. I suppose it would be much better on public display."

"I agree. In the meantime, Mr. Knight, I shall have to review your new security before signing the release papers."

"Of course. Come any time, I'm sure you'll be impressed."

Abbott felt like walking, he needed a breather. From the centre of town, he headed past the 14th century church. Made of local flint the building stood in the hazy January sun, it's steeple casting a long faint shadow across the road. In spite of the greyness and the lack of warmth in the atmosphere it was a very pleasant winter day, just right if you were wrapped up properly for a brisk breath of fresh air.

When Abbott arrived at Froghole farm, the shiny doors of the hangar were resplendent in green and brown camouflage paint. They were a standard factory fit with a side door on the left. There was a combination lock and a new alarm system. The alarm was deafening.

"At least I'll be able to hear it in the house," said Robert "I'm going to have it connected by phone to a security company, one of those organisations who attend for you, if it's set off. Besides, I'm too old to be rushing around after villains, don't you think?"

"I would certainly prefer you to let the police deal with villains rather than tackle them yourself, but I am glad you've made it more difficult for thieves to take advantage."

"Yes, quite. I can't believe Jack was involved. He was such a good friend. Still it was daft of me not to have done something about the security before this. It's the old adage, it won't happen to me. We never take action to prevent crime until it's too late. Barn doors and horses."

"That just leaves the matter of moving the tank."

"Well, we'll need a crane and manpower for the operation. How about next Sunday? Would that be best, from a traffic point of view?" asked Robert.

"Yes. If I sign the release orders tonight, you can come round on Sunday. I'll have some of my men there to supervise and assist."

"Fine, about ten?"

"Excellent." Abbott returned to the station and posted a memo requesting volunteers for extra work on Sunday. He was sure he'd get a good response with the prospect of overtime pay. It would be a nice little earner, for which Robert Knight would have to foot the bill.

* * *

By 9.30 a.m. on Sunday, the road at the back of the police station had been closed and all parked cars had been removed from the compound. Robert Knight drove up in his U.S. Army M26 transporter ready to receive the tank. The huge vehicle only just fitted into the street. He parked on the opposite side of the road from the police station. Six burly looking workmen, brought to handle guide ropes and direct the lift, bundled out of the huge cab. The crane arrived ten minutes later.

Hydraulic sponsons set, the crane swung into motion carrying a large steel frame with eight, five-tonne straps dangling in expectation. Abbott, in control of the policing staff, watched the operation from the roadside. When the main hook was over the tank's turret, the frame was lowered and the straps were attached to the eight suspension units. Guide ropes were fitted to both ends of the hull at the towing lugs.

The lift went smoothly as the tank was raised over the wall. Very slowly, the crane lowered away until the tank was just inches from the deck of the transporter. Final adjustments on the guide lines and the tank settled comfortably in the middle of the trailer. Lines and straps were stowed in the crane's lockers while the tank was secured with chains and chocks. By 11.00 a.m. the crane had left.

"I'll be quite sorry to see this lady go, Mr. Knight. I've become quite attached to her over the past few weeks."

"I have to say I am greatly relieved to have her back, Inspector. I've missed her."

"I'm sure you have. Drive carefully."

Soon afterwards, the low-loader left with the Panzer. Inspector Abbott watched as the now familiar vehicle disappeared.

When Robert arrived back at his farm, he arranged the equipment in the hangar so everything was back to normal again. There was still the problem of repairs to the gun where it had been rammed against the wall. He would look into it tomorrow. Rex Cadman at the War and Peace Show might know where to find a replacement, but right now, Robert wanted his lunch.

22

Museum

Robert took another glass of champagne. The last one had gone flat as he'd chatted. There had been a constant run of well-wishers and congratulations to acknowledge.

"Tell you what Robert," George Bailey shook Robert's hand, "if this place is a success, I'll design a whole line of museums for you to spread across the Nation."

"If I can find the exhibits, I may just take you up on that."

George moved on and another face appeared.

"Inspector Abbott, so glad you could come." Robert shook the Inspector's hand.

"*Chief* Inspector. I have a lot to thank you for," said Abbott. "Your tank was a big influence in my promotion."

"Congratulations, Chief Inspector."

"Please, call me Chris." Abbott looked at the Panzer. "I suppose that is the same tank? It looks different somehow, like the gun is smaller."

"It's the same vehicle, almost. Rather than pay a huge amount to have the old gun repaired, I replaced it with a gun assembly from a Normandy Tobruk turret. This is an L24 barrel like the one she would have started out with." Robert pointed to the back of the Panzer, "The old gun is to the side there with the recoil housing cut away."

"Oh yes, I see," said Abbott. Robert continued his explanation.

"I also removed a lot of the bolt on armour from around the turret and front plate."

"Was it difficult finding a replacement gun?"

Robert smiled to himself.

"It wasn't easy, but like most things, if you want something enough and are willing to search and pay for it, you will find it somewhere. I've been offered three more tanks and two guns since I bought that one."

"Will you buy them?"

"Not for this museum, I've nearly run out of space as it is."

"I wonder what the original crew would say if they were to see it now." Abbott looked round as if searching for German uniformed

303

intruders. "They're not here are they?"

"Ha, ha. No they're not here, and if they were, they would probably babble at me in German and tell me it was all wrong. I know the original driver. I sent him an invite, but I never heard back. I expect he's passed on by now." Robert felt sad about Jürgen not being present.

"It must have been quite a shock to you, to meet someone who had actually driven her."

"I think, it was more of a shock to him to realise this was actually his old tank. We chatted for hours. He seemed so attached to it."

"As you are now?" said Abbott smiling.

"I suppose so, but in a different way and for different reasons. Jürgen loved the tank as though it had saved his life."

"Maybe it had."

* * *

The policeman walked away and Robert looked round. Dorothy quickly guided a woman pushing a wheelchair, to greet her husband.

"Excuse me, is this your Panzer IV? I am wondering if I might be permitted to sit inside?"

Robert immediately recognised the old man but was shocked at how frail he looked. "Jürgen! I thought you weren't coming."

"I have been here some time but you seemed occupied, I did not want to disturb you, Robert."

"I'm sorry, I was wondering what had happened to you."

"It is of no consequence. Robert, may I introduce my daughter, Krista."

"I am very pleased to meet you, Krista."

"It is lovely to meet you too. My father has told me so much about you."

"I hope your father said only good things about me." Robert smiled at Jürgen.

"Naturally, my friend." Jürgen butted in. "Here, I have something for you. Krista, give the cases to Robert, please."

Krista reached for something hidden under the wheelchair.

"My Father was insistent we should bring all this stuff. He said you would be interested." She held out two small suitcases.

"What is all this, Jürgen?"

"Memorabilia. My side of the Panzer story if you like." Jürgen explained.

"You had better come to my office." Robert led them to the back of the Main Hall. "Do you want the cases back now?"

"Oh, no. They are for you also. Every article there is documented so there should be no difficulty identifying them."

"Thank you very much. Is there anything I can get for you? Some champagne perhaps and something to eat."

"I would like to take some photographs of the Museum." Krista drew a small camera from her purse.

"Please, take as many as you like. And if you need anything, do let me know."

"Thank you, I shall leave you to discuss those bags now."

"Do not stay away too long, my daughter. This will only take a short while I think… Robert, why don't you open the plain case first?"

Both cases were old, made of brown leather, one plain, the other embossed with the German eagle and Swastika on the lid. Robert opened the plain case.

Inside was an N.C.O.'s black woollen uniform pressed and neatly folded with badges and insignia in place. The accompanying wool cap had a roundel badge plus the eagle with Swastika. There were gloves, medals, a Luger and holster, a dagger, a pair of binoculars, an inscribed pocket knife, a *Soldbuch*, a Hitler Youth uniform and a list describing each item.

Robert read the list quickly checking off each item.

"You have been very thorough, Jürgen. I shall have hardly any work to do before these can go on display. I think I just need a suitable cabinet," Robert inspected Jürgen's pay book, turning the pages one by one. "I would like to have a translation of this."

"There is one in the other case," said Jürgen. "Krista has documented it page by page for you."

"Really, I must thank her when she returns." Robert picked up the Luger. "Not loaded I hope?"

"No, Robert. The authorities removed the firing pin and magazine before I was permitted to transport it. Fortunately I have replacements."

Robert turned to the eagle crested case, it was half filled with a sheaf of papers. Underneath was a later German Leutnant's uniform with insignia and at the bottom was a Russian quilted Tank-Lieutenant's vest. Robert opened it out with puzzlement.

"What's the story behind this?"

"I will tell you at dinner. For old time's sake, I have arranged a table at the Red Lion. I know you like it there."

"Have you, by jingo. I can't wait."

Robert repacked the cases. Dorothy and Krista stepped into the office as he was closing the latches.

"Hello, darling, has everyone left?" Robert asked.

"Yes, we're the last ones now."

"Good. It seems that Jürgen has invited us to dinner at the Red Lion."

How wonderful, thank you Jürgen." Dorothy bent to kiss him.

"What did you want to do between now and dinner, Jürgen?"

"I would like to sit in *my* Panzer again."

"All right, let's go and put you in *my* Panzer for a while."

Krista looked at Dorothy, an amused smile on her face. "Men!"

The End

Acknowledgements

A work such as this cannot be accomplished without the help of many additional people from many different backgrounds. Inevitably while researching history, one comes up against discrepancies, or statements that are just contradictory.

For their help in guiding me through the maze of information I would like to offer thanks to the staff at the Imperial War Museum reading rooms, London, to Janice Tate and Stuart Wheeler at the library of The Tank Museum, Bovington Camp, Wareham, to The Engineering and Maintenance Department at the Tank Museum Bovington with a special mention to David Willey (Curator) and Mike Hayton (Workshop Manager) for their enthusiasm and assistance in answering technical questions.

Thanks also go to the staff at RAF Duxford, and The RAF Museum Hendon for their excellent exhibitions of aircraft and land vehicles. I would also like to say *Vielen Dank* to the staff at Munster Tank Museum, near Hamburg, for their assistance with understanding the markings on tank ammunition.

Thanks to Peter Owen (General Manager) at the Royal Air Force Club for his help in feeling the atmosphere of the club and understanding some of the everyday running of the club now and in the past.

I would also like to thank the staff at the Shoreham Harbour lock gates for the information about operating procedures, to the Coast Guard staff at Dover and Solent for their insight into the problems presented by small craft.

The Hop Farm Country Park at Beltring have been wonderful in letting me examine their showground and a big thank you to Rex Cadman for his help in showing the workings of the world's biggest military orientated show, *The War and Peace Show*, held every year at this venue in Kent.

Thank you to my wife Simone, Daphne Green and particularly Nina Milton for their help in proof reading and other aspects of writing.

Warm thanks to the members of my family who have been so helpful and supportive over the past years, particularly to my Uncle Richard and my cousin Enid for all the snippets of information.

But most of all, I would like to thank my mother for her ardent support over the past three years and Simone for her patience and encouragement.

Bibliography

Allison Nigel. Collecting World War II German Military Pay and Service Books. Ulric, 2007. ISBN 1-905142-10-2

Ambrose Stephen E. Pegasus Bridge. Pocket Books, 2003. ISBN 0-7434-5068-X

Atkin Ronald. Dieppe 1942, the Jubilee Disaster. Book Club Association. 1980. In association with MacMillan.

Attenborough David. Life on Air. BBC Books, 2003. ISBN 056348780-1Badsey Stephen. Normandy 1944. Osprey Publishing Ltd, 1990. ISBN 0-85045-921-4

Badsey Stephen. Normandy 1944, Allied Landings and Breakout. Osprey Publishing Ltd., 1990. ISBN 0-85045-921-4

Bance Professor Alan. (Translator). Blitzkrieg in Their Own Words, First Hand Accounts from German Soldiers 1939-1940.Amber Books Ltd, 2005. ISBN1-84415-276-6

Bard Michael Ph.d. World War II, The Complete Idiot's Guide to. Alpha Books, 2004. ISBN 1-59257-204-9

Bastable Jonathan. Voices from D-Day, Eye-witness accounts of 6th June 1944. David & Charles, 2006. ISBN 978-0-7153-2553-7

Baxter Ian. German Panzer Markings, from Wartime Photographs. The Crowood Press, 2007. ISBN 978-1-86126-897-6

Benamou Jean-Pierre. Sword Beach, Album Souvenir collection memory 1944, Normandy 1944. OREP Editions, 2004. ISBN 2-912925-70-3

Besnard Josephine. La Cote des Prenoms en 2007. Michel Lafon 2006. ISBN 2-7499-0528-1

Binney Marcus. Secret War Heroes. Hodder Paperback, 2006 ISBN 0-340-82910-9

Blitzkrieg in their own words, First hand accounts from soldiers 1939-1940. Pen & Sword Military, 2005. ISBN 1-84415-276-6

Bombs to Butterflies, From Ruddington Depot to Rushcliffe County Park. Ruddington Local History & Amenity Society 2003. ISBN 0-903929-10-4

Booth Nicholas. ZigZag, The Incredible Wartime Exploits of Double Agent Eddie Chapman. Portrait, 2007.

ISBN 978-0-7499-5156-6

Bradford George. German Early War Armoured Fighting Vehicles. Stackpole Books, 2007. ISBN 0-8117-3341-6

Brayley Martin. The British Army, 1939-45(1). Osprey Publishing Ltd, 2001. ISBN 1-84176-052-8

Brook Henry. True Stories of D-Day. Ushborne Publishing Ltd, 2006, in association with the Imperial War Museum.

Brown Mike. A Child's War, Growing Up on the Home Font 1939-45. Sutton, 2000. ISBN 0-7509-2441-1

Bull Stephen Ph.d. World War II Infantry Tactics (1). Osprey Publishing Ltd, 2004. ISBN 1-84176-662-3

Canpbell John P. Dieppe revisited, a Documentary Investigation. Cassell 1993. ISBN 0-7146-3496-4

Carruthers Bob & Trew Simon. The Normandy Battles. Cassell & Co, 2000. ISBN 0-304-35396-5

Cawthorne Nigel. Fighting them on the Beaches, The D-Day Landings June 6, 1944. Index Books Ltd., 2004. ISBN 1-84193-113-6

Chappell Mike. British Battle Insignia 2 1939-45. Osprey Publishing Ltd, 1991. ISBN 0-85045-739-4

Clark Lloyd. Battle Zone Normandy, Operation Epsom. Sutton Publishing, 2004 ISBN 0-7509 3008-X

Clark Lloyd. Battle Zone Normandy, Orne Bridgehead. Sutton Publishing, 2004 ISBN 0-7509-3009-8

Clostermann Pierre. The Big Show, The Greatest Pilot's Story of World War II. Cassell Military Paperbacks, 2004. ISBN 0-3043-6624-2

Compagnon General Jean. 6 June 1944, The Normandy Landings, The strategic Victory of World War II. Editions Ouest France, 2001. ISBN 2-7373-2641-9

Crown Copyright 1962, Battery Press official History Series. Battery Press Inc. 1993 ISBN 0-89839-193-8

Cullen Simon MBE. Soldier Talk, A squaddies Handbook. Lee Cooper, 1995. ISBN 0-85052-459-8

Dalglish Ian. Battleground Europe, Normandy, Operation Goodwood, The Great Tank Charge July 1944. Pen and Sword Military, 2004. ISBN 1-84415-030-5

Deighton Len. Blitzkrieg, from the rise of Hitler to the fall of Dunkirk. Triad/Granada, 1981. ISBN 0-586-05207-0

Delaforce Patrick. Monty's Ironsides, From The Normandy Beaches to Bremen With The Third Division. Alan Sutton Publishing Ltd, 1995. ISBN 0-7509-0781-9

Delaforce Patric. The Black Bull. Chancellor Press, 2000. ISBN 0-75370-350-5

Doyle Hilary & Jentz Tom. Stug III Assault Gun 1940-1942. Osprey Publishing Ltd, 1996. ISBN 1-85532-537-3

Dunphie Christopher. The Pendulum of Battle, Operation Goodwood July 1944. Leo Cooper, 2004. ISBN 1-84415-010-0

Ethell Jeffrey L. Blitzkrieg in the West 1029-1042. Greenhill Books, 1997. ISBN 1-85367-283-1

Farndale Nigel. Haw-Haw, The tragedy of William and Margaret Joyce. Pan, 2006. ISBN 0-330-49284-5

Ford Ken. Battle Zone Normandy, Sword Beach. Sutton Publishing, 2004. ISBN 0-7509-3019-5

Ford Ken. Caen 1944, Montgomery's Break-out Attempt. Osprey Publishing, 2004. ISBN 1-84176-625-9

Ford Ken. D-Day 1944 (3) Sword Beach & the British Airborne Landings. Osprey 2002. ISBN 1-84176-366-7

Ford Ken. Dieppe 1942, Prelude to D-Day. Osprey Publishing, 2004. ISBN 1-84176-624-0

Forty Jonathan. Tanks in Detail, PzKpfw III Ausf A to N. Ian Allan, 2004. ISBN 0-7110-3015-4

Forty Jonathan. Tanks in Detail, Panzer IV, PzKpfw IV Ausf A to J. Ian Allen, 2002. ISBN 0-7110-2931-8

Fowler Will. Blitzkrieg 2, France, Holland and Belgium 1940-1944. Ian Allan, 2002. ISBN 0-7110-2944-X

Fraser David. Knight's Cross, a Life of Field Marshal Erwin Rommel. Harper Collins Publishing, 1993. ISBN 0-00-215936-8

Gander Terry J. Tanks in Detail, Panzer III, PzKpfw III Ausf A to N. Ian Allen, 2004. ISBN 0-7110-3015-4

Gawthorne Nigel. Fighting Them on the Beaches, The D-Day Landings June 6, 1944. Index, 2004. ISBN 1-84193-113-6.

Military High Command. German Invasion Plans for the British Isles 1940. Bodleian Library, University of Oxford, 2007. ISBN 1-85124-356-9

Germany 1944, The British Soldier's Handbook. The National Archives 2006. ISBN 1-903365-91-0
313

German Invasion Plans for the British Isles 1940. Bodleian Library, 2007. ISBN 978-1-85124-356-3

Green Michael & Gladys. Panzers at War. Zenith Press, 2005 ISBN 0-7603-2152-3

Green William. Famous Fighters of the Second World War. Purnell Book Services Ltd, 1975

Guderian Heinz. Achtung-Panzer! The Development of Tank Warfare. (in English) Cassell Military Paperbacks, 1999. ISBN 0-304-35285-3

Guderian Heinz. Panzer Leader. Penguin Books, Classic Military History, 2000. ISBN 0-141-39027-1

Haining Peter. World War II Stories, Where The Eagle Landed, The Mystery of the German Invasion of Britain , 1940. Conway, 2007. ISBN 9781844860517

Hargreaves Richard. The Germans in Normandy. Pen & Sword Military, 2006. ISBN 1-84415-447-5

Harris Robert. Enigma. Arrow Books, 1995. ISBN 978-0-09999-200-4

Hastings Max. Overlord, D-Day and the Battle for Normandy 1944. Pan Books, 1999. ISBN 0-330-39012-0

Healey John. Panzers in North Africa. Concord Publishing Company, 2004. ISBN 962-361-685-6

Hills Stuart. By Tank into Normandy. Cassell Military Paperbacks, 2003. ISBN 0-304-36640-4

Hitler Adolf. Mein Kampf. Pimlico, 1992. ISBN 0-7126-5254-X

Hitler's War Machine. Salamander Books Ltd, 1996. ISBN 0-517-15961-9

Hue Andre and Southby-Tailyour Ewen. The Next Moon. Penguin Books, 2004. ISBN 0-141-01580-2

Irving David. Rommel, Trail of the Fox. Wandsworth Military Library, 1999. ISBN 1084022-205-0

Jackson Julian. France. The Dark Years 1040-1944. Oxford University Press, 2003. ISBN 0-19-925457-5

Jackson Robert. Dunkirk, the British Evacuation, 1940. Cassell Military Paperbacks, 1976. ISBN 0-304-35968-8.

Jappy M.J. Danger UXB. Channel 4 books, 2001. ISBN 0-7522-1576-0

Jordan William. The Normandy Mulberry Harbours. Pitkin Guides, 2004. ISBN 1-84165-157-5

Kessler Leo. Kommando, Hitler's special forces in the second world war. Leo Cooper, 1995. ISBN 0-85052-464-4

Kirchubel Robert. Operation Barbarossa 1941(1), Army Group South. Osprey Publishing Ltd. 2003
ISBN 978-1-84176-697-3

Kirchubel Robert. Operation Barbarossa 1941(2), Army Group North. Osprey Publishing Ltd. 2005
ISBN 978-1-84176-857-1

Kirchubel Robert. Operation Barbarossa 1941(3), Army Group Centre. Osprey Publishing Ltd. 2007
ISBN 978-1-84603-107-6

Knock Heinz. I Flew for the Fuhrer. Cassell Military Paperbacks, 2003. ISBN 0-304-36638-2

Kohne-Lindenlaub Renate. The Villa Hugel, An Entrepreeur's Residence in the Course of Time. Alfried Krupp von Bohlen und Holback-Stiftung, Deutscher Kunstverlag Munchen Berlin, 2003. ISBN 3-422-06449-4

Krawczyk Wade. The Panzer Soldier. The Crowood Press, 2006. ISBN 978-1-86126-856-3

Laffin John. The Man the Nazis Couldn't Catch. Sutton Books Ltd., 2004. ISBN 0-7509-3547-2

Legout Colonel Gerard. D-Day and the battle for Normandy. OREP Editions, 2007. ISBN 978-2-912925-02-2

Le Port D'Arromanches, Album Souvenir collection memory 1944, Normandy 1944. OREP Editions, 2004.
ISBN 2-912925-54-1

Lewin Ronald. Rommel as Military Commander. B.T. Batsford Ltd. 1968

Lindau Christian Friedrich. Die Schonsten Vornamen Fur Ihr Baby. Urania, 2004. ISBN 3-332-01494-3

Longden Sean. To The Victor the Spoils, D-Day to VE Day, The Reality Behind the Heroism. Arris Books, 2004.
ISBN 1-84437-038-0

Lord Walter. The Miracle of Dunkirk. Wordsworth Military Library, 1998. ISBN 1-85326-685-X

Lumsden Robin. The Allgemeine-SS. Osprey Publishing Ltd, 1993.ISBN 1-85532-358-3

Michulec Robert. Panzer Division 1935-1945, (1) The Early Years 1935-1941. Concord Publications Company, 2000.
ISBN 962-361-666-X
Milson John & Chamberlain Peter. German Armoured Cars of the World 2. Arms and Armour Press 1974.
ISBN 85268-239-9
Mitcham Samuel W. Jr. The Panzer Legions, a guide to German Army Tank Divisions of WWII and their Commanders. Stackpole Paperback, 2007. ISBN0-8117-3353-X
Morgan Mike. D-Day Hero, CSM Stanley Hollis VC. Sutton Publishing, 2004. ISBN 0-7509-3694-0
Munson Kenneth. Bombers 1939-1945, Patrol and Transport Aircraft. Blandford Colour Series, 1969. ISBN 0-7137-0379-2
Munson Kenneth. Fighters 1939-1945, Attack and Training Aircraft. Blandford Colour Series, 1969. ISBN0-7537-0917-1
Natkiel Richard. Atlas of World War II. W.H.Smith and Son Ltd, 1985. ISBN 0-86124-208-4
Neillands Robin. The Dieppe Raid. Aurum. 2005.
ISBN 1-84513-116-9
Neillands Robin. The Battle of Normandy 1944. 2003.
ISBN 0-304-36563-7
Norris John. 88 mm Flak 18 / 36 / 37 / 41 & Pak 43 1936-45. Osprey Publishing Ltd, 2002. ISBN 1-84176-341-1
Ousby Ian. Occupation, the ordeal of France 1940-1944. Pimlico, 1999. ISBN 0-7126-6513-7
Panzers on the Eastern Front, General Erhard Raus and his Panzer Divisions in Russia 1941-1945. Greenhill Books, 2002.
ISBN 978-1-85367-682-6
Patmore Chris. Get Started in Short Filmmaking. A&C Black Publishers Limited, 2005. ISBN 978-0-7136-7340-1
Perrett Bryan. German Light Panzers 1932-1942. Osprey Publishing Ltd, 1998. ISBN 1085532-844-5
Perrett Bryan. Iron Fist. Cassell Military Paperbacks,
ISBN 0-304-35128-8
Perrett Bryan. My Story, D-Day, Lieutenant Andy Pope, Normandy 1944. Scholastic Children's Books, 2004.
ISBN 0439-96789-9
Perrett Bryan. Panzerkampfwagen IV Medium Tank. Osprey Publishing Ltd, 1999. ISBN 1-85532-843-7
316

Perrett Bryan. Taste of Battle. Cassell Military Paperbacks, ISBN 0-304-35863-0

Piekalkiewicz Janusz. Tank War, 1939-1945. Blandford Press, 1986. ISBN0-7137-1666-5

Price Alfred. The Legendary Spitfire Mk I/II 1939-41. Osprey Publishing Ltd, 1996. ISBN 84-8372-204-6

Price Alfred. The Spitfire Story. Cassell & Co, 2002. ISBN 1-85605-702-X

Probert Air Commodore Henry & Gilbert Wing commander Michael. '128' The History of the Royal Air Force Club. Royal Air Force Club, 2004. ISBN 0-9547840-0-1

Purnell's History of the World Wars Special, D-Day Invasion of Hitler's Europe. Phoebus Publishing Co. 1975

Rawson Andy. Images of War Victory in Europe, Rare Photographs from Wartime Archives. Pen &Sword Military 2005. ISBN 1-84415-274-X

Rees Laurence. The Nazis, a warning from history. BBC Books, 2005. ISBN 978-0-563-49333-4

Reynolds Michael. Eagles and Bulldogs in Normandy 1944. Spellmount Ltd, 2003. ISBN 1-86227-201-8

Robinson Derek. Invasion 1940, The Explosive Truth About the Battle of Britain. Constable and Robinson, 2005. ISBN 1-84529-441-6

Rommel Erwin General Field Marshal. Infantry Attacks. Greenhill Books, 1990. ISBN 1-85367-064-2

Rottman Gordon L. Fubar, soldier slang of world war II. Osprey Publishing Ltd, 2007. ISBN 978-1-84603-176-2

Rottman Gordon L. German Combat Equipment 1939-45. Osprey Publishing Ltd, 1991. ISBN 0-85045-952-4

Rottman Gordon L. Landing Ship, Tank (LST) 1942-2002. Osprey Publishing Ltd, 2005. ISBN 1-84176-923-1

Rottman Gordon L. World War II Infantry Anti-Tank Tactics. Osprey Publishing Ltd, 2005. ISBN 1-84176-842-1

Ryan Cornelius. The Longest Day. Wordsworth Military Library, 1999. ISBN 1-84022-212-3

Sebag-Montefiore Hugh. Dunkirk, fight to the last man. Penguin, 2007. ISBN 978-0-141-02437-0

Shepperd Alen. France 1940, Blitzkrieg in the West. Osprey 1990. ISBN 0-85045-958-3

Scutts Jerry. Messerschmitt Bf 109. Airlife Publishing Ltd, 2002. ISBN 80-7236-319-0

Sectional Maps of Britain's Railways, Revised Edition. Ian Allan Ltd. 1985. ISBN 0-7110-1458-2

Sebag-Montefiore Hugh. Enigma, the battle for the code. Cassell. 2000. ISBN 987-03-43-6662-0

Shacklady Edward. Messerschmitt Bf 109. Tempus Publishing Ltd, 2002. ISBN 0-7524-2003-8

Shepperd Alan. France 1940 Blitzkrieg in the West. Osprey Publishing Ltd., 1990. ISBN 0-85045-958-3

Smith Peter C. Stuka Spearhead, The Lightning War from Poland to Dunkirk, 1939-1940. Greenhill Books 1998. ISBN 1-85367-329-3

Snyder Louius L. Encyclopedia of the Third Reich. Promotional reprint Company, 1995. ISBN 1-85648-219-7

Spielberger Walter J. Panzer IV & its Variants, The Spielberger German Armour & Military Vehiclles Series, Vol IV. Schiffer Publishing Ltd. 1993. ISBN 0-88740-515-0

The Observer's Book of Railway Locomotives of Britain. Revised and Edited by H. C. Casserley. Frederick Warne & Co. Ltd. 1964.

The Royal Air Force Club. Memorandum and Articled of Association.

The Royal Air Force Club. Rules 2005.

Thomas Donald. An Underworld at War. John Murray, 2004. ISBN 0-7195-6340-2

Thomas Hugh. Spirit of The Blue, Peter Ayerst-A Fighter Pilot's Story. Sutton, 2004. ISBN 0-7509-4253-3

Trew Simon. Battle Zone Normandy, Battle for Caen. Sutton Publishing, 2004. ISBN 0-7509-3010-1

Villa Brian Loring. Unauthorizer Action, Mountbatten and the Dieppe Raid. Oxford University Press, 1989. ISBN 0-19-540679-6

Vinen Richard. The Unfree French, Life Under the Occupation. Penguin Books, 2006. ISBN 978-0-140-29684-6

Von-Luck Hans. Panzer Commander, The Memoirs of Colonel Hans von-Luck. Cassell Military Paperbacks, 2002. ISBN 0-304-36401-0

Warner Philip. The Battle of France 1940. Cassell Military Paperbacks, 2001. ISBN 0-304-35644-1

Weir Adrian. Last Flight of the Luftwaffe. Cassell Military Paperbacks, ISBN 0-304-35447-3

Wheeled Vehicles of the Wehrmacht. Taste International Publications Ltd. 1074. ISBN 0-903234-04-5

Whitaker Brigadier General Denis & Shelagh. Dieppe, Tragedy or Triumph. Loe Cooper. 1992. ISBN 0-85052-309-5

Williamson Gordon. German Security and Police Soldier 1939-45. Osprey Publishing Ltd, 2002. ISBN 1-84176-416-7

Windrow Martin. The Panzer Divisions. Osprey Publishing Ltd, 1982. ISBN 0-85045-434-4

Zaloga Steven J. D-Day Fortifications in Normandy Osprey Publishing Ltd., 2005. ISBN 1-84176-876-6

Zaloga Steven J. V-1 Flying Bomb 1942-52, Hitler's famous doodlebug. Osprey Publishing Ltd, 2005. ISBN 1-84176-791-3

Zetterling Niklas. Normandy 1944, German Military Organisation, Combat Power and Organizational Effectiveness. J. J. Fodorowicz Publishing Inc. 2000. ISBN 0-921991-56-8